BARS
THE WRATH OF KHAN

THIS IS A WORK OF FICTION. ALL NAMES, PLACES, CHARACTERS, EVENTS, AND INCIDENTS ARE EITHER PRODUCTS OF THE AUTHOR'S IMAGINATION OR USED FICTITIOUSLY. ANY SIMILARITY TO ACTUAL EVENTS OR LOCALES OR PERSONS, LIVING OR DEAD IS ENTIRELY COINCIDENTAL.

BY KING 44

Copyright © 2024 DaleeSpitz Publications

All rights reserved. No part of this publication may be reproduced, distributed, or transmitted in any form or by any means, including photocopying, recording, or other electronic or mechanical methods, without the prior written permission of the publisher, except in the case of brief quotations embodied in critical reviews and certain other noncommercial uses permitted by copyright law. For permission requests, write to the publisher, addressed "Attention: Permissions Coordinator," at the address below.

Printed by DaleeSpitz Publications, in the United States of America.

First printing, 2024

DaleeSpitz

P.O. Box 53

Highspire, Pa 17034

www.daleespitz.com

DEDICATION

This book is dedicated to my Angels. My Angels were the ones that helped me inch closer and closer to the stars every day. The ones that never broke me down, only built me up. My Angels showed me how to live a life I could never imagine, and also showed me the repercussions in balanced contrast. I am forever in debt to my Angels and I love you all. Now sit back and watch Daddy get this bag.

It's DaleeSpitz Nugga!

SHOUT OUTS

I would like to give a shout out to all of the fans and supporters of my work. Big Love to the Battle Rap Community, Big Love to the Hip-Hop Community and Big Love to the P's holding it down like they suppose to. Shout Out to Smoov T.V. for getting my face out there and also Shout Out to Akbar Pray for the advice. Shout Out to my family, my kids and my mama, and the general. Shout out to my Babygirl for the inspiration and Shout Out to my Babycakes for the motivation.

Table of Contents

Chapter One _____ 9
    The Yard _____ 9

Chapter Two _____ 17
    Daddy Issues _____ 17

Chapter Three _____ 26
    Back to the Block _____ 26

Chapter Four _____ 47
    Love Hurts _____ 47

Chapter Five _____ 61
    Angel of Mine _____ 61

Chapter Six _____ 77
    Red Mask _____ 77

Chapter Seven _____ 81
    Squared Up _____ 81

Chapter Eight _____ 87
    All in the Family _____ 87

Chapter Nine _____ 92

Weekend Warrior _____ 92

Chapter Ten _____ *103*

   A Girl Can Dream _____ 103

Chapter Eleven _____ *112*

   Facebook _____ 112

Chapter Twelve _____ *128*

   Time to leave the Nest _____ 128

Chapter Thirteen _____ *135*

   Give Us, Us Free _____ 135

Chapter Fourteen _____ *142*

   Workin' Girls _____ 142

Chapter Fifteen _____ *152*

   99 Problems _____ 152

Chapter Sixteen _____ *167*

   Bad Break-Up _____ 167

Chapter Seventeen _____ *176*

   One Final Salute _____ 176

Chapter Eighteen _____ *188*

   Focus Bitch _____ 188

Chapter Nineteen _____ *196*

Stars n Stripes _____ 196

Chapter Twenty _____ 213
Small World _____ 213

Chapter Twenty-One _____ 221
The Freaks Come Out at Night _____ 221

Chapter Twenty-Two _____ 239
Pigs in a Blanket _____ 239

Chapter Twenty-Three _____ 246
Learning How to Fish _____ 246

Chapter Twenty-Four _____ 260
Good Times _____ 260

Chapter Twenty-Five _____ 273
Bad Boys, Bad Boys...Whatchu Gonna Do _____ 273

Chapter Twenty-Six _____ 276
Boy meets Girl _____ 276

Chapter Twenty-Seven _____ 290
I got a pocket full of Sunshine _____ 290

Chapter Twenty- Eight _____ 310
The Lion King _____ 310

Chapter Twenty-Nine _____ 319

    When it Rains, it pours _____ 319

Chapter Thirty _____ *330*
    Whip it like a Slave Master _____ 330

Chapter Thirty-One _____ *333*
    Eviction Notice _____ 333

Chapter Thirty-Two _____ *340*
    When life gives you Lemons _____ 340

Chapter Thirty-Three _____ *350*
    Time to Plant the Seed _____ 350

Chapter Thirty-Four _____ *353*
    Family over Everything _____ 353

Chapter Thirty-Five _____ *369*
    Captain Save -A- Hoe _____ 369

Chapter Thirty-Six _____ *378*
    Sunday Funday _____ 378

Chapter Thirty- Seven _____ *390*
    Theres a Ghost in the Basement _____ 390

Chapter Thirty-Eight _____ *396*
    Never Judge a Book by Its Cover _____ 396

Chapter Thirty- Nine _____ *404*

Lady Pimp	404
Chapter Forty	*415*
Family Matters	415
Chapter Forty-One	*425*
Time to Wake Up	425
Chapter Forty-Two	*432*
Little Child, Running Wild	432
Chapter Forty-Three	*438*
The Final Showdown	438
Chapter Forty-Four	*465*
Double Entendre	465

Chapter One
THE YARD

"Hey Khan, you ready Moe?" questioned an anxious Kyree in his strong D.C. accent.

"I'm gucci pimpin." Khan muttered while nervously rolling a joint.

The two cell buddies had a ritual of getting high before they went to **The Yard**, but this wasn't your typical day at the isolated prison located in the mountains of Western Maryland.

M.C.T.C was a medium level prison that housed over 2000 inmates with security levels ranging from low to medium. Even inmates with life sentences resided at the college campus styled facility. There were eight housing units and three dormitories for lower-level inmates. Khan was housed in Unit 7 a.k.a **"The Island."** **The Island** was reserved for gang members and troublemakers. Unit 7 sat by itself furthest away from the main compound. Its newly built design made privacy for the inmates virtually impossible with over 300 cameras and state of the art cell doors which made them impervious to escape. The showers were also timed, and the temperature controlled by staff who monitored the inmates closely.

"Don't tell me you trippin' bout Big Mammoth?" said Kyree in between the puffs.

"Naw dug, dat nigga ain't even on my mind" lied Khan.

"You wellin' like shit Joe." giggled Kyree, who was now feeling the effects of the weed.

"I'ont do no bluffin' bruh, I can show you betta than I can tell you doe." challenged Khan.

"Chill Moe, let's just go handle business, they fit'na pop da doors in a minute. Where dat smell good at?"

The walk to **The Yard** seemed longer than usual. Possibly due to the effects of the weed, but Khan knew what it was. He had butterflies in his stomach. When Big Mammoth called Khan out in front of everyone, his pride wouldn't allow him to back down. Big Mammoth stood 6 and a half feet tall and weighed a little under 300 lbs. He had a mid-night black complexion with dusty dread locks that hung over his perpetual cocky scowl. Big Mammoth only challenged Khan to avenge his comrade 9 Milly, whom was effortlessly man handled by Khan in a prior duel. As Khan made his way closer to the center of the yard, he noticed the large flock of spectators that started to gather at the sight of his presence. Scanning the crowd, Khan finally spotted Big Mammoth, he also noticed that 9 Milly and the rest of their click the Empire were also in attendance.

"Yo, this shit bout to be good" yelled someone from the crowd.

"Khan, I can't believe you had the balls to show up" snickered Big Mammoth.

"Only thing I run from is da law nigga" retorted Khan.

After a few minutes of getting the vastly growing group of enthused inmates to quiet down, a short middle aged brown skinned man named Bob-Cat walked in between Big Mammoth and Khan. Bob-Cat was the prisons designated referee and facilitator for all events, all prisons had one.

"Everybody quiet down…. Chill out y'all… shut da fuck up!" screamed Bob-Cat.

"Alright now, y'all know how we do…. We got two very talented M. C's out here today, ya boy Big Mammoth is undefeated representing them country ass niggas from da Eastern Shore"

The crowd erupted in laughter at Bob-Cat's trademark humor and showmanship.

"With an impressive record of 22 wins and no losses. I'm tellin' y'all this nigga ain't to be played with…. y'all give it up for Big Mammoth!" Bob- Cat paused as the crowd cheered for their champion before introducing the challenger.

"Now I know we don't know much about the challenger but that ass whopping he put on 9 Milly should speak plenty for itself. With a record of one win, no losses, show some love for Gangas Khan!" The cheers continued as the gathered inmates placed multiple side bets while Bob-Cat continued his introduction.

"Khan where you from?" questioned Bob-Cat.

"Eastside." said Khan while staring Big Mammoth directly in his eyes.

"Okay lil nigga, Big Mammoth where you reppin'?" laughed Bob-Cat.

"Salisbury stand up!" shouted Big Mammoth while returning a menacing stare-back at Khan.

"Place y'all bets now, this gonna be for three rounds, I'mma judge rounds one and two then leave the third one up to the people."

As Khan glanced around the busy group of gambling spectators, Khan got the feeling that he would once again be considered the underdog. Fortunately for him, that's exactly how he wanted it to be. Khan's homeboys were taking bets on his behalf as four to one underdog odds, which could really put some money in his pockets, if he pulled off the upset. Khan had recently transferred from the Jessup Region, which was located about twenty minutes South of Baltimore. His transfer occurred due to behavioral issues at the minimum-security institution. He had a few months left on his sentence before he was pre-release eligible, so now Khan was trying to be on his best behavior. The only reason Khan involved himself in the potentially dangerous sport of battle rap was because the money orders from his family came few and far in-between. His long duration of seven years in the system for a robbery charge had finally taken a toll on everybody's pockets. Khan understood and found new ways to hustle to avoid putting so much stress on his loved ones.

"Hey, Yo Khan, since you da challenger, you go first" instructed Bob-Cat.

"Naw Bob-Cat, I'mma go first. I ain't scared of this nigga" demanded Big Mammoth as the crowd echoed a series of ooh's.

"If you tryin' go toe to toe, come on nigga, I'm wit it/ Cuz when I roll up my sleeves, boy my wrist be glistenin'/ Now ya mama gotta miss you cuz my A.K. didn't/ Plus all my lines and hooks reel (real), don't confuse it with fishin'/

"Daaaamn" uttered someone in the crowd as Big Mammoth smirked then continued...

"Bitch I'mma pro an' lil nigga you'z a walk-on/ Ya bootleg bars bout to get ya team stomped on/ You can't buy ya stripes on commissary, niggas gotta earn em/ I done moved so many chickens in da hood they calling me Colonel/"

Everyone went crazy over Big Mammoth's first round, now it was Khan's turn to even the score. As Khan took a few deep breaths. He mentally prepared himself by clearing his thoughts and relinquishing full control of his mind, body and soul to new ownership.... Gangas Khan!

"Now that was fair for a square, but you can't be serious Mam/ Cuz if you goin shoot ya shot just don't let that 9 Milly jam/ Boi fuck ya fam, cuz we could do whateva/ Nigga I got a choppa so big, I needed some help from NASA just to put it together/ Da pistol grip got extended clips with a nice range/ And that bitch got one purpose, that's to get rid of Mammoth like da end of da ice age/ So, you movin' chickens huh?... I guess you got ya pawns thinkin' you a real Chess Master/ Nigga you a junkie, they wouldn't give Mam a gram if he had breast cancer/ Ya priorities fucked up nigga, focus on getting profit/ Instead of running round da jail chasing tail like Dr. Robotnik/ Plus, ya team on some hot shit/

"Khan spoke while staring directly at 9 Milly.

"Check Milly paperwork, I heard he singing songs to them cats/ Come on Mammoth, God dammit, I thought elephants didn't get along with rats/"

Mammoth shook his head in disgust as he noticed a visibly distraught 9 Milly shake in nervousness while the crowd laughed at his crew. After the conclusion of the first round, the crowd roared with excitement. Khan also noticed something that he had yet to see upon arriving at the prison. The arrogant smirk that usually laid permanent on Big Mammoth's face was now replaced with a look that Khan and every other apex predator knew too well. Fear! Khan's second round was much more aggressive than the first and his bars possessed a wit and creativity that couldn't be matched. Big Mammoth's punchlines were well constructed but it was evident that he already knew his undefeated record would come to an end today. In the midst of the third round Big Mammoth started stuttering and stumbling over his words. His team had no choice but to throw in the towel.

"Y'all just witnessed history in the making, we got a new champ out this bitch and his name is Khan!" announced Bob-Cat as he grabbed Khan's arm and hoisted it in the air.

The crowd went insane as a wide smiling Kyree approached Khan as he jumped up and down. Kyree was a very social person, his young age of 19 kept him on the move. He was a tall dark-skinned kid with a slim build. Khan never witnessed a more gifted and agile person at the quarter back position. Not even on the streets. Khan's favorite position was defensive end because he loved the challenge of chasing down Kyree. Khan was six years Kyree's senior, but the love of football and the Deen of Islam had them joined at the hip.

"You did that Joe" Kyree complimented then gave Khan a

quick embrace, half hug.

"Good lookin' bro" said Khan with a matching smile.

"Joe, we banked off them niggas, at least 600 in side bets" said Kyree, while thumbing through the stamps their team won.

"I guess you cooking tonight since I did all the hard work"

"Yea I'm gonna cook that ass in Madden when we get back" retorted Kyree as the two cell buddies took a lap around the track.

A few days later Khan received a Knock on his cell door from a C.O. informing him that it was time to pack up and transfer to the work-release prison back in the city. Khan and Kyree shared a slightly tearful embrace, then Khan gathered his belongings and briskly walked down the long pathway of the compound that he called home for the last year and some change, for the last time.

"On my momma I will never come back to this place again" Khan shouted while pushing the raggedy yellow chart with his personal belongings towards the R&D Unit. Khan took one last glace over his shoulder and prepared for making the transition to "The Free World".

Chapter Two
"DADDY ISSUES"

It was almost 2:00 a.m. When Walter Biggs came in stumbling through his front door. The aroma of alcohol and failure flooded the living room as he made his way towards his Lazy boy chair. Finally able to relax, he reclined his 5'10-inch body as he spotted the mail. "God, I hate my life" Walter spoke to himself while sorting through a large stack of bills and cut off notices.

Walter was a middle-aged white man that once had high hopes to play baseball in the major leagues but suffering a career ending injury to his knee, forced him to relinquish those pipe dreams and face reality as a janitor for the local elementary public school system. It seemed that only "Grandpa's Ol' cough syrup" could remedy his proverbial wounds. The only light in his tunnel was a young woman named Stacey. Stacey had never been with a white man before, Walter. Being from a heavily black populated area in North-East Baltimore didn't give her many options. Walter and Stacey met at a batting cage in Loch Raven. She was hired to work at the concession stands. Walter took one look at Stacey's 5 foot 7-inch beautiful brown skinned frame, and it was love at first sight. Stacey eventually got pregnant and decided to ride it out with Walter when his career took a crushing blow. Two kids later, and a mountain of debt to go along with their problems, made Stacey question her life choices.

"Let's see what's on T.V. before they cut the cable off" snickered Walter.

"Owwww skin-a-max" slurred a drunken Walter while grabbing for his penis.

As the two college co-eds playfully engaged in a pillow fight. Walter's fantasy consumed him while masturbating to the duo of young Asian women. In the midst of his fictional threesome, Walter barely noticed his youngest daughter, eleven-year-old Khadeja, watching him from the staircase.

"Got dammit girl, whatchu doing up there?"

She hesitated for a second before responding.

"Nothing daddy"

"Well come on down here and give ya pops some sugah" Walter uttered with a drunken smirk.

Young Khadeja did as she was told as Walter continued his self indulgement. She kissed him on the cheek while watching him massage his erection at a frantic pace.

"You like what you see?" Walter asked while noticing her curiosity.

"I just came down here cuz I heard you come in... I'm going to go to bed now daddy, good night." she said quickly while attempting to retreat to her bedroom.

"Not so fast bitch, you wanna spy on me and be in grown folk business so I'mma put some grown folk's business in you." He spat while rubbing on her small butt.

"Daddy, I'm sorry," cried Khadeja.

"Whateva! Take them clothes off, daddy got something for your little sneaky ass." He lustfully commanded.

Khadeja started at a snail's pace while removing one pant leg at a time. She assumed she was about to receive a butt whippin' for sneaking out of her bed. Agitated by his daughter's slow haste, Walter started tugging at her pajamas until they fell to the floor. Walter then picked her up and placed her flat on the coffee table, as she laid face up in deep confusion to what her father was attempting to do while he mounted her, she felt his stiff erection slowly invade her most private of places.

"Daddy what are you doing...it hurts....awww!" she cried.

In a state of drunken rage, anger and sexual deprivation, Walter relentlessly took his frustration out on his own child while ignoring all the blood and tears. During the commotion, Stacey was jolted from yet another husband-less sleep. She was caught in-between not wanting Walter around, but not wanting to be alone as well. Hearing the screams again, propelled Stacey to her feet to investigate her home. She opened sixteen-year-old Jasmines room first, and closed the door when she noticed her sleeping soundly. Her next destination was Khadeja's room until she heard both voices so clear it re-routed her downstairs towards the living room. Slowly walking down the steps, she peeked from behind the wall and witnessed a scene so terrifying, she almost fainted.

"Walter!" screamed Stacey.

Walter was so focused on reaching his climax that he never noticed his wife standing inches away from him with a small .22 caliber pistol aimed at his head.

"Walter!" She screamed even louder now demanding his attention.

"Huh?" he muttered while almost shitting himself at the sight of the gun.

"Get off my child you sick son of a bitch!" she spoke with eyes full of rage.

"Mama..." cried a worn-out Khadeja.

"Come here baby" said Stacey through misty red eyes.

"Put the gun down or I'mma kill both of y'all." spat Walter.

"Fuck you" screamed Stacey while attempting to pull the trigger, but to her surprise no bullets were fired.

"Stupid bitch don't know how to take the safety off." thought Walter.

Suddenly Walter charged Stacey and out of instinct Stacey threw the gun at Walter, striking him in the head, which caused him to fall, giving Stacey and her daughter enough time to run upstairs and lock themselves in Jasmine's room.

"Where's your phone?" yelled Stacey to a startled Jasmine.

"Huh?" Jasmine replied slightly disoriented from being awakened unexpectedly.

"Phone! I need it now!"

"It's on the dresser" Jasmine managed to say while grasping the severity in her mother's voice.

"Yes 911... I need help!"

Walter was seeing stars as he finally started to recover. The reality of what he'd just done finally hit him like a ton of bricks.

"What the fuck is wrong witchu Walt." he said to himself while picking up the .22 from the floor.

"Cops are probably on the way; I can't go to jail no way! I ain't got nothing to live for! My family don't want me now! I'm broke as fuck! My life is shit!"

Knock- Knock the door sounded.

"Baltimore County Police! Open up!"

"Fuck... I'm sorry Stacey...I'm sorry Jasmine...I'm sorry Dee, I'm so fucking sorry!" he yelled loud enough for everyone to hear with cold tears running down his cheeks.

Khadeja sat with her mother, confused and traumatized by her father's perverted actions and even though she was in a great deal of physical and emotional pain, after hearing the despair in her fathers' voice she jumped up, unlocked the door and ran to her father. Khadeja didn't want her father to go to jail for something she thought was her fault.

"Khadeja!" Stacey yelled after her.

"Daddy!" Khadeja screamed while moving as fast as her little sore body could muster.

"I'm sorry princess" were Walter's last words before removing the safety from the .22 and placing it at his temple.

The second he pulled the trigger; a team of policemen rushed the house but not before young Khadeja witnessed her dad, decorate the living room with his brain matter.

"Khadeja!" screamed Stacey.

"Khadeja!"

"Khadeja!"

"Dee!" screamed Valita in an attempt to wake Khadeja from yet another night of terror.

"Huh..What..Yea.. Sup Lita" Khadeja spoke slightly conscious.

"You had another nightmare?" questioned Valita.

"Yea, shit just pops up from time to time" said Khadeja while searching for her phone.

"Look, I know I ain't no doctor or nuffin' but it's been like eight years now, so you gotta let that shit go." said Valita while rubbing Khadeja's shoulder.

"I'm trying...I really am..I got raped and watched my dad literally blew his brains out in the same day." Khadeja closed her eyes to halt the tears.

"I feel you on all that girl, but right now we gotta start working on our future." Valita replied while standing up to retrieve Khadeja's phone from the nightstand.

    Valita was three years younger than Khadeja, and like Khadeja, she was also a product of bi-racial parents, except Valita's father was black and her mother was white. Her father, Oscar, was arrested for a string of armed bank robberies when Valita was just nine-years old, and he still had another ten years left on his sentence. Joyce, Valita's mom was killed in a car accident four years after Oscar's arrest which caused a young and very frail Valita to almost go crazy if it wasn't for the comfort of her older cousin Khadeja. After her mother's demise, Valita moved in with her aunt Sissy. Sissy had always shared a close bond with Joyce so taking Valita into her custody went without saying. It was a tough transition for young Valita, without the constant love and attention that Valita used to receive from her parents, Valita felt as if she was placed on the back burner because Sissy had several young kids of her own to tend to.

    Valita also had a younger sister named Valinda whom Joyce took under her wing as well. At the age of sixteen, Valita's body and shape started to blossom; resembling the look of a woman in her mid-twenties. Valita stood five foot three inches with a thick figure that was hard for most to ignore. She had long dark curly hair and very fair skin, even for a mixed girl. Valita and Khadeja could've passed for sisters, but Khadeja was a few inches taller and her complexion was just a shade darker. Valita allowed all of the attention she received from her male counterparts to alter her mindset. Once a sweet innocent girl, she was now a loud, rebellious, young diva that played by her own rules. Valita was a wild child but she had a sweet spot in her heart for Khadeja. The two were notorious party girls and craved the attention they received. They were more than cousins, they were sisters.

"Best Friend!" Valita screamed.

"What bitch!" yelled Khadeja while checking her texts.

"That nigga Brent hit my phone, him and his man's K-Willz trying to meet up for a smoke ride or something."

"And.." Khadeja stated flatly.

"Is you wit it?" Valita asked with a scrunched-up face.

"What they pockets looking like cuz you be sweatin' dem dusty ass niggas.' Khadeja smirked.

"Bitch you trippin, plus you know they gotta come correct if they fuckin' wit' Lita" Valita countered.

"Alright then, bet" said Khadeja while responding to her text.

"Bet bitch!" Valita smiled then called Brent to share the good news.

Chapter Three
"BACK TO THE BLOCK"

"You have a collect call from...Deez Nutz" announced the automated voice. "To accept the call please press one, to reject, please hang up."

Shaking her head in disgust while trying to mask the smile which slowly crept across her face, Renee promptly pressed the one button.

"Mama!" shouted Khan

"Don't be playing on my phone like that boi!" retorted Renee.

"I love you too mama." replied Khan.

"I see you back around the way" mentioned Renee while glancing at the display screen on her phone.

"How you know that? I ain't called nobody butchu so far." questioned Khan.

"The caller ID silly, when you was calling from them mountains you was calling from some long-distance number. This is a local number your calling from." she explained.

"Alright Matlock."

"I gotcha Matlock"

"Hey, can you help me find a job? I can't leave here until I work for six months."

"I will see what I can do, but do me a favor, I'm driving right now, talk to my home girl until we get to IHOP."

"Man, ain't nobody tryin' talk to none of ya old ass fri"

"Hello" the sweet voice stopped Khan in mid-sentence.

"Hey, who dis?" questioned Khan.

"My name is Lakia, ya mother had told me so much about you."

"Oh yea, you sound a lil young to be hanging wit' my old ass ma dukes." joked Khan.

"Well, I'm twenty-two, all of our kids go to the same school and your mother offered me a ride one day when I was walking my son, Thomas to school." Lakia declared.

"That's what's up, are our kid's friends?"

"Absolutely...they are best friends...Thomas can't go a day without hanging out with his two best friends."

"Well, watch his lil ass round my daughter." Khan half joked.

"Everyone plays nice, I make sure of it." Lakia confirmed.

"What about you?" asked Khan.

"What about me?" Lakia asked in confusion.

"Do you play nice?" Khan asked in a serious tone.

"I see you got a lot of jokes, I'mma have to watch myself around you Mr. Larson."

"Nah you good mama, I got a feeling we goin' get along just fine...so um, you got a man, or is you one of them ugly girls with a pretty voice?" cracked Khan.

"I am far from ugly Mr. Larson, and yes someone does claim this." Lakia clarified.

"Damn...time for plan B." Khan thought to himself.

"Well since our kids are already friends, you know that means by law that we must be friends as well." Khan jived.

"Is that so?" Lakia spoke while blushing at his charm.

"Fraid so miss Lady."

"Well, if thats the law, lord knows I'm not trying to end up in there with you... no offense."

"I see you got jokes too." Khan spoke slightly impressed.

"Yea we can be cool, besides my boyfriend just joined the army so I will definitely be in need of a friend.

"*Got one!*" Khan thought to himself.

"Alright well lem'me get ya number and I'mma make sure I keep you outta trouble while Ole' boi out saving da world."

"Funny....its 443 572..."

Khan spent the next few days rummaging through "The Yellow Pages" and any other sources to find a job that would not only hire a convict but hire a convict that was still incarcerated. On his third day of fruitless leads, Khan finally lucked out when a young lady named Gina said that she would give Khan a shot. Khan hung up the phone and jumped for joy. He was so excited that he bumped into someone while celebrating.

"Damn my bad...oh hey Blackman!" Khan spoke excitedly.

"Hey Khan, you damn near took a nigga out, fuck gotchu all hype fo?" Black asked.

"Man, I just got off da phone with this chick that said I could come in for da inna-view." Khan beamed.

"Good shit. I'm glad you taking this shit serious, cuz I couldn't have imagined you ever taking anything serious when I first met you at da old jail." Black reminisced.

"Yea that ain't me no more. I've grown since then."

Black was a very knowledgeable person whom Khan became close with partially due to their similar attitudes and perspectives on life, but mostly due to their love for the Green Bay Packers. Black was as dark as two closed eye lids and cut up like a bag of dope. He could pass for Wesley Snipes on any day of the week.

"Bruh, I'm on my way to the case workers office now to see if Ms. Gina called and set- up my inna-view time." Khan spoke on the pivot.

"Alright lil brova..I'mma see you when I see you, oh and if you land that gig, see if you can get a brova in there withcu." Black requested.

"No problem BlackMan...peace fam."

"Blackman need to give his kid back them little ass tank tops he keep wearing." laughed Khan as he bopped that East Baltimore bop all the way to the case workers office. He bypassed the round smiling face of Ms. Julie in the finance office on the way as he gave her a slight nod of acknowledgement and kept it moving. The hallway was a long but narrow corridor with several offices that split between case workers, supervisors and the finance department. Once outside his caseworker's office, he noticed. Ms. Johnson was in the midst of a telephone conversation. He almost decided to leave and return later until she motioned him in by pointing to the small wooden chair across from her desk. The Niecy Nash look alike, held a delicately manicured finger up symbolizing that she would only be a minute. Khan scanned her office and wondered why the state made so much money, yet they crammed their employees in such small areas, her desk was littered with office supply paraphernalia. The object that stuck out the most amongst the clutter was a Donovan McNabb bobble head that represented her proud Philly upbringing.

"Khanstantine Larson" Ms. Johnson brought Khan back from his daze.

"Yes, ma'am."

"I already spoke with a...ah, Ms. Gina Kyle, your interview will be on Wednesday at 1:30 p.m. Tell your family they can drop you off an initial package containing your interview clothing, under garments, socks, ect... oh and a coat, gloves and hat." Johnson informed.

"Thank you, ma'am...is my mom allowed to drive me to work?"

"No, you are only permitted to travel with the M.T.A. bus lines."

"I will issue you some bus tokens until your first paycheck if you don't already have the funds in your account."

"Cool." Khan replied while watching Ms. Johnson's breast bounce as she spoke.

"Once a week you can visit Ms. Julie in finance, and she will give you $40.00 a week to use for your expenses which will be deducted from your account."

"Is there anything else I need to know?" questioned Khan.

"Yes, .. don't fuck up. I'm tired of seeing guys like you that spent so many years locked up, then do something stupid as soon as they hit the streets. Be smart and be on time. We are very strict here and I noticed this store doesn't have any of our work- release inmates working there."

"Yup, I'm da first one." Khan spoke with pride.

"Don't refer any other inmates to your boss, because if they fuck up, they may take you down with them." Ms. Johnson warned.

"Good medicine Ms. J" said Khan while nodding.

Khan made a mental note of all the precious gems Ms. Johnson dropped on him as he made his way back to his cell. Time seemed to move in slow motion as Khan tossed and turned in his bed. It was now Wednesday and Khan's eye lids would no longer shut as he stared at this alarm clock that read 5:17 a.m. Anxiety got the best of Khan as he sat up in his bed.

"In just a few more hours, I'mma be in that world." he thought. He pondered everything from what food to eat, to what places he wanted to visit, to whose daughter he would wreck.

Anticipation had him excited yet nervous at the same time. In the other corner of the dark two- man cell, Khan noticed his celly, Jynx sit up in his bed as well.

"Top of da mornin' to ya, ya old fuck!" greeted Khan.

"Hey young man, I guess you got the jitters huh?" replied Jynx.

"You guessed right" smiled Khan.

Jynx was a veteran convict that had over 20 years in the system. He was in his mid-fifties but was in better shape than most guys half his age. He was a short man with a light red complexion and sported a head full of grey waves. He wasn't very social, unless he was speaking with one of the female C.O's, but he and Khan got along fine.

"Sup, youngsta...wanna move the earth with me for a lil bit, might help ya with dem jitters?" Jynx asked while turning the light on in the cell.

"Yea we can do a couple sets of push-ups right quick, get swole for theses bitches before a pimp hit da streets." joked Khan

"I hope you can keep up."

"Chill wit all that before I mop ya old ass in here, they going have you runnin' round this bitch with a life alert keychain around ya neck...ha." Khan said while laughing.

"Don't let da grey hair fool you."

"Sup gramps." Khan said while charging at Jynx. Jynx quickly sidestepped him then applied a choke hold.

"Alright you got that, damn nigga you fast." Khan spoke surprised by his speed.

"Fuck is y'all faggots doin' in there?" shouted SGT Wallace while flashing his flashlight in the eye's of the inmates as he conducted his rounds.

"Man, eat a dick bitch." shouted Khan.

"I gotcha bitch." muttered SGT Wallace as he calmly continued on with his rounds.

SGT Wallace was the senior officer on his shift. He had to be the oldest employee in the system. The inmates all respected him because he kept it real. He was one of the few officers that you could talk to about anything, but he would talk that shit, to inmates and co-workers alike. He had a swag all of his own and you either loved him or you hated him... but you respected him.

After stepping out of the shower, Khan glanced in the mirror to inspect his fresh haircut, courtesy of the jail house barbershop.

"Not bad...They got a nigga waves spinning like a mug." Khan smiled.

Khan also noticed his 6'2-inch frame which carried a definition that only prison could provide. He stared at the reflection of the young co-co complexion of a man, and his big dimples gave way to a huge slightly gaped tooth smile that read... "I'm ready."

After checking out with the lobby officer, Khan was on his way. As he stepped outside, the sight of the surreal urban tranquility only lasted a few seconds because his bus was vastly approaching. Khan's long legs made easy work of the 30-yard dash to the bus stop. Once aboard the bus, Khan's nostrils were violated by a combination of urine, coffee, and cuss words. Nevertheless, the jovial experience made Khan numb to any and all negativities. Khan couldn't contain his smile as he walked down the dirty bus dressed like a black stockbroker on Wall Street, sporting a white short- sleeve polo dress shirt and brown slacks with a pair of brown dress shoes his mother found at the last second from Walmart. Khan didn't give a fuck. He was just happy to be free... even if it were temporary. The only available seat on the crowded bus was next to any elderly dark-skinned woman who appeared to be homeless. Khan waited for her to slide her large bag of empty cans to the side so that Khan could sit. She smiled a toothless smile when Khan sat down, and Khan smiled back at her.

"This bitch smell like alligator sex." Khan thought while still smiling.

"Hello, young man, where you on ya way to dressed all nice like that?" questioned the homeless woman.

"I stay at the work release spot, I'm on my way to a job inna-view." Khan answered.

"Well, that's wonderful... I like to see our black people puttin' they self in a position to take over the world." she spoke while adjusting her wig.

"Yea...well I dunno about takin' over da world,

I'mma just be flippin' burgers."

"Well, you gotta start somewhere...all you have to do is start, some folks don't even wanna start."

Khan sat and thought how a homeless woman could possibly

give him any advice on trying to better himself when she interrupted his thoughts and answered him.

"I know what your thinkin'...and your right, I ain't shit, so use me as an example on what not to do... I didn't have a strong young man like you in my corner, cuz if I did, I reckon we would'a took ova da world." she smiled with her eyes closed.

"Next stop. Baltimore street." the automated voice yelled.

"This my stop Ms.?"

"Sunshine."

"I like that, a'ight Sunshine, I'mma see you when I see you." Khan stood to leave.

As Khan walked down the steps of the bus, he turned around and ran back as he yelled to the bus driver.

"Hold up one second!"

Khan dashed back to Sunshine and reached in his pocket to retrieve a twenty-dollar bill which he gave to the very appreciative homeless woman. Feeling a sense of pride, Khan patiently waited for his second bus to take him to work while taking in the sights of all the hustle and bustle of beautiful downtown Baltimore.

"So, let's talk about your strengths and weaknesses." Gina

inquired.

"Well, my strengths are that I have no weakness." shot Khan.

"I like that you're taking my interview as a joke."

"Neva that, I'm being for real…The only thing I can't do is …lose, I'm a natural born leader, and I'm a good guy that got caught in a bad situation. I'm not gonna waste ya time. If you hire me, I will do such a great job that you will only exclusively hire convicts. I'm tryin' to raise the bar here. I come dressed for success and I only play to win." Khan delivered with conviction.

"Well, Mr. Larson, you are a very smart and handsome young man, and judging from your constant glances to that group of people over there in the corner, that must be your family." Gina observed.

"Yes, ma'am. That's my folks, I didn't know we would be conducting this inna-view in the dining area, I would'a told they loud ass'es stay in da car." Khan joked.

"Everything is fine... I tell you what, just let me know what size shirt and pants you wear so I can get outta ya face, tell ya family you got the job, and y'all can have a free meal on me." Gina smiled.

"Thank you so much." Khan said while noticing that Gina may have been a white woman, but she was built like a sista.

She was in her mid-thirties with a short, cropped hairdo. As she stood up to leave Khan with his family, Khan observed the tan khakis ride up her ass as it jiggled all the way behind the counter.

"Daddy!" screamed his eight-year-old daughter Khannie.

"Hey ladybug...come here Jr." Khan said while hugging both his children.

"Look atchu Jr... I see you getting big. Khan smiled.

"Yup...I'm seven now!" Jr beamed.

"Hey mama... bring it on in." Khan gave Renee a bear hug.

"Lemme go boi!" Renee protested.

"Yella... Scrap" Khan's younger brothers approached.

"Yella, what's good you still rapping?" Khan asked while embracing his slim built light skinned brother with a half hug.

Yella's nickname was given to him due to his light complexion. He was about 5 foot 11 inches and weighed about 155lbs. Scrap and Yella had the same father, but Scrap was the same height as Yella but was a bit more muscular, as he boxed for a semi pro league.

"Khan... you know I stay in da booth bro." Yella replied.

"Come here lil nigga, put ya dukes up. Khan gestured by

standing in a fighting stance in front of Scrap.

"I'mma spare you big bro...I missed you nigga." Scrap spoke while ducking one of Khan's playful swings then bear hugging him.

"Excuse me!" Lakia interrupted the boys embrace.

"Damn my fault lil mama, I recognized ya heavenly voice, but I didn't know da face." Khan spoke while giving Lakia a complete optical pat down.

"Well, here I am... I heard the good news, congrats." Lakia replied.

"This is truly a good day, good lookin' family, good lookin' food, now I got a good lookin' best friend." Khan said while admiring the petite yet thick in all the right places young lady.

She had long hair that Khan assumed was weave but she was making it work for her. After Khan got reunited with his family and friends, they dropped him off back on Baltimore Street where he could catch his second bus to keep the wondering eyes of the C.O.'s at bay. Waving goodbye to his family, Khan glanced at his G-shock.

"Damn, I still got like an hour of travel time left." Khan said to himself while finally taking the opportunity to appreciate his surroundings. Baltimore Street or as the underground world, knew it as "The Block" was infamously known for its array of strip clubs, pimps, hookers, drug transactions, and many other forms of seedy activity, Khan was at home. Nothing personified the city of Baltimore more to Khan than The Block. The food, the drugs, the women, and yes, the women!

"Geez even the snow bunnies getting phat now." mused Khan while staring a little too hard at the young white woman smoking a cigarette dressed in a pair of skintight jeans that hugged her very plump yet firm ass.

As Khan decided to "shoot his jumper" the young lady reacted to another young woman's voice calling the name "Kitty" from inside the doorway of the strip club that she stood several feet from.

"Kitty you're on in ten minutes hunny." yelled a small white woman with a head full of blonde highlights.

"Okay, Mona" replied Kitty as she almost inhaled the filter of the cigarette before flicking it towards the street. She briefly made eye contact with Khan, smiled then headed into the club titled "Oasis" which Khan observed as he read the large sign overhead the entry.

"Shit I got a couple minutes to spare." thought Khan as he followed his penis into the dark tinted doorway. To his surprise there was no bouncer. He was greeted by a tall slender, bright smiling, honey toned bartender with a set of breasts that could give the most articulated man a speech impediment.

"Hey sweetie, can I get you something to drink." she asked.

"Um...A sprite on da rocks." Khan laughed, knowing that the jails sometimes did surprise breath checks.

As Khan slowly sipped his drink, he was in stripper heaven as he vividly scanned the club's small variety of well-toned dancers.

"Now coming to the stage...The wild, the feisty, kitty cat!" screamed the DJ as the small group of patrons gathered closer to the stage. Khan decided to follow suit and move closer when someone called his name from a dark corner of the club.

"Khan!" screamed the unknown voice.

"Who that?" Khan replied while walking slowly in the direction of the voice in question.

"This me nigga...Gutta!"

"Ha... Sup my nigga?" Khan replied as the voice and image of the man finally made recognition. Khan met Gutta earlier in his prison sentence. Gutta was a small brown skinned man in his mid-twenties. He was a member of The Empire and was a notorious shit talker. Dressed in black from head to toe, he escorted Khan to his booth in the back of the club after sharing a small half embrace. Khan never considered Gutta an actual friend, but fucked with him on the strength of his east Baltimore ties.

"How's life treating you?" Khan asked while enjoying Kitty's performance.

"Man I been on da streets fo' like two years now...shit cool, but them blood niggas tryin' fuck with a nigga bread."

"Oh yea?" Khan questioned only half listening.

"Yea..that's a small thing to a giant, matter fact I'm 'bout to go see one of they bitches in Latrobe after I leave this joint."

"I'mma be headed in that direction too. I just came back from a inna-view at McDonalds out in Dundalk. I got the job too."

"That's what's up, I was wondering why you was in da titty bar wearing ya church clothes." joked Gutta.

"Man, it is what it is, I gotta stay at B.P.R.U. for at least six months before I can go home."

"You on ya way pimp, well lets bounce because the bus comes in like ten minutes and you don't want to be late ya first day out."

"True shit...I just wanted to see that white bitch shake sumthang but I'm good now." said Khan while downing the rest of his seven-dollar Sprite then exiting the club with Gutta on his heels.

As the two departed from the bus, Khan walked very slow with Gutta as he listened to Gutta talk shit about how many females he conquered and his plans to take over the streets.

"Yo, lem'me get a fug." Khan asked while looking at his

watch.

"Relax nigga, you still got a half hour and shawty right around the corner." replied Gutta while sending a text on his phone, then handing Khan a cigarette.

"Good lookin', what shawty talkin' bout?" asked Khan while inhaling deep on the cigarette.

"She keeps asking where I'm at and shit. Dumb bitch can't wait to get some of that Gutta dick." boasted Gutta. Khan continued to enjoy his smoke as he watched Gutta text message back and forth at the speed of light.

"Everything cool Broski?"

"Yea, she say she at the park on Chase Street with her homegirl."

"Homegirl?!!" Khan replied with the Scooby Doo Face.

"Yea nigga, I bet you tryin' roll with me now?" laughed Gutta.

"Oh, yea we can do that, she only up the street from the jail, plus I still got a few ticks." said Khan while throwing his cigarette and caution into the wind.

The walk to Chase Street took only a few minutes as Gutta continuously pounded the display screen of his phone with his thumbs.

"Fuck is this bitch at?" mused Gutta.

"If she don't show soon, I'mma be on my way yo."

"Nigga chill I'm tryinna-" Gutta words were cut off by the sight of a large group of men clad in crimson red attire that suddenly approached them.

"Sup blood." sounded from the group as they surrounded the pair of unsuspected victims.

"Hey, Gutta." said the young fair skinned female dressed in red.

"Bitch done set me up. Fuck!" screamed Gutta.

"Ayo, lem'me holla atchu." spoke the largest man in the group while directing a finger at Khan.

"Ain't this 'bout a bitch." thought Khan as he and the large man walked away from the scene about to unfold.

"Yo, this ain't about you dug, so as long as you give me ya word that you ain't see shit, you good to go." said the large man.

"Bruh, I don't bang, and I definitely don't snitch." replied Khan with a straight face.

"Say no more." said the big guy after searching Khan's eyes

for validation, then he returned back to his entourage.

"I don't feel right leaving this nigga, but he ain't my peoples and this ain't my business." Khan rationalized to himself while moving slowly in the direction of the jail as if he was in a dream-like state. As Khan neared the entrance of the prison, he never bothered to look behind him because the thunderous sound of..."Boom! Boom! Boom!" were enough to confirm his suspicions.

Now in most neighborhoods, the sounds of gunfire would frighten and send people into panic, but Baltimore wasn't like most cities. As the shots rang, no one flinched, no one moved, not even the children playing double dutch in the street missed a beat. Gutta's death was listed as another cold case and never made the news. It was never discussed because as usual... no one saw a thing.

Chapter Four
LOVE HURTS

"Pass that blunt!" Khadeja screamed over the eardrum shattering bass speakers.

K-Willz turned the music down then extended his long arm to the back seat with the blunt in hand.

"Here woman, you fuckin' up a gansta's vibe." spat K-Willz.

"Man... I dunno who that was rapping on that song but yo was some straight trash." Khadeja replied while snatching the blunt.

"Umm - hmm." snickered Brent from the driver seat as he already knew that K-Willz would take offense to Khadeja's statement.

"That was some gansta shit shawty, you dunno good music." K-Willz defended.

"Nah, that was a nigga just rhyming words and talking shit."

"Bitch that was me rapping and I'm da best in da city!" claimed K-Willz..

"*Damn.*" thought Khadeja.

"You know I knew that was you... I'm just fuckin' witchu." lied Khadeja.

"Yea right." K-Willz replied still not buying it.

"Hey, well at least the beat was nice." Khadeja countered while trying to save face.

"Ha!!!" shouted Brent, unable to hold his laughter at his homies embarrassment.

"Brent, baby this is such a nice ride, is this the newest Impala out right now?" Valita interjected trying to lighten the mood.

"Yea Lita, with da gansta red custom paint job too." Brent boasted.

"I love it." Valita sang sweetly while elbowing Khadeja in an attempt to tell her to chill out.

"K-Willz, how long you been rapping?" questioned Khadeja.

"All my life... this what I do, I gotta battle some white boy next month."

"What's his name?"

"The Baltimore Crazy Cracker!" laughed K-Willz.

"Seriously!!!! He's nice as shit, I didn't know you was fuckin' wit guys on his level." Khadeja stated surprised.

"First off... he ain't on my level, and secondly, how da fuck you know so much about these battle niggas?"

"For your information, I've always had love for hip-hop, I even write... well mostly poetry but anyone making any noise from our city, I checks on 'em." Khadeja informed.

"Well check this, you riding wit a winning team so act right, and I might let you rock wit me."

"Is that your way of asking me out?" Khadeja asked with a squinted face.

"I ain't stutter." said K-Willz while unwrapping his red bandana from around his wrist to remove another bag of weed.

"What girl could resist that?" Khadeja replied sarcastically.

A few weeks passed and Khadeja found herself spending much more time with K-Willz than she intended. At first she wasn't attracted to K-Willz, he was about 6'4 inches and weighed at least 280 lbs... He wasn't what you'd call a pretty boy by any means, in fact he had a face only a mother could love. The attribute that eventually snagged Khadeja was his confidence. He carried himself like he was king of the world and the fact that he was the head of the local Blood organization brought a lot of perks that could benefit Khadeja. She played her position and took a lot of verbal abuse from him, which slowly turned into physical abuse, but being the solider that she was, she hung in there in hopes that he would one day change. She desperately wanted to experience love for the first time, and she had no problem sacrificing her mind, body and soul for just a quick hit of that emotional high. She was socially introverted throughout most of high school and if it wasn't for Valita constantly nagging her to go out, she wouldn't have had a social life at all. Khadeja turned to poetry and music as an outlet for her frustrations.

As Khadeja sat alone in the one bedroom apartment in the projects that she shared with K-Willz, she held an ice pack to her swollen right eye as she located her notebook and began to write her pain away..

Daddy Issues

Never nice, always the aggressor/ Being gentle never brought me pleasure /Pull my hair, then slam me into the dresser/ He is my lover and my oppressor/ I've been told I have daddy issues/ Beat me, hurt me, break me, bruise me/ But say you love me, and it will soothe me/ I am aware, I have daddy issues./

Starships were meant to flyyyyy, hands up and touch the skyyy." Khadeja's poetic therapy was interrupted by her Nicki Minaj ringtone.

"Sup, girl." Khadeja greeted while placing her notebook in her dresser.

"Ain't shit, is you going to the show tonight?" asked Valita.

"Do I have a choice; I mean my man is the main event." replied Khadeja.

"Crazy cracker going kill that boi." laughed Valita.

"I know right, but I gotta root for the home team."

"True, ain't nothing you can do but be supportive. I just hope he don't take his loss out on you." said a concerned Valita.

"Mind ya business hoe, I'mma big girl besides the sex is always better after we fight."

"Alright if you say so, I was just checkin' up on ya, I'mma get dressed and we can all meet up later before we go."

"A'ight shawty."

"A'ight Dee."

As Khadeja ended the call, she opened her make-up kit then

stared in her vanity mirror at the dark ring around her eye.

"Okay, M.A.C. lets work ya magic." She did her best to hide the evidence of her boyfriend's temper.

"*All in the name of love.*" she mused while searching for the perfect outfit for tonight's festivities.

The grand opening of Club Sonar filled the entire city with anticipation. Trending on every social media platform, it was indeed the place to be. The small parking lot was quickly packed to capacity while others found parking close by. All walks of life from ballers to broke nigga's, rappers to managers, side pieces to wifey's and even those who just wanted to be seen, all gathered at the central downtown location for a night of entertainment.

K-Willz and his small army of goons ignored the long line as they bypassed a multitude of hateful gawks and made their way to the front of the club.

"Schuze me." spat an arrogant K-Willz as the bouncer quickly stepped aside and made room for the sea of red that flooded the club.

"Yo, we on some boss shit." screamed an excited Valita as she made the path to the V.I.P. section her personal runway while strutting extra hard in her all red jump suit with matching pumps.

"Indeed." Khadeja concurred as she walked alongside her cousin wearing a red miniskirt that left little to the imagination.

Khadeja was still amazed at the power of her hubby's influence as she noticed guys were purposely trying not to glance at the amount of cleavage showing from her banana republic v-neck top. She couldn't help but laugh, then she took a second to take in the scenery of the beautifully plush furniture that gave the VIP section a nostalgic vibe. There were sofas spread along the outskirts of the large dance floor with an adjoining room for alternate functions. The club had two bars and a large stage. The white décor was something new for Khadeja, usually clubs had more of a dark theme but this gave the place that "Brand New" feeling.

Khadeja slowly sipped on her Bacardi cocktail as her attention, along with the rest of the energized club goers, suddenly diverted to the large stage once Yo Gotti's DM song abruptly cut off and was followed by a bright spotlight. A large dark-skinned man walked towards the center stage with a microphone in his hand.

"That's Slick fat ass!" shouted someone from the crowd.

Slick's round face was all smiles as he stood in awe. Taking a moment before speaking, as he appreciated the large crowd at his feet. Coming from humbled beginnings, Slick's path to success started at a young age. He was obsessed with stardom and wanted to be the face of his own franchise. Using freestyle battles at local basketball courts helped launch Slick and his highly sought– after events, "Slick- Talk" as a house – hold name in the Hip- Hop community. Everything Slick touched sold out. He went from producing events, to party promoting. He eventually ventured into comedy showcases and variety shows, but headlining for the biggest club in Baltimore took Slick's status to a whole new level.

"What's happening y'all!" Slick finally yelled, breaking his trance as the crowd went nuts.

"First and foremost, I wanna give a shout out to all the good folks with the Sonar family for letting a young nigga rock with 'em. I am truly honored to bring Baltimore Hop-Hop at this beautiful venue. We done made it a long way y'all." Slick spoke almost on the verge of tears as he regained his composure then winked at his wife who sat in the far corner of the club smiling at her man.

"A'ight, so let's get this party started. We got some real talented artist in da building tonight, but the main event....yeah this main event... will be talked about for ages. So do me a favor, let's enjoy this night and leave all the drama to the entertainers, tip ya bartenders and please no recording at this event."

"This is the Club Sonar Grand Opening, and I Slick now present to you. Slick- Talk!" Slick dropped the mic as the crowd roared.

It seemed everyone was in good spirits for the exception of Khadeja who stood stone-faced as she watched K-Willz smile like a gitty schoolgirl while in the company of some Spanish looking scallywag that somehow managed to sneak in their VIP section.

"So, this nigga just goin' play me like this right in front of my face, huh." she said to no one in particular.

K-Willz felt like a superstar as countless groupies flagged for his attention, lost in the sauce he completely forgot about Khadeja until he felt someone burning a hole in the side of his head. Now in damage control mode, K-Willz quickly shook hands with his newest admirer and yelled.

"Thank you for your support and I will give the best performance that you've ever saw." Loud enough for Khadeja to believe that their conversation was purely professional.

"Sup baby." K-Willz greeted with a nervous smile.

"You ain't slick nigga." Khadeja spat while crossing her arms.

"Man, that hoe was just talking about the show."

"I hear that bullshit, please refill my cup then get outta my face." Khadeja replied while tossing the empty cup towards K-Willz and picking up her phone

"Whoa... that was close." thought K-Willz as he headed towards the bar.

"And the winner of this battle with the judge's decision being 2 to 1... is Piff" Slick shouted while raising Piff's arm in the air.

"Alright, ladies and gentlemen, now for the moment y'all been waiting for... it's time for our main event!" Slick broadcasted while scanning the room to make sure all of his cameramen were in the proper positions.

K-Willz and his crew stepped on the stage throwing gang signs to the audience as they stood to the left side of the stage. Crazy cracker was nowhere in sight as the members of K-Willz crew started to suggest, Crazy cracker was too scared to show up. Just as K-Willz was about to start talking shit, a team of loud obnoxious young men stormed through the club making the crowd of on lookers give way to Crazy Cracker and his team known as "The Hooligans."

Crazy Cracker and his posse had a presence about them that demanded your attention... and Khadeja was not exempt. Noticing the admiring glare, K-Willz grabbed Khadeja's chin and said, "Ya eyes tellin' on you." This caused Khadeja to regain focus.

"I was just seeing what all the fuss was about."

"I hear that bullshit." replied K-Willz with a slight grin.

"Crazy Cracker in da house y'all!" screamed Slick loving the dramatic entrance.

As Crazy Cracker and his crew walked on stage, you would've thought he was the mayor of the city, the way the crowd erupted.

Crazy Cracker took his positon on the right side of the stage with the Hooligans standing directly behind him as he stood nose to nose with K-Willz.

"This lil nigga got some balls." mused K-Willz while mean-muggin' Crazy Cracker and his crew.

"A'ight let's get this show on the road, tonight's main event between Crazy Cracker and K-Willz will be judged by three of "Slick-Talks" seasoned veterans. From Sandtown, give it up for Kill- Moe. Next, representing Cherry Hill, show some love for the O.G. Big Nelly, and last but not least... holding it down for dem "Down da Hill" nigga's, let's make some noise for E- Money." The crowd was loud, it seemed to have doubled in size.

"Okay, okay lets simma' down now, Challenger please introduce yourself." Slick announced while pointing at K-Willz.

"Man, you nigga's know what da fuck it is...K-Willz holding down Latrobe Projects." K-Willz proclaimed while throwing up his set.

"And our champion please let the folks who live under rocks know who you are." screamed Slick.

"Southside... Crazy Cracker...Let's go!!" Crazy Cracker said nonchalantly.

"You heard the man... it's customary to let the challenger go first, so do ya thang K- Willz." said Slick.

K-Will stared at Crazy Cracker searching for a hint of nervous energy, but came up empty, so he decided he would deliver his bars as aggressive as possible.

"Aye Yo... I say when we throw dem signs up, call it gansta vernacular/ I went and scooped ya bitch in all red Acura/ Now she suckin' bloods like Dracula/ She be yellin' Willz you spectacular/ Then flipped her like a spatula/ Kicked her out the whip then told da bitch I'll get back atcha/

K-Willz first round continued to be solid but Crazy Cracker seemed unfazed as he prepared to recite.

"Hey, Baltimore." greeted Crazy Cracker.

"I love you Crazy." screamed a female fanatic.

"I love you too bitch." replied Crazy Cracker with a smirk.

"So they say, I got a Vic..via battle tonight/ Well watch me step up in da spot and bring this venue to life/ Aye Willz fuck how you feel cuz this is still no bout/ And since ya name Willz, I hope you filled one out/ So if the pressure get high from you and ya thug members/ I got two 45's ... I call em my blood thinners/ I got destruction on my mind, so I'm winning by all means/ Ya bitch ate da Cracker up, now she callin' me saltine/

Crazy Cracker struck a nerve with K-Willz with that reference to his girl. There was a considerable difference in height. K-Willz dwarfed Crazy Cracker by at least six inches, but the lyrics of the young, fearless, black hooded Crazy Cracker made him seem as tall as a giant. Crazy Cracker was a young white kid in his early twenties that had short dark hair with an average build. He was one of those white guys that grew up around black folks so he always had respect from the community. The more Crazy Cracker spit, the more the audience fell in love.

His stage presence combined with his street savvy swagg commanded your attention. K- Willz couldn't take it anymore as he stepped closer to Crazy Cracker and stared him down.

"Yo!" K-Willz said while interrupting Crazy Cracker's verse.

"Hold up K-Willz, let the man finish his shit." Slick yelled as he continued to maintain order.

"Man fuck that. This bitch ain't bout none of that shit be talking." challenged K-Willz.

"Yo man." Crazy Cracker giggled.

"Fuck you" spat K-Willz

"Fuck wit me." rebuttaled Crazy Cracker while closing in the distance between them and standing nose to nose with K-Willz.

K-Willz could no longer handle the disrespect and shoved Crazy Cracker into the arms of the Hooligans, and as if on cue all hell broke loose. The two groups of men charge one another as the crowd mimicked the chaos. Everything from alcohol bottles to sneakers and high heels were being used as air-borne ammunition. During the hectic battle royal, K-Willz scanned the crowd in search of Khadeja. He suddenly spotted her, Brent and Valita ducking for cover over by the bar. As he roughly pushed his way through the bio-traffic, he felt someone tap his shoulder.

"What!" K- Willz's question was answered by a gallon sized bottle of Cîroc to his head.

CRACK

"Bottle's up bitch!" laughed Crazy Cracker while making a mad dash out the exit.

Chapter Five
ANGEL OF MINE

"Next Stop!" yelled Khan as the bus slowed to a halt and he exited.

Today was Khan's first day of work. The skies were blue, and the sunshine seemed to spotlight his every move. Khan's smile could be seen from a mile away, as the birds chirped, the bee's buzzed and countless streetwalkers turned tricks up and down Dundalk Ave. Khan stood in the parking lot of the McDonald's basking in the ambience, until his senses were compromised by the allure of nicotine.

"Hey, my man, you got a extra Fug on you?" Khan addressed the tobacco tooting teenager.

"Uh..oh yea, I gotchu dug." replied the young faced teen as he reached in his hoodie and produced a pack of Newport's.

"Here Yo, take two."

"Good looking my nigga, I appreciate that. Khan said thankfully as the young man placed his ear buds back in his ears and continued to strut across the street.

As Khan enjoyed his cigarette, he stole a glance from one of the parked car's windowed reflections.

"I'm really in a fuckin' McDonald's uniform." Khan said while smiling at his own humility.

"Oh well let's get this paper" Khan said while flicking the cigarette in the large trash can ashtray then making his was inside his newest place of employment.

"Khan!" Gina greeted while in the company of another female.

"Good afternoon Ms. Gina, I just wanna say thank you again." Khan replied.

"It's no problem, I'm glad I could help, now I want you to meet somebody. This is Angel, she'll be training you on register today."

"Sup, Angel." Khan said while eyeing his prey.

She was about 5'7 inches with olive skin and very large hips with a smile that read "Come get it."

"Hello, Khan, it's nice to meet you." Angel greeted as her thick gorgeous figure extended a hand to Khan.

"Oh and just to let you know, she is also my daughter so no funny business." Gina interjected causing Khan to abort all prior thoughts, well for now.

"But of course, Boss lady." Khan smiled.

The inside of the restaurant was very well kept. All of the napkins and soda dispensers were up to date, there was a large television displaying the news for customers as they sat in the modern – sheik style dining area. It was just after the lunch rush and the hungry traffic had finally slowed down.

"Let's start your training now, follow me to the back so I can give you a tour of the store." Angel spoke while turning on her heels.

The moment she turned around Khan was in love. This was the biggest backside Khan have ever saw in his 26 years on the planet earth.

"Good lawd." Khan uttered a little too loud causing Angel to giggle.

Angel knew her body had a certain effect on men, hell even some women couldn't resist the dangerous curves of the bi-racial 19-year-old. She wore a pair a glasses that gave her a more approachable look with a short hair style that slightly resembled her mother's. Angel took it upon herself to train Khan, hell she wasn't even a manager, but as the saying goes "Whatever Angel wants, Angel gets." As Khan followed Angel closely behind, he lustfully watched as her large hips struggled to maneuver through the cramped grill area.

"This is the grill team, that's Dalvin and T." Angel announced as the two skinny black youngsters nodded in acknowledgement.

"Sup." nodded Khan.

"That white kid over by the fries is P-Rock." she pointed towards the short teen.

"And the nosey ass bitch up in ya face working the drive-thru window is Jamie." Angel joked while Jamie smiled at Khan then shook her head at Angel for putting her on blast.

"This is the breakroom." Angel directed while making her way towards the back of the store.

The breakroom was small and had a table that sat four, with a tiny window positioned above the coat rack. In the far corner of the breakroom, there was a desktop computer which was used for the training process.

"I have to log you in, then you can get your punch-card info. You'll need that in order to get paid. My mom's gonna log you in manually today, but you'll have to do it yourself the next time you come in." Khan's mind remained on tunnel vision. His only thought was bending Angel over that breakroom table, and it seemed by the way Angel kept prancing around the room, finding every reason to bend over and pick random objects up from the floor gave Khan all the confirmation that he needed.

"So how long have you been at the work- release prison or jail or whateva it's called?" questioned Angel while finally sitting next to Khan.

"Two cheeks... I mean ah, two weeks." stumbled Khan.

"Ha - ha, I'm guessing you ain't got ya rocks off yet?" she inquired.

"My rocks off?" Khan scrunched his face.

"Yea... you know, did you fuck anyone yet?"

"Damn, no filter huh?" Khan asked slightly stunned.

"Nah, I just say what's on my mind. I'm not a fan of beating around the bush."

"I see... well I haven't really had the chance. I tried to hit a strip club after my inna-view but that didn't work out how I was hoping."

"So, your plan was to fuck some nasty ass stripper?" Angel spoke while shaking her head.

"Look I've been locked up for seven long years. When I stepped outside there was nothing but lovely women everywhere. I needed my fix, you know I'm long overdue." Khan explained while stealing a glance at Angel's fat pussy print through her tight work pants.

"Well maybe you shouldn't rush, you've already waited seven years. What's a few more days or weeks to see if you could find your soul mate?"

"And where would I search for this soul mate of mine?"

"Sometimes you don't have to go looking for her, sometimes, maybe she'll find you." Angel stated with a shy smile.

"*Got one*" thought Khan.

"Do me a favor, I like you, and I want you to take my number and call me from the prison, when you get off work." Angel suggested while scribbling her digits on the back of an old receipt.

"Bet, I get off at 7 P.M. so I will hit you around 9

P.M."

"Cool... don't forget." Angel said while her big brown eyes penetrated Khan's soul.

"How could I... I'm honestly waiting for someone to pinch me and wake me up from this dream."

"Ahh, your so sweet. You betta not be playing me, my mama warned me about your type." Angel confessed.

"Listen, here are the facts, your a great girl with a big heart and a gorgeous smile. Your assertive and you speak your mind. I can tell you come from a good family, and speaking of family, ya moms is the boss and on top of that, ... that ass doe!" Angel blushed at Khan's candid response.

"Now on paper I could see why you would have doubts... mainly thinking that since I've been locked down for so long, I'm about to fuck everything walking, but I would much rather be with someone that has a good head on their shoulders. This ain't no "Playa talk", I fucks witchu heavy and I'mma play fair as long as you play fair with me." Khan replied while folding the paper which contained Angel's number then placing it inside his wallet.

After two hours of simulated training on the computer, eventually Khan found himself standing in front of the register dealing with real customers.

"Welcome to McDonalds, how may I help you?" greeted Khan with a well-rehearsed smile.

"Let me get a um... number one" The large dark-skinned woman asked while briefly removing her phone from her ear.

"Will that be all?"

"Yea thats it." she replied then continued her phone conversation.

Angel watched from afar as her pupil, soon to be husband,

conducted himself professionally.

"I see you got it from here, it's almost 4:00 so me and my mom's about to leave. She's waiting for me in the parking lot...don't forget to call me." she spoke with a face draped in apprehension.

"I'mma call you."

"Promise..." Angel asked with "The Puppy dogs".

"You got my word mockin' bird, now goin'...get before ya moms run up in here and fire my black ass on my first day!" smiled Khan as he watched Angel's traffic stopper sashay out the glass door.

"Even in Khakis that ass phatter than a mug." Khan mused as one of the street walkers that Khan noticed from earlier stole his attention.

"Yes... umm how may I help you?" Khan greeted the young red bone whose skin slightly glistened in the white halter top and yellow shorts that barely contained her plump ass.

"Yea lem'me get a ice cream please."

"Cone or cup?" Khan asked while stealing a quick cleavage shot.

"Cup please, can I get some extra sprinkles too?" she winked.

"I gotchu." Khan replied while turning around to make her ice cream.

"That'll be one dollar and six cent."

"You goin make me pay for it?" she asked while batting her long lashes.

"Not if you eat it in front of me." Khan smirked.

"I could eat more than this ice cream... but it might cost a lil more than a dollar." she countered.

Suddenly Angel appeared out of nowhere with a vexed expression plastered on her face.

"So, I see you making friends already huh?" Angel questioned.

"Huh..Oh naww... this a customer, I ain't see you come in here, everything cool?" Khan replied dumbfoundly.

"I bet you didn't see me come in here, ya ass was too busy flirting with this bitch." Angel spat.

"If you see a bitch, smack a -" Angel's ninja- like reflexes slapped the ending from her sentence.

"Here bitch, you forgot ya ice cream." screamed Angel while picking up the remains of the fallen ice cream cup and hurling it at her retreating adversary.

Khan stood flabbergasted while Angel mean mugged him without words.

"I thought you was leaving?" were the first words to break the silence.

"I forgot my phone, but just 'cause I'm not here don't mean you can disrespect me like that."

"Oh she crazy for real" Khan thought while becoming turned on by her anger.

"Look... that was a misunderstanding, we wasn't doin' shit...If you really giving me a chance to be with you, I'm not goin' to fuck that up. Stop getting ghetto in McDonalds, go home, rest ya feets, and wait for a nigga call."

"Alright." Angel replied then pursed her lips with her eyes closed.

"Yo, she really crazy." Khan said to himself while reciprocating to her kiss.

"Hmm... your lips are soft... call me." Angel moaned as her face went from irate to jovial in a split second, then bolted back thru the glass doors.

"What da hell did I get myself into?" Khan asked himself out loud.

"Trust me, you don't wanna know." replied an eavesdropping Jamie.

"Oh, yea?" Khan questioned.

"Yeah she my best friend, but that bitch ain't all there." snickered Jamie while chewing bubble gum in the drive – thru section.

Jamie was a quiet pale skin white girl that wore her blonde hair in an up-dew ponytail with a large pair of pink framed glasses that sat atop of her small nose. Her loosely fitting uniform did a poor job of concealing her large breast and shapely butt.

"Why didn't the manager come out here when Angel was causing a scene?" questioned Khan.

"Who, Tyler? Tyler ain't worried about nothing but smoking weed." Jamie's nosey ass announced.

"He probably out back getting high now, as soon as Gina and Angel leave, he dips out back, it's like clockwork." she assured him.

"Speak of the devil." Khan said as Tyler came in slowly strutting from the back of the store smelling like the inside of the Mystery Machine.

"Sup, Khan... Angel said you was a fast learner, I hope you

didn't mind me stepping off for a sec and holding down the fort...I had to um..um..handle some business." Tyler slurred through red eyes.

"You good family, shit ain't shit." Khan assured.

"Awesome...hey why don't you take a load off, sit back, grab something to eat, be back in 30." Tyler suggested.

"No prob." Khan said while grabbing a ten piece nugget and taking his food to the breakroom.

As Khan put out his cigarette and headed back inside the building to finish his shift, he stopped dead in his tracks as he observed his frightened manager Tyler get bombarded with a slew of obscenities and death threats from a very short man dressed from head to toe in hot pink Versace.

"Sir, I apologize for what happened, but I wasn't here." Tyler said with wide eyes.

"Bitch shut-up, I don't want no apologies, I want compensation." demanded the man in pink.

"Compensation...for what sir?" Tyler questioned.

"For what! For damaging my god damn merchandise." the man in pink said while pointing towards the young woman that Angel assaulted earlier.

"Take off them glasses, Suga." the man in pink ordered, as the young woman removed her glasses, the rest of the staff accompanied by the few remaining customers all gathered to watch the ordeal unfold.

"See that ...there.. Hows a pimp suppose to make money off that trainwreck..." he commented while pointing at the woman's bruised left eye.

"Suga, had at least two more jawns to service... so if my pimp-rithmetic is correct, which it always is... I calculate two Ben Franks, minimum." he surmised.

Tyler's body shook nervously as his pale face became a shade lighter. His cool demeanor was replaced with fear as he frantically rubbed his dark hair searching for a solution. Noticing the sudden change of his composure, Khan intervened.

"Excuse me...Mr...ah -" Khan interceded.

"Pimp...Flamingo Pimp." Flamingo Pimp replied while shifting his eyes towards the newest edition of their party.

"Look it wasn't his fault, ole girl had a misunderstanding with my lady friend... and well you know how women are. She thought ya folks was trying to make a play at me, and before I could diffuse the situation. Emotions got the best of my gal so she spoke with her hands, instead of using her words." Khan clarified while opening his register withdrawing two one-hundred- dollar bills.

"It's my fault, I shouldn't have tried to shit where I eat at, please take this money and have a meal on us, you and your lady friend." Khan offered while Tyler stood looking like a scared frat boy.

"What's ya name, play boi?" questioned Flamingo Pimp.

"Khan"

"Khan huh. Well Khan I like ya style, I was about to put that white boy on the streets and make him get my money, but you displayed great diplomacy. Oh and Suga, fuck you doin' in here tryin' run game behind a pimps back?" Flamingo Pimps eyes shifted to Suga who remain quiet.

"Uh...no daddy...I -" Flamingo Pimp cut her words short by saying...

"Oh yes you was so you know you sleeping in the hole tonight!"

"Mr. Flamingo.." Khan interrupted.

"Mr. Flamingo Pimp" Flamingo Pimp corrected.

"Mr. Flamingo Pimp, she wasn't doin' nothing either man, she just asked for a ice cream."

"Don't cover up for this bitch, that's the mascara's job."

Flamingo Pimp preached.

"Bitch, grab us a twenty piece and go wait in my Cadillac truck." ordered Flamingo Pimp.

"What kinda sauce you want Daddy?" asked Suga.

"Bitch, sweet n sour!" screamed Flamingo Pimp.

Tyler broke his scared trance long enough to fetch Flamingo Pimp's order, then rapidly retreated from harm's way.

"*Bitch ass nigga.*" thought Khan as Flamingo Pimp reached in his pockets to retrieve the $200, Khan gave him.

"Take this back pimp, ain't no need in you getting in trouble with ya girl and a theft charge."

"Respect." Khan replied while placing the money back in the drawer.

"Respect... that's what it's all about. As long as you have respect, you can do whateva you want...some try to earn respect through fear, but that ain't respect, that's just-folks being punks. When you got respect nigga and bitch alike do as you command." Flamingo Pimp dropped a gem while heading towards the exit.

"I appreciate that Flamingo Pimp, get at me sometime."

Khan spoke while watching Flamingo Pimp head towards the doors.

"Will do... stick with ya job black man, it may not seem like much, but trust me this a blessing."

The gentleman saluted one another as Flamingo Pimp slid in the back seat of his bright pink truck while Suga checked the rear-view mirror before pulling off.

Chapter Six
RED MASK

"Red mask on… call me Rafael/ I'mma keep it gansta' til I burn in hell/ Keep them thangs on my side, call me Rafael/ I'mma keep it gansta, til I burn in hell/"

Blasted from the speakers of Brent's Impala as K-Willz rode shot gun in search of their prey.

"You sure Crazy Cracker stay round here?" asked K-Willz as he carefully examined his chrome plated .380.

"Yea yo, I know this bitch that used to fuck wit 'em, she say he live in the apartment complex across from the Walmart in Rosedale, and this it nigga!" Brent stated while turning down K-Willz played out mixtape.

"Yo, why you turn down my shit!" reacted K-Willz while searching the faces of the pedestrian traffic.

"Cuz nigga we supposed to be on a recon mission right now and ya hot ass making dumb noise."

"Recon! Nigga this search and destroy!"

"Regardless how you put it, it's easier to hit an unsuspecting target, than a moving target." K-Willz sat back in his seat unable to deny Brent's logic until he suddenly spotted his objective.

"Yo!, Yo there that bitch go right there, ova by da ice cream truck!" yelled K-Willz while opening the door before the car came to a complete stop.

"Hold up lem'me scope da scene befo -" Brent's words were cut short by the slam of a car door.

K-Willz stood out like a NBA player in China as he swiftly crept to the rear of the ice cream truck, donned in a all red sweat suit with a bandana covering his lower face to match. He gripped the handle of the .380 firmly, while delicately resting his index finger on the trigger. Noticing that his target was surrounded by children as he purchased them all ice cream, K-Willz thoughts ran rapid.

"So what, he with kids, this bitch done had me laying up in a fucking hospital bed for a week straight lookin' like a fuckin' mummy and shit, nah this bitch gotta die... today!" K-Willz concluded as he advanced in on his prey.

Extending his arms with the gun in hand, K-Willz rounded the corner of the truck startling the small group of children along with his intended victim.

"Yea nigga what's up now!" shouted K-Willz as he pointed the gun at the innocent bystander then shook his head in disbelief.

"Sir, you can take my wallet...or whateva, just please don't harm me or my kids." begged the Crazy Cracker look-a-like.

"Everybody just get on the ground." shouted K-Willz while jogging back to the Impala.

As K-Willz jumped back in the car he motioned for Brent to take-off ASAP. Brent complied and gave K-Willz a side-eyed look with a smug expression on his face.

"Don't say shit nigga just drive." ordered K-Willz.

Brent continued to drive toward the exit of the complex until a large black Suburban truck cut off the route. Another black truck pulled up behind Brent's car as several men with guns in hand surrounded the vehicle.

"Yo, you got ya banga too?" asked K-Willz in a hush tone.

"Fuck... nah, I left my shit at 'Lita house." Brent confessed.

"Fuck, what we goin' do wit one gun, against all these niggas?" K-Willz questions were answered once his eyes met with his intended mark.

"Yo... I know that ain't my boy K-Willz runnin' round here playing Rambo lookin' like da Kool-Aid man with all that red on!"

laughed Crazy Cracker as members of the Hooligans took aim at the four wheeled dark red casket.

"Fuck you bitch!" screamed K-Willz as he prepared to go out like a G.

"Nah... Fuck with me!" retorted Crazy Cracker as the distinct clicking sounds of guns cracked back in preparation of death, K-Willz quickly aimed his gun at the windshield towards the direction of Crazy Cracker and pulled the trigger.

Click..Cha..

"Fuck da gun jammed." K-Willz shouted while a bug-eyed Brent said his prayers in silence.

"Rambo you just won't learn will you." Crazy Cracker taunted while secretly thanking the good lord for his own blessing of the malfunctioning weapon.

"Enough of this shit... wet 'em up!" ordered Crazy Cracker.

Boom! Boom! Boom! Boom!

After the hail of gunfire the large group dispersed leaving the car decorated in red.

Chapter Seven
SQUARED UP

Slurp...Slurp....Slurp.

"Yeah suck that shit bitch." coached Khan as he firmly grabbed a hand full of Suga's hair to get a better view of her succulent pink lips devour his glossed erection.

Slurp...Slurp...Slurp...

"Oh my God!" Khan chanted as Suga's head game brought the bitch out of him.

"You like that shit daddy?" Suga moaned between slurps.

"Please stop talking." Khan uttered while doing his best to maintain his seated position on the toilet of the McDonald's restroom.

Suga could feel his testicles tightening as she massaged his sack then allowed her throat to relax for her signature deep throat fatality. Khan's ass cheeks clenched as he became a statistic to Suga's talented tongue while exploding down her throat, the penned-up rage and frustration of seven long years.

"Well, worth the price of admission." Khan smiled.

"I aim to please, just lem'me know when you ready for another go around." replied Suga, while checking the two twenty-dollar bills Khan gave her for authenticity.

"That money just as real as them contacts you wearing." joked Khan while peeking out the stall.

"Lem'me see if the coast is clear, wait for a knock on the door." instructed Khan.

"Okay." replied Suga, while fixing her hair using the mirror as a guide.

Khan stepped out of the men's restroom casually scanning the hall for co-workers or anyone else that might throw a wrench in his plans. Seeing no signs of danger to his employment, Khan knocked on the men's room door then walked away as if nothing happened.

"Well don't we look five pounds lighter." sang Jamie as she caught Khan off-guard by the soda machines.

"Huh... Nah...Oh.. You mean I was shitting." Khan stumbled then smiled at Jamie's ambiguity.

"Ah Duh! You was in there for a while, I thought you fell in." joked Jamie.

"Wow, this bitch is nosey as fuck." Khan mused.

Khan had finally adjusted to "The square life", in just a few short weeks he was making amazing progress with his job and Angel as well. He learned that as long as he stayed clean during the day shift, when Angel and Gina worked, he could run wild during the evening shifts. He kept most of his affair's secret and did his best to avoid the ever-inquisitive Jamie at all costs.

Khan checked his watch that read 7:42 p.m. "Eighteen more minutes till I can bounce." Khan said to himself while standing idly behind his register.

"Hey, Khan by the looks of things you can leave early if you want, business is pretty dead right now." Tyler spoke while spraying Axe body spray on his clothes to hide his non-professional scent.

"A'ight.. That'll work." Khan said as he went to the breakroom to retrieve his jacket and two loose cigarettes. As Khan made his way back to his register to clock out, Tyler approached him.

"Hey... since I see that your cool now, if you ever wanna step outside and partake in the delights of Sir Granddaddy Kush, you are more than welcomed." Tyler offered.

"I'mma have to take a rain check on that for now, even though I am a ganja guru, I can't take the chance of pissing dirty until I leave this work release spot."

Well, just let me know when you all clear to party." stated

Tyler as he went to the drive- thru window to bother Jamie.

Khan rode in silence as he allowed the cornucopia of characters of the bus to entertain him. He observed a trio of young black males, sit behind a tall slender white male, talking aimlessly on his phone, moments later one of the young black men snatched the phone as all three made a mad dash once the bus doors opened.

"Hey, they stole my phone!" screamed the white man as he abandoned his small carry-on bag and gave chase to the suspects.

The bus driver calmly put the bus in drive and continued on as this was a mundane event. Homeless vultures circled the white man's forgotten parcel then tore it apart in search of valuables. Two homeless men argued over a wallet that was dropped to the floor during a scuffle between the two bums, a third homeless man picked up the wallet and discovered it was empty and the tussle ceased. Just as Khan thought the festivities of public transportation died down, a chocolate angel with a familiar face entered the bus and made her way in his direction.

"Khan!" Lakia screamed girlishly. "Lakia!" Khan mimicked playfully.

"Shut- up, why you ain't been calling lately?" questioned Lakia while squeezing next to Khan in the two-man seat.

"Well, last time I spoke to you, you told me ole boy was back in town from basic training, so I figured I'd chill and let you get ya quality time."

"Oh... I thought it was because Angel had you on lockdown or something." Lakia smirked.

"What? How you know about her?"

"It's all over Facebook, my baby Khan this...my hubby Khan that...that girl love her some Khan." Lakia stated with a hint of jealousy and Khan quickly picked up on it.

"So whatchu mad or something?"

"Mad? Boi bye, I'm on my way to see my nigga now."

"What kinda man allows his woman to ride the fuckin' bus this late at night, he must not give a damn." Khan surmised.

"Boi its only 8 p.m., don't worry about mines. You just make sure you wrap up ya lil ding- a- ling with Angel hot ass."

"I haven't touched that girl yet." Khan stated truthfully.

"Yea right!"

"Scouts honor." Khan held two fingers up like the boy scouts.

"Then why you with her, I'm sure you find all dat ass attractive."

"Yea she straight, we just ain't had the time, I only see her at work and I'm not gonna disrespect her by trying to fuck her in the bathroom or anything like that. I ain't rushing, besides I get my home pass next weekend. I'mma slay her then." Khan assured.

"Okay, lover boy, oh and my man is leaving in the morning so I would appreciate a phone call now and then. I might even swing by ya moms house next weekend, ya know... to check on my best friend." said Lakia while standing up to depart from the bus.

"I would love that." Khan said with a wink as he wrapped his arms around Lakia for a quick off-balanced embrace.

"I'mma call you." Khan shouted as she walked away.

"Okay." Lakia replied while waving goodbye.

Chapter Eight
ALL IN THE FAMILY

"You have reached the voicemail box of 443-622 -" Khadeja ended the call after hearing K-Willz's voicemail for the twentieth time.

"Why won't this nigga answer the phone? He still can't be trippin' about that Crazy Cracker shit." wondered Khadeja.

After the incident at the club, K-Willz asked the staff at the hospital to deny her visitation. He completely ignored all of her calls and made no effort to contact her. If it wasn't for Brent informing Valita about K-Willz status, she would've been in the dark in regards to K-Willz health. Valita laid in her queen size bed in nothing, but her matching Victoria secret bra and pantie set as Khadeja sat on the edge of the bed, drinking an off-brand vodka straight from the bottle. Poetry wasn't the only thing that soothed her mind when she was upset. The alcohol helped with the pain, but formed new emotions to stir up as she eyed her cousin's voluptuous half-naked body spread out on the bed like a tasty dessert.

"Yo, you woke?" Khadeja said to Valita while slapping her ass causing it to ripple slightly.

"What...Huh?" Valita said waking her from a drunken slumber.

Khadeja said nothing as she grabbed both of Valita soft ass cheeks and slowly spread them apart. She then caressed her phat pussy lips through the thin material of her pink panties causing Valita to moan quietly. Khadeja continued to fondle Valita's kitty cat with one hand, while using her other hand to remove her jean shorts. Khadeja never wore underwear so undressing was never a strenuous task. After shedding her t-shirt, Khadeja tugged at Valita's panties until she had a clear view of Valita's prized possession. The bright yellow hue of Valita's bubble shaped asset caused Khadeja's mouth to water. Khadeja orally attacked Valita from behind, pressing her nose into the crack of Valita's ass and viciously munched away at her sweetness. The alcohol started to wear off as Valita tried to pull away from Khadeja's grasp, but Khadeja being the bigger, older and stronger of the two, kept Valita hostage as she swallowed nut after nut.

Khadeja finally released her cousin as she laid on the bed with her legs spread wide.

"Now, it's my turn, eat this pussy or I'mma get Mr. Charlie." Khadeja said while smiling and rubbing on her own clit.

"Mr. Charlie! I told you, chill out wit that big ass dildo...I'mma eat ya shit, but this the last time... this shit ain't right.

I'm only doing this 'cause I know K-Willz been M.I.A...So let's get this over with." said Valita while slowly positioning her face directly above Khadeja's hot box.

Since the incident with Khadeja's father, she no longer considered any sexual act, "Taboo". Everything and everyone was fair game. Khadeja wasn't bi-sexual, she was "tri-sexual' meaning that she was willing to try anything at least once. Initially she was never attracted to women, let alone her own cousin, but the constant drinking coupled with her cousin's awesome body, always snuggled up with her every night, made her throw normal thinking out the window. Khadeja never considered herself into girls, she just liked a little taste every now and again.

"Ahhh! Yea 'lita...just like that, please don't stop....I'm cummin' awww." Khadeja screamed before reaching her third climax.

"Thank you lil mama, I knew that mouth of yours could do more than just talk shit."

"I can suck a mean dick too!" Valita bragged.

"Don't make me get Mr. Charlie and find out." laughed Khadeja while wiping sweat from her forehead.

"A'ight. Stop playing, that big ass dick be hurting, that thing got Brent beat by at least five inches." stated Valita while searching for her switch blade to open a Dutch Master cigar.

"You keep fucking with them lil ass dick niggas."

"Hey, ya dick can be small as long as ya pockets big." Valita chimed as both girls gave each other a high five.

"Break that weed up while I gut this blunt."

"Where the weed at?" questioned Khadeja.

"Over by my phone, on the nightstand." replied Valita while locating her knife in the depths of her knock-off Prada purse.

As Khadeja stoop up in her birthday suit to fetch the weed, she felt light-headed as the walls of the small basement slowly spun in her head.

"Whew. This cheap ass vodka ain't no whore." Khadeja said as she noticed how junky Valita's bedroom basement was kept.

Valita didn't have much furniture, just a small nightstand, a long dresser with a vanity mirror made of oak wood, her infamously unmade queen size bed that sat in the center of the room, and a 27-inch flat screen T.V. that was mounted on the wall to the left of her bed. Khadeja rarely went to visit her mom's, not because of a dislike towards her mother, but because of an eerie feeling that came to her whenever she entered "that house". Valita was everything to her, and she truly appreciated the comfort Valita provided. They would be lost without one another.

K-Willz literally pinched himself to see if he was still alive, this was confirmed when he realized Brent was staring at him thinking the same thing. Brent's car was indeed decorated in red. Crazy Cracker and his crew of delinquents opened fire on the vehicle with an array of paint ball guns leaving the car covered in red paint while also leaving Brent and K-Willz shocked and stupefied.

"Hey, yo...on my mama this the last time that white boy goin' make me look stupid my nigga." K-Willz spat embarrassed.

Brent nodded his head then thanked his lucky stars for allowing him to breathe and put the pedal to the metal en route to route 40.

Chapter Nine
WEEKEND WARRIOR

"Oh my god, you got approved for your home pass!"

"Yup and that ain't even the best part, Ms. Johnson, said that since I been doing so well at this facility and at my job that she extended my 24-hour home pass for the entire weekend." Khan beamed with joy as he relayed his good news to Lakia over the prison phone aka "The Bluebird".

Khan's behavior improved drastically during the course of his stay at B.P.R.U., which was strange in the eyes of Ms. Johnson. When inmates that served the kind of time that Khan served hit the streets, they usually collapse under pressure from the temptations of the streets. After observing Khan's behavior at the prison, and learning through conversations with Ms. Gina, that Khan has made employee of the month twice and Ms. Gina was also considering enrolling Khan in the management program, it almost brought tears to Ms. Johnson's eyes. Extending Khan's home pass was the least she felt she could do, to encourage the noble precedent.

"Yea so umm... clear ya weekend for a nigga." Khan said while lightly massaging his semi through his sweatpants.

"Oh, I'll be there, just make sure you-know-who ain't trippin."

"Damn, I almost forgot about Angel crazy ass." thought Khan.

"Hey, ... everything is everything. I'mma always make time for my best friend." Khan charmed.

"Whateva, lemme finish cleaning up before Thomas gets outta school. I'mma drive up there witcha mama to pick you up in the morning." replied Lakia.

"Good shit, and tell her ass to be here at 8:00 a.m. sharp, cuz when they let me out this bitch... I ain't looking back!" laughed Khan as he said his goodbyes with Lakia and sat by the Bluebirds with a contagious smile plastered on his face.

Khan was so excited for tomorrow's events that it almost made his bladder burst. Passing several inmates which Khan slightly acknowledged, he finally reached his destination. After washing his hands from a piss that could've filled a swimming pool. Khan was greeted by Black as he slowly stepped in the communal restroom.

"Black man... what's good brova?"

"Ain't shit, bout to get faded right quick...you tryin' ride wit me?" asked Black while he removed a small baggie and started rolling up the contents in white rolling paper.

"Bruh... ya know niggas wit jobs get piss tested every week." Khan protested.

"Man, fuck I like? Boo-Boo da fool.. This ain't weed nigga, this that Kiesha."

"Kiesha?" Khan replied with unfamiliarity.

"Yes, nigga.. Kiesha, Dukey, that dumb shit, spice... K2 nigga!"

"Yea I ain't neva fuck with nothin but E- pills and weed dug."

"This shit like weed on steroids, and the best thang about it is... it don't show up in ya piss."

"Word?" Khan gawked at the revelation.

"I am still here ain't I, I been tested like 20 fucking times." Black bragged.

Khan had been drug free for almost 90 days now, and he was hell-bent on staying out of trouble for his kids' sake. He had missed most of their lives and wanted to prove to himself that he could be a great dad... but that wouldn't start today.

"Fire that shit up nigga." Khan yelled while rubbing his hands together like a big ass Fly.

"My nigga... we bout to get fried!" sang Black while passing

Khan the lit stick of K2.

"Ahh" Khan yelled after an array of coughs from the chemically laced cigarette.

"Take it easy lil bruh, you don't need much of it." Black cautioned.

"Nigga I been smoking since I was two." Khan mimicked Smokey.

"A'ight nigga, watch-whadda tell ya."

As the two longtime friends departed from the bathroom, a thick cloud of smoke stalked their trail.

"Yo, let's go to your room, my celly old ass prolly in my cell working out." Khan suggested.

Black's cell was closer, and even though Black was a workout junkie as well, he kept a locker full of sweets which Khan thought could be useful when or if, the munchies set in.

"Yo, I don't even feel this shit Blackman."

"Just give it another second, trust me."

As the two entered the cell, Bone, Blacks celly was nowhere in sight.

"Where ya celly dug?"

"He at work, he got a job at Moe's downtown."

"Good shit, that place be-" Khan's body felt like he had just been dropped from a cliff.

"Da fuck..." Khan said out loud as his head started spinning.

"Yea, nigga, I told you that's that shit." Black boasted.

Unable to respond, Khan slowly rubbed his temples with his index fingers while attempting to ease the tension his brain was feeling. *Boom-Boom Boom-Boom* Khan could hear his heart beating, louder and louder *Boom-Boom*. His eyes felt misty as his head slowly nodded without consent.

"What da fuck is happening to me?" Khan thought to himself as he still could not speak. *Boom- Boom!* His heart sounded while his brain continued to spin as if in competition with his heart. Khan felt like his soul was being removed from his body as he slowly extended his arms above his head, in an attempt to clasp his spirit in the omnipresent tug of war.

"Fuck is this nigga doin'?" questioned Black while crushing a bag of hot chips and enjoying his homeboy's K2 episode.

Suddenly the white tiles on the floor started to crack as Khan sat there in panic as the hand of Satan emerged through the floor surrounded by hell fire.

"This is it, I'm done, so much in my life I ain't get a chance to do... Mama I love you."

The large molten hand opened wide as it centered Khan's motionless body, preparing to snatch him away to the depths of hell. One last tear escaped his bloodshot eyes as he said his final goodbyes and awaited for the inevitable.

"Yo, is you cool?" Black said, placing his hand on Khan's shoulder.

"What." Khan replied visibly shook.

"Nigga.. You geekin' drink something nigga." as

Khan took a swig from the orange soda Black passed him, he looked Black directly in the eyes and said.

"Yo, I need some more of that shit!"

"Daddy." Khan's kids yelled as he approached the car.

"Hey, my little ones, and who is this little man y'all got with y'all?" Khan asked knowingly.

"This is Thomas, Thomas say hello to Mr. Khan." instructed Lakia while getting out of the front passenger side of the car.

"Hello, Mr. Khan." greeted Thomas bashfully.

"Hey, lil man, boy you sure got a head on your shoulders." joked Khan while grabbing Thomas's head.

"Leave my son alone, his head is just fine the way it is." Lakia defended while smiling at her smaller chocolate twin.

"You got a big head too Mr. Khan!" continued Thomas.

"And don't you forget it." Khan replied slyly while winking at Lakia before jumping in the back seat with little Khannie on his lap.

"Hey baby." greeted Renee as she waited for everyone to buckle up before pulling off.

"Home sweet home." sang Renee as she pulled up to her home in her black Nissan Pathfinder.

Khan nearly broke his neck as he ejected from the back seat of the SUV like one of the children. Giddy with excitement, Khan surveyed his old neighborhood of Dundalk, in search of familiar faces. In nearly a seven-year hiatus, it amazed Khan that nothing really changed, yet everything seemed so surreal. The nosey old neighbors were still on post, watching everything and everyone. The bad-ass little kids were now bad ass teenagers, and the foul signature smell of the local sewage company confirmed that indeed... Khan was home.

"Baby, you hungry?" questioned Renee as she unlocked the front door.

"Hell yeah...whatchu cookin'?" answered Khan while taking a seat in the white lawn chair on the porch.

"Ya brothers should be out back, I told them to fire up the grill." replied Renee while entering her home.

"Tell them niggas come holla at me." yelled Khan as Lakia took a seat in the empty chair adjacent to Khan.

"So Khan.. How does it feel to be home?" asked Lakia while noticing how handsome Khan looked in such simple attire of Levi blue jeans and a white tee-shirt.

"I ain't goin' front, this shit feel like a dream." Khan said while admiring how plump Lakia's thighs looked in her hip hugging black Seven jeans. Khan was always a thigh man but a pretty pair of feet was his kryptonite.

"If she got some nice toes I'mma wife this bitch." thought

Khan while staring at Lakia's all- white jordan sneakers.

"Something wrong with my tennis?" asked Lakia while watching Khan, stare at her shoes.

"Oh, Nah...dem joins hard, what they the 11's?" lied Khan.

"Yea... I bought me and Thomas matching pairs."

"Cool, you mind if I hit this fug?" asked Khan while preparing to light the cigarette.

"Do ya thang, this your world." replied Lakia

"Good answer, good answer." Khan smiled while inhaling his cigarette.

"Broski!!" shouted Yella as he and Scrap came barging through the screen door.

"Look at y'all two ugly muthafuka's." shouted Khan.

"My nigga, what's good, sup Lakia." greeted Scrap.

"Peace and love baby boy." Khan replied as Lakia nodded.

"So, what's da deal for today, I heard you out for the whole weekend." Yella beamed.

"Yea...I'mma just sit back today, prolly do a lil sight-seeing tomorrow."

"Cool, I'mma take you to my new crib, you know I got the state of da art recording studio now." Yella said proudly.

"Good shit, lil bro, I'mma check it out."

"Yo, we got some burgers and hot dugs for you whenever you get hungry." Scrap chimed.

"Always on time, I'mma come out after I finish this Fug." Khan said while slightly nodding his head in the direction of Lakia. Picking up the hint, both Scrap and Yella stood up to leave.

"I know you can't smoke, so we bout to go out back and burn something. Holla when you finish big bruh." said Yella while he and Scrap went back inside the house.

"So what are your plans today Khan?" asked Lakia.

"You." Khan said seductively.

"What about Angel, ain't she coming ova?"

"Nah, I didn't tell her I had a pass for the entire weekend. I told her it was just for Sunday."

"Sneaky, Sneaky" Lakia laughed.

"It ain't like that, I just wanted to manage my time correctly."
"Sure... you ain't gotta lie Craig." Lakia said in her Felicia voice.

"So...Thank you for coming ova here and spending my first pass with me. It means a lot."

"It's no problem, and when the kids go to sleep, I got a little surprise for you." smiled Lakia.

"Really... kids! Bedtime!" Khan yelled while opening the door startling the children as they played Nintendo.

"Stop it, it's like 9:30 in the morning." laughed Lakia.

"Oh... a'ight, I guess we can wait until after lunch." Lakia just shook her head as she pondered what life would actually be like if they were more than just friends.

Chapter Ten
A GIRL CAN DREAM

"What!" Khadeja spoke slightly upset that she was disturbed during her mid-day nap, but somewhat excited that K-Willz finally called her back.

"Hey Ma, I'm sorry about ignoring ya calls and shit, I been just going thru a lot of shit and I didn't wanna take none of that out on you." K-Willz justified while signaling to the young Spanish broad that he met in the V.I.P. section, during his battle with Crazy Cracker, to keep quiet.

"You didn't have to ignore me for so long, all I ever wanted in life was to be loved." Khadeja replied with tears starting to build up as she closed her eyes tightly.

"I know baby, but that's just how I handle my business. It ain't nothin' personal, sometimes I need my space -" K- Willz words jumped as the groupie gargled on his dick.

"What!" What are you doing?" asked Khadeja.

"Huh?....um...nothing. I hit my toe."

"Okay... so when can I see you?"

"Tonight, but do you think you can do me a favor?"

"It depends." said Khadeja while picking up the half smoked blunt from the ashtray.

"Look, I need you to go holla at Slick and get that bread he owe me from that battle."

"Why can't you go get it?" questioned Khadeja.

"Cuz I got some shit to attend to in these streets." lied K-Willz.

Truth be told, he was still embarrassed about being knocked out by Crazy Cracker, and on top of that, the latest stunt by Crazy Cracker didn't do much to help the already, destroyed image of K-Willz.

"You my bit -, woman, and I need you to grab that chedda' for me while I get this money from the streets."

"Okay, when Valita wake up we goin' go grab it for you baby." Khadeja finally gave in.

"Thank you, bae." K-Willz replied while shoving his dick further down his new fan's throat.

"Are you sure this is the place?" asked Khadeja while verifying the address in her text message.

"Yes, bitch, Slick has shows here all the time, he usually comes here like twice a month." assured Valita, while checking her hair, using her compact mirror.

The two girls walked inside a small building. The layout of the venue was very simple, it had a small center stage floor, with a dozen tables scattered around the outskirts of the room. A lone mini bar sat caddy corner, while two microphones grabbed the attention of Khadeja as they were placed center stage.

"Where da fuck is Slick?" asked Valita while eyeing the unattended mini bar.

"This nigga just got all this shit out here without nobody watching." said Valita as she went to the mini bar and made herself at home.

Khadeja was fascinated by the allure of the microphone as she slowly approached it, while running a delicate finger along the mic stand. She removed the microphone from its stand and gripped it firm as she closed her eyes picturing the small stage being surrounded by a fictional audience. She was a writer, not a performer, and her introverted lifestyle made these thoughts something she could only phantasm.

"Here bitch." Valita interrupted her trance with a glass of Cîroc.

As Khadeja stood with the mic in one hand and the vodka in the other, she playfully imitated the battle rapper "Goodz" as she gave Valita a few bars.

"Hey Vee, errrbody know you ain't fuckin' wit' me/ And if you is, then I'm charging a fee/ So how you want it/ Run them lips and its Mr. Charlie all in ya stomach/"

Khadeja paused once she heard someone clapping as Slick appeared walking towards the impromptu performance with a huge smile on his face and dollar signs in his eyes.

"Damn, that shit was fire!" yelled Slick.

"You ain't gotta pump my head up, I was just fuckin' around." Khadeja retorted embarrassed.

"That was awesome, what's ya name first off?" asked Slick.

"I'm Khadeja, the girl you spoke to about coming to get that money for K-Willz."

"Oh, you K-Willz girl, well you rap a lot better than he does...

would you ever cons-" Khadeja cut him off mid-sentence.

"I already see where your scheming ass is goin' at with this and the answer is no, I write from time to time, but I'll be damn if I'mma be looking stupid on stage while somebody dis the fuck out me!" Khadeja spat.

"I dunno Dee, you sounded real good to me." interjected Valita while smiling at Slick.

"That's what I'm saying." Slick concurred.

"Blah Blah Blah, could you please just give me my man's money so we can leave." Khadeja said while becoming agitated.

"Khadeja….come here." said Valita as she walked Khadeja to an isolated area of the venue.

"Listen, this is a chance for you to do something with your life, you're so fuckin' talented and if anyone deserves to be on stage, it's you. K-Willz sucks, and I know you don't have much experience but with Slicks help we can run this shit. You know I got ya back all the way sis." smiled Valita.

Khadeja took a second to think over the proposal, then walked towards Slick.

"Do you think I could be good at this?" Khadeja asked Slick.

"I know talent when I see it, I wouldn't waste your time, and I damn sure wouldn't waste my money." Slick said as he draped his arms around both girls, smiling from ear to ear.

"I'll tell ya what, let's go have lunch so this way we can go over all the details and if your still having doubts, I'll leave you be." said Slick as he removed his arms from around the girls to cover his quickly formed erection that stemmed from the thought of making money, and love with the two beautiful exotic looking women.

After a lovely lunch consisting of lobster, shrimp and clams from Moe's Seafood, Slick dropped the girls back off at Valita's home.

"Bye, Slick I'll be in touch." said Khadeja as she walked towards the porch but not before noticing Brent's Impala parked across the street.

"Here we go." said Khadeja as she and Valita re-directed towards Brent's car.

"Hey baby." said Khadeja as K-Willz sat shotgun mean mugging the rear of Slick's fleeing Yukon.

"So you just rippin' and runnin' wit any ole nigga's now?"

questioned K-Willz.

"Don't start wit me, you asked me to handle some business for you and that's what I did, trust me bae, it ain't even like that....eww." said Khadeja from the back seat.

"I hit ya phone mad times, what's up wit that?"

"I was having a business meeting with Slick, so I put my phone on silent."

"Business.... What business y'all got? You was sent to get my ducketts then bounce!" yelled K-Willz.

"Well I wanted to surprise you, but Slick thought it would be a good idea to make me a battle rapper."

"Get da fuck outta here, Slick must be high." K-Willz said while taking the blunt from Brent.

"That's what I said but he heard me spit a few bars and"

"Bars...what you know 'bout bars?" questioned a smiling K-Willz.

"*I know that's something you ain't got.*" Khadeja mused.

"I know how to rap baby, I just neva' performed in front of people. I been writing for a long time." Khadeja informed.

"You know what, maybe Slick is on to something, we ain't really got no female battle rappers in B-more so as long as you take it serious, I'mma rock witchu."

"That's the best news I heard all day, and here is the money Slick told me to give to you." said Khadeja while removing several one hundred dollar bills from her clutch.

Being back in the confines of K-Willz's small apartment brought back many memories, some good but mostly bad. Nevertheless, Khadeja felt invigorated with her new lease on life, a fresh start with her lover, and finally a way to earn an income of her own. She was hell-bent on becoming less dependent on men, and planned to use this newest venture to jump start her life on the right track. As Khadeja sat alone in the love nest, she scrambled through K-Willz's dresser drawers in search of her infamous notebook, which she had been without through the course of their momentary hiccup in their relationship.

"Where's my damn notebook." Khadeja said out loud as she stumbled on a gold earring with the name "Carla" embroidered in cursive.

"I can't believe this nigga bringing bitches into our home."

Khadeja fumed as she punched the wall in anger.

"Fuck that shit hurt." screamed Khadeja while shaking her hand frantically.

"You know what…I ain't even goin' trip, I got a trick for this nigga." huffed Khadeja while picking up her phone to alert her partner in crime.

Chapter Eleven
FACEBOOK

Khan was exhausted after a long day of horse playing with the kids, two-hand touch football with the local teens, and stomach full of BBQ. Khan sluggishly removed his all-white Air Max's as he attempted to get comfortable on the sofa next to Lakia.

"I didn't think them kids would ever go to sleep." yawned Khan.

"Me neither…but we can relax now." replied Lakia while rising from the sofa.

"Where you going?" questioned Khan while admiring her small but jiggly backside, as she vanished from the living room.

"To get your surprise." Lakia yelled from the kitchen.

"'Bout time… lem'me do some push-ups first." smiled Khan as his energy suddenly re- emerged. Lakia entered the living room carrying a bottle of Paul Masson and two glasses.

"That's my shit." Khan smiled while accepting one of the glasses from Lakia.

"I know, ya brova told me." replied Lakia as she topped off both glasses.

"So." Lakia said while taking a seat next to Khan and sipping slowly from her glass.

"What's on ya mind Khan?" she asked while staring into Khan's eyes.

"Honestly." Khan replied while staring back.

"Yea.. Be honest."

"I wanna see your feet." Khan said seriously.

"Why?" Lakia replied slightly confused and shocked.

"Cuz yo, everything about you seems perfect, and if ya feet's is up to par, then we may have to re-evaluate this friendship."

"Boi you crazy, ain't nothing wrong with my feet."

"Man gim'me them sneakers." Khan yelled as he dove for her right leg.

Lakia struggled to pull her foot free from Khan as he removed her shoe and sock. As Khan examined her naked foot, he smiled at how cute and soft her freshly pedicured toes were squirming in his hands.

"So it's settled...pending you don't have a penis, you are the perfect woman." Khan announced while releasing Lakia's foot.

"You are an idiot." shouted Lakia while removing her other sneaker and picking up her glass.

The two friends took this opportunity to open up on a more personal level, Khan went into detail about his criminal past, and Lakia shared tales of her struggle being a single mother and the hardships that came with it. Lakia revealed that her boyfriend was a good person but he didn't portray any qualities to father a child that didn't belong to him. Their conversation included everything from past relationships, to their favorite pets as children. As time passed Khan could feel the effects of the alcohol, and judging by the looks of Lakia's low eyes, she too was feeling it.

"If you trying to lay back, I got a bed in the basement." Khan slyly suggested.

"You ain't slick, but I am getting a lil tired." replied Lakia.

Khan led the way down to the basement steps, to his childhood bedroom with Lakia in tow. The large bed in the middle of the floor made up most of the décor. There was a large screen television and a desktop computer which completed the basement's furnishings. Khan neglected to turn on the main light of the bedroom, opting to use the dim lighting of the half bathroom that occupied the corner of the room.

"Make ya self at home." said Khan while surfing the channels of his T.V.

"Put some music on." slurred Lakia.

"You got it." Khan retorted while settling for the R&B channel.

"I'm not trying to pressure you/ Just can't stop thinking 'bout you/ You ain't even really gotta be my girlfriend/"

The smooth sounds of Musiq Soul child serenaded the atmosphere.

"I love this song." said Lakia as she sang along while subconsciously caressing her breast.

"Yea…this dat." replied Khan, as he enjoyed Lakia's one woman show.

Khan's penis could take no more as he slid over to Lakia and lightly massaged her neck and shoulders. Lakia welcomed his touch as her eyes closed while Khan's massage quickly turned into a TSA pat down. Khan started to peel every layer of clothing from Lakia as she mimicked his aggressiveness' by tugging at his belt and pulling down his jeans. The two were stripped down to their underwear as they gazed at one another, slowly inching forward to the inevitable…once their lips met, their bodies were filled with a euphoric sensation that neither of the two had ever experienced. The kiss started slow… innocent, as their hungry tongues darted with eager exploration. Khan's hands calmly unclasped Lakia's bra as he inhaled on Lakia's breast while fondling the other. Lakia faintly stroked Khan's tool into complete stiffness. Lakia grabbed Khan's erection with both hands as she placed light kisses on the tip, out of nowhere, Lakia started bobbing on Khan's pole at a rapid pace, until she noticed Khan's moans rise in octave. She then removed his penis, which was shiny with saliva, turned around and positioned herself on all fours and yelled.

"Beat this shit up!"

Khan was more than up for the challenge as her ass clapped for motivation. Once Khan adjusted to the small canal of her woman hood, he pounded her petite frame with all he had. Smack! Smack! Smack! Her cheeks sounded after every thrust. When Khan felt his legs shake, he knew that his time on this ride was coming to an end.

"Fuck!" Khan shouted as he shot warm nut in the depths of Lakia's sweetness. Khan was in heaven as he enjoyed the best ten seconds of his entire life.

"You can't be serious?" Lakia spat upset that Khan was already getting under the covers preparing to go to sleep.

"I'm sorry, but fuck you expect, I ain't had sex in seven years. Just lem'me recharge and I got you on the rebound." Khan spoke while fluffing his pillow.

"Whateva." Lakia said while channel surfing and waiting for Khan to pick up where he left off.

As a few minutes passed, Lakia was startled by Khan's snoring.

"This muthafucka!" said Lakia as she laid back in the bed and started to finger herself, determined to get her nut off, one way or another.

"Oh shit." Khan said while he was suddenly awakened by a head bobbin on his dick underneath the blanket.

"Damn this bitch can't get enough of the boy." Khan mused while enjoying the early morning performance.

Khan watched as the head under the blanket moved faster and sucked harder as he eventually unloaded his seed into the warm host.

"Damn baby that was the shit." Khan said as he removed the blanket from her head.

"What da fuck!" shouted Khan as he laid eyes on the last

person he thought he would see.

"Fuck you doin' here... what happen to-"

"Ya lil girlfriend, she left like an hour ago, I was at my mom's house, up the street and decided to see how my man was doing."

"Bitch I ain't ya man, you just my fuckin' babymama."

Helen was the biological mother of Khan's kids, due to the constant struggle with drug abuse and countless rehab facilities, she allowed Khan's mother Renee, to legally adopt her children. Helen barely involved herself in her kid's life, she only came to see them when Khan was present. Renee only tolerated her behavior for the kids' sake.

"You ain't glad to see me?" asked Helen with a mouth covered in semen.

She was as beautiful as they came, she was a white girl that had porn star tits and a video vixen's ass, and she was short in height, barely reaching five foot with long blonde hair and blue eyes. As pretty as she was on the outside, she was indeed as ugly on the inside, always putting her needs before everyone including her own children.

"Man you gotta roll." Khan said while searching for his jeans.

"How did you know I was coming home this weekend anyway?" Khan questioned.

"Facebook, ya shit all over Facebook." Helen stated while using an old towel to wipe her face.

"I don't even own a Facebook." Khan shouted as he grabbed Helen by the hand and escorted her up the stairs and out the front door. As soon as Khan opened the door he stood, face to face with Angel.

"So lem'me get this straight, you lie to me about what day you coming home, just to creep around with this bitch." Angel spat while eyeing the much shorter Helen.

"What… how did you know when I came -"

"Facebook." Angel answered.

"Fuckin' Facebook." Khan said while shaking his head.

"Look Ma, I did come home yesterday but that was just to spend a little quality time with the fam so I could devote all my attention to you today."

"But what about that bitch Lak-" Helen's words were cut short when Khan pulled out a twenty- dollar bill and stuffed it in Helens face.

"Helen just stopped by to get this money that I owed her from way back, isn't that right?" Khan said with pleading eyes.

"Um... yup, and I'mma get the rest from you next time I see ya...Bye." replied Helen as she made a bee-line straight to the dope man.

"*Fuckin' bitch.*" Khan thought as he noticed Angel's face soften a bit.

"Oh, I'm sorry baby, I guess I need to stop blowing up on you so fast. Huh?"

"You good mama, don't change a thang."

After showering and throwing on the fresh gear that Angel brought Khan, Khan sat dumbfounded as Angel explained how to operate his new cellphone, she also purchased for him.

"But it don't got no buttons." Khan said while holding the thin Verizon phone as if it had A.I.D.S.

"It's not supposed to, geez Fred Flintstone, get outta the stone ages and pay attention." instructed Angel as Khan vividly listened to her explain how to make calls, send text messages and most importantly, create a Facebook.

Angel took Khan on a shopping spree, then the couple went to dine at one of Khan's favorite restaurants in Fells Point. Angel was very touchy feely as she continued to rub on Khan's thigh while he drove her white Honda Accord to his brother Yella's condo in Cedonia.

"Baby, I want that dick now." cried Angel and Khan did his best to obey all traffic commands.

"Mama Chill, you goin' make a nigga crash, my brova got a extra room, after we kick da bo-bo for a minute, I'mma gutcha…I promise." Khan smile as he noticed the wet spot forming in Angel's pants.

"Damn, she horny forreal!" Khan thought while driving 10 and 2. As they pulled up on Goodnow Road, Khan found a parking spot in front of Yella's complex. Without the assistance of Angel, Khan managed to send a text to Yella letting him know of their arrival. After being buzzed in, Khan was briefly mesmerized by Angel's enormous ass, as he followed behind her up the stairs.

"Yurrrrp!" yelled Swine as he greeted Khan and Angel in the stairway.

Swine was introduced to Khan through Yella, he was very young, at the age of 19, but carried himself extremely mature. Swine was Yella's engineer and best friend. He stood about 5 foot 10 inches and was very thin and lanky. He was the goofball of the group, but wouldn't hesitate to pull that iron on you if you violated him or his people. He had a big heart and contagious smile that always brighten up everyone's mood.

"How you been fam?" Khan greeted with a half hug.

"Well.. I got like two more bitches pregnant, but besides that, everything is everything." replied Swine.

"Whoa… bruh, you betta start wrappin it up."

"Man what's done is done, who this you got with you?" Swine said while eyeing Angel's thick frame.

"This my lady…. Go drank some water witcha thirsty ass." laughed Khan.

"Respect… you did that doe." Swine said while giving Khan a thumbs up.

Angel smiled then walked past the guys into the living room.

"This is such a nice place." Angel commented.

"Thank you." replied Yella as he entered the living room and gave Khan a half hug and a smile.

"Bro-time!" greeted Yella.

"My nigga….Man fuck all the pleasantries, let a nigga see this studio you keep braggin' about." shouted Khan.

"To the Bat Cave!" shouted Swine while attempting to steal one last glance at Angel's rump.

Yella's condo was a sight to see, he had a large living room with a balcony that extended over the surrounding wooded area, a kitchen with all up to date appliances including a smart stove and fridge, a modest sized dining room, furnished with a small wooden table completed with four wooden chairs and three bedrooms. Yella used one of the bedrooms for his studio, one for himself and the third bedroom doubled as a guest room, aka Swine's hotel. As Khan entered the studio, he was immediately impressed by the quality of equipment that Yella had sprawled out all over the room.

"Yo you got a nice set up here." Khan praised.

"Thank you big bro.... all my team is missing is you." Yella said with a wink.

"Look yo... I ain't really tryin' to fuck wit that rap shit no more, I'm passing the torch to you nigga, matter fact lem'me hear whatchu got." Khan stated in an attempt to take the heat off of him.

Yella was in a rap group called M.F.I. (Made for It). It consisted of two other members, Swine and their older cousin Duke, who was currently sitting in the city jail for Breaking and Entering.

"I'mma let you hear my newest shit, but we goin' get back to you getting down wit us Khan... ain't nobody forget about ya skills nigga." Yella promised.

"You rap Khan?" questioned Angel.

"A lil something but I'm retired now, it's a young man's sport." laughed Khan.

"Nigga whateva, tell that shit to someone who don't know…Hey, yo Swine!" interrupted Yella.

"Yurrp."

"Spin that shit." shouted Yella.

"Hey yo its Baltimore Bitch, that's Big Blunts and crab cakes/ Man you couldn't see my paper if you was my classmate/"

Yella sang along with the song as the entire room nodded their head with the catchy hook.

"I'm on my way to Marz/ I'm on my way to Marz/ I'm on my ways to Marz/ Bitch I'm on my way to Marz."

Blasted from the speakers as Khan gave Yella, dap for producing a Banga.

"Hey yo on some real shit, I fucks wit it." said Khan.

"Thank you yo, ya opinion be the only one I be looking for." said Yella as he licked his – thumb to wipe away an imaginary stain from his yellow Air Force ones that matched his all yellow Nike sweat suit.

Swine, whom was dressed down in fatigues and a white tank top started rolling a blunt as the foursome continued to vibe to Yella's mixtape.

A few hours later, Khan escorted a very impatient Angel to the guest room, where she wasted no time stripping down to her birthday suit. As she sat on the bed, Khan walked up on her and positioned his semi erect penis in her face.

"I know you don't think I'm sucking that thang. Do you?" questioned an appalled Angel.

"Um... yea, you my woman….that's what you suppose to do." Khan stated while rubbing his penis to prevent it from going soft.

"You can't even get that shit hard." yelled Angel.

"That's cuz you keep talking, I'm tryin' to see if ya mouth know any other tricks." smiled Khan.

Angel stood up and slowly massaged Khan's dick as she stuck her tongue in his mouth and roughly swapped spit. Angel's kiss was a far cry from the magic Khan experienced with Lakia. If it wasn't for the amount of booty meat that Khan cuffed while kissing Angel, he feared his dick would've never rose to the occasion.

As Khan, finally stiffened, Angel slowly bent over as Khan wasted no time sliding in, Khan barely got the tip in when Angel screamed out in pain.

"*Oh, I'm 'bout to murder this.*" Khan thought while inching in more.

"Go slow, this shit hurts." cautioned Angel.

"Yea a'ight." Khan replied while inserting his entire wood.

"Stop!" Angel screamed.

Khan was starting to become frustrated with Angel's intolerance to his penis. At first he assumed she was simply acting to play towards his ego, but the agonizing look on her face told Khan that she was in pain for real.

"Yo all this damn ass and you can't take no type of dick?" Khan shouted as he pulled his boxer shorts back up and fished through his pants for his pack of Newports.

"I'm sorry bae, I thought I could hang."

"Bitch you in da way." Khan said without looking at her.

"You want a hand job or something." begged Angel.

"Hey, yo… on da real, just go-head and bounce, I'mma see you when I see you."

Angel's face threaten to flood the room with her tears as she quickly dressed and stormed out the house. Khan just smiled as he opened the small baggie that Black gave him and rolled up a fat stick of Kiesha.

"Fuck that bitch." said Khan while blowing smoke rings in the air.

Chapter Twelve
TIME TO LEAVE THE NEST

The Macy's department store was packed to capacity with shoppers, which made it easier for Khadeja to blend in. She was here on a mission, to tuck away as many designer garments as possible without getting caught. Giving K-Willz the silent treatment led to Khadeja being dead- broke, even though she wasn't new to this lifestyle, she desperately begged for a way out.

"Oh.... This is Prada, I should get a pretty penny for this." thought Khadeja as she quickly slid her security tag remover from her hoodie and undid the tag. Khadeja had about ten bands worth of merch on her, so she decided to call it a day, as she casually walked towards the exit door, a hand grabbed her shoulder.

"Excuse me miss, I'mma need you to come with me." ordered the short stocky dark- skinned bull dike security officer.

"For what? Y'all always messing with black people in this store, get da fuck off me!" shouted Khadeja.

"Look lady I been following you since you walked in here, and if you wanna cause as scene then that's on you." replied the guard as she shook her dreadlocked head anticipating a fight.

"Fuck!" Khadeja yelled as she was slowly escorted to an office in the back of the store, while countless customers observed the humiliating spectacle.

As soon as they reached the office door, a young woman fell to the ground and started convulsing.

"She's having a seizure!" screamed Khadeja as the dike contemplated between detaining her perp or providing medical care to the fallen customer.

Years of lawsuits led to the decision to assist with the safety of the shopper as she reluctantly released Khadeja and rushed to the customers' aide.

"*I know I got a horse shoe up my ass.*" thought Khadeja as she gave thanks to The Most High, then snatched a few more items before disappearing into the crowd of vastly forming spectators.

Khadeja sat in the car with her older cousin, Yemi as she gave her the recap of her narrow escape when suddenly the back door flew open and Valita jumped in smiling.

"Bitch, you wild as shit." said Khadeja with a smile.

"And bitch you blessed! If it wasn't for me thinking fast on my feet, that strong face security bitch would'a put her Mr. Charlie all up in you." Valita shot back.

"So you was really rolling around the floor?" questioned Yemi, whom looked like an older version of Valita but her hair was dyed blonde.

"Yup, like a fuckin' fish, anything for the family." smiled Valita.

The trio drove out of the Towson Town Center Mall parking lot and made their way back to 695.

"I'mma call you once I get rid of this shit." said Khadeja as she stepped out of Yemi's dark green, late model Toyota Camry.

"Don't forget a bitch, I needs mines." replied Yemi as she waited for the girls to close her doors before pulling off.

Khadeja waved to her cousin then proceeded to high-tail it to Valita's bedroom before Sissy or any of the other nosey occupants of the crowed house notice the large amount of shopping bags, containing designer clothes.

"Hurry up and unlock that door before Sissy see this shit

bitch." coached Khadeja.

"It's hard to unlock a door and carry a billion bags…bitch!" spat Valita while searching through her purse for the keys.

"Got 'em!" yelled Valita but her victory was shorted lived as Sissy appeared in front of them as she opened the door wide and stood with arms crossed followed by a face of disapproval.

"So y'all still boostin'….hmm..hm..hmmm." as Sissy shook her head.

"What! No Brent and K-Willz bought this for us." lied Khadeja as they both brushed passed Sissy's tiny frame.

Sissy had her hazel eyes in small slits as she followed the girls in the house determined to make the girls hear her out.

"Khadeja, I know you're the one putting 'Lita up to this. Your suppose to be setting an example for your younger cousin, but you got her out here shoplifting. What happens, if y'all get locked up? I ain't bailing none of you bitches out so I hope them lil gang bangers y'all run around with got y'all's back." Sissy spoke while eyeing the clothes.

"Sissy, I'm sorry if I'm such a bad person and a terrible role model, but what about you, you lay around this bitch collecting checks from the state. You think your so high and mighty, you stealing too…just in a legal way." replied Khadeja while dropping her bags on the floor and approaching the much shorter Sissy.

Sissy was a very petite natural red head of Irish decent, her sister and Valita's mother Joyce, also shared the red hair and heavy Irish features. Sissy was small, but she was also rowdy and ghetto, and this ghetto white woman wasn't about to back down from someone young enough to be her child.

"Bitch." Sissy started while stepping in Khadeja's space.

"You don't run shit here, and ya broke ass don't pay no bills. If you wanna talk that talk, then walk that walk." yelled Sissy while pointing towards the door.

Valita had a "scared shitless" expression on her face as she awaited for Khadeja's response.

"You know what, fuck you, you section 8, welfare, government cheese eatin' piece of white trash!" shouted Khadeja as she scooped up as many of the shopping bags that she could carry and stomped out the front door.

Valita looked at Sissy with pleading eyes as Sissy broke eye contact staring away from Valita. Valita pondered the outcome of leaving with Khadeja as Sissy read her mind.

"If you walk out this door, don't come back. I did my best with you but some girls that think their women, have to learn the hard way. If you follow that train wreck out this house, I'm changing the locks."

"Train wreck! That's your blood, I can't leave her by herself out there in them streets. She needs me, shit, she needs you. I'm not tripping, we goin' be alright." Valita said calmly as she picked up the rest of the bags and headed out the door.

"*I hope this bitch knows what she doing.*" thought Valita as her body shook from the vibrations of her aunt slamming the door behind her.

"You sure it was him?" questioned K-Willz as he, Brent and Cannon sat inside Cannon's Black Ford Explorer awaiting their unsuspecting victim.

"Yea blood, I saw him wit some bad ass red bone bitch when I was coming outta footlocker." replied Cannon as they scoped the scene from behind tinted windows in the East Point Mall parking lot.

"Yo, let's just pull up on this nigga and dump! Don't nobody get out the whip." ordered K-Willz.

The trio all nodded to the sounds of Future as they carefully examined their hand guns, not wanting his gun to jam again, K-Willz spent a few extra seconds looking over his new .45 as Cannon broke his study.

"Yo, there that nigga go right there, I told you that bitch he got was bad." Yapped Cannon while briefly forgetting about the task at hand.

"Nigga let's move, fuck that hoe, and if she get in the way, spray her ass too!" shouted K- Willz as Cannon put the truck in drive and headed towards Jiffy, Crazy Crackers right hand man.

Jiffy was a short Dominican that favored the rapper Common. As Jiffy strolled aimlessly hand in hand with his female companion, a screeching truck came to an abrupt stop directly in front of him.

"Charge it to da game Fam!" greeted K-Willz with a smirk, as a barrage of bullets riddled the young couple's bodies.

A flock of innocent by-standers dove for cover as the chaos erupted. Once the clips were empty, the truck burned rubber as it quickly sped from the scene. Moments later, most of the mall-goers slowly emerged to witness the horrific sight of the disfigured corpses. Everyone reached for their phones in a synchronized matter, ironically not to alert the police, but to share their experience on…. Facebook.

Chapter Thirteen
GIVE US, US FREE

"Boom!" Jynx kicked the side of Khan's bed, jolting him from a deep sleep.

"What da fuck nigga!" Khan yelled slightly disoriented.

"They calling you on da innacom, Ms. Johnson want you." replied Jynx as he plopped back on his bed and went back to his crossword puzzle.

"Thanks but a nigga was dreaming up something nice, now I ain't neva' gonna be able to fuck Alicia Keys." uttered Khan as he grabbed his tooth brush, then headed to the bathroom.

After handling his hygiene, Khan rushed to Ms. Johnson's office, but before reaching her office he decided to make a quick pit stop to see Ms. Julie in the finance department. The finance office was setup like a bank teller booth. It had a small glass window which stood as a partition to provide some security to the cash which was issued once a week in $40.00 increments.

"Ms. Julie." greeted Khan as Ms. Julie notice him then slid some large envelops under her desk before standing to approach Khan with a smile.

"Hey, Chile." Ms. Julie replied with her strong Jamaican accent.

Ms. Julie was a large woman with very short grey hair. She always seemed to be in a festive mood which made transactions with her very pleasant.

"I was just dropping by to get my lil money right quick." Khan stated as Ms. Julie already knew Khan's weekly routine.

"Me know Chile, erry Wednesday you come by for de money, Ya no have 'ta tell me, me gotcha." Ms. Julie smiled as she retrieved one twenty dollar bill, one ten dollar bill, one five dollar bill and five one dollar bills.

"Here ye go boi, now get, Ms. Johnson's waiting for ye…I hear she's she got some good news!" smiled Ms. Julie as she left the glass window and walked back to her small desk.

After hearing Ms. Julie's last statement, Khan wasted no time getting to Ms. Johnson's office.

"Well, about time Mr. Larson!" said Ms. Johnson while pointing towards the small chair that sat in front of her desk.

"Take a seat, I have some news for you."

"What's up Ms. Johnson?" replied an excited Khan, thinking

that she approved him for another weekend pass.

"Well let me get straight to the point, this prison is getting over crowded, so I contacted the home detention office and made them aware of your progress here. If I'm not mistaken, you should have another three months left before home detention eligibility. I spoke to the supervisor…and… long story short, they will be here within the next seven business days to pick you up."

"What!" shouted Khan while jumping out of his seat.

"Calm down, I know this is good news but-"

"Great news!"

"I know but you must remain employed and you must pay a weekly fee for being on home detention. I'm not sure of the exact amount but…Blah Blah Blah Blah." was all that Khan heard once he learned that he would be finally leaving prison.

Khan stood up and shook Ms. Johnson's hand then strolled out of her office en route to hang with his favorite two people to celebrate, Black and Kiesha.

A few weeks passed since Khan's official return home and for the most part, things were going pretty good for Khan. He had no problem reconnecting with his kids, he recently made manager at his job, and he was now single and could do whatever and whoever he wanted to do. Just like clockwork every night after putting his kids to sleep, with the help of his new best friend, Facebook, Khan would entertain guest. Being home was beautiful but confined to these walls proved to be somewhat stressful, not just for Khan, as Renee was also starting to reach her boiling point with her oldest child. As Renee peaked from her window, she noticed a tall white girl open her front gate and head towards her porch. Renee was in her late 40's, and possessed the body of someone half her age. She was about average height and had a glow to her that only Hershey chocolate skin could generate.

"I can't believe this boy is bringing another girl into my house." said Renee as she jumped from her bed and located her house coat.

Khan led the tall pale skinned social media slut into his chambers as he wasted no time "matching parts" without even knowing the girls real name. He had only met the girl a few hours prior on Facebook before learning that she was single, she was horny, and she was close by.

Khan was balls deep in the Lindsey Lohan look-a-like until he heard a loud..*Boom!* Followed by a variety of slightly softer, yet highly irritating knock's at his bedroom door.

"Khan!" shouted Renee.

"Khan, open this damn door!" she screamed while banging on the door simultaneously.

"Really..." said Khan as he pulled out his instantly soft penis then frantically ordered the flavor of the night to quickly get dressed.

"Who's that?" questioned the portable pothole as she stared at Khan with confusion.

"Please just get dressed."

"Whateva!" she snapped then reluctantly complied.

As the two made their way towards the door, Khan's heart was reminiscent of past childhood ass whoppings, as it beat loud and uncontrollable, because standing on the other side of that door, neither Navy Seal nor Marines could combat with ...an angry black woman.

"Boy if you don't open this door right now. I swear to the lord and baby Jesus I'mma-" Renee stopped talking once Khan opened the door. She stood silent with a look of disgust, as Khan's once talkative guest finally understood the severity of the situation and took off running like a bat out of hell straight to her car without saying a word.

"Ma-" Khan started, but Renee finished by saying....

"Let's get one thing straight. I am more than blessed to have you home with me and your children, but once you start taking advantage of our love and kind hearts, please believe I will protect those kids. What? You think I'm either deaf, dumb or blind? You think I don't see you, sneaking them damn trifling ass bitches in my house every damn night? You been here for seventeen days, and so far I counted twenty different girls. Yea, I saw when you had multiple women come here at the same time too! You got the nerve to send ya kids to bed early just so you can do, God knows what, with them nasty little girls." Renee paused to catch her breath for a second.

"I love you son, but you clearly got your priorities fucked up, you working less hours, and what ever happened to that nice young girl that worked at your job with you?"

"We brok-"

"Shut Up!" Renee cut him off and continued.

"You need to find somewhere else to live, cuz this ain't working no more." Renee concluded.

"So you just gonna kick me out, cuz late at night when everyone is sleep, I like to have a little company." Khan stated modestly.

"Company, negro this ain't no hotel, and we ain't ya maids, you don't cook nothin', you don't clean nothin', you just play video games with the kids, then let the XBOX babysit them until bed time, and don't think bringing your kids home a twenty piece is considered making them a home cooked meal, you lazy, like I said I tried…Lord knows I've tried, but there's only one King around here and it's me. I'mma give you thirty days to find somewhere to go, I'm sorry baby." Renee said as she shook her head then vanished from Khan's view.

"Fuck I'mma do now?" Khan spoke out loud, then headed out the backyard to smoke a stick of Kiesha and make a phone call to the only person that he thought could help.

Chapter Fourteen
WORKIN' GIRLS

Valita's feet felt as if they were on fire as she and her cousin marched alongside the busy traffic of Holabird Ave. Khadeja had no idea where to go, as her pride wouldn't allow her to apologize to Aunt Sissy or forgive K-Willz for his treachery. Unable to withstand any further pain to her feet, Valita dropped the shopping bags as she screamed.

"You know what, since you don't have a clue on what to do right now, I'm 'bout to take action."

"What… you goin' call Brent, I ain't trying to see him right now cuz he goin' have K- Willz all in my business." replied Khadeja as she dropped her bags to contain a hysterical Valita.

"Nah, he don't fuck wit me no more, he all in his feelings cuz he saw a couple dick pics in my inbox."

"You's a trip girl." laughed Khadeja as she was finally able to make light of her troubles.

"Whateva, fuck him, he shouldn't have been goin' through a bitch phone anyway." retorted Valita as she unzipped her pink windbreaker and started walking to the edge of the street.

"Fuck are you doing?" questioned Khadeja.

"Taking action." replied Valita as she stood bow-legged while her breast threaten to pop out of the helpless white tank top.

Valita used her headlights to flag down some much needed assistance, as a white pickup truck parallel parked next to his damsel in distress.

"You need a ride?" questioned the elderly white man as he was so caught up in Valita's glistening display of cleavage, he didn't notice Khadeja standing just a few feet away.

"Actually I would." said Valita as she sauntered to the front seat of the passenger door and entered the truck.

After a few minutes of giggles and seductive shoulder and thigh rubbing, Valita poked her head out the window and yelled for Khadeja to get in the truck. Khadeja assumed her cousin abandoned all her bags and expected Khadeja to carry them all until the pudgy, John Deer hat wearing man, jumped from his seat and scooped all the bags then threw them in the cab of his truck as he gave Khadeja a wicked smile. Khadeja didn't ask any questions as she slid in the passenger's seat, while Valita gave directions to the Best Western Hotel.

About ten minutes later, the truck arrived at the hotel as Khadeja had a puzzled look on her face as to how they would pay for a room. Khadeja had about ten dollars to her name and she knew that her cousin was flat broke as well.

As if, Valita could read minds, she whispered "He's gonna pay for the room, don't trip, I got this."

"Okie dokie." replied Khadeja as the trio made their way to the hotel.

After unloading the shopping bags, Khadeja started to get a funny feeling when she noticed the old white man take a seat on the queen size bed and kick his feet up.

"Valita can I talk to you in the bathroom real quick." demanded Khadeja before storming off.

"What's up?" said Valita while closing the bathroom door behind her.

"Why is this old ass man still here, I didn't know he was staying the night with us!"

"He's not, he just wants us to do him a little favor in exchange for this room, and he's giving us a couple dollars too." smiled Valita.

"Are you serious, I ain't no fuckin' prostitute!" yelled Khadeja.

"Me neither, I'm a survivor, and since you ain't have no plan, then its next bitch up." stated a straight faced Valita.

"Fuck… I ain't never think shit would get this bad." replied Khadeja nearly in tears.

"Me too, but I'm tired of people trying to control us, it's time we get our own money and live life by our rules."

"Damn…so what favor does he want?" questioned Khadeja felling ashamed.

"All he want is for us to suck his dick that shit ain't goin' take but two minutes."

"I'm not sucking his dick girl." replied Khadeja.

"All you gotta do is play with his balls, I'mma handle all the hard stuff… get it?" smiled Valita.

"This ain't the time to be making jokes silly." smiled Khadeja as a slight chuckle escaped from her throat.

"Come on girl, its game time." encouraged Valita as the two

exited the bathroom to find their courteous stranger butt naked, laying on his back with a huge smile.

"'Bout time, dang I thought y'all fell asleep, y'all can take turns, I don't care who goes first, but let's hurry up and get this show on the road. I gotta handle some business soon." The old man stated as he fondled his penis into a small erection.

"Well, since you in a rush we goin' suck it at the same time." suggested Valita as both girls crawled beneath his pale hairy legs.

"Whateva." replied the old man as his eyes closed to enjoy Valita's firm grip of his chap- stick sized manhood.

Valita wasted no time as she easily deep throated the old man's length, causing his toes to curl. Khadeja lightly massaged his testicles as they became tight to her touch. Valita wrapped her tongue around the tip of his penis while Khadeja planted soft kisses on his inner thigh, as the old man pulled his penis from Valita's mouth and started to jerk wildly on his pink girth until a glob of semen exploded on Khadeja's face.

One would have thought that Khadeja was drenched in acid, as she nearly broke her neck while racing to the bathroom.

"She sure is a character." said the satisfied old man.

"Yup, she sure is." smiled Valita.

"Can I stop by later, after I deal with the wife and kids?" asked her newest sponsor.

"Sure….what's ya name by the way."

"They call me, Bill."

"Alright Bill, can I get that money from you before you leave."

Bill gave one hundred dollars with promises to return later. A few minutes later, Khadeja returned to the bed with a look of disgust on her face.

"That old fuck got cum all over my face."

"Chill girl, he left you something." replied Valita as she gave Khadeja one of the fifty dollar bills and laid back on the bed while checking her messages.

"So you not even gonna brush ya teeth, you just goin' lay back like ain't none of that shit just happen?" questioned Khadeja while shaking her head.

"Bitch relax, besides you the only one that got dirty." laughed Valita.

"Ha ha very funny."

"You need to be on ya grind right now, you be stressing ova

the wrong shit, like we gotta get rid of them clothes and I think, I know where to start."

"You know somebody?" asked Khadeja

"You didn't see all these bitches running around in the lobby when we checked in, they probably working girls, so that mean they got money!" surmised Valita.

"You might be on to something." smiled Khadeja as she started taking pictures of her inventory; to post on Facebook.

"I'mma hit a few people online, see if they want something too." stated Khadeja as she continued to take pictures of the clothing.

"You think this looks nice on me?"

"Of course girl, Gucci looks nice on everyone." said Khadeja as she went into full salesman mode trying to convince Tammy, a well-known hooker, to purchase the blouse.

Tammy was a former high school teacher with a secret fetish for bad boys. One day, Tammy decided to take Carlos, a dope dealing fifth year senior, up on his invitation to hang out with him. After their first encounter, Tammy was in love, so in love that Tammy offered

Carlos her home to stash dope. Eventually, Carlos got tired of Tammy's desperate and controlling attitude, in which Carlos broke up with Tammy. In a last-ditch effort to make Carlos come back, Tammy secretly stole from Carlos's stash and told him he would only get the dope back if he gave her another chance. Once Tammy realized that not even money could bring him back, she started sniffing the dope in an attempt to ease some of the pain. Tammy eventually found someone that was more than willing to commit to her, his name was heroin. Her new found love caused her to lose her job, her house and the respect of all her family and friends as the statuesque brunette now made a living in America's oldest past time…selling that ass. Tammy took one final glance in the mirror as her tall, large breasted figure filled the ensemble nicely while yelling at Khadeja.

"I'll take it."

Khadeja charged her $150.00 for the top and allowed Tammy to rummage through the rest of her inventory.

"So are y'all working girls too?" asked Tammy.

"It's a long story." replied Valita while texting Bill.

"It usually is." smiled Tammy.

"Y'all seem a little young but it ain't my business. I don't really get along with the other girls here, but if y'all ever need anything lem'me kno…y'all got a cool vibe." stated Tammy as she held up a pair of jeans.

"How much are these?"

"Gimme $200.00 for 'em." said Khadeja as she stared at Tammy with a thousand and one questions in her mind.

"What?" asked Tammy noticing Khadeja's glare.

"Nothing." replied Khadeja while shifting her eyes to the television.

"You can asked me anything…we girls now." assured Tammy.

"How can you just sell ya body, it don't make you feel cheap?" asked a curious Khadeja.

"It makes me feel powerful. Knowing that guys will spend their hard earned money on this pussy. I ain't goin' lie, I was scared at first, but when I realized that this pussy was the only valuable thing I had, it left me with no choice but to get my money's worth."

"I'm fucked up right now, and I really don't know what I'm doin'." replied Khadeja while staring at the floor.

"Look lil mama, I know all the tricks of the trade, so if y'all wanna work together, we could save a lot of money and split hotel cost. I can show you how to setup shop and get paid." Tammy said while pulling a cigarette from her bra.

"Do y'all mind?" asked Tammy before she lit the cigarette.

"You good. Let's do it, what's the best way to get started?" asked Khadeja with a hint of excitement.

"Well for starters, have any of y'all ever heard of Back Page…"

Chapter Fifteen
99 PROBLEMS

"Fuck that hoe!" spat Khan as he sat in the back of the MTA bus angered by Angel's theatrics'.

Gina decided to send Khan home early from work, due to a screaming match that occurred between Angel and Khan. Khan was busy enjoying the single life as he laid his mac game down hard on a pretty young thang at his register. Khan never noticed Angel standing behind him burning a hole in the back of his head as she stood with her arms crossed, mean mugging Khan and the lovely innocent bystander.

"So you just goin' sling dick everywhere now huh?" shouted a heated Angel as she approached Khan and company.

"Mama we not even together no more, so please miss me with that." Khan responded while focusing his attention back to his newest chum.

With fire in her eyes, Angel stepped into Khan's space then grabbed his dick.

"Look bitch…this is mine…all mine, now get the fuck outta

my man's face before I toss you out this bitch!" screamed Angel as the young lady quickly fled from the restaurant.

Fed up with Angel and her drama, Khan snatched Angel's hand from his groin and spazzed on her.

"You got one more time to put ya fuckin' hands on me and I'mma move some McFurniture up in this bitch!" Khan spat.

"But.."

"But shit yo, I'm done witchu yo, you too much. You play too many games, and ya pussy trash."

"Khan!" shouted Gina.

"I'm sorry Ms. Gina, but she keep trying me, like I work for her, Like I'm her slave or some shit. I love working here but this bitch crazy." stated Khan as co-workers and customers all gathered around to witness the latest episode of Angel and Khan.

"Khan, I told you on day one to leave her alone, but no, you had to bite that apple, do me a favor and take a few days off, just calm down a little and come back when your good to go."

Khan knew Gina was right, she told him to stay away from Angel, but he couldn't resist that big butt and a smile.

"I shouldn't have lost my cool." Khan said to himself while

looking out the window of the bus.

Khan stretched his long legs as he prepared for his long bus ride home. His once twenty minute trip was now an exhausting three hour journey across town, to the southwest area of Baltimore; known as Pigtown. Dundalk to Pigtown was a 30 minute drive in a car, but the slow pace of stop and go traffic of the MTA bus line was a completely different story. Khan no longer had the luxury of working minutes away from home since his mother kicked him to the curb, but to his surprise his grandfather was more than willing to allow Khan to move in with him, provided that he keep after himself, and of course chip in with the rent.

"Next Stop... Monroe Street."

Khan lit his cigarette as he took in the scenery of Wilkens and Monroe Street. Just as Dundalk Ave, the strip was littered with streetwalkers, pimps, addicts and dealers. The only difference was the abundance of homeless people that cluttered the sidewalks and bus stops. Khan dodged, dashed and stiff-armed through numerous bums asking for change and cigarettes until he noticed a familiar face flagging down tricks in the middle of the street.

"I know this bitch ain't...muthafucker." uttered Khan as he made his way towards the preoccupied prostitute. The working girl was so busy trying to find her next customer that she never noticed Khan creep up on her.

"Helen...fuck you doing out here!"

"What..." Helen replied, not accustomed to Johns calling her by her government name.

"My name is Babygirl." said Helen while attempting to regain sobriety.

"Bitch ya name is Helen, is you that high you don't even know ya own name, betta yet, do you even know who I am?" questioned Khan while attempting to reach for her hand to pull her from the middle of the street. Helen became combative as she pulled her hand from Khan's grip.

"Get the fuck off me!" screamed Helen still not able to recognize the stranger in front of her.

"It's me yo, ya baby daddy." Khan said as Helens once beautiful blue eyes stared at him with a dark red gloss.

"Khan?"

"Yes, woman."

"What are you -"

"Don't trip, come with me." Khan cut her off and pulled her to his grandfather's house.

"Where we going?"

"My house, you gotta get some clothes on and you need to sleep that shit off." Khan said while dragging Helen like a child across the street.

"I gotta get money…Snake is gonna be mad." uttered Helen as she reluctantly followed Khan inside a large row home.

"Khan! That's you?" shouted Grandpa

"Yea GP."

"You home early, next time call a nigga before you pop up here like that, I coulda had one of my freak-a-leaks up in here." shouted GP.

"I'mma remember that, guess who I got with me?" asked Khan as he and Helen walked over to GP's tan recliner to greet him.

"I know that scent anywhere, that's Harriot!"   "Helen GP…Helen." laughed Khan.

Grandpa or GP as Khan called him, was diagnosed with Diabetes some years back and eventually lost his vision, thus enhancing his other senses. He couldn't remember names but he would never forget a female's fragrance. He wasn't your typical "Bill Cosby" grandfather, he was down to earth and had a great sense of humor, and was born and raised at the local church and even sang in the choir. He played drums in the church band and attended every event held by the ministry. He was beloved by all, but he was a straight shooter. Even though he never missed a Sunday at church, he cussed like a sailor and would trick frequently.

GP extended his short arms and yelled "Girl get over here and give grandpa some lovin'" Helen bent over to hug GP as he squeezed her butt in the process.

"Grandpa!" shouted Helen.

"My bad jitter bug, you know my vision done left me, honest Abe I'm sorry." replied GP as he smiled.

Helen couldn't help but smile at the old man as she looked around the home.

"This house looks so much bigger than the outside." said Helen while walking back to Khan.

"Yea, it was a fixer upper, but the church sold it to me for a low price, so I had to jump on it" replied GP.

"Yea, I love this spot, I just wish it was closer to my job." said Khan as he led Helen upstairs.

"GP, we going up stairs, you need anything before I dip?"

"Yea, come holla at me real quick."

"Helen go upstairs, I'mma be up in a sec." said Khan as he walked back towards GP.

"Hey grandson, check this out, now I don't mind you bringing company over here but I do got a couple rules."

"Okay?" Khan stated while rolling his eyes.

"Don't roll your eyes nigga!"

"What, I didn't … how did you?" questioned Khan.

"I heard them shits." GP retorted.

Khan shook his head and smiled while GP prepared to lay down the law.

"Rule number one… Don't smoke that shit in my house! Keep this damn house clean! Don't be eating up all my damn food! And if you plan on trickin' up in this bitch, you betta' make-sho grandpa get a slice!"

"Ain't no fun if the homies can't get none" laughed Khan.

"Damn skippy." chimed GP.

"But my baby mama off limits nigga!"

"Hey, I told you that was a mistake."

"Mistake my ass, but I gotchu doe." said Khan as he prepared to leave.

"Hey." GP called out.

"Yo."

"Don't bring no bitches in here if they don't know they ABC's."

"ABC's?"

"Yea… ABC's… Always Be Contributing. Don't be no captain save-a-hoe. If they ain't bringing nothing to the table, you got's to swerve on 'em." preached GP.

"You sounding like a real pimp old man." laughed Khan.

"Don't hate da playa, learn from him."

"Will do GP… will do." said Khan as he climbed the stairs and entered his bedroom.

Khan heard the shower running as he flopped down on his queen size mattress.

"I know this bitch was up here snooping through my shit." said Khan as he scanned his large bedroom.

The room was practically empty aside from the small dresser and 13 inch television, which Khan played his XBOX on in his spare time. Khan's mattress laid on top of a frameless box spring which acted as the rooms' center piece. The only good feature about the room was the private bathroom, which gave Khan an excellent view of Helen's naked body as she made her way towards the bed.

"I really don't like you, but for a junkie… you got a bangin' ass body." said Khan as he watched Helen dry off her legs, then wrap the towel around her long blonde hair.

"Thank you… I guess." said Helen while laying on her stomach making no attempt to hide her nakedness.

"So… Snake got you out on them streets like that huh?" said Khan while eyeing her bubbly backside.

"We gotta eat." Helen responded nonchalantly.

"Tell that nigga get a job, or here's an even better idea…how about you get a job."

"Yo, don't be acting like you give a fuck, cuz you don't. I ain't got nobody in this world but that man, and I'mma do what I gotta do to make sure we straight." said Helen while staring at Khan in the eyes.

"Well I wish you had that same attitude about our family, we coulda been a great team, but you so worried about chasing that monkey. You put the high over everything."

"And you don't?" asked Helen.

"Fuck you talkin' bout!" Khan retorted.

"Nigga…you chase highs too…you chase the highs of pussy and getting money all day. I left you because you can't keep ya dick in ya pants, and I gave the kids to ya moms, so they could have a chance. I'm real, I know I ain't shit, and those kids don't deserve to be sleeping in crack houses with me." cried Helen.

"You know what, we both some fuck ups, you can't get off da drugs and I can't stay outta jail, but we don't have to give up. Maybe the whole picture-perfect family thing is dead, but we can at least strive to give our kids more of our time."

"You right, I'm about to go to a rehab and-"

"Chill, I done heard that shit a thousand times, let's just start with something simple…. Like a phone call to the kids." Khan spoke while placing an arm around Helen to comfort her.

Khan hated Helen, but he still loved her, in fact she was his first love. He wanted nothing more than to be with this girl forever. When she first got pregnant, Khan was ecstatic, but when prison got in the way, Khan realized that Helen wasn't a girl that would stick around and wait for him. Khan was a hustler on the streets, so Helen was accustomed to fast money and nice things, which unfortunately for Khan, put Helen in a tough position being left with two kids and absolutely no job skills made it hard on her to provide for herself, let alone her kids. The longer Khan was away, the more involved in drugs Helen became. Now at the point of no return, Khan struggled with his emotions towards Helen.

"I wanna talk to them, but let's take a nap first and call them later." suggested Helen as she removed the towel from her hair allowing it to cascade onto her shoulders while giving Khan a seductive look.

"Yea that's what's up." said Khan as he stared at Helen's large peach colored breast.

"See something you like?" Helen teased while grabbing both breast and squeezing them.

"Maybe." said Khan as he felt an erection brewing in his work pants.

Helen wasted no time attacking the khakis which caged her kryptonite, tugging on his pants until she freed his tool. Helen gripped his meat firm as she planted lite kisses on the tip.

"You miss me Daddy?" Helen asked in-between kisses.

"A lil sumthang." uttered Khan with his eyes closed.

"Can I suck it, please Daddy?" Helen begged while placing one of her small hands on Khan's ball sack.

"Yea go head." Khan whispered.

"Huh…what was that Daddy, I couldn't hear you?" Helen playfully stated while running her tongue around his balls to the tip of his wood.

"Yes suck it." Khan said a little bit louder while struggling to keep composure.

Helen grabbed his hard dick with both hands and held it in front of her mouth like a sword swallower, then slowly inched it into the warmth of her throat, then she suddenly removed it.

"Are you sure I won't get in trouble like I did last time Daddy?" Helen said while pouting, then licking some of the precum from the tip of his dick.

"Bitch, if you don't suck that dick I'mma -" Khan's words were quickly replaced by loud moans as Helen skillfully slurped down every inch, thus up holding her title as the undisputed heavy weight dick sucking champion of the world.

Weeks passed by as Khan successfully completed his home detention program and aside from the mandatory parole, Khan was a free man. Khan breathed a little easier since Angel finally gave Khan his space, making his job a much more enjoyable experience. Khan's relationship with Lakia also blossomed into something greater than friendship. Lakia started meeting Khan at his job after work and they would ride the bus together to Grandpa's house completely lost in each other's company.

"Yo, you might aswell stay with me since ya baby daddy taking ya son for the whole summer." suggested Khan while rubbing Lakia's feet.

"You serious?" asked Lakia while sitting up in Khan's bed to look at him directly in his eyes.

"Yes, I know I've been all over the place with theses females but lately, these last few weeks since we've been together.. I ain't been thinking 'bout nobody but you." Khan admitted.

Lakia rented a room at her Aunt's house which her and her son, Thomas shared. She loved her family but her Aunt was taxing her something serious for the small bedroom that her young cousins constantly raided in search of her clothing whenever Lakia was away at school or work. Lakia also worked at McDonalds, but she worked at the Eastpoint Mall location. Lakia shared custody of Thomas …well sometimes. It was a miracle that Thomas Sr. actually texted Lakia and said that he would be taking his son for the summer. She also suspected that Kenny, her boyfriend, was cheating on her with a young lady in the army due to all the pictures Kenny shared of the two on social media. Every picture of the duo displayed some type of affection, hugging sitting in close quarters. Call it women's intuition but a lack of phone calls gave Lakia all the confirmation she needed. She knew that life with Khan was like rolling the dice, but had it set in her mind, that his words were true and he could change for her.

"Do you think GP would mind me living here?" asked Lakia.

"I'm pretty sure he thinks you live here already, you here damn near everyday anyway." Khan assured her as he kissed the top of her head then started to get dressed for work.

"Fuck it… I'mma roll da dice witchu… but I'm warning you now, if you fuck wit my heart…oww-" Lakia spoke with closed eyes.

"Mama…chill out, you not the only one with they heart on da line. I'm putting myself out there with you, I'm in it for the long haul." Khan replied while lightly kissing the small developing tears forming in the corners of Lakia's eyes.

"Okay… I trust you." Lakia smiled weakly.

"Good so whats da game plan mama?"

"I'mma get my uncle to help me pack and bring my stuff here while your at work, gimme ya key so I can copy it. Good thing I have off today so everything should run smooth."

"Cool well let's get rollin' cuz the bus will be here shortly."

Chapter Sixteen
BAD BREAK-UP

"Oh my God Papi, take it easy on me!" shouted Khadeja as the hung African cab driver punished Khadeja's pussy.

"You like dat bitch!" grunted the African as he pushed her head down and fucked her even harder in the doggy style position.

Suddenly he stopped stroking her swollen vagina, pulled his dick out then positioned the head of his dick on Khadeja's virgin asshole.

"Whoa...whoa... whoa!" screamed Khadeja.

"Huh?" replied the African with a puzzled look.

"You done already killed my pussy, ain't no way in hell I'mma let you fuck up my ass!"

"But da ad said anything goes." pleaded the trick.

"*I knew I shoulda read them damn Back page ads 'litas freak ass be posting.*" Khadeja thought.

"Me want 'dem cheeks!" whined the African.

"I'mma go get someone who can help you out with that." said Khadeja as she pulled up her leggings and ran into the hallway in search of 'Lita.

"Dee... you cool?" said Tammy as she noticed the flustered look on Khadeja's face.

"That long dick trick tryin' to take my butt." cried Khadeja.

"What?" laughed Tammy.

"You heard me... I ain't even let K-Willz do that so I'm damn sure not gonna let no damn trick get it first." Khadeja protested.

"It's cool, I'mma soulja mama... just split the take with me." said Tammy as she walked back into the hotel room to finish the job.

Khadeja wondered the hotel lobby in search of Valita. She came across the ice machine, grabbed a few cubes and stuck them in her pants to soothe her throbbing vagina. It had been almost a month since Khadeja and Valita left Sissy's house and Khadeja was slowly coming to terms with her new career choice. She bedded about three tricks a day and still had some trouble adjusting to "The Life." Now Valita on the other hand took it all in stride. She felt that she could finally get paid for something she was good at. Valita was a child living in an adult world. So she took pride in making grown men beg. She would literally milk them for all they were worth. The two girls manage to put away a little over $3,500 for a rainy day. They hid the money under the mattress. Tammy did about ten tricks a day so needless to say, saving money was never her thing. All of her cash went directly to the dope man. As Khadeja continued to ice her kitty cat, she spotted Valita talkin' to the desk clerk.

"Whateva nigga... Fuck you!" Valita screamed as she noticed Khadeja and walked towards her.

"What was all that about?" questioned Khadeja while chucking the soiled ice cubes behind the soda machine.

"Girl, can you believe that fat ass Bin Laden nigga gonna tell me he knows we working girls and if we don't suck his dick for free whenever he wants he's gonna call the cops on us." yelled Valita.

"He must have found our ads on Backpage." said Khadeja.

"Probably so, I made like a hunnid of them damn ads." said Valita while waiting for the elevator to take them back to their room.

"Damn the whole city gonna know we some sluts now."

"Bitch we been that." laughed Valita.

When the girls reached their floor, the African brushed by them smiling at Khadeja with a large grin on his face. Khadeja shook her head and immediately grabbed her vagina which still hurt.

"Here's your cut." said Tammy as she made her way towards

the elevator.

"Where you going?" asked Valita.

"I got a pocket full of money, do ya have to ask?" smiled Tammy.

"The Dopeman." both girls said in unison.

"Duces." sang Tammy as she made her exit.

"Well things are finally starting to look good for a change. We got a couple dollars saved up and enough steady tricks, to have us wanting for nothing." Valita spoke while splitting a Dutch.

"So what's up with that rap shit, have you spoke to Slick?"

"I told him to give me some time to get my shit together."

"Okay… well let's just stack this paper in da meantime in between time."

Knock-Knock-Knock the door shook.

"Tammy must've left her key card." Valita spoke while opening the door without looking thru the peek hole.

"What da fuck!" yelled Valita.

SLAP! – Valita caught a violent hand across her face.

"So y'all bitches up in here selling pussy ignoring niggas and shit." yelled K-Willz with Brent in tow.

"Get da fuck out now!" shouted Khadeja while running to her cousin's aide.

"Bitch shut up…since y'all wanna be hoes maybe we wanna be pimps. Now kick that money out!" demanded K-Willz.

"We broke, now please leave.." Khadeja cried.

"Wrong answer." replied K-Willz, as he pistol whipped Khadeja with his brand new .45 and laughed while Khadeja slipped in to an unconscious slumber.

Alone in her bedroom little Khadeja sat on her bed with her face buried in her knees, while clutching her favorite baseball glove as tears poured from her big brown eyes.

"What's the matter, sweetheart?" asked Walter as he heard his daughters whimpers from outside her bedroom.

"Nothing." spat Khadeja as her pig-tails shook with her response.

"Come on now, tell daddy what's bothering you." Walter spoke while taking a seat next to his youngest daughter.

"Stupid Jasmine said that girls can't play baseball. She said that it's only for boys!" cried Khadeja.

"Your sister probably just wishes she could throw a ball like you. Never let anyone tell you that you can't do something. You can do anything you put your mind and heart into. Jasmine just thinks like your mom, she wants you to do more girlie things like ballet class." said Walter as he smiled at Khadeja.

"I'm going to be the best baseball player in the world. Even better than those stupid boys!" announced Khadeja.

"That's the spirit Dee, now who wants ice cream?" asked Walter proudly.

"Me!" screamed an excited Khadeja, but as she jumped off the bed to follow her father he suddenly vanished leaving Khadeja puzzled. She looked around her bedroom and it too started to morph into a fuzzy darkness.

"Daddy!" she screamed while noticing her voice maturing into an adult tone, her arms started to stretch along with her legs and before she knew it, she was now a little girl trapped in an adult body.

"Daddy!" she cried out again, yet no answer.

The joy that she felt from the ice cream was replaced by an awful pain that traveled throughout her entire body. The darkness started to fade away as her eye lids began to flicker.

When Khadeja's eyes opened, they slowly adjusted to the familiar setting of her hotel room. She attempted to yell for Valita but her tongue was met with a foul mixture of blood and semen. The salty combination caused Khadeja's face to grimace and immediately puke the contents of her stomach all over the cheap hotel carpet. Feeling slightly light headed, she wiped her mouth with her forearm and she felt the remains of more dried up excrement imbrued on the sides of her face. A gentle breeze caressed her skin alerting her that she was completely nude as she spotted her once stylish ensemble, scattered on the floor as if it had been ravaged by animals. An enormous knot quickly formed on the top of Khadeja's head. Her entire body was consumed in pain, but the most excruciating sensation came from the depths of Khadeja's rectum. She rubbed her anus and discovered small droplets of blood.

"What the fuck!" screamed Khadeja out of frustration?

Being sodomized was one thing, but she had been raped…again. The fact that she just had every orifice on her body violated almost pushed Khadeja over the edge until she remembered that she was not the only victim, Khadeja gathered the rest of her strength and made her way towards Valita, who also laid disrobed and unconscious.

"Lita! 'Lita! Wake up baby." coached Khadeja while shaking Valita's nude bruised body from her daze.

"Huh…what happened?" asked a befuddled Valita.

"They raped us…I can't believe this shit." said

Khadeja as she noticed two things while glancing around the ransacked hotel room.

The mattress where Khadeja stashed their cash was flipped over, and all of Tammy's belongings were gone.

"I think ole girl set us up." said Khadeja while staring at the spot where their small fortune once sat.

"Damn." was all that Valita could muster.

"I can't believe this shit." Khadeja repeated.

Khadeja tried to shake the feeling of revenge for the larceny as she helped her cousin from the floor. There was an eerie silence as the girls inspected the damage done to themselves and each other until Valita asked.

"So what now…" Khadeja stared at the heavens searching for the right answer to comfort her cousin, but opted to speak from the heart. Khadeja made direct eye contact and said.

"I guess it's back to square one."

Chapter Seventeen
ONE FINAL SALUTE

"Baby its youuuu…you're the one I love…you're the one I need." Lakia sang along with Beyonce as she prepared dinner for Khan and GP.

Lakia had officially moved into the house and she was a welcomed addition. GP enjoyed the home cooking, and Khan enjoyed everything else Lakia had to offer. Having a regular job and a Live-in girlfriend was a first for Khan. He vowed to become a better man for his new woman, his kids and himself. Lakia got Khan to leave the drugs along, and Khan convinced himself to leave all the other girls alone. This was definitely something new for Khan but he was more than up for the challenge.

"I'mma make my boys a nice steak dinner tonight." smiled Lakia while searching through her playlist on her phone for a new song as she prepared dinner.

"Aww!" screamed an unknown female voice coming from upstairs.

"Who in da hell is that?" questioned Lakia while running upstairs to investigate.

Lakia noticed the frantic sounds were coming from GP's bedroom. She almost turned around and went back downstairs to finish cooking, assuming that Grandpa was simply entertaining one of his many "Freak-A-Leeks", but another scream more horrific than the first, indicated that this was a scream of fear not pleasure. **Boom.** Lakia barged into GP's bedroom as a look of complete confusion over took her face.

Gp's handcuffed body laid sprawled across his bed, butt-naked as his body convulsed while his eyes rolled to the back of his head.

"Oh my God!" screamed Lakia as four young Asian women ran past her dressed in schoolgirl uniforms. Lakia quickly called 911, then covered GP's still hard penis with a blanket while searching for the key to the handcuffs.

Khan stood outside in the parking lot of his job taking a much needed smoke break, He pondered if he had what it took to actually live a square life. One woman, one very small source of income, no car, no drugs, just him against the world.

"It is what it is." said Khan as he noticed Flamingo Pimp making his rounds to collect his money up and down Dundalk Ave.

"Now that's da life….that's how I wanna live. All them women, all that money… I want that, well everything except for that big ass pink truck." laughed Khan as he shook the thought, then made his way back inside the McDonalds to finish his shift.

As Khan walked behind the counter a middle aged brown-skinned woman approached Khan with a ghetto swagger.

"May I help you ma'am?" Khan asked politely.

"Yea lem'me talk to a manager." demanded the belligerent customer.

"I am a manager, how may I help you?"

"I was in the drive-thru, I ordered three twenty piece nuggets and y'all only gave me six damn BBQ sauces." she smacked.

"So you just want some BBQ sauce?" asked Khan while still trying to maintain a professional tone.

"Ah…duh! Fuck is all y'all stupid or something?" she patronized.

"Ma'am there's no need for name calling. I can correct this." assured Khan.

"You need to correct ya life, fuck is you like 30 years old, still working at McDonalds. And y'all is too stupid to give a bitch that's spending good money, enough BBQ sauce for her damn food." She raved while Khan felt his cool quickly slipping away as the rowdy customer continued.

"Then y'all got da nerve to make me get out of my car, walk up in here and ain't even offer me no free food for my troubles!"

"Would you like an apple pie ma'am?" Khan offered while rubbing his temples to nullify some of the stress.

"A pie?!...Fuck is that gonna do for me? Y'all got me wasting all my damn time in this stupid store with you stupid people. Y'all can't even work in McDonalds without fucking shit up!"

"Then what would you like ma'am?" asked Khan through clinched teeth.

"Not no damn pie, I want something else to eat."

"You want something else to eat ma'am?"

"Yaas Bitch!" she smiled, then crossed her arms over her chest.

"How's about you eat a dick, you dirty bargain basement smut. Fuck outta my face before I come around this counter and violate my parole!" fumed Khan as he started walking towards the woman.

Gina had just come from her office and caught the tail end of the heated exchange. She quickly jumped in-between Khan and the customer to de-escalate the situation. After receiving a free meal the customer continued to talk shit as she walked out of the store, threatening to call the corporate office for Khan's unethical behavior.

"Gina…. I know… I'm sorr-" Gina cut Khan off.

"Go home, take a few weeks to get ya life together. I'll decide what I'm going to do about your job here."

"Damn Gina, that wasn't even my fault doe." pleaded Khan.

"Just give me a little time to see what I can do." said Gina as she walked away.

Khan was upset and was about to follow Gina to plead his case but his phone vibrated and the text message from Lakia caused him to stop in his tracks. Khan jetted to the break room to retrieve his coat, then bolted out the double glass doors to the bus stop.

"Damn, bus ain't neva here when you need it." said Khan with a worried expression stamped all over his face.

"Everything okay?" questioned a nosey ass Jamie from out of nowhere.

"Where da fuck you come from?" asked a startled Khan.

"I'm everywhere…now what's da matter, pancake platter?"

Khan smiled involuntary, as he was unable to keep his worried gaze. Jamie, although nosey as hell, was a person that always displayed positive vibes and high spirits. It was almost impossible for Khan not to smile when in Jamie's presence. She had a very bubbly personality, and a bunch of corny jokes to keep everyone around her smiling.

"Well... I got into it with another customer, so Gina sent me home again." said Khan as he finally gave in.

"Is that all?" Jamie asked.

"No, I think it's for good this time... I'm pretty sure once that customer complains to corporate, not even Gina will be able to save me."

"I hear all that, but what's really bothering you?" asked Jamie while sensing this wasn't the real reason behind Khan's distress.

"My girl just told me that my Grandpa's in the hospital, he had a heart attack." Khan spoke while fighting tears.

"Geez...well I hope he recovers. I'm sorry to hear that." said Jamie while wrapping her arms around Khan.

Khan hated to cry around people, especially females, but for some strange reason he let himself go. It felt safe for him to let his guard down around her. He took in her sweet scent and warm embrace. Khan felt his entire body tingle as Jamie pressed her large breast firmly against his chest and whispered...

"If you ever need me, just give me a call." she gently grabbed his phone and input her number then walked away.

Khan shook his head in disbelief as the weight of today's activities were almost too much to bare. Khan watched Jamie vanish into the restaurant as the number ten bus finally arrived.

"What's the patient's last name sir?" asked the middle aged Hispanic receptionist.

"Larson... Victor Larson." replied Khan as he anxiously awaited the location of his grandfather.

"He's in the emergency ward, directly down the hall to your left, pass the double doors. I will let the clerk know your coming, so just wait in the lobby until someone calls you."

"Thank you." said Khan as he navigated his way through the University of Maryland Medical Center.

Khan moved swiftly through the long off-white themed hallway, as he desperately tried to ignore the stale smell of the hospital. Khan hated everything about hospitals, the smell, the slow staff, the possibility of catching an airborne virus from another sickly visitor, or not knowing if your loved one would ever leave. As Khan reached his destination, he quickly spotted Lakia wearing an identical look of agony. Lakia never noticed Khan approach as he gently tapped her shoulder. No words were exchanged as the two embraced. The pair took a seat in the waiting room, as Khan finally broke the silence.

"I hope he pulls thru." Lakia simply nodded her head as the thoughts of this kind old man dying before her eyes brought long streams of tears to her face.

"Mama, he's gonna be good." Khan spoke while kissing her forehead.

Khan was blessed to have someone in his life that cared so dearly for someone that she barely knew. In the midst of dealing with his own fears and tears, a young white male wearing a long doctor's jacket appeared and called for Khan and Lakia.

"Here we are Doc…Can we see him now?" asked Khan without acknowledging his grandfather's status.

"Well…Mr.." said the doctor while shuffling through paperwork.

"Well.. Mr. Larson, I'm afraid your grandfather didn't make it." said the docor while giving Khan direct eye contact.

"What!" screamed Lakia.

"I'm sorry." said the doctor through a stoic expression.

"Can we see him?" asked Khan while fighting emotions.

"Room 7." said the doctor while walking away without saying another word.

"How can someone just die, and you act like it's not a big deal!" said Lakia to the doctor as he continued to walk unmoved by Lakia's comment.

"Come on ma." said Khan as he led Lakia to GP's room.

Upon entering the small quiet room, Khan smiled when he noticed that GP still had an erection. Lakia couldn't help but smile too once she noticed Khan's grin.

"I told that man about using all them damn Viagra pills." Khan spoke while grabbing GP's hand. GP had a very peaceful look to him as he took his final rest with his eyes closed and what Khan thought to be, his trademark smirk.

"I thought those pills would have worn off by now." commented Lakia.

"Ain't nothing wrong with a soldier going out with one final salute." Khan spoke while using humor to diffuse his true feelings of gloom.

Khan pondered how life would be now, knowing that the last

person who had his back was now gone. The sudden feeling of grief struck Khan as he released Gp's hand and headed towards the door.

"Where are you going?" questioned Lakia.

"I need some air." Khan responded without waiting for a reply.

"Damn I need a fug." said Khan as he retrieved a cigarette from the pocket of his Carhartt jacket.

While Khan was in the midst of the famous "Where's my lighter" dance, a young woman wearing a hospital gown handed Khan her lighter.

"Good lookin' out." said Khan as he closed his eyes and allowed the Newport to do its job.

"No problem…you looked like you could use a helping hand." replied the young woman as she puffed on a Black and Mild.

Khan was so caught up in his emotional state the he never noticed the kind stranger standing in the hospital parking lot when he arrived. After the third hit of his cigarette his craving for nicotine finally subsided allowing him the opportunity to also notice the breathtaking features of his hospitable, hospitalized, heroine. She had a light almond complexion with a shapely figure. Considering the fact that she'd also looked as if she had been struck by a truck, her warm smile and perfect white teeth gave way to some of the most hypnotic brown eyes Khan had ever saw in his life.

"Damn what happened to you?" Khan asked in-between puffs.

"Oh…nothing…just an accident." She nervously replied.

Throughout Khan's many experiences with the opposite sex, made Khan a master at reading women, and he knew something was up.

"An accident huh…well I hope you stay away from this "accident" " Khan said while making air quotes.

The young woman's silence gave Khan all the validation he needed. Khan didn't know this young woman from Adam and Eve but felt the sudden urge to protect her.

"Is there anything I can do to help?" asked Khan, not sure why he felt so concerned for her wellbeing.

"I'm cool, guy… don't trip, I'mma big girl. I can handle myself."

"What's your name sweetheart?" asked Khan while studying the young lady more intensely.

"It's-"

* Beep Beep*

A pick-up truck sounded as the older white male pulled up in front of Khan and the strange woman. Another younger looking female opened the passenger side door as the mysterious stranger walked to the truck, leaving Khan without giving him a name. As Khan got a better view of the other female in the truck, he thought that he recognized the passenger from somewhere. Without saying another word, the young woman and Khan locked eyes. There was a mutual non-verbal message that read "We will meet again." They both smiled at one another as the trucked pulled away, leaving Khan emotionally perplexed.

Chapter Eighteen
FOCUS BITCH

"Who was that cute guy you were talking to Dee?" inquired Valita while rolling up a blunt in Bills truck.

"Just some guy." Khadeja replied modestly.

"Some guy huh…well I saw how y'all was looking at each other. Smiling all hard and shit."

"It ain't nothing like that. He just seemed so sad and he looked like he was getting ready to go crazy because he couldn't find his lighter." informed Khadeja as she grabbed the blunt from Valita.

"Roll down the window, y'all keep blowing that shit on my side." coughed Bill while driving.

"My bad boo, anyway well it seemed like y'all made a little connection out there. It's not often that I see a guy make you smile like that."

"True, but I don't even know that nigga, but if I ever see him again I'mma get to know him."

Cough! Cough! "Blow that shit the other way" yelled Bill again.

"My bad Bill, oh and thanks for picking us up from the hospital. I know the doctor didn't buy that story we told him about being in an accident. And it would only be a matter of time before he sent the police to us, asking a bunch of stupid questions." said Khadeja as she passed the small blunt back to Valita.

"I just wanted to get a prescription for oxy's, fuck all that police paper work." Smiled Valita.

Yea, besides from a mild concussion, the doctor said we were good to go." announced Khadeja.

"That's all great news girls but y'all gonna have to think of a new game plan. I can't afford to keep putting y'all up in these damn hotel rooms. Eventually my wife is gonna start asking questions." said Bill while keeping his short stubby fingers gripped ten and two on the steering wheel.

"Bill's right Dee. We need money and it's not safe to post any ads right now because of K- Willz and they might try some more bullshit." stated a concerned Valita.

"I'm in the works with Slick now." replied Khadeja while typing on her phone.

"What are you gonna do…sell Slick some pussy?"

"No bitch, I'm trying to see how much money he will pay me to rap." smiled Khadeja.

"For real…that's what's up, but what if, K-Willz shows up to the event?" asked Valita as she noticed Bill's wallet slightly peaking from his back pocket.

"K-Willz is still embarrassed about that Crazy Cracker shit, I think we should be fine." assured Khadeja as she laughed at her cousin's pick-pocketing skills.

Valita gently caressed Bill's back while slowly removing a few twenty dollar bills from his exposed wallet.

"Bill when can I see you again?" Valita cooed.

"Let me get straight with my family and I'll come yelling for ya." Bill said as he pulled up at the Regal Motel on Route 40.

"Thanks Bill." said Khadeja while hopping out of the truck with her younger cousin.

"I'll see y'all soon." said Bill while pulling out his wallet.

"Here's sixty bucks for the room…I thought I had a little more than this." said Bill as he handed the girls three twenty dollar bills.

"Oh well… see ya girls and stay safe." said Bill while pulling off.

"Thanks guys. Give me a ring if y'all ever need me…for anything." waved Tammy as she walked away towards the truck stop diner.

"Yo that bitch wild ass shit." said Brent while putting the Impala in drive and heading towards the highway.

"Shawty sold them bitches out for a couple of rocks." laughed K-Willz.

"They was holding mad bread too." surmised Brent.

"I'm surprised they dusty asses could pull in that kinda cash. I think we in the wrong business." replied K-Willz.

"So you trying to hit the studio first?"

"Yea.. I got some fire for the booth, it's time to get back on the map baby!" sang K-Willz as he thumbed through a stack of stolen money courtesy of Khadeja and Valita.

"What about Crazy? You know he still buzzing right now."

"Man, I gotta let shit die down right now, I can't have no heat coming my way from smoking his mans."

"So we putting that beef on ice?" asked Brent while snaking through the traffic.

"First I'mma kill 'em in this rap shit…then I'mma just kill 'em." laughed K-Willz.

"Cool… speaking of that rap shit, I heard Khadeja suppose to be at the next Slick-Talk."

"Word?" asked a stunned K-Willz.

"Yea, word on da street is she battling Big Pam."

"Ha…Khadeja dumb ass gonna get fried."

"You wanna go check it out?" questioned Brent.

"Slick's security ain't gonna let that shit fly, especially not after what happened at his last show."

"Damn, I kinda wanted to see that shit."

"You know what…fuck it, I still might make my presence felt…after all, this is My City."

Khadeja and Valita did their best to maintain with the help of Bill and a few other sponsors that Valita and Khadeja served on a regular basis, they made just enough to make ends meet. Khadeja desperately wanted a way out. She hoped and prayed that Slick could provide her with a new way of life.

"What ya doing?" asked Valita while painting her toenails.

"Getting my material together for the show." said Khadeja while opening her notebook and flopping down on the bed next to Valita.

"Damn bitch, you almost made me fuck up my feets."

"Shut up bitch." mocked Khadeja as she laid on her stomach with a pen in hand.

"So, ….Big Pam…..that bitch nice." stated Valita.

"Yea, hopefully I can pull this off, Slick is paying five hundred bucks to the winner."

"You about to be doing all this writing and shit, what if you lose…you don't win shit?" questioned Valita.

"Yea I think he said like fifty bucks or something, all I heard was the five hundred so I don't plan on losing." Khadeja replied confidently.

"Okay well I'mma go get a soda and leave you to your writing…you want anything?"

"Yea some peace and quiet."

"Okay Miss Rap Star, you got that." Valita spoke while leaving the motel room.

"Finally." sighed Khadeja as she focused her attention to the blank pages of her notebook.

"How to start…how to start….should I watch some Rap battles on YouTube to get a better idea? No because that would be swagger-jacking. Come on Dee you can do this…just write from the heart."

"Big Pam…you big bitch…No. No. No." said Khadeja as she scratched out her first line.

"Big Pam or should I say Big Spam." laughed Khadeja as she continued to scratch out every line she wrote. Khadeja closed her eyes and allowed her poetic spirit to take control of her pen.

"I am in love with a stranger/ A man that I've only met one time/ And even though he is a stranger/ He is the only thing on my mind/ I am in debt to this stranger/ Yet he has done nothing at all/ For the eyes of this stranger/ Show a future where I am involved/"

Valita suddenly entered the room and noticed her cousin's eyes on the verge of tearing up.

"You okay?" asked Valita as she tried to see what Khadeja

was writing.

"Oh yea I'm straight. Just getting my rap right for shawty." Khadeja lied while quickly closing her notebook.

"You sure?"

"Yea fuck you coming running back in here all fast for?"

"Stupid vending machine don't take nothing over ten dollar bills." said Valita while rummaging through her dresser for smaller bills.

"Oh a'ight…I'mma roll with you. I could use a Ho-Ho."

"Bitch you is a Ho-Ho."

Chapter Nineteen
STARS N STRIPES

Nearly a month passed since Gp's funeral. It was a beautiful ceremony and a vast majority of Khalil's family and friends showed up to pay his father their respect. Khalil noticed his son's somber mood and promised to meet with him once his own mourning was resolved. Later that week Khalil met with his son Khan to check on his mental and financial status.

"How you holding up son-son?" asked a smaller, older yet identical version of Khan, as he extended his arms for a quick embrace.

"As good as I can be." replied a misty eyed Khan. Khalil stroked his graying beard as he jumped directly to his main reason for visiting.

"Looks like you having some money problems son."

"What gave that away?" Khan replied sarcastically while rubbing the top of his unkept mini-afro.

It was apparent that Khan was having money issues. He usually maintained great grooming and took pride in his appearance, but when Khan showed up to the funeral, wearing a dingy white tee and some off-white sneakers, this confirmed Khalil's suspicions.

"A'ight well check this out son-son, I got my hands in something right now, and if you can assure me you won't fuck this up, I could float a little something ya way."

"Oh yea…well what's good?" inquired Khan enthusiastically.

"I got a little weed connect, I know it's probably not what you had in mind but you fucked up that last package when you let that non-cooking baby mama of yours, fuck my coke up. So now I refuse to let you put me in that position again. I'm going to give you a quarter pound of Afghan Kush. Just bring me back half and I will give you another QP to flip. As long as you don't fuck me, we will be good and I will make sure you get back on your feet."

"Thanks Pops, I won't let you down."

"I hope not because if you burn me again…you on ya own."

"I got this Pops."

"We will see…. Assalamu Walaakum."

"Walaakum Salaam."

The church allowed Lakia to take over responsibilities of GP's house since Khan didn't have a job and the members of the church didn't want to see GP's grandson out on the streets. Lakia was ecstatic to finally have her own home but this excitement was short lived once she realized that maintaining a house was tough, especially when you were paying all of the bills by yourself.

"Khan...Khan... wake up." Lakia yelled as she poked Khan's chest.

"What!" yelled Khan as he drifted in and out of a Kush induced coma.

"It's time to find a job, I can't keep working all these double shifts. I need your help."

"I got a job mama, I worked these streets." replied Khan as he submerged himself in the comforter.

"Boi stop, you smoking up all of your product, look I'm on my way to work and I'll be back at ten so please take this five dollars and get you a bus pass, so you can do some job hunting." Khan's eyes opened wide at the sound of free money.

"Where that five dollars at?"

"Here… please have some good news for me when I get back. I love you but the landlord don't care about being depressed. Get ya shit together baby boy." said Lakia as she fastened up her light brown Northface jacket, kissed Khan on the lips, then headed out the door.

"*I gotta get away from this bitch.*" thought Khan as he pocketed the crumbled five dollar bill in his basketball shorts and reached on the night stand for his phone.

Khan had already smoked up his half of the weed, leaving him with just his fathers' share to flip. Khan tried his best to uphold his end of the deal but allowed his depression to justify smoking just one blunt, which led to two, which led to two OZ's. Khan always denied labeling himself as a drug addict, but his actions spoke otherwise.

"Fuck do she want?" asked Khan while opening Jamie's text message.

"HOW YOU BEEN BUDDY?" Khan read as he replied to Jamie's text letting her know that he was still hurting from his Grandfather's demise. A few seconds later Jamie called Khan.

"Hey it's good to finally hear from you, I had to get ya number from Tyler since you don't know how to call nobody." screamed Jamie.

"My bad, I ain't been too social lately."

"It's all good, hey do you know anyone that has any good green."

"Hell yeah…I could make something shake for you, how much you need?" Khan asked while sitting up on his bed.

"Whateva two hunnid bucks will get me, I'm trying to turn up tonight."

"Oh yea, what's the occasion?"

"A sista finally got her child support check." Jamie gleefully shouted.

"Where you at now?" laughed Khan.

"I'm downtown at the Gallery."

"A'ight you ain't but ten minutes from me, I'mma text you my address now."

"See you soon, hey can we burn one when I get there?"

"Damn Skippy, oh and grab me a bottle of Paul Masson too."

"Why you drinking so early." replied Jamie in her usually nosey inquiry.

"I'm trying to celebrate too." smiled Khan as he prepared his room for his houseguest.

"Thanks for the ride Sandy." waved Lakia as she felt blessed to be getting off work two hours early.

"I hope he'll surprise me with some good news." thought Lakia as she unlocked the door to her home. Upon entering the living room, her nostrils were immediately violated with the strong sent of Afghan Kush.

"You know what, I don't even feel like fussing tonight. I'm gonna shower then fuck the shit outta my man." smiled Lakia as she made her way upstairs. Rick James "Fire and Desire" blared from the bedroom as Lakia neared the door.

"He's always listening to this old ass shit when he's high." laughed Lakia as she turned the door knob.

Lakia barely cracked the door when the once cheerful expression was replaced by sudden rage. Lakia couldn't believe her eyes as Khan laid on his back with his hands behind his head as some big titty white girl rode him reverse cowgirl. Her hipster glasses barely clung to her face as she slammed her ass on Khan, so hard it threatened to break the box spring. Lakia quietly walked away as Khan's full attention was focused on the soft milky white ass cheeks bouncing before him.

"Oh my God." screamed Khan as Jamie hammered Khan's pelvis with thunderous smacks of ass meat.

Jamie cuffed Khan's testicles and noticed them getting tighter and once she knew he was getting ready to blow, she jumped off of Khan's dick and swallowed him whole as he exploded down her throat. Khan thought he was in heaven as he stared at the ceiling smiling while Jamie continued to suck on his half hardness.

"I guess you ready for round two huh?" asked Khan while squeezing Jamie's soft butt cheeks.

"If she not, I'm ready." said Lakia while standing in the doorway gripping GP's Cal Ripken autographed baseball bat.

"Lakia… oh shit, look it's not what-" Lakia silenced him with a finger to her lips.

"I told you a long time ago not to play with me Khanstantine, now you goin' bring another bitch to My House that I pay all the bills at and disrespect me like this!" yelled Lakia while removing her earrings and starting to tear up.

"I'm sorry yo." Khan said with his head down.

"You are sorry, so sorry, ya broke ass don't deserve no Queen like me. You and this trash get the fuck outta my house now." said Lakia while pointing the bat at Khan, then the white girl attempting to cover herself with the bed spread.

Khan, wearing nothing but a pair of Hanes tube socks, took a step towards Lakia.

"Look ma-" Khan halted as Lakia cocked the bat back.

"Look ma shit, get out!" Lakia's eyes were glossed with red hot anger.

"Khan I'mma get out of here before things get crazy." said Jamie as she tried to slide pass Lakia.

"Before things get crazy..Bitch its girls like you that's always trying to fuck up somebody's happy home." screamed Lakia inches from Jamie.

"Happy home? He looked pretty happy a few minutes ago." Jamie boasted while sizing up a much smaller Lakia.

"Oh yea?" said Lakia while cracking a sinister grin.

"*Oh no.*" thought Khan.

"Yup!" replied Jamie while rolling her eyes.

CRACK

Sounded Jamie's skull as Lakia swung with enough force to make Babe Ruth proud.

"Aww." said Jamie while folded up on the floor, howling in

pain as Lakia stepped on her shattered glasses while walking in Khan's direction.

Lakia threw the bat on the floor and Khan felt some relief until she produced a box cutter. Khan, completely naked and defenseless backed towards the window which over looked the back yard.

"Mama… chill out…we can fix this." Khan pleaded.

"Lemme see them dirty ass nuts, I'm 'bout to fix you." laughed Lakia with a deranged look in her eyes.

"Hold up!" yelled Khan while barely dodging Lakia and the wild swings of her blade.

With no other option, Khan jumped from the second story window and landed ass first on a box shaped air condition unit. He stumbled to his feet, grabbed a neighbors' American flag that hung from their back patio and fled the scene before Lakia returned to finish the job.

"Hey Captain America, you trying to hop on this new track with me and Swine?" asked Yella, whom came to Khan's rescue once Khan explained his situation over a borrowed good samaritan's cell phone.

After an hour long roast session on Khan's American Flag covered body, and barely escaping death by a girl two inches taller than a midget, Swine and Yella finally cut Khan some slack and offered him a blunt to relax.

"Don't trip big bruh, I won't let her little ass sneak up on you." laughed Yella, a little too hard for Khan's liking.

"Nigga, I almost died!" declared Khan in an attempt to earn some pity instead of laughter, as he snatched Swine's phone from his hands.

"I know, but that's what makes it funny." interjected Swine while sparking another blunt as Yella took the other blunt into the bedroom.

"Y'all niggas terrible." said Khan while finally cracking a smile.

Yella offered Khan refuge in his living room but Khan needed his own space to let his dick swing. Khan messaged every female on Facebook looking for a place to lay his head until he came across Mary Jane. Khan met Mary Jane on XBOX Live while playing Halo 4. She was mixed with Puerto Rican and white with a tomboy swag. She was the most attractive gamer Khan ever met, but it wasn't just the games, she loved football, Bruce Lee flicks, Superhero movies and not the mention she was a stone cold freak. Khan smiled when

Mary Jane replied back saying that she lived alone and Khan was more than welcomed to stay with her as long as he followed her rules. Khan interrupted Mary Jane when she started to explain the rules and said.

"Just give me the run down when I get there. I'm sure I won't have an issue with Mary's Law." smiled Khan as he reminisced about a few wild encounters he had with Mary Jane.

Swine noticed Khan smiling hard while talking on his phone.

"I'mma tell Lakia!" shouted Swine in his young high pitched voice.

"Nigga! Hey Mary I'm with the fam right now, I will give you a heads up when I'm en route." said Khan while throwing an empty Top Pop bottle at Swine's head.

Khan started to body slam Swine until he realized how tight and restricting Yella's sweatpants were on his much bigger frame.

"You lucky, these tight ass pants saved you."

"Yea yea yea…you don't want no smoke nigga, now let's lay this verse down before Yella come out the room bitchin'." said Swine while mixing the chorus to their latest masterpiece.

"Fuck is Yella doing in the room?" asked Khan while opening the notepad app on Swine's phone to start the brainstorm process of writing a 16.

"He back there with his Russian bitch, some bad little broad we call Jaws." smiled Swine.

"Jaws huh..might have to test that out." said Khan.

"Good luck, Yella been trying to charge niggas for da head, yo think he a pimp, he only bring Jaws here when his girl be outta town."

"Who his girl?" questioned Khan.

"Jo-Jo, this Jamaican girl he met from New York, and she crazy as shit. I don't think she fucking with your little slugger though." laughed Swine while searching for another cigar to gut and fill with Sour Diesel.

"Yo we got a problem." warned Swine.

"What's up yo?" asked Khan while standing up in the tight yellow sweat suit.

"We forgot to get blunts yo…we fresh out."

"Fuck, it's like three in da morning, is any stores open?"

"Yea the gas station but I ain't walking all da way up that bitch." protested Swine.

"Let's just get the keys to Yella's whip. I'm sure won't trip."

"Yea right, that Camaro brand new, and plus that nigga fucking Jaws right now. He not coming out here for another two or three hour's bruh. She be fucking that nigga like she trying to get a ring." laughed Swine.

"Man fuck all that." said Khan as he approached Yella's bedroom door.

"Yo...lemme see the keys yo. I gotta make a blunt run." Khan heard nothing but moans as he pushed his ear to the door.

"Yo..." Swine yelled.

"Let's just walk man, I can't finish these tracks until I get my medicine."

"Fuck it." Khan spoke as he finally gave up.

The walk to the gas station allowed Swine and Khan to catch up on old times. Swine suggested that they take the short cut through the woods which would save them about fifteen minutes. Khan agreed as they now traveled in silence through the eerie darkness of the wooded area. There wasn't a soul outside as Khan followed Swine's lead down the dirt path. The tall trees seem to dance in the lite breeze which caused Khan's eyes to dart back and forth as they reached a sloped hill next to a large fence that separated a private wooded area.

As Khan cautiously moved down the dirt trail, he felt a presence watching him. Khan sped his pace as his paranoia started to get the best of him. Khan's peripheral vision saw what looked to be a large humanoid figure walking stride for stride with him on the other side of the fence. Khan thought his eyes were playing tricks on him until he turned his head and looked directly at the large being. The features were very much disoriented as Khan could only make out the large faceless head on a very thin dark frame. The pale face on the creature looked in Khan's direction as Khan finally snapped out of his trance like state.

"Yo Swine!" screamed Khan.

"Yo." replied Swine without turning around.

"Yo, Do you see that shit?" shouted Khan while pointing to the fences.

"Huh.." Swine turned around and looked in the direction of Khan's pointed finger.

"That big ass thing with the white head." answered Swine.

"Yea yo." confirmed Khan.

Without warning Swine took off like a bat out of hell, completely ignoring the laws of physics as he repelled the rest of the hill without hesitation. Khan shook ass also for fear of not knowing the creatures' intentions.

"So you telling me y'all saw Big Foot?" laughed Yella while brushing the young Russian's hand from his shoulder.

Yella hated to be touched after sex, he also hated public displays of affection. Jaws or Nina desperately wanted to be wifed up and had no plans on being someone's side piece. Regardless of what degrading act she had to perform for Yella or any of his paying homeboys, she was down for the shits as long as she thought she was his girl. Yella made it perfectly clear that his baby mama was his main bitch but she was willing to "play along" until Yella or someone put a ring on her finger.

"No it wasn't no damn Big Foot, actually I dunno what the hell I saw." replied Khan as he made eye contact with Nina.

Nina took notice as she slightly blushed and diverted her crystal blue eyes away from Khan's enticing smile. Khan's lips made Nina's pussy moist as she crossed her long shapely thighs to conceal her secret. Nina stood 5'9 and had a lean athletic build with a set of perky C cups which complimented her round high sat rear. Nina decided to join the conversation before someone noticed the glances she threw at Khan.

"May I ask…what did this thing, look like?" questioned Nina

with an excuse to stare at Khan's face.

"It was tall, like twenty feet tall with a big ass white face with no features. Like no eyes or nose or nothing."

"I think it could have been Slender Man." surmised Nina as she made her way towards the studio desktop.

She minimized the Protools Project and opened the browser. She went to YouTube and typed "Slender Man encounters" then clicked on the first link. Everyone watched in awe as Swine and Khan both said in unison…

"That's him!"

The foursome continued to watch the rest of the Slender Man videos in the dark until they were all startled by a loud crack of broken glass coming from outside.

"Yo I know y'all ain't bring no damn Slender Man back to my house." said Yella while Swine grabbed a small hand gun and opened the front door to investigate.

Swine peeked his head out the front door and shook his head slowly at Yella.

"What, is it Slender?" asked Yella scared shitless.

"Nah dug, much worst…it's ya crazy ass baby mama."

Jo-Jo stood next to Yella's prized all yellow Camaro with her arms crossed over her large pregnant belly admiring the brick she flung through the windshield.

"So-me leave for one blood clot night and ye already got that damn white girl in me house." Jo-Jo ranted.

"I can't go through this shit again." thought Khan as he retrieved Swine's phone to let Mary Jane know he was on the way.

Chapter Twenty
SMALL WORLD

"Hey everybody welcome back to Slick-Talk's One-on-One, where we give you behind the scenes access and the most exclusive interviews from the people that the streets wanna hear from. I got with me now… all the way from Belair road, Miss Big Pam. Big Pam, the streets been buzzing about your up and coming battle with a new artist that goes by the name of Deja- Vu. How do you feel about you opponent and her lack of experience in the ring?" asked Slick in his best Vince McMahon impression.

"First of all…shout outs to Slick-Talk for giving ya girl a cage to fuck theses bitches up in, secondly Deja-who? Fuck outta here with that off brand bitch…I'm only taking this battle 'cause a bitch need a new purse. Pammy not playing, please believe." Big Pam answered in her usual cocky swag as she threw up three fingers in the form of the letter "E" and shouted…

"Empire! We 'bout to do girl dirty."

The rest of the Empire click responded in similar fashion as Slick quietly counted all the dollar signs in his head, anticipating a huge turnout for the biggest lyrical cat fight in the city.

"You heard it live from Big Pam, herself and this Slick-Talk event will be the place to be. I hope to see everybody in the building."

Khadeja just stared at her phone as the YouTube video ended with Slick's round face froze with a huge greedy smile plastered on his grill that stretched a mile long.

"I betta make sure my shits up to par. I might have to cut that big ass bitch if she try to play me." mused Khadeja as she sat on a curb in the parking lot of The Regal Motel, while waiting for Valita to finish up with one of her regulars.

Moments later Khadeja finally saw Valita step out of the motel room with her John, Valita motioned for the John to call her by extending her thumb and pinky finger, then headed in Khadeja's direction. As Valita passed a large pink truck, the window rolled down a bit and Valita had a small conversation with the occupant of the flashy vehicle. Valita's eyes got bright as she smiled then sprinted towards Khadeja to share her good news.

"Dee…don't trip but I think our money problems are over." announced Valita still hyper with excitement.

"I'm listening." Khadeja replied slightly skeptical.

"The guy in that truck says that he can help us make some money, like big money and he would personally protect us if someone tries some bullshit."

"So he's a pimp?" Khadeja said dryly.

"He's a guy that offers his assistance if things get out of hand…for a small cut." corrected Valita.

"Oh…Okay, so he's definitely a pimp." Khadeja repeated.

"Oh my God, look negative Nancy he wants to talk to you. He says if we don't like what he has to say then he won't ask again."

"Fuck it, should we go to his truck?" asked Khadeja.

"No he gave me his room key, he's staying in a suite."

"I didn't even know this raggedy motel had suites." laughed Khadeja as the duo searched for room 113.

After circling the entire complex they finally located the small wing of the motel which contained the suites. Valita inserted the key card and was completely shocked at the large suite's layout. It looked like an apartment rather than a motel room. The girls thought they finally made a good decision as they scanned the lavish layout. The room had a beige living room set with brand new furnishings surrounding the multi room design. A large flat screen TV with a DVD player made the girls feel right at home. A gorgeous redbone, with a body of a video vixen appeared out of nowhere as she greeted the two startled additions.

"Hey y'all...I assume Flamingo Pimp sent y'all."

"Yea he said to wait for him in here." answered Valita as she made her way to the minibar.

"Cool, well my name is Suga...I'm happy to have y'all with us. All I'mma say is, if you trying to eat, your in the right place." Suga laid her game on thick.

Yes Flamingo Pimp was the face of this operation but Suga actually ran the show. She realized the more girls she had working on the team, the less work she would have to do. Plus she received a small commission for every job she booked for the girls. Suga was just your average hustler trying to find her way, just like everybody else from the hood.

"We make big bank here girls." smiled Suga.

"How much do we have to give him?" asked Khadeja.

"We give him half, but here's the thing, I'm willing to bet you can't pull the type of clientele he has. So the way I sees it, half of something is more than all of nothing." Suga schooled.

"I like ya style...you on Facebook?" asked Valita.

"Yea it's Suga, Spice and everything Nasty." All the girls laughed at her Facebook link as Khadeja heard some commotion coming from the bathroom.

"Is there another girl here?" questioned Khadeja.

"Oh yea I almost forgot. Y'all not the only girls he found today. I think her name is Torri or Tasha… something with a T." replied Suga.

"What is she doing?" asked Valita.

"Smoking…doing a little pregame before her next John.

"Oh word, shit I'm trying blow too. I ain't had no grass all day." shouted Valita.

"She ain't smoking no weed, that's that rock you smelling." answered Suga while prepping her hair in the vanity mirror.

"Daddy don't smoke nothing so he hates the smell, he makes everyone smoke in the bathroom with the fan on. I told Tanya or Tina, whateva her name is…to smoke in the bathroom and she caught a attitude."

"Well, I guess I'll just have me a drink until that man gets here." said Khadeja as she poured a glass of Hennessy, and took a small sip.

Khadeja heard the bathroom door knob jiggling and waited to see the other new girl with anticipation.

"Girl do you have another lighter because-" Khadeja cut her

off by yelling her name.

"Tammy!"

"Yea Tammy, that's her name." replied Suga while completely oblivious to their history or the scene getting ready to unfold.

"Oh..Hey Dee." A nervous Tammy responded while discreetly clutching her pocket knife in her back pocket. Tammy was high but she was well aware that something was about to pop- off.

"Don't hey Dee me, I want my money bitch!"

"I have no idea what your talking about, them guys did what they did and I ain't have nothing to do with it." lied Tammy while trying to sound sincere.

"Bitch yous a lie!" yelled Valita while stepping up to Tammy alongside her cousin.

"Y'all chill out, Daddy gonna kill all of us if something jumps off in here." cautioned Suga after realizing the severity of the situation.

"These bitches ain't 'bout shit, they young asses don't want no grown-up problems." Tammy spat.

"Whad-up then bitch." said Khadeja as she put up her dukes and closed in on Tammy.

Tammy quickly produced her pocket knife, ready to slash at anyone in arms reach. Khadeja didn't know how Tammy's knife game was and had no intentions on finding out, so she took the glass of Henny she passed to Valita and tossed it in the face of Tammy. Tammy was temporarily blinded as she swung the blade wildly. During her frantic melee, Tammy bumped into a wall causing her to drop the knife. Her visibility partially returned as she dove for the knife along with Khadeja. Tammy and Khadeja wrestled for the deadly weapon, as Valita went for Tammy's feet to pull her away from the knife but Valita was met by a Michael Koors flip-flop to the face, sending her tumbling across the room. Khadeja outweighed Tammy by twenty pounds but the energetic crack high combined with the rush of adrenaline felt as if Khadeja was tangled up with an anaconda. Khadeja finally got ahold of the knife as Tammy dove on Khadeja trying to rip it away but the tip of the blade penetrated her stomach when she landed on Khadeja, causing blood to leak rapidly from her abdomen.

Suddenly all of the fight in Tammy ceased as she tried to catch the red fluid with shaky hands as it flooded the motel's carpeted floor. Her eyes got wide as she attempted to remove the knife which was plunged deep within her, to no avail, she allowed her body to slip into the depths of the unknown while awaiting the inevitable. Khadeja stood up and ran to her cousin who was still dazed from the kick to the head. Suga calmly walked towards the young girls and said…

"Don't trip, Daddy has a clean-up crew on payroll for situations like this; it's usually for the tricks when they get out of line. Just get far from here and lay low. Y'all got my Facebook, just message me if you need anything."

The girls nodded then headed towards the door after saying their goodbyes. As they attempted to exit the room, they were met by a straight-faced Flamingo Pimp.

"I can't leave you bitches alone for one damn minute." spat Flamingo Pimp as he glanced at the bloody white girl lying motionless on the motel floor.

"And y'all done dirtied up a pimp's carpet. Suga, that carpet stain and the fees for the clean-up crew is coming outta ya ass. So start booking ya tricks, ain't no sitting on ya yellow ass watching Love and Hip-Hop tonight hoe!"

"Yes Daddy, I'll get right to it." replied Suga as she escorted the girls outside and shut the door on them without saying another word.

Chapter Twenty-One
THE FREAKS COME OUT AT NIGHT

"Okay so let's hear these rules of yours?"

"Well there's only one rule, and that rule is to do whatever I say, whenever I say to do it." said MaryJane while sitting on the floor eating sushi from her traditional Japanese dining table in her kitchen.

Khan loved her style. She lived in a two bedroom apartment in Cherry Hill. Her living room had a small tan couch in the center that faced a large flat screen television. To the left of the sofa there was a large display of Japanese Katanas accompanied by a Marvel comic custom china plate collection. She had a small kitchen with two large bedrooms. The master bedroom had a large walk-in closet but the main feature was a queen sized waterbed with princess draping. She had a style all her own along with a feisty personality to match.

"Whatever you say huh?" Khan asked while becoming aroused.

"Whenever I say it." MaryJane reminded as she stood from her small table completely naked and motioned for Khan to put her plate in the sink.

"So you on some Slave and Master type shit?" asked Khan as he played along and placed her plate in the dishwasher.

"Oh you have no idea." smiled MaryJane as she invaded Khan's space standing nose to nose.

"For our first order of business, once you enter this house you shower and you must remain naked until I give the consent to dress." Khan nodded as she continued.

"I make more than enough money so you contributing on a monetary scale is not a necessity, however your obedience is paramount." Khan nodded while staring at her small perky breast as her pointy pink nipples stared back at him.

"You will cook, clean and all in-between. I don't want company in my home and you will be required to work-out every day. Also-" Khan tuned MaryJane out as she continued to explain "Mary's Law."

Khan was just happy to have a nice home with a bad bitch, but he knew he had to find a job because a job meant money, and money meant options, and options brought opportunity which was all Khan needed. He refused to let another female call him broke.

"Hey, I appreciate everything you doing for me mama and I'm

sure we will click just fine but I'm about to shower up and go job hunting. I gotta have my own money." MaryJane studied Khan for a moment, then walked away switching her ivory ass cheeks with every step.

"May I use the shower?" Khan asked mockingly.

"Granted." said MaryJane as she sat in front of her television, plugged in her headphones and turned on her XBOX.

"Yo you got a razor in here?" shouted Khan from the bathroom.

"What?" asked MaryJane as she removed her Turtle Beach headphones?

"You got a razor, I'm trying to make myself more presentable."

"Gotcha…there should be a pack in the towel closet."

"Good looking mama." said Khan as he vanished to the back of the apartment.

Khan scoured through the city in pursuit of employment.

Finding a job with a record was a rigorous task. Khan went to shoe stores, department stores, even fast food places were now doing background checks. Khan almost gave up until he found himself on his stomping grounds in Eastpoint Mall.

"Now hiring for Masseuse" read the sign displayed in the window for the new salon. "The Palace" was having its grand opening and still had some positions available. Khan had absolutely no experience in hair care or in cosmetology but had plenty experience in massaging women. It was his go-to move. Khan had actually enrolled in a course at the Baltimore school of Massage, which was short lived once the instructor discovered Khan's only intention for the class was to pick up chicks.

Khan walked inside the large salon, scanning the new equipment and hair supplies. The salon was split into three sections. The hair dryers and shampoo station sat on the right wing. The nail and eye brow station occupied the left wing, and the back of the salon housed the massage area. The staff consisted of Black and Dominican female's stylist and one man. The man's name was Jerry. Jerry was the proud black owner of "The Palace". He made it his business to hire only minorities. Jerry grew up from humble beginnings in the city of New York. He had a few run in's with the law and vowed to turn his life around.

"Hey Jer… a young man here is interested in the masseuse position." called Ester, the workplace grandmother to everyone at

"The Palace."

"Oh wurd, send him over." replied Jerry from behind the counter in the far corner of the salon.

Ester nodded and wobbled her large frame back to the waiting area which sat in-between the hair and nail wings. Khan got the "Okay" from Ester to walk to the back in search of Jerry. Khan found him reading a newspaper while eating a bowl of milk-less cornflakes. Dressed in a black leather jacket with a V-neck white Tee shirt, blue jeans, Timberlands and topped with an "NY" fitted, Jerry spoke first.

"Welcome young brother. I hear your interested in the position?"

"Yes sir, massage therapy has been a passion of mine for a long time."

"Good to know, do you have any experience?"

"I recently just graduated from The Baltimore School of Massage." Khan lied as he produced a name tag that he received from the school hoping that would deter him from asking to see an actual license.

"Congrats young man." Jerry was from the streets and could tell that Khan wasn't being completely honest, but admired the young man's style and decided to not press for more proof.

"Usually I wait until I have all of your credentials but I'm in desperate need for a masseuse right now so in other words...When can you start?"

"Yesterday." replied Khan as the two men shook hands.

Business was slow but Khan was happy to have a job. Khan serviced about three customers a day which was just enough to put a little change in his pockets. As Khan closed up the massage station for a quick lunch break, he bumped into a young woman.

"Sorry about that" said Khan to the very cute petite light brown skinned nail technician.

"It was my fault, I-I-I- shoulda been more a-a-a- aware of my surroundings." she stuttered.

"Khan" Khan introduced himself while extending a hand.

"Olivia" Olivia replied while taking Khan's hand into her own.

Olivia was mesmerized by Khan the second he walked through the door. She was upset that she had a customer in her chair or it would've been her greeting Khan instead of Ester.

"Well it's nice to meet you. Ya little ass should think about wearing a bell around your neck so you don't get stepped on." joked Khan.

"Big things come in little packages." retorted Olivia.

"*I'm trying to cum in that little package.*" thought Khan while changing the subject.

"You hungry?" asked Khan.

"Yea, I can eat, but let me lock up my station." Khan watched Olivia walk away as her round ass bounced every direction in her black leggings.

After a quick meet and greet over taco bell in the mall's dining area, the two returned to the salon and back to their respected stations. A few hours passed and Olivia notice Khan had a disheartening look on his face as she approached him. Khan saw her nearing as he applied a fake smile on his face.

"Sup O"

"What's up with you…why you look so down?"

"Business is so slow, I dunno how I am suppose make money for myself and pay a weekly booth rental." said Khan while staring off.

"Everything will work out for you, just allow God to work at his own speed." Olivia comforted.

"Good medicine mama."

"Hey well since it looks like your not too busy…How much massage can I get for ten bucks?" asked Olivia in attempts to put that handsome smile back on Khan's face.

"It's not much but it's all I have for now."

"Don't worry about it O, the first one's always free." laughed Khan as he led Olivia into the small intimate massage room.

Khan had a single massage table setup in the center of the room with a shelf of oils and lotions that stood in the rear corner. A small table next to the shelf held a Sony disc player which played nature sounds and other tranquil melodies. Olivia's nostrils invited the sweet smells of the cinnamon scented candles as she sat on the table.

"I'm going to step out for a sec, just remove as much clothing as your comfortable with then lay under the sheet on the table." said Khan while noticing the hesitant look on Olivia face.

"Your in good hands mama." Khan assured then gave Olivia her privacy.

"*I can't let this man see me naked, we just met…were still meeting.*" thought Olivia as she removed her shoes and slid under the sheet. A few moments later he returned and Olivia was greeted by that handsome smile that she already came to love.

"What?" asked Olivia while laying on her side staring at Khan's goofy smile?

"So you only comfortable taking off ya shoes around me?" replied Khan still laughing.

"Well... I don't know you yet. I am not one of these fast girls your probably used to being around." said a straight face Olivia.

"O.. I am a professional massage therapist. I understand your apprehension but your safe with me. We will start slow, take off your shirt but leave your bra on. I will start with your shoulders and back."

"Okay." agreed Olivia as she slowly removed her red sweater and tossed it on the neighboring chair. Khan coated his hands in mango oil and slowly applied some pressure to Olivia's neck and shoulders.

"Is this too hard." asked Khan while pinching her skin softly to loosen up the muscles.

"No its fine." said Olivia as she too started to loosen up while Khan had her on cloud nine. Khan worked her back next by using the Swedish technique. Olivia was completely relaxed until she felt Khan pulling down her leggings.

"Hey what's up?" question Olivia while looking back at Khan.

"Relax mama, I'm just getting ready to do your lower body."

"Um...I don't-" shuddered Olivia as Khan's touch gave her sensations she never felt.

"Shh" Khan cut her off as she stopped resisting and allowed Khan to slide her leggings off by lifting up her midsection while Khan pulled the last pant leg over her small foot. Khan stared at her honey colored ass while oiling up the lower half of her body. Khan started with her small feet as she playfully kicked from the tickling sensation from Khan's warm hands. Khan then proceeded to caress her shapely thighs as the tips of his fingers "accidentally" scraped the outskirts of her woman hood. Khan could see a small wet spot forming in the center of Olivia's purple cotton panties. Khan inched up her soft body as he grabbed her ass cheeks. He gently spread them apart and allowed them to clap back together on their own. He used his knuckles to push on the fatty part of her ass which caused Olivia to shake. Khan then reached around her waist and applied pressure to her small pelvis. The closer he got to her honey pot, the more Olivia began to quiver. Khan knew she was on the verge of climax and decided to play his hand. Khan moved his fingers inches away from her clit and watched as her eyes tightened behind shut eye lids. Once Khan felt the precum flowing he abruptly stopped and said...

"All finish" smiled Khan.

"Huh..What." spat a confused Olivia

"Did you enjoy ya massage?"

"Yea…well…I wasn't done.. I mean." Olivia stumbled.

"You weren't done…what are you talking about?" Khan played dumb.

"That's fucked up…you funny…but that's fucked up." replied Olivia.

"I know you didn't think I offered happy endings…what kinda guy do you think I am?" joked Khan while handing Olivia her clothes.

"Two can play it that way, what are you doing after work?"

"Shit." replied Khan.

"Wanna come over."

"*Got one!*" thought Khan while nodding and helping Olivia from the table.

Khan was shocked to see a girl that worked in a hair salon own a home like this in Essex, It was a large two bedroom dwelling with a large living room and dining room. The kitchen was small but it also had a set of glass sliding back doors. The only thing that seemed odd to Khan was there was no furniture for the exception of the queen size bed in the master bedroom and a small box shaped television that sat on a small dresser. Khan also saw a large black and white cat that jumped in her arms as soon as she stepped foot in her bedroom.

"Whats ya cat's name?"

"Gabby." Olivia smiled as she gently stroked Gabby's fur.

"I love cats too, she pretty." Khan stated then patted Gabby's head.

"Thank you."

"So did you just move in here?"

"I've been here for four months."

"Why don't you have furniture?"

"I want to open my own salon in the living room and besides it's just me and my Gabby here so I don't need much."

"Cool well what do you wanna do?" asked Khan while already scheming and plotting.

"Follow me." Olivia led Khan to the bathroom where she

removed his clothes and set the temperature of the water at a reasonable setting. Olivia's shy girl demeanor went out the window when she grabbed Khan's dick and started to lather it up with soap which caused Khan to become fully aroused. Olivia continued to glide a small sponge all over Khan's body as Khan found another sponge to bathe Olivia. Suddenly Olivia dropped to her knees and attacked Khan's sausage like it was the last supper. She crammed as much of his meat in her tiny mouth as she could muster and bobbed her head at lightning speed until Khan showed signs of climax in which she abruptly stopped.

"What's up." asked Khan, upset about the sudden pause in action.

"I told you, two can play that game." smiled Olivia.

Khan wasn't going for any of that as he picked Olivia's small body up and started hammering her like a jack rabbit. The two fucked like animals until the wee hours of the night. When Olivia's eyes opened she was surprised at the delicious spread that Khan presented. Khan made scrambled eggs, turkey sausage, waffles and grits.

"This smells wonderful." replied Olivia in a state of shock.

"Why you look like that?" asked Khan.

"Honestly, I never had a man bring me breakfast in bed."

"Well…you deserve it, especially after that performance last night."

Olivia smiled then thought long and hard about what she was about to say next. Khan noticed her in deep thought as he asked if everything was okay.

"You wanna move in?" Olivia asked through wide eyes.

"Let me get back to you on that." Khan replied and smiled on the inside.

Khan thought about Olivia's proposal as he rode the bus from Essex to Cherry Hill.

"*I could probably have my way with Olivia if I moved in with her. I could turn her house into my house, but MaryJane caked up, I know Olivia got that house off section 8. I'mma just chill with my white girl for right now.*" Khan mused as he exited the bus and entered the home he shared with MaryJane.

"Where have you been?" yelled a nude MaryJane while giving Khan an evil glare.

"Damn I didn't know I had a curfew mama, I was out with my

peoples." said Khan as he tried to walk away but MaryJane signaled for him to come to her by curling her index finger.

"I have a sink full of dirty dishes, laundry that needs to be washed and it's time for breakfast."

"Breakfast...I'm good I just ate-"

"Not that kinda breakfast...come here now." Khan obliged and stood next to MaryJane. She ordered him to kneel down in-front of her as she spread her legs while sitting on her sofa.

"Eat up!" commanded MaryJane.

Khan did as he was told until MaryJane exploded all over his face. Then stood up to leave for the bathroom.

"Hold up where are you going?"

"To brush my teeth and shower"

"Don't brush your teeth...savor the flava"

"Are you serious, I really can't brush my teeth?"

"Please don't make me repeat myself, now hurry up and shower. I feel like fucking the shit out of you." responded MaryJane as she sashayed into the bedroom.

After a long shower, Khan was starting to have second

thoughts about his new living conditions. "*Maybe moving with Olivia wouldn't be so bad*" thought Khan as MaryJane's impatient yelling reminded him that he had some grade A pussy waiting for him. Khan quickly dried off and rushed to the bedroom as MaryJane sat on the water bed holding a bottle of baby oil.

"Bring ya black ass on, I'm ready to fuck." MaryJane motioned for Khan to lay on the bed. Khan carefully climbed into the rickety waterbed and laid next to

MaryJane.

"Turn on your stomach, I'm about to oil you up."

"Okay" said Khan as he enjoyed the quick rub down.

When MaryJane got to Khan's ass she applied extra oil in-between his legs and buttocks.

"Whoa mama, my ass ain't that ashy is it?" laughed Khan.

"You will thank me later…trust me." replied MaryJane devilishly.

After rubbing oil over Khan's body, MaryJane stood up and disappeared in her walk-in closet.

"Fuck you going?" said Khan while fondling himself.

"I got a surprise for you" MaryJane answered seductively.

"Awesome, I hope it's that batgirl costume again."

As MaryJane stepped out of the closet, Khan's stiffening penis went limp as he couldn't believe the sight before his eyes.

"I said I wanted to fuck the shit outta you."

"A'ight mama you done and lost ya fuckin' mind." said Khan while standing up and getting dressed.

"Aw come on, it's just a kinky toy I found" said MaryJane as she slowly stroked her twelve inch strap-on.

"Besides you know the rules now bend over" spat MaryJane.

"Keep playing with me woman" said Khan while gathering what little clothes Yella gave him then shoving them into a trash bag.

"Where are you going, I thought you didn't have anywhere to live?" asked MaryJane while following Khan into the living room.

"So you try to take advantage of my situation….Damn."

"Why not, you fucking men have been doing the same shit to us for centuries."

"I'm out bruh" said Khan while heading towards the bus stop.

"Fine, don't call me no more when ya black ass needs help." MaryJane screamed then slammed the door.

Knock Knock

Olivia jumped from her sleep as she and Gabby walked down the steps to investigate the late night disturbance.

"Who is it?" asked a nervous Olivia

"You know who it is" Olivia smiled as she opened the door.

"What took you so long?" asked Olivia as she jumped into Khan's arms.

Chapter Twenty-Two
PIGS IN A BLANKET

Further down the highway, about three blocks from The Regal motel, Valita persuaded a very gullible young man to purchase the girls a room at the El Rich Motel. The El Rich Motel was the lowest of the low. It was a collection of closet sized, filthy, bed bug infested rooms that exclusively catered to pimps, hoe's, dealers, addicts and any other vice that the city had to offer.

"Do you think we're going to jail?" asked a terrified Khadeja while frantically pacing the stained carpet of the cheap motel.

"I think we cool..for some reason I trust Suga" assured Valita.

"Me too but I'm still a little paranoid about the whole situation."

"Don't nobody know our names so all we gotta do is sit back and play it cool." said Valita while fishing through her purse for a tampon.

"You on ya damn period now…fuck, how we gonna eat now!"

"Chill Bitch, I got a mouth too….plus ain't nothing wrong

with that thing between your legs." retorted Valita as she walked into the bathroom.

Khadeja's mind flooded with hysteria as she did her best to calm her emotional state. The prostitution, being broke, ducking K-Willz, her battle with Big Pam, and not to mention recently stabbing a bitch all added to her seemingly endless list of problems.

"I just know the cops are looking for me" thought Khadeja while flopping down on the full size bed. Khadeja decided to watch some T.V. to take her mind away from her dreadful reality. As she surfed through the limited local cable channels, Valita re-emerged from the bathroom with her hair and make-up done to perfection.

"Where you going?" asked Khadeja while eyeing her cousin up and down.

"We damn near broke, I gotta go see what I can round up." replied Valita as she walked out the door.

Khadeja admired the "Go-Getter" mentality of her younger cousin. Considering that Valita was prostitutionally handicap by being on her period, she still made getting paper her number one priority. Khadeja's paranoia finally subsided as she allowed the comedy of Tyler Perry to distract her from her distress.

"Madea dumb as shit" said Khadeja as several knocks on the door diverted her attention.

Khadeja's cheerful mood was quickly erased as she stood from the bed and slowly took baby steps in the direction of the door. Her bowels almost emptied in her pants upon witnessing what appeared to be a uniformed officer through the rounded lens of the peep hole.

"Fuck…I'mma just get this over with." said Khadeja as she "soldiered- up" and opened the door to reveal a tall lanky middle age white police officer staring her in the face.

"You Dee?" questioned the policeman.

"Yes, sir." cried Khadeja as she slowly turned around with her hands clinched behind her back opting not to fight with a member of the law enforcement.

"Fuck is wrong with this bitch?..I guess she's into the Cops and Robbers type stuff" thought the cop as he stepped into the room and closed the door behind him. He removed his cuffs and proceeded to play along with the young girl's sexual act. He cuffed Khadeja and pushed her on the bed, face first with her ass hanging high in the air as he tugged at her pants until Khadeja golden globes jiggled slightly.

"Oh my God, I'm about to get raped again" screamed Khadeja as she closed her eyes and prepared for the inevitable.

"Rape?" thought the cop as he unbuckled his polyester pants and pulled out his penis.

"*Damn, that little bitch outside said Khadeja would be a great fuck but she's taking this role play stuff to a whole new level...fuck it I'll play along*" mused the cop while spreading Khadeja ass cheeks then sliding his fingers roughly in and out of her vagina.

"Yea, I'm about to rape the shit outta you!" yelled the cop.

"I knew it...Listen I'll do whateva you say just don't take me to jail...it was self- defense!" screamed Khadeja with her eyes still closed.

"*Self-Defense...What is she talking about? Who cares, let me just screw this bitch and leave before dispatch calls for me*" thought the cop while placing a condom on his erected penis.

"I don't care what law you broke, just take this dick like a good girl and I'll think about setting you free."

"Yes sir" replied Khadeja as she threw her ass back on the policeman like her life literally depended on it.

"Yea just like that, you fucking criminal" coached the cop.

"Yes officer" replied a frightened Khadeja as the cop firmly grabbed Khadeja's hips and plunged his penis in as deep as his below average length would allow.

Khadeja continued to slam her ass back on the cop until she heard the distinct grunt from the officer alerting her that the deed was almost done. The cop's face screwed up as he gave Khadeja a few more pumps until he released his seed into the loosely fitted condom. Khadeja anxiously awaited for the cop's decision as he stepped into the bathroom to dispose of the condom and proof of his illegal venture. The cop walked out of the bathroom with a smile as he adjusted his heavy policeman belt.

"Ya friend was right…you are a great fuck, I will be in touch." said the cop as Khadeja finally took notice of the bronze name plate which read Officer McFarley.

"That's a bet." replied Khadeja as the satisfied officer McFarley vanished from the small chamber.

"Whew" sighed Khadeja as she sat Indian style on the bed counting her blessings.

"Wait until Valita hears about this" Khadeja said out loud.

"Hear about what?" questioned Valita as she appeared from out of nowhere.

"Girllll, the cops tried to arrest me but he let me off the hook in exchange for a shot of ass" explained a relieved Khadeja.

"Word?" said Valita with a smile.

"Yea I thought it was a wrap but you know I gotta do what a

bitch gotta do…I'm too pretty to be sitting in somebodies prison." stated Khadeja through wide eyes.

"Valita I am truly blessed, I wasn't trying to serve no life sentence for a dumb bitch like Tammy."

"You blessed huh?" said Valita while shaking her head.

"I am blessed." replied a thankful Khadeja

"You ain't blessed, Bitch you dumb." laughed Valita.

"Huh..What?" questioned Khadeja in confusion?

"I sent that cop here dummy"

"What??"

"Yea, when I took a walk, the cop flagged me down and asked how much for some pussy. I told him it was that time of the month and all I could do was give him some head…he started crying about all he wanted was some pussy until I told him I had a beautiful friend that had the best pussy in the world and he broke his neck running to you." explained Valita while searching through her purse.

"You can't be serious…I thought I was really going to jail."

"Yea he mentioned that…he thought you were really into role playing. He said that fetish shit really turned him on." smiled Valita as she removed a fresh hundred dollar bill from her purse and handed it to Khadeja.

"I am a dumb bitch." Khadeja smiled from the embarrassment then stuffed the bill into her bra.

"I second that shit." laughed Valita as she searched her phone for her next vic.

"Next time give me a little heads up before you send a trick in here. I'm all about the money, I just wanna be on point."

"No problem Queen."

"Cool, why don't you line up some work while I continue working on my rhymes for Big Pam. We need all the money we can get if we plan on making it on our own." said Khadeja while opening her notebook.

"Sounds like a plan…Slick-Talk is coming up soon and I'mma need you to have ya shit together because if that bitch beat you I'mma dis- own you." laughed Valita

"Whateva hoe"

"Ya mama!"

Chapter Twenty-Three
LEARNING HOW TO FISH

Khan's new living situation couldn't have been better. The difference between living with Lakia, MaryJane and even his mother was a total culture shock when Khan moved in with Olivia. Olivia was subservient to Khan's every wish. She cooked, she cleaned and she left Khan sexually fulfilled. Olivia wasn't the most sexually experience but was up to any challenge Khan threw her way. She even allowed Khan to turn her spare bedroom into Khan's game room. She bought Khan a new Xbox with the little money she did have, and she even made sure Khan had all the weed he could smoke by working another job at a department store.

The best feature about Olivia that separated her from the other women that Khan lived with was that she never pressured Khan to do anything, and being in such a comfortable situation Khan once again found himself without a job. Khan quit the salon job because of a new gym called "Old Faithful's" which was a Gym/Health Center that specialized in the fitness of senior citizens. Old Faithful's open next door to The Palace, and when the old women discovered the young stud working at the massage station, they became frequent visitors. At first Khan loved the money, but the constant sight of the naked, decrepit, wrinkly bodies became too much for Khan to stomach. Jerry was outraged when Khan suddenly stopped showing up. His business was sky rocketing due to the surge of senior patrons. Khan stuck to his guns, and promised Olivia he would find a new source of income, and like a good girl, she smiled and picked up the slack.

"I will see you after work babe" said Olivia while waving Khan Good-Bye.

Khan never took his eyes from the television as he shooed her away with the flick of a wrist then returned to his online gaming. Khan was about to score a touchdown as his Madden 14 game disconnected from online play.

"What da fuck?" yelled Khan as he tried to sign back into the internet.

"Fuck is up with da Wi-Fi?" said Khan as he pulled out the phone that Olivia recently purchased him to call the internet company.

"You've reached The Plug internet service how may I help you?" asked the representative.

"Yea umm... my innanet ain't working...sup wit dat?"

"May I have your account number sir?"

"Yea its 224-679-8453"

"Okay …one second…okay sir, well this is an easy fix. It says the reason your internet doesn't work is because you need to pay the bill." said the rep in a sly tone.

"Damn we just paid that damn bill." Khan spat.

"Yes sir, you paid it 30 days ago, our service requires payment every month!" Khan could hear the rep laughing.

"Look niggas know how bills work!" screamed Khan.

"Well obviously niggas don't or else you would be enjoying our wonderful service instead of making this phone call… now if you would like to make a payment we can restore your service."

"Look I ain't got no mon .. No more time for you right now, I'mma call later." Khan hung up then called Olivia.

"Hello sweetheart you miss me already." smiled Olivia.

"Huh…oh yea, and also why you ain't pay the innanet bill."

"I'm sorry Khan, I spent the last of my money on that weed that you told me to get. I thought the internet company was suppose to send us a notice when it's close to being due." asked Olivia while walking off the bus.

"Man that ghetto ass company don't do shit, the bitch in

customer service got smart with me and everything." Khan fumed while rolling a blunt to calm down.

"I have an idea..but you might not wanna hear it."

"Sup O…if I can get my innanet back I'm all in."

"Well theres gonna be a job fair at-"

Click

Khan hung up the phone and decided to call Yella. A year before Khan got released from prison, Yella was awarded a quarter million dollar check from being exposed to lead as an infant. Actually all of Khan's brothers, including Khan himself suffered from lead poisoning but Khan and Scrap both missed the age cut off required by the state to receive the funds. Khan never turned down anything but his collar, but Khan had an issue accepting money from other men. He viewed it as a sign of weakness but right now he was tired of being broke and figured his little brother wouldn't put him through any bullshit if Khan needed a helping hand.

"Yo." answered Yella on the first ring.

"Bruh-Bruh whats good?" Khan smiled as he spoke.

"Shit…whatchu need nigga?" asked Yella getting straight to the point.

"What, why you say…fuck it Bruh, I need some scratch man, shit ain't going my way right now."

"I knew this day would come." said Yella while flushing the toilet.

"Is you shittin'?"

"Don't worry about that, now as far as this money shit go, I'mma tell you just like I told Scrap."

"*Here we go.*" thought Khan while Yella spoke like he was the older brother.

"I just bought a brand new Camaro, a brand new windshield for that Camaro, a condo, a new wardrobe, and I got a pregnant bitch, so that's a wardrobe for her and my seed, new studio equipment, new.." Khan took the phone from his ear momentarily then placed it back to his ear as Yella continued.

"Now I may not have no extra cash for you but I got something way better than money." now Yella had Khan's attention as Khan sat up straight.

"Better than money? What's that?" asked Khan.

"Well remember that old saying…you can give a Nigga a fish and he goin' keep asking for fish every day, or you can teach a Nigga how to fish and the nigga should be straight."

"I think you paraphrasing a bit, but I'm still not getting you."

"Don't trip. Give me a few hours and it will all make sense to you shortly." Khan hung up the phone and anxiously awaited whatever Yella had in store.

Khan dosed off after smoking a blunt, his slumber was abruptly interrupted with several knocks on the front door. Khan wiped the eye boogies from his face and made haste to the front room. Looking out the living room window, all Khan could do was smile once he saw his brother's surprise standing on the other side of the door.

"Wow..I didn't expect my lil bro to send you."

"Well you better believe it." said Nina in her strong Russian accent as she brushed past an ogling Khan wearing a large Jan Sport book bag. Khan noticed the book bag.

"What's in the bag?" asked Khan as he took the bag and her coat.

"My clothes silly, Yella said I am yours now…I belong to you."

"What!" screamed Khan as Nina took her book bag back from Khan.

"Yes..Now where can I put my belongings, I have clients on the vay." replied Nina with a straight face.

"Put your things? You got clients?" Khan was beyond confused.

"Listen, Yella has a pregnant woman which means no room for me, you have a big house and you need money. I make money for you. I belong to you now. You understand, yes?"

"Yea… I guess" Khan replied befuddled.

"Yella said something about we go fishing later."

"Fishing? Oh…Okay, teach a Nigga how to fish.

Whats better than money? A money making machine." smiled Khan as he put two and two together then escorted Nina to his game room.

"Just put ya shit in the closet. I got a futon in here, I hope this will do for now, but there's another girl that lives here. I'mma have to finesse this shit when she gets home." Khan spoke while retrieving a sheet and blanket from the hallway closet for Nina.

"Yella said that your in charge of household, Yes?"

"Yea I got this mama" Nina's phone rung while Khan found her a pillow.

"Okay Khan go hide in the other room, my John is here" said Nina while ushering Khan out of the bedroom.

"But-" Nina cut Khan off.

"Go…time for making money" said Nina as she descended the stairway. Khan walked into the master bedroom as he was left with only his thoughts.

"I dunno what I'mma tell Olivia, she goes for a lot of shit but I know she ain't going for this." Khan picked up Gabby as she purred in his lap.

"Fuck I'mma do Gabby…huh.. ya mama gonna whip my ass." laughed Khan while twirling Gabby's tail with his finger.

"I'mma just be straight up with her. She gotta respect honesty." Khan surmised as he heard a knock on the bedroom door.

"Come in" Nina opened the door and presented Khan with two twenty dollar bills.

"Damn that was quick" Khan said in amazement.

"Yes, I am the best. They don't call me Jaws for nothing" said Nina.

"Well shit I may need a sample of that" said Khan while standing up with Gabby.

"Let me finish next John first, he's already outside." said Nina as she closed the bedroom door and went to work.

The rest of the day ran smooth like clockwork. The only downside to Khan's newest venture was the amount of money Nina received for her services. Nina had a plethora of clientele but made next to nothing. To be blunt, she was charging dope fiend prices. The most Nina made off of one John was fifty dollars. Yella wasn't a pimp, he was just fascinated with the power of making girls fuck for money to simply please him. Khan quickly understood this as he conjured a way to make Nina more profitable.

"I'm going to take shower." said Nina in her broken English.

"A'ight mama" said Khan as he thumbed through five hundred dollars.

Moments later Khan heard Olivia's keys jiggling in the door knob as Khan rushed down stairs to meet her.

"Hey baby" said Khan as he removed the bag of groceries from Olivia's arms and carried it to the kitchen.

"Khan you seem chipper" said Olivia with a shocked expression.

"Of course I'm chipper, my Queen is home."

"And you are my King, after I finish cooking we can try

calling the internet company again. I made some good tips today at the Salon."

"Don't worry about that mama, as a matter fact I got some good news today." announced Khan.

"Did you get a job?" Olivia asked a bit too excitedly.

"Well something like that..."

"Okay what is it-" Olivia paused once she saw the tall goddess of a woman standing in her living room wearing only a towel.

"Khan I need conditioner" said Nina while completely ignoring Olivia.

"Olivia meet Nina" said Khan as Olivia simply stared at the beautiful Amazon.

Khan's whole game plan went out the window as a brainfart caused Khan to have a mental freeze. Nevertheless, Khan was always quick on his feet as he shot his jumper.

"Nina is my cousin"

"Your cousin?" said Olivia as she tried to find a comprehensible comparison between the pale woman and the black man.

"My cousin in law" Khan rebounded knowing that Olivia

knew about Helen and his kids having white relatives.

"Well not really in-law because I ain't never marry Helen but she's my baby mama's kin-folk."

"Okay...." Olivia stood still confused as to why she was standing in her living room half naked.

"Well her and her boyfriend had a bad fight and she asked me could she stay here until she finds a place to go." said Khan while digging in his pocket.

"Here she already gave me two hundred dollars for the rent so I set her up in the guest room."

"You mean your game room."

"Bloods thicker than water, and sometimes in life we have to make sacrifices." Olivia just stood with a stoic expression as Khan continued.

"Also, she too is in the massage therapy field, so instead of that being a game room, I think we should allow her to set up shop and service her customers. This way we will have additional income and you won't have to work all these hours." Khan noticed his words were starting to penetrate Olivia's barriers as he went for the gusto.

"Plus that means more time that I can spend with the love of my life."

"What, your XBOX" Olivia replied jokingly.

"No mama...you ... I love you" said Khan with a stern expression.

"You don't love me.." Olivia spoke while looking down. Khan walked closer to Olivia and raised her head by lifting her chin.

"Listen to me...I love you and if you allow me to steer this ship I can promise you nothing but a life of happiness.

Sometimes I may do somethings that the average woman might frown upon but your not the average woman. You can see the bigger picture. Put your trust into me and allow me to think for the both of us. If you take one step towards me, I will take ten steps towards you. I will be the brains. No woman has ever allowed me to be who I am destined to be... will you be the first, will you take my hand and sail the oceans of the unknown all in the name of love mama...will you grow with me?" Olivia closed her eyes for a moment. Then opened them as a lone tear slid slowly down her right cheek. She took a deep breath, then turned around to face Nina.

"I'll show you where the conditioner is, follow me."

As Khan was in the middle of some of the best head he'd ever received, his phone rang.

"Yell what's good?" said Khan as he watched his dick scream for help.

"Just here to collect" said Yella with a grin.

"Collect...oh I gotchu, how much you want for shawty."

"Nah I don't want money, remember that verse that you was suppose to do on my new song?"

"Yea my bad bruh-bruh, I finished writing it but that Slender Man shit made me forget about recording it.

"Not to mention ya wild ass baby mama chucking bricks and shit."

"Look I just need you to come with me and perform ya verse live. We can record it later."

"Live? Bruh I ain't trying to get back into all that shit, I've out grown that club shit."

"Really yo? I know that Russian bitch done put some cake in ya pockets by now, don't do me like this. Plus them niggas be wildin' out at Slick-Talk so I gotta have some niggas with me that will go."

"Damn man, you always trying to get me back into this rap

shit."

"Because you like that, nigga you too talented to be letting ya skills go to waste. Just do this one performance and we'll call it even?"

"Word"

"Yes nigga, it's in a couple of days so make sure you get a haircut and use some of that hoe-money to get some new gear." laughed Yella.

"A'ight nigga… always crying and shit." teased Khan.

"Good looking….see you soon." as the brothers ended the phone call, Khan laid back on the futon and pondered the notion of being back in the rap scene.

His thoughts were quickly interrupted as Nina continued her oral assault on Khan's manhood. Khan felt his toes curl as Nina showed Khan exactly why they call her Jaws.

Chapter Twenty-Four
GOOD TIMES

The usually placid intersection of West Baltimore street and Gilmore Ave was hit by a barrage of traffic crowding around the famous Good Times Lounge. Swarms of people bum rushed the establishment and for those who arrived late, formed a line more than a block long. This was the night everyone and their mama waited for, this was Slick-Talk.

"Don't scratch my shit dug." said Yella as he tossed the skinny black valet his car keys.

Yella, Swine and Khan by passed the long line of agitated spectators and made their way through the V.I.P. entrance. The bouncer checked their names on the guest list before allowing them access into the venue. Swine and Yella looked like walking advertisements as they entered the venue, wearing their teams name branded all over their clothing. Swine had a black hoodie with M.F.I. (Made for It) plastered on the back and Yella wore a M.F.I Tee-shirt with his signature yellow Nike windbreaker to top it off. Khan went simple with a black Polo thermal, blue Levis and all three gentlemen rocked the latest Nike boots. Khan never had much style. His thing was making money. His theory was, if you spent all of your money on designer jeans, then what would you put in the pockets?

Slick couldn't believe the turnout of tonight's event. He assumed since the venue was in the middle of the hood, that it could possibly deter some of the fans from attending. Slick got love from the city, county, state and now he was getting recognition nationwide. He was up and coming and knew that is was only a matter of time before Slick-Talk was a household name.

"Okay. Okay. Okay…Y'all about to make a black man blush out this bitch." said a cheesing Slick as the crowd made him feel like royalty.

"Boy, do I have a treat in store for y'all tonight. Not only do I have the best artist's in the city ready to rock da mic. I also have some great battles for y'all aswell. We got the undefeated Crazy Cracker in the building set to battle an out of town cat from Philly.

I'm sure y'all heard of a guy named.. Ten-fold." The venue erupted in cheers at the mention of Ten-fold.

Ten-fold was quickly making a name for himself by destroying every battle rapper on the east coast. He had a large social media following and Slick wasted no time booking Ten-fold before his asking price became too high.

"I can't wait to see those two rap gods lock horns! We also have our very first girl on girl co-main event. Big Pam will face off against Deja-Vu for a cash prize of $500. Don't sleep on the new comer because I promise this will be talked about for years to come!" Slick followed up by reading the rest of the jam packed card then decided to pay some bills by promoting everyone that sponsored him before introducing his opening act.

"Let's kick this shit off right y'all…give it up for M.F.I!" The beat dropped as the trio hit the stage with Yella leading off with the opening verse to his new song "Colorful Life"

"Yellow wrist, yellow kicks, Yellow whip, Yellow bitch/ Yella hit, then Yella dip, now Yella that n Yella this/ (Ha!) Canary diamonds got me getting' all da puddy cat/ I took my dick up out that hoe, she yellin' Put it back/"

Yella continued his verse until Swine, aka Captain Hook, delivered the chorus.

"I got black, white, red, different color hoes jockin'/

I got brown, orange, green, different color wrist watches/…Boy stop it, you know I keep some options/ Euros, Yins, and Pesos. I got different color profit/"

Swine smiled as the audience nodded in sync while he stepped aside to allow Khan to take center stage…The closer it came to Khan's verse, the more sober Khan became. The drugs in Khan's system started to fade as the butterflies in his stomach resurfaced.

Khan closed his eyes tight behind his Raban shades and allowed the music to flow through his body. He opened his eyes and focused in on a familiar face in the crowd, then he spit his bars.

"Orange Kush, eye's red, when I'm coming thru/ Black hoddie when I'm ducking all them boys in blue/ White Russian, I ain't talkin' bout da drink dawg/ 'Cause she goin' fuck ya like she tryin' get a green card/"

Khadeja marveled at Khan's ability to use a color word play scheme while incorporating quality punchlines. As Khan's verse came to an end Swine retook center stage and as he recited the chorus the audience sang along. Yella cracked a huge smile as he jumped around the stage instigating the crowd to make more noise. Khan was feeling the vibe also as he did a few fist pumps then nodded his head to the hook.

Khan and the M.F.I boys stepped offstage to a thunderous ovation. Swine and Yella gave Khan his props then gave some of their new female admires some attention. Khan wasted no time hunting down Khadeja as she stood by the bar with two glasses in her hands awaiting Khan's arrival.

"It's you!" yelled Khan over the music.

"Live in the flesh…you were awesome." Khadeja complimented.

"Thank you miss…" Khan asked still unaware of the young womans name.

"Khadeja." she replied while handing Khan a glass.

"Khadeja…what a beautiful name and thanks for the drink."

"No problem, let's have a toast." Khadeja said with her glass held high in the air.

"A toast to what sweetheart?"

"A toast to those nice lines you spit." smiled Khadeja.

"Nice lines? We call 'em bars mama." Khan laughed.

"Bars huh… I like that, To Bars!" Khadeja announced.

"To Bars" replied Khan as their glasses met.

Khan took a long gulp from his drink then wiped his mouth with the sleeve of his shirt.

"Damn what was that?" asked Khan while licking his lips.

"It's called a Blue Mother Fucker" answered Khadeja as she glanced over Khan's tall frame. Khan caught her eyeing him up as he flexed a bicep.

"You see something you like?" joked Khan.

"Maybe." said Khadeja with a little help from the liquor.

"The feelings mutual...I can't lie, I been thinking about you ever since the last time I saw you."

"Word?" Khadeja replied bashfully.

"Real shit, then you ain't even tell a nigga ya name, shit drove me crazy...but anyway what brought you out here tonight?"

"I'm performing..."

"Oh yea...you sing?"

"Nah, I got a battle...I'm battling Big Pam."

"Get da fuck outta here!" Khan was stunned.

"Yea it's my first time, that's why I'm sipping on this Blue Mother Fucker so slow" laughed Khadeja.

Khan walked closer to Khadeja and grabbed her hand.

"Don't be nervous, shawty ain't shit but a lot of noise. All you gotta do is match her aggression and maintain eye contact. Even if ya bars don't hit with everyone in the crowd, just spit that shit with confidence and I promise she will crumble." Khan coached as he gently massaged her shaky hand.

"Sounds like you know a little something about this battle

shit."

"A little something." Khan could feel Khadeja's body starting to relax as he placed a lite kiss on Khadeja's hand.

"I gotchu mama, I will be in your corner." said Khan as the same familiar female walked up to Khadeja.

"Hey Khadeja, hey stranger" waved Valita to Khan.

"Khan and your name?"

"Valita"

"Valita…I think my homie Gutta knew a Valita" said Khan as he finally remembered Valita was the girl that set Gutta up with a group of Bloods on Chase street.

"Gutta….oh shit, look them niggas forced me-" Khan silenced her with a raised index finger.

"I'm not tripping about that shit mama, Gutta knew what came with that life and I ain't no banger so we good on my end."

Valita released a sigh of relief then her bright smile returned as she put her arms on the shoulders of Khan and Khadeja.

"Well enough about that, tell me about this shit going on over here" Khadeja blushed and shook her head from side to side.

"We are just friends." uttered Khadeja while taking another sip of her drink as Valita gave her a "Bitch Please" glare.

"Whateva, Khan are you gonna stay and watch ya girl put in work later?" asked Valita as she snatched Khadeja's drink and took it to the head.

"I wouldn't miss it for the world" replied Khan while studying Khadeja's thick frame.

"Oh you did ya thang too Khan…I didn't know you could rap." Valita congradulated.

"Appreciate it mama"

The rest of the night went well for Khan and Khadeja as they took this time to socialize and learn about each other's past and future plans. Khan could tell Khadeja was only giving him small bits and pieces about her life but he was captivated by her mystery. Khadeja also detected that Khan was withholding information but nevertheless, she enjoyed his company. Several more groups and solo artist performed giving the Slick-Talk fans a night to remember but now it was time to give the people what they really came to see, the battles. The undercard had its ups and downs as Bullets da Maniac destroyed

Smoke Grey, and Afta-Thought barely edged Kris Swag. It was now time for the co-main event as Slick made his way back to the stage.

"Is y'all having fun thus far?" the crowd replied with a series of "Yea's and Yurrps" as Slick continued.

"Well it's time for Slick-Talk to make history with its first girl on girl battle!" as all parties met on stage Khadeja remembered Khan's words and locked eyes with Big Pam.

Big Pam was a few inches shorter than Khadeja but she was as wide as all outdoors. Big Pam sported a large Green Football Jersey with the words "The Empire" on the back. Tight black jeans and a pair of white reebok classics. Her small group of Empire thugs had her six as she returned the mean mug Khadeja shot her way.

Khadeja had on a pair of leopard print leggin's with a tight brown tank top that hugged her ample breast. She decided to wear a pair of Valita's black Timberland boots in case she had to stomp a bitch. Both girls met in the middle of the stage as everyone gathered around them as close as possible. Slick pulled a coin from his pocket.

"Deja-Vu call it in the air"

"Heads" said Khadeja without removing her eyes from Big Pam.

"Heads it is!"

"She got it" Khadeja uttered as she pointed at Big Pam.

"Alright Big Pam this will be for two rounds as previously discussed. We will go a third round if y'all tie. My judges for tonight are Slim Jim from Coldspring, Knuckles representing York Rd, and Miss Carla holding down the four by four…a'ight Pammy we ready when you ready" Big Pam took her time before speaking as she took in the scenery.

"All these people came here to see me" thought Big Pam as she reflected back to her humble beginnings. Big Pam or Pamela Lopez was a twenty-five year old Cubana. She was raised in the gang life on the lower end of Belair road. Being around the guys all her life caused her to also have the same desires which led Pamela to becoming a lesbian. It was hard for Big Pam to grow up in a man's world but she fought for every crumb. Once Big Pam discovered her rap skills, she became a hot commodity battling some of the neighborhoods best male M.C.'s. Now Big Pam was in a position to give her and her family a better life and she had no intentions on letting Khadeja stand in her way.

"Empire…we outchea!..Hey yo! Slick you done fucked up by giving me this bitch/ But if she volunteered then this must be her death wish/ Now don't take this shit personal, I'm just doin' it for da wealth/ They say it's a man's world so its every bitch for herself/ Say something crazy out ya mouth, and watch how I react babe/ Don't

make me fuck up that pretty face, wont that hurt ya business on back page/

"Wow!" said Yella as he and Swine found Khan standing behind a visibly shook Khadeja. The crowd went nuts as Big Pam, continued her first round.

"Relax mama...don't let her see you sweat" whispered Khan as Khadeja prepared to recite her first round.

Big Pam gave Khadeja a wink as she finished her round then awaited for Deja-Vu's rebuttal. Khadeja took several deep breaths as she did her best to remain cool. She took a few steps towards Big Pam and replied...

"If that was ya best work...sweetie I am not impressed/ Y'all think Big Pam gonna beat me? Maybe at a pie eating contest/ Cause bitch I'mma soldier, and I don't need a bunch of thugs to command the field/ Yous a flunky and you funky, Big bitch probably sweat standing still/ It's obvious the more I rap, the more you lose faith/ And when the shotty pump connect with ya sloppy gut...it'll help ya lose weight/"

Khadeja continued to insult Big Pam as her first round concluded with roars of laughter and cheers. Khan gave Khadeja a pat on the back as Slick announced it was time for round two. Big Pam wasted no time as she stepped face to face with Khadeja.

"If a nigga pay to fuck you, he either desperate or retarded/ You had to know this shit was over before it started/ Now this broke hoe think she a rapper, somebody throw her some cash/ Cause even them fuck ass bloods like K-Willz said that pussy trash/"

Khadeja was beyond heated as Big Pam finished the rest of the round leaving spectators anxious for Deja-Vu's response.

"If I slapped da shit outta you right now, you probably get one of them Empire nigga's to do the fighting for ya/ Which makes me believe they probably did the writing for ya/ And yea I'm in the streets, and can't nothing you say get me discouraged/ You just mad 'cause my pussy so good I could fuck up Slick's marriage/"

Slick's wife gave Khadeja the "stink eye" as Khadeja continued to pick Big Pam apart. After Khadeja spit her last bar she returned the same wink that Big Pam gave her earlier in the round as both ladies awaited the judges' decision.

"What I tell y'all …I knew this battle would be fire. Let's give it up for both contestants!"

The entire venue showed their appreciation by clapping until their hands hurt. Slick huddled up with the three judges as they rendered their decision. Once confirmed, Slick attempted to quiet the crowd by fanning his hands downward before speaking.

"Alright the results are in…with two judges in favor of the

victor, the winner is Deja- Vu!" Khadeja couldn't believe her ears as she and Valita jumped around screaming, Big Pam shook her head and walked off stage. Slick walked over to Khadeja and raised her arm in the air then asked her if she would like to say a few words.

"Well I have two things to say actually….one, thank you to everyone who believed in me." Khadeja shot Khan a quick smile.

"And two, where my money at Slick?"

Chapter Twenty-Five
BAD BOYS, BAD BOYS... WHATCHU GONNA DO

"Good work McFarley. Throw that lowlife pimp in cell 5" spat Detective Clark while ice grilling the handcuffed man dressed in all pink.

Detective Sterling Clark was a proud member of the Baltimore City Police Department. He was a faithful servant of his community. Detective Clark was a mild manner middle age man with a head full of grey hair and a tall muscular build. He had seen it all and done it all. Living in the city of Baltimore gave the detective a tough demeanor. Very few things got under his skin, well for the exception of anyone involved in the sex working industry. Everyone from the pimps to the prostitutes to the Johns, received the harshest of treatment while in the detectives' custody. This was a touchy subject to him because his mother was a streetwalker, and his alleged father, was an abusive pimp. His mother neglected him and left a young Sterling to deal with life on the mean streets of Baltimore all by himself. Growing up in the predominantly white neighborhood of Canton, Sterling found it daunting task for a young white male to avoid the massive outbreak of addiction and pledged to himself that he would make a change in the community.

Officer McFarley returned from the cell block section of the precinct and poured himself a cup of coffee.

"You want some coffee Clark?" offered McFarley.

"No thank you, hey what's going on with our city?" asked Clark

"Huh?" replied McFarley while sipping his coffee.

"That's like the fourth pimp we've arrested this month, they are growing. There are a lot more girls walking these streets too!"

"I guess there's something in the water." replied McFarley.

Steven McFarley didn't take prostitution as serious as Detective Clark, unless the pimp had white girls in his stable. If there was one thing McFarley couldn't stand, it was a good white woman serving a nigger. The only reason McFarley brought the pimp in pink into custody was because he was beating a young white hooker down in the broad daylight. McFarley was aware of the pimp's operations in the area but didn't know the low life now had white women on his roster. McFarley was in an unmarked sedan receiving some head from Suga, one of McFarley's favorite working girls as he radioed for back up, then several officers beat the pimp down like a gang initiation before cuffing him and dragging him to the precinct.

Suga was so into pleasing the cop, she never noticed Flamingo Pimp disciplining his newest recruit for short changing his money, until McFarley tossed her a C-note and bolted from the car with his pants halfway down. Suga crept back to the motel, gathered her belongings and headed towards the truck stop without looking back.

Chapter Twenty-Six
BOY MEETS GIRL

"Fuck you mean you ain't coming? I done already paid you in advance plus spent mad money on promotions" screamed Slick into his phone while his wife tried to make out what was troubling her man.

"Is everything okay baby?" asked Tee as Slick held up his index finger signaling her to wait for a second.

"Fuck you nigga, ya scary ass just making up an excuse so you don't get bodied by a white boy. I'll see you in hell pussy!" Slick slammed his phone on the ledge of the bar as Tee waited for him to inform her of the bad news.

"Ten-fold is a no-show, he said his camp advised him that battling a "nobody" like Crazy Cracker would hurt his credibility." said Slick while thinking of a way to salvage his main event and save his reputation.

Slick knew that once he announced that Ten-fold canceled, this would be detrimental to his brand and future endeavors.

"Maybe you could tell everyone that Ten-fold backed out of

the battle because he's scared of Crazy Cracker, and if anyone is willing to battle Crazy Cracker on the spot, you would give them a cash prize if they win." suggested Tee.

"What? Fuck no that shit sounds dumb as shit" said Slick as Wayne, Slicks camera and production crew leader, located Slick in the rear of the venue and approached him.

"Wayne whats good?" said Slick as Wayne could read the stress on his face.

"Just checking to see what's going on, we can't keep having the D.J. spin records to entertain the crowd. What's up with the main event?" Slick scratched his head for a second and yelled.

"I got it!" Tee and Wayne looked at each other than at Slick.

"Look Ten-fold gonna be a no show, so I'm about to try something new."

"Okay?" replied Wayne.

"I'm gonna tell everyone that Ten-fold backed out of the battle because he's scared of Crazy Cracker. Then to add my special touch, I will offer a open challenge for Crazy

Cracker with a chance for a cash prize." Tee simply shook her head and walked away as slick finished "His" proposal.

"I love it" said Wayne as he rushed to inform the rest of the crew, the new turn of events.

"Tee! I'm sorry baby" yelled Slick as he chased after his wife.

"I wonder what the holdup is?" asked Khadeja as she stood close to the stage with Valita, Khan, Yella, and Swine, waiting for the battle of the night.

"Me too…I can't wait for this shit" Khan commented as he sipped from a fresh glass of Blue Mother fucker.

"There go Slick now" yelled someone from the crowd.

"Okay so here's the deal y'all….it appears Big Bad Ten-Fold was bluffing the whole time. I guess I created a monster when I let the Crazy Cracker out of the gate." said Slick as numerous fan's expressed their displeasure in Ten-Fold's absence.

"Hold up now…. As they say in show biz…the show must go on. With that being said, if anyone can defeat Crazy Cracker I will pay them one thousand dollars cash money!"

Slick could see the eyes of damn near everyone in the audience grow wide at the sound of possibly winning a stack of Slicks money.

Slick assumed at the very mention of a thousand dollars people would bum rush the stage to get at Cracker but to his surprise, no one flinched. Crazy Cracker walked on stage next to Slick as he snatched the microphone from Slick's grasp. "Let me find out I got this whole city shook." laughed Crazy Cracker and a few members of the Hooligans.

"This my city Slick and everybody here knows it. Ain't nobody in this bitch got the balls to fuck with me, Y'all on social media all day talking shit, but when y'all get a chance to step up to a real villain y'all bitch out." Crazy Cracker taunted as he scanned the group of spectators.

"Black? Tre? Lil Chunky? Why all y'all ducking?" asked Crazy Cracker while signaling out different M.C.'s in the crowd.

"I'm a little too tipsy dug" replied lil Chunky while trying to save face in front of his lady friend.

"Yella? Whats up…you running around like you the hottest in da streets, step up bruh!"

"Yo, you know I don't battle, I make music and fuck niggas bitches" Yella replied cool and calm.

"Shit sounds good" spat Crazy Cracker.

"I got somebody for you though…" said Yella as Khan already

knew where his brother was going with his statement.

"Yo, Khan…Kill that white boy" said Yella while Swine and Valita cosigned.

"Man don't put me in this shit bruh" said Khan.

"Whats ya name…Khan…come on man I won't go too hard on you" laughed Crazy Cracker.

"Khan, you ain't gonna let him talk to you like that are you?" questioned Khadeja with a smile.

"I'm not trying to get caught up in this rap shit again, every time I jump in this rap world bad things happen. I get too caught up in trying to fit that image and almost always end up in prison" Khan thought to himself as everyone around him continued to rally Khan to the stage.

"What if I give two thousand to the winner?" shouted Slick as he had already took notice in Khan's unique skill set when he performed with Yella.

"Shit that's a bet" said Khan as he climbed the stage while an excited group of fans cheered him on.

The rest of Khan's crew joined him as Slick stood in-between the two parties to explain the rules of the impromptu showdown.

"This will be for one round, winner take all. You've already met my judges and they will continue to call a fair decision. We already know who Crazy Cracker is…how about you introduce yourself challenger."

"Khan…Gangas Khan…east side, let's work" Gangas Khan was the identity that Khan strived so hard to stay away from.

He was a ruthless force that only cared about three things…Money, Power, and Respect. Making music was one thing, but when it came to battling, Gangas Khan took no prisoners. If he spit it, then he lived it. There was no faking when it came to Gangas Khan and the world had no idea what had just been unleased.

"Gangas call it in the air" said Slick while flipping the coin.

"Tails"

"Tails it is, you wanna go first or second"

"Let him speak" said Gangas Khan while getting his thoughts together.

Yes Khan was officially out of the rap game but like any vet, you always possessed the tools of the trade. Khan had a collection of "Uni-Bars" which was a term that Khan coined meaning universal bars that could be used at his disposal for occasions such as this. Khan had the ability to combine a plethora of pre-meditated lyrics with improvised punchlines to lyrically assault any M.C. stupid enough to step in his path. Crazy Cracker displayed no fear as he removed his black bomber jacket to reveal a medium muscular physique covered with a white tank top and a variety of prison tattoos.

"You look like a playa, but you ain't neva been in this type of game/ They can't be ya friends if they gassed you up for this type of pain/ Ya know what...let me explain/ Fear in my heart is something da best cardiologist can't find/ So if I catch you in public, I will let da K spray with no regard for mankind/ We could do da fist but if you got a piece, I'd advise you to bring one/ Cause I got a hollow tip for you and da pussy you came from/ Hey whats wrong with guy?/ Don't he know I keep da metal in the van like Johnny Five/"

Crazy Cracker spit several more aggressive gun bars before grabbing his crotch and blowing a kiss at Khadeja. Khan remained cool as he allowed Gangas to take control. Gangas Khan waited for the roaring crowd to subdue, then said...

"Bars like that, be da reason all you bitches stay local/ Cuz nigga you is too small to make me take any of ya threats outside of rap vocals/ Say for instance we was locked up, like I'm talkin bout a real prison/ You'd come in a stand up guy, but I'd make ya sit down pissin/ And chill with all that gunplay talk before I mask up wit da bandana/ Cuz from 500 yards away, I got something that could clip a cockroach antenna/ Fuck da police, if you really 'bout that life then let them bullets dance/ But if you scared of jail, we can do it in braille...that means I can see you with the hands/"

The entire venue exploded in cheers as Khan quietly thanked Gangas Khan for the stellar performance. Yella's smile couldn't be contained as he continuously shoved Khan's chest in excitement.

"Chill nigga!" said Khan while playfully bear hugging Yella.

"Nigga you killed that cracker!" shouted Swine as the girls nodded their heads in agreement.

Khadeja wrapped her arms around Khan from behind and whispered…

"That shit got a bitch panties wet, oops I ain't wearing none." laughed Khadeja as Khan smiled then awaited for the judges' decision.

Slick huddled up with the judges as it appeared to be a bit of confusion.

"So Slim is in favor of Crazy, and Knuckles going with Khan…well Carla I hate to put so much pressure on you but for political reasons, I can't have my main attraction losing to a new comer." said Slick.

"I thought we were suppose to judge this fairly?" asked Miss Carla.

"Fair? Don't I pay you a fair piece of change to judge these events? And if you want me to continue paying you, I need you to get with the program!" threatened Slick as Miss Carla thought about the steady cash Slick sent her way, she reluctantly voted in favor of

Crazy Cracker.

"Alright y'all the results are in, and the winner of this heavy weight bout…with a split decision, the Baltimore Crazy Cracker!"

Khan was hot as Crazy Cracker gave Khan the "I told ya so" look.

"Ain't this a bitch" muttered Khan as everyone in Khan's corner shouted their frustrations at Slick and the judges.

Slick knew it was dirty but it was a business decision that he figured was the right move to make. On the other hand Slick had no intentions on allowing this diamond in the ruff to slip through his hands. Slick jogged over to Khan as he and his people were exiting the stage.

"Hey for what it's worth I think you won." said Slick as he caught up with Khan.

"Well it ain't worth two g's" laughed Khan as the others stepped aside to give Khan and Slick some privacy.

"It could be worth more than that if you let me take you under my wing."

"Not interested bruh, I refuse to be apart of anything that let's bullshit bars beat out the type of fire that I gave you nigga's tonight…and for free at that."

"I completely understand my dude, but in life you win some and ya-" Khan cut him off.

"I only win…"

"Well not tonight, but…if you give me a chance I could put you in a position where even if you lose, you still win." Khan understood where Slick was coming from but decided to take baby steps with the slick talking young entrepreneur.

"Get my info from Yella" said Khan

"Will do" replied an animated Slick as he happily skipped his way off stage.

Khan noticed the large herd slowly dispersing through the exit doors. Khan followed suit as he made his way out in the parking lot searching the sea of faces for Khadeja. Khan spotted a small assemblage of guys dressed in red. The closer Khan got to the men he recognized Khadeja standing in the center with a man twice her size. Khan almost walked away, thinking that Khadeja was choosing until he heard some of their conversation.

"Bitch you think this a game, I own ya dumbass. You leave

when I say you can. Now get in the fuckin' car before I throw you in that bitch" said K-Willz while staring Khadeja in the eyes.

"I'm not fucking with you…leave me alone, you lucky I ain't go to the cops for that bullshit. I want my fucking money back too!" yelled Khadeja.

"Bitch you ain't getting shit, and if you went to the cops I woulda killed you and everybody close to you…now get in the car!" K-Willz grew impatient with Khadeja's attitude and decided to take action.

K-Willz grabbed Khadeja by her hair and pulled her to the car. Valita broke free of Brents grasp and pulled at K-Willz arm until he released his grip from Khadeja's hair. He then back handed Valita as she quickly dropped to the ground. K-Willz raised his large boot over her head to finish the job until Khan appeared in K-Willz space.

"Fuck is this nigga?" said K-Willz to his homies.

"I don't want no smoke bruh, but leave the girls alone before you force my hand" replied Khan as he stood nose to nose with a slightly taller K-Willz.

K-Willz was confused then angry at the stranger for interfering with his affairs.

"Walk nigga" said K-Willz while reaching for his 45.

"You need all these niggas and a gun to deal with me bruh…shoot me a fair one" challenged Khan as K-Willz goons anticipated K-Willz response.

"I don't need shit to deal with you" said K-Willz while taking his hand off of his gun handle. K-Willz put his fist in the air, in a fighting position and waited for Khan to take a fighters stance before dropping his hands and yelling….

"Sike…niggas don't fight no more, and if memory serves me correct, I believe I spared your life one time already." said K-Willz while drawing his pistol at Khan's head.

"*Spared me before?*" thought Khan while looking the gun straight down the barrel.

"*Oh he was the nigga that pulled me from the Gutta situation*" thought Khan as he prepared for the inevitable. As K-Willz prepared to pull the trigger, someone called K-Willz's name.

"Hey bitch….you take one of ours, we take all of yours….this for Gutta bitch!" yelled Big Pam as her and her team produced several pistol's in hand and aimed them at K-Willz and his set.

Khan took advantage of the distraction and threw a strong right hook that connected with the tip of K-Willz chin causing him to fall backwards into the hands of his homies as Khan grabbed Khadeja and Valita by the hand and high tailed it out of the parking lot. Khan knew

Allah was on his side, as Yella's Camaro pulled up a few feet away and waited for Khan and the girls to jump in the backseat before the 700 plus horse powered engine catapulted them from the bullet spraying warzone.

An hour and ten blunts later Khan and the crew ended up at the Boulevard Diner on Eastern Ave. While under the influence of Grand Daddy Kush, the five-some managed to turn a life threatening situation into a humorous discussion as they all sat in the booth smiling and smashing a table full of chicken and waffles.

"Why it seem like every time I leave you, somebody always try to kill you" laughed Yella as Khan shrugged his shoulders and continued to punish the helpless platter of waffles.

"I dunno my nigga…but the key word is try. If Slender Man couldn't do it, K-Willz ain't got a chance." everyone laughed accept for the girls.

"Who's Slender Man?" asked Khadeja through red eyes.

"Long story… so where y'all staying so I can tell Yella where to drop y'all off?"

"Long story" replied Khadeja while staring off in the distance.

"I'm listening mama" said Khan while looking her in the eyes.

"We staying at El Rich" confessed Khadeja.

"You mean that piss hole on route 40." retorted Khan.

"The one and only" when Khan heard Big Pam mention Khadeja was on Backpage, Khan understood why Khadeja chose her words so carefully. Khan could see the pain in her eyes and decided from here on out that he would protect her at all cost.

"Y'all ready to roll?" asked Yella while standing up from the booth.

"Yea drop us all at my spot" said Khan while looking at Khadeja.

Khadeja blushed uncontrollably when Khan followed up with

"We will pick y'all stuff up from that motel in the morning. Y'all with me now…like I said before, I'm in ya corner."

Chapter Twenty-Seven
I GOT A POCKET FULL OF SUNSHINE

"Olivia, Nina...meet Khadeja and Valita" said Khan as the quartet examined one another in the empty living room. Neither girl made a sound as Khan could sense Olivia starting to reach her boiling point.

"Let me guess Khan, more cousins of yours?" said Olivia in a sarcastic tone.

"Actually, yes they are....and like I told you before sweetheart, I need you to trust me. I don't get along with a lot of my family members but for the few who are like minded, we have big plans and it's time to put shit in motion."

"Whateva Khan...do what you want, I don't even care anymore!" said Olivia then stormed upstairs and slammed her bedroom door.

"Nina...since we don't have much furniture here, please allow my guest to room with you" asked Khan while placing a gentle hand on Nina's shoulder.

"Finally...I don't have to sleep alone anymore" laughed Nina as she ushered the girls upstairs to her room.

Khan took advantage of the momentary silence as he removed a pack of Dutch Masters Cigarillos from his pant pocket. He used his thumbnails to split the cigar in half and dumped its contents in the trash can. Khan walked to the kitchen table and pulled out a small dime size bag of Grand Daddy Kush. He then spread the Kush evenly throughout the empty cigar and rolled the cigarillo into a perfect circumference.

"*I hope I ain't putting too much on Olivia's plate.*" mused Khan while inhaling the potent smoke.

"She'll get over it...I got a good thing going on and I gotta ride this until the wheels fall off."

After finishing the blunt, Khan was much more relaxed and decided to check in on the girls before fussing with Olivia. Khan walked into the girl's room without knocking as all three sets of eyes surveyed his presence.

"Sup Y'all" said Khan while taking a seat on the futon next to Khadeja and Nina.

Valita sat indian style on the floor as she read old text messages on her phone.

"Sup...oh here Khan before I forget" Nina spoke while taking two hundred dollars from her purse and handing it to Khan.

Khadeja watched the transaction as she started to really question what type of man Khan was, Khan saw the bewildered look on Khadeja's face as he thought it was now time to come clean and lay it all out on the table.

"I know what you thinking" said Khan while looking at Khadeja.

"You do..." Khadeja played dumb.

"Yup, you see a guy living in an empty house with two different women and one of which giving him money."

"Yea I peeked that" said Khadeja nonchalantly.

"I ain't no pimp, I ain't no rapper, I ain't no playa, I ain't shit. Truth is...I dunno what I am, but I do know that I am destined for greatness" Valita put her phone down as Khan's words commanded her attention.

"I am just a man that's trying to make the most out of this piece of shit they call life. I been struggling for a while, but I won't give up until I get my slice of the pie. I also see your struggle, but I can tell you got some fight in you too." Khadeja nodded as she remained silent while Khan continued.

"Look around, everyone here has been struggling, including Olivia out there, but the difference is we have the smarts to come together and create a winning team. Yes this probably ain't the way you imagined it as a kid with dreams of being a doctor or runway model or marrying some athlete. This is real world so we gotta make real moves."

"Khan you don't have to explain this to me, I'm a lot smarter than you think. I know that team work makes da dream work so this is for you" said Khadeja while pulling out the five hundred dollars she won from her battle with Big Pam.

Khan gave her a perplexed stare then took the money.

"What's this for?"

"It's for a lot of things…it's for that battle they cheated you out of, it's for saving my life, it's for also being in my corner. Honestly, I wish I had more to give you but I see ya vision and I'm ready to give you my life and put this family in a position to win" Khadeja smiled as she gave Nina a high five.

"Nina how much did you make?" asked Khadeja.

"I made two hundred dollars" Nina said with pride.

"How many Johns?" asked Valita.

"Five, I do head for them, forty dollars each" said Nina in broken English.

"No offense but you are way too pretty to be charging crack head prices…I am about to upgrade you. I can get you a least three times what your making now." explained Khadeja.

"Valita you take care of Nina's hair and make-up so we can take some better pictures for her backpage profile."

"What is Backpage?" asked Nina.

"It's a social media app that helps us working girls get dates"

"Oh…like Tagged" responded Nina.

"Tagged…oh no! That's the reason why your not making any real money.

Nothin but corner hustlers use Tagged. Those niggas are cheap. Backpage is mostly older white tricks with tons of money to spend." said Khadeja as Khan listened to Khadeja, school him and his girl.

Khan knew that there was something special about Khadeja as she reminded him of a female version of himself.

"Well I gotta go straighten things out with Olivia before she kicks us all out" laughed Khan.

"But if any of y'all have any ideas to bring money in, I'm all ears, oh and Khadeja I'm going to help develop your rapping skills too. For that being ya first time, you did great."

"I honestly think you could be the next big thing. But y'all need to understand we gonna be more than just a bunch of hookers and hustla's. We gotta be on our shit. Once you get lazy, you gotta go…remember anyone under this roof must be on they ABC's."

"ABC's?" questioned Valita.

"ABC's…Always Be Contributing" Khan smiled as he paid homage to the late G.P.

"A'ight well I'mma leave y'all to it…if y'all wanna chill tonight I'm cool with that but we on the move in the morning." said Khan while standing up to leave.

"Hey Khan if you serious about making money, I got another girl that's interested in joining our family." said Valita while texting on her phone.

"Oh yea…" smiled Khan.

"Yup and she say's she already knows who you are" added Valita.

"What..Who is it?" Khan's curiosity had the best of him.

"This red bone named Suga"

"Good ole Suga" said Khan while reminiscing about his brief encounters with Suga.

"Yea she's downtown and don't have no way out here. She's at a hotel now so she straight but she has to leave in the morning." stated Valita.

"How do y'all feel about another girl coming?" asked Khan while searching the girl's faces for any resistance.

"More bitches mean more money" said Nina as Khadeja nodded in approval.

"But when we start making money, we gotta get some furniture in this house!" spat Khadeja.

"No prob…tell Suga we'll be there after we get y'all shit from El Rich."

"I vant come" said Nina in her second language.

"Cool" said Khan as he went to handle Olivia.

The next morning Khan was exhausted from a long night of apologetic sex with Olivia. Olivia made Khan fuck her until she no longer cared that Khan was slowly transforming her house into a circus.

"Why we gotta take the bus, I know you sitting on at least seven hundred dollars….lets just get a cab" cried Valita as the group hiked to the bus stop.

"Because sweetheart" replied Khan.

"Because what!" Valita spat with an early morning attitude.

"It would cost at least sixty dollars for a round trip from here to downtown, not to mention our pit stop on route 40"

"So, we got the money…why you ain't got no car like your brother. His shits nice"

"In due time mama….if I spend every dime we make on senseless things then how will we ever climb from this hole. If we take the bus it will only cost three dollars and fifty cent per person, which adds up to fourteen dollars. Sometimes you gotta see the big picture if you really wanna advance in life." Khan did his best to explain his frugal ideology to an ornery Valita.

"Once you get a little older you'll understand why saving ya money is important...how old are you anyway?" asked Khan as they finally reached the bus stop.

"I'm...ah...nineteen" lied Valita.

"Yea you will one day see what I'm talking about." smiled Khan as the bus arrived.

After grabbing their belongings from the El Rich Motel, Khan and company jumped back on the bus and headed downtown. The long bus ride to downtown Baltimore took a little over an hour before Khan pulled the yellow rope for the bus to stop at St. Paul and Fayette Street.

"Is she at the Burger King now?" asked Khan to Valita.

"Yup" replied Valita as she texted Suga to let her know of their location.

"A'ight well the Burger King is right up the street." said Khan as the girls followed his lead.

Once they arrived at the Burger King, Khan spotted Suga

immediately sitting on her phone sipping on an ice coffee, looking like million bucks.

"Hey girlll!" shouted Valita.

"Heeey!" replied Suga as she hugged Valita then Khadeja like they were long lost friends.

"Hello" Suga greeted Nina as Nina smiled back at her and waved.

"So you don't see me huh?" questioned Khan while eyeing Suga's tight body.

She had on a pair of skin tight jeans with a long sleeve form fitting pink shirt which displayed enough cleavage to make men and women sneak a peek.

"You know I was saving the best for last Daddy"

"Show ya right" smiled Khan as he grabbed a little ass during their embrace.

"Alright let's get outta here…where'd you park?"

"Nigga ain't got no car" said Valita.

"I'm working on that right now…just bare with me" said Khan while shooting Valita a distasteful glare.

"Where's your house?" asked Suga.

"I got a little cozy spot out Essex. It's not much but once we get our money up, I'mma find something better" assured Khan as Suga gave him a quick smile then commenced in mindless chatter with the rest of the girls.

Khan allowed the girls to lead the way to the bus stop as he surveyed his surroundings from the rear of the group. As the girls rambled on about the latest gossip in pop culture. Khan took notice that every man and even some women had their eyes on his stable. Businessmen, bums, beat cops and block boys all eyed his girls hungrily. Khan smiled as the young women turned Charles Street into their own personal runway. A young kid, no older than twelve damn near ran into a street light while ogling the girls intensely.

"You good lil man?" asked Khan with a grin.

"Yea…damn, which one of them yours" asked the kid while pointing to the girls.

"All of 'em" smiled Khan as the kid gave him a confused look.

"For real…I wanna be like you when I grow up" Khan laughed and gave the kid a thumbs up then picked up his pace to return with the girls as the bus was fast approaching.

Khan took a seat away from the girls, as the girls found refuge in the back of the bus. Khan used this time on the bus ride to check his messages.

"Damn this nigga don't give up" said Khan while ignoring yet another message from Slick.

As Khan strolled down his newsfeed on Facebook, someone called Khan's name. When Khan looked up, he saw a familiar toothless smile.

"Sunshine!" yelled Khan while jumping up to embrace her and squeeze into the seat next to her.

"How have you been Sugah?" asked Sunshine while adjusting her wig that Khan almost knocked off.

"Couldn't be better and you?"

"Well I'm still trucking...I see you done and came up in the world." said Sunshine while pointing towards the gorgeous group of Divas lost in conversation.

"Something like that" Khan replied modestly.

"Who you think you talking to Khan...I can smell a pimp from a mile away" Khan was shocked then replied.

"I ain't no pimp, I'm just a nigga trying to make it."

"Call it what you want, but know this…if that white man gets a hold of you, he don't give a damn what you call ya self. He just know where to throw ya black ass at when it's all said and done" cautioned Sunshine.

"So you saying I should stop while I'm ahead?"

"Huh…fuck no, I'm saying if you gonna do something…do the shit right. Go hard or go home because they goin' smash ya black ass if you get knocked regardless if you got ten bitches or ten thousand." Sunshine informed while popping a peppermint in her mouth.

"You want some candy?"

"Nah I'm cool, so how do you know so much about this life?" questioned Khan while studying Sunshine's eyes.

"Have you ever heard of Freddie Flip-flop?"

"Freddie who?"

"Freddie Flip-flop was one of Baltimore's most successful pimps, if you ever spent a dime on pussy back in the mid 80's, I can promise you it went in his pockets."

"And how do you know about Freddie Flip-flop?" asked Khan.

"I was his bottom bitch, well until he got jammed up with the Feds a few years later. Since then it's been a rocky ride, but there ain't shit about this game that I ain't hip to."

"Is that so" said Khan while the wheels started turning in his head.

"Yup" Sunshine smiled.

"What are your plans today?" Khan questioned.

"Well I was on my way to the soup kitchen but besides that I'm as free as the wind blows." Khan wasted no time putting his plan into motion.

"Would you be willing to come back to the house with me and drop a few gems on the girls for me? Most of them are rookies and could benefit from some advice of a vet like yaself." Khan proposed.

"I dunno…it's hard to get a seat at the soup kitchen, if you get there late." Sunshine replied.

"Lunch, Dinner, whateva, it's all on me. I will compensate you for your time. You know I gotchu." pleaded Khan.

"Okay baby….Sunshine gotchu too"

Sunshine slowly paced back and forth throughout the

bedroom, as Khan and the girls sat on the futon giving her their undivided attention like anxious pupils. Sunshine's old heavy frame, finally came to a halt directly in front of her platoon as she spoke with the militant command of a drill sergeant.

"First of all, if you's a scared bitch, this ain't the line of work for you. So my advice would be to leave now. My name is Sunshine, I'm a seasoned vet with over forty years of experience so if I tell you something…its law. Khan wouldn't have brought me here to waste anyone's time, and speaking of wasting time, that will be the first topic of discussion. Time and Money. That is the most important thing you need to understand in this business. Money is what we want and time is something we will never have. This job is more of a sport, and the game is to make as much money as possible in as little time as possible. Remember these two names Tim and Kim which are acronyms meaning Time is Money, and Keep it moving. If a john pays for one hour of your time, send him packing in 30 minutes. If he pays for 30 minutes, finish him in 15 minutes, and if he pays for anything less, tell him to keep his engine running…" The entire room erupted in laughter as Khan and the girls soaked up everything the old vet said like good students.

"Now who sucks the best dick outta all y'all" said Sunshine as Nina jumped up and shouted…

"Me!!! I am the best"

"Okay…stand up and come here" Nina complied as the other women prepared to see what Sunshine had up her sleeve.

"How long does it take you to make a man bust a nut?" Nina thought about Sunshine's question before responding.

"No more than five minutes…easy" Nina proudly answered.

"Only five minutes, huh?" asked Sunshine.

"Yup…they don't call me Jaws for nothing" smiled Nina.

"Okay Khan I'm going to need your help for this next demonstration…"

"Alright" Khan replied hesitantly.

"Come here baby" coached Sunshine as Khan stood up to join Nina and Sunshine at the front of the room.

"Now drop 'em" said Sunshine with a smile.

"Drop 'em?" questioned Khan beyond confusion.

"Yea drop ya draws baby, I'm about to see exactly how long it take for little miss Russia to make you nut." Khan nodded his head and slowly began unbuckling his jeans as the girls started giggling at Khan's bashfulness.

"Hurry up baby, this ain't nothing old Sunshine ain't neva saw before" smiled Sunshine as Khan stood before the entire room with his flaccid penis exposed for the world to see.

"Please no flash photography" joked Khan as he tried to make light of the situation.

"Alright now, once I figure out how to use the stop watch on this Obama phone you can begin"

"Okay" replied Nina as she got on her knees in front of Khan's limp penis.

"Damnit…how do you use this shit….okay I got it working"

"Can I start now?" asked Nina.

"Yea, ready ….Go!" shouted Sunshine as Nina placed Khan's soft dick in her warm mouth.

Khan's penis reached his full length once Nina's mouth started making loud suction sounds. Nina's head moved up and down at supersonic speed as she disdainfully showed off her ability to swallow an entire dick without gagging. Khan felt his toes curling as he closed his eyes in attempt to block out the woman old enough to be his grandmother, as he shot his load down Nina's throat.

"How long was that?" smiled Nina with a face full of baby Khan's.

"Well you did a lot better than I thought…it only took you

three minutes" announced Sunshine as Nina did the old "raise the roof" dance and wiped her mouth with an old towel she picked up from the floor.

"Now if I asked you to suck his dick again, how long would it take you?"

"It would take a little longer, man have to recharge" said Nina in her accent.

Sunshine gave Nina her phone and got on her knees in front of Khan as everyone made the same astonished expression.

"Whoa mama whatchu doing old gal?" said Khan as Sunshine grabbed Khan's wood.

"You brought me here to teach these youngsters how to do shit the right way…right?" asked Sunshine while looking up at Khan on her knees.

"Um yea…but-"

"But shit, let me earn my keep"

"Yea Khan stop being a bitch and let Grandma show us what she's got" laughed Valita.

"Damn alright" said Khan as he closed his eyes and pictured Megan Good about to blow him.

"Go!" shouted Nina as Sunshine slowly licked Khan's soft penis into stiffness.

She then reached her hands around Khan's back and started squeezing on Khan's ass cheek as she devoured Khan whole, while wrapping her tongue around Khan's girth like a small hand. Sunshine continued to squeeze on Khan's ass cheeks while manipulating her tongue in a quick jerking motion. Khan felt his knees starting to buckle as his nut was quickly approaching.

"Oh shit…I'm cumming!" yelled Khan as he busted a mega nut and let out a huge fart at the same time.

"Damn excuse me" said Khan as he took a seat next to the choir of laughing females.

Khan felt light-headed from busting one of the biggest nuts he'd ever experienced. Sunshine picked up the same towel Nina used, as she wiped her mouth dry and asked how long was that?

"Fifty-two seconds" said Nina barely above a whisper, in complete shock that she was dethroned by a senior citizen.

Khan laid back on the futon completely spaced out as he told Khadeja to roll a blunt for him. Sunshine approached him and said.

"I think my job here is done, my only advice would be to get you a few more white girls. You don't want to over work Nina with the clients that prefer snow bunnies. Get you a big girl or two also.

These tricks will always want what you don't got. Remember that and if you ever need me just hit me on this Obama phone." Sunshine kissed Khan on his forehead and left the house one hundred dollars richer, thanks to Khan.

Khan was still in La-La land as he waved bye to an already departed Sunshine then took a pull of the freshly rolled blunt Khadeja passed him. Khan could feel his team growing stronger by the day as he grabbed his crotch and smiled…

"Money well spent"

Chapter Twenty-Eight
THE LION KING

Khadeja laid cuddled up with Khan as the two recovered from yet another early morning fuck session in Olivia's bed. Like clockwork, Khadeja would routinely creep into their bedroom as soon as Olivia left for work. Khadeja peered deep into Khan's eyes as he intensely watched an animal planet documentary on a West African Lion Pride. Khadeja played in Khan's chest hair as Khan pointed to the television and smiled.

"You listening to this shit mama?" Khan asked while having an epiphany.

"Not really why?" replied Khadeja while tracing Khan's nipples with her finger.

"Because this real shit they talking, they say the key to the lion being the King of the jungle is because of its unique ability to work with his lioness. Yes the lion by himself is more than a formidable force, but combine that with several lionesses, unstoppable.

"Okay...?" asked Khadeja still not comprehending Khan's

words.

"It's the lioness's job to hunt and protect the cubs" stated Khan.

"So what does the lion do since the women do all the work?"

"The most important job, he protects the territory. Think about it…yes you can make a few bucks here and there by turning a few tricks in they car or seedy motels, but eventually one of those hyenas will get you. But in this house or territory, you are free to make as much money or hunt as many antelopes as you can sink your teeth into." Khadeja smiled as Khan's jungle logic finally made sense.

"I get it now daddy, so we ya little lionesses' sang Khadeja.

"Yup y'all are my Pride, and speaking of The Pride…you got any work set up for the girls yet?" asked Khan while stretching both arms wide and yawning.

"I got Suga and Nina some work around noon and Sabrina's trick should be here in an hour."

Khan took notice of Khadeja's selflessness and appointed her the role of Bottom Bitch. Khadeja made sure that not only her and her cousin got dates, she also found dates for the other girls. This infuriated Nina as she thought she should have been Khan's right hand but Nina couldn't compete with Khadeja's networking skills.

Nina decided to keep her thoughts to herself with the hopes that one day Khan would see that she was the only girl that had his best interest at heart.

"A'ight well go wake, Sabrina's big ass up and get them other girls up too!" said Khan as he kissed Khadeja's neck.

"Can we fool around one mo'time first?" said Khadeja while getting horny from Khan's soft lips.

"No bitch! Get!" screamed Khan as he turned her on her side and smacked her ass.

Khadeja jumped from the bed and blew Khan a kiss as she vanished from the bedroom.

Khadeja convinced Khan to spend a few dollars on some furniture. He added a large sofa bed in the living room along with a queen-size bed in the girl's room. Khadeja was grateful for the sofa bed because Khan took Sunshine's advice and brought in some new talent. Two white girls, Rain and Heidi, and one heavy set black girl named Sabrina. Rain was a cute girl with long brown curly hair with high cheek bones which she claimed she got from having some Indian in her family, and her body was well put together by being thick in all the right places. Heidi was Khan's baby's mother's twin sister. They were identical twins with two totally different personalities. While Helen was loud and belligerent, Heidi was more quiet and docile. Heidi started off on the right track by pursuing a career in medicine, but spending one too many nights around her sister caused her to drop out of medical school to pursue a degree chasing that monkey. Helen got Heidi hooked on damn near every drug on the market. Some say Helen did this out of jealously.

Rain was also an addict but their bodies showed no signs of drug abuse, which was the reason Khan allowed the two snow bunnies to join The Pride. Sabrina was a big girl, but she was a big sexy girl and she knew it. She wasn't sloppy with her weight as her large breast took from the sight of her not so flat stomach. She also had an ass that you could sit a whole twelve pack on, with a face of an angel. Sabrina was once a plus size model for a local agency until life's tough demands caught up with her and sent her to the streets for answers. Now she models for Instagram.

The living room served as resting quarters for the new girls and also a work station for their tricks. Khadeja glided down the stair way in search of Sabrina. When she reached the bottom of the stairs, Khadeja was bombarded by a huge cloud of crack smoke.

"Ahh Shit!" spoke Khadeja while coughing and fanning her hands wildly through the fog.

"Hey Dee" greeted a red-eyed Heidi while sucking on a glass

dick.

"Hey…damn y'all bitches don't be playing when it comes to y'all wake and bake." said Khadeja while standing next to a sleeping Sabrina.

"Shit, we been up. I done already did two car dates." smiled Rain while handing Khadeja some crumbled bills.

"How can she sleep through this fucking smoke?" said Khadeja while eyeing Sabrina's large ass.

Khadeja took a seat next to Sabrina causing her ass to jiggle like jello. Khadeja smiled to herself while thinking lustful thoughts as she slapped Sabrina on her massive money maker, jolting her from her sleep.

"Wake up bitch, you got money on da way. Go shower and get ready, he should be here in like forty five minutes."

"Huh…damn Dee you know a bitch need her beauty rest" Sabrina groggily replied while rolling out of the sofa bed like a zombie.

"I know but it's time to get this paper." said Khadeja as she watched Sabrina march upstairs while her ass cheeks completely devoured the small Buttmuncher boy shorts.

"*Damn*" thought Khadeja as she then shifted her attention to

Rain and Heidi.

"I got some dates for y'all too" Khadeja spoke while smiling.

"Good shit..Oh and hey when you gonna stop hoggin' up all Khan's free time and let another bitch hop on that dick?" grinned Rain as Khadeja's smile quickly faded, she cut her eye's at Rain and went back upstairs without answering her question.

Khan had big plans for today as he texted his brother Yella to come pick him up. Yella assured him he would be there shortly as Khan thought about the look on the girls faces once Khan returned with his surprise. As Khan got dressed, a lite knock on the bedroom door caused Khan to shift in its direction.

"Hey daddy, I vas just checking on you" said Nina as she planted a big kiss on Khan's cheek.

"Fuck I tell you about putting them Dick-Suckers on me!" yelled Khan as Nina smiled and stared at Khan seductively.

"Relax, I brush teeth every morning…you vant head?" asked Nina while tugging at Khan's waistline.

"Nah not right now, I'm about to go handle some business."

said Khan as he playfully stiff-armed Nina. Nina felt slightly rejected as she sat on the bed.

"What business…I come with?"

"Nah me and Yella got some shit to do, I need you here to help Khadeja run the show while I'm gone." Nina shook her head in disgust as she struggled hard to swallow her words.

"Why must I help her, she should be helping me run the show." cried Nina while staring at Khan for empathy.

"Mama, we all have our strengths and weaknesses. She is good at making these girls listen and she's good at getting clients, high paying clients, for everyone. You are good at servicing those clients, she's like my quarterback and your my star receiver." said Khan while patting her on the head.

"You don't spend time with me like you do with her."

"I gotchu…that's because I be having a lot to discuss with her, these girls get lazy when I'm not around and she's the only one who keeps the ship floating. I'mma do something special for you, just chill mama…okay?"

"You promise?" asked Nina with puppy dog eyes.

"I promise" smiled Khan as Nina grabbed Khan by the sides of his face and planted a big wet kiss on his lips then bolted from the bedroom.

"Aww you dirty bitch!" screamed Khan as he chased after her.

A few hours later Khan returned to the house with the girl's surprise.

Honk Honk

"Do somebody got a date waiting for them?" screamed Sabrina while peeking through the curtains at the vehicle responsible for disturbing her afternoon nap.

"Not me" said Rain as Heidi also shook her head no.

"Dee!" Sabrina screamed upstairs as Khadeja and the other girls came out into the hallway to see why Sabrina was making so much noise.

"What girl?" said Khadeja as she and the other nosey girls came downstairs to investigate?

"Is this truck out here for you?"

"The only client I have is for 5pm, I dunno who that is."

"I'm going to go see before this nigga puts us on blast in front of the whole neighborhood" said Suga while stepping outside in her pink bunny slippers.

"Come out here, y'all ain't gonna believe this!" shouted Suga.

The girls all stood in awe as Khan had his arms crossed leaning on the side of his brand new 2014 Black Lincoln Navigator. Sabrina wasted no time snapping endless pictures of her posing with the truck for her Instagram. The truck was a rental but as long as Khan kept up with the payments, the girls would never know. In due time he would have enough money saved up to actually own a vehicle like this but for now Khan was content with at least looking the part.

Chapter Twenty-Nine
WHEN IT RAINS, IT POURS

"I'm on that good Kush and Alcohol" Lil Wayne's song blared through the Navigator's speakers as Khan and his Pride sang along.

"I got some down bitches I can call…I dunno what I would do wit-out cha'll, but I'mma ball to the day I fall!" Khan decided to give the girls a day off and take his Pride out to dine at The Cheesecake Factory.

Khan and his entire crew rocked Raban sunglasses as they drove the speed limit, not because Khan was a law abiding citizen, but to prevent the girls from spilling some of the that good kush on the floor as they rolled blunt after blunt. Nina could barely contain her wide smile as Khan suggested she ride shotgun, and made due on his promise by giving Nina some additional attention.

Khan pulled up to the valet parking area of The Cheesecake Factory and smiled as he glanced in his rear view mirror.

"Y'all is some bad bitches" commented Khan as every girl

blushed then exited the truck when the valet approached. Khan handed the young Spanish looking kid his keys then led his Pride into the restaurant. Every girl in his squad wore a little black dress and dark sunglasses that coordinated with Khan's all black polo outfit. Every patron in the establishment seemed to take notice of The Pride as the hostess escorted them to their make-shift, extended table.

"And what can I start you fine people off with today?" greeted a pale lanky waiter, while staring a second too long at Rain's cleavage as her breast threatened to escape from the low cut prison of a dress.

"I want some chicken and shit" shouted Suga in her ghetto East Baltimore dialect.

"Suge….this is not Hip-Hop chicken, we are at a fancy, upscale, eatery. Why don't you take a second to actually check out the menu and try something a bit more cultured." suggested Khan as he opened the menu.

After a moment of scrunching his face in disgust while attempting to pronounce the foreign dishes, Khan quickly recanted…

"Yea my dude, just bring us some chicken and shit."

The girls all smiled as Khan also ordered two bottles of house champagne, along with a variety of appetizers.

"We about to go to the powder room for a sec…Valita you wanna come with?" asked Rain as she and Heidi stood from the table to feed their nostrils.

"Nah, she's good!" yelled Khadeja while giving Rain a menacing glare.

"Let the girl speak for her herself, besides this ain't her first rodeo" countered Rain, as she matched Khadeja's stare.

"She what!" screamed Khadeja while standing from her seat.

"Relax cuzzo, a little sniff-sniff ain't neva hurt nobody." said Valita as she walked off with Heidi and a smiling Rain.

"Let her live Dee…we chilling tonight, no drama" said Khan in attempt to keep some of the wondering eyes from their table.

"Whateva yo….that bitch is trippin'." fumed Khadeja while finally sitting back down and taking a sip of her water.

Khan used a cloth napkin to wipe the crumbs of fried chicken from his mouth as he picked up a spoon and tapped it several times against his half empty glass of champagne.

"May I have y'all attention please, as I look at each and every one of y'all pretty faces, I know that I made the right choice by selecting you girls to help start this Pride. We been making money, but I think we can do so much better. I plan on expanding soon. I want to develop everyone of y'all into leaders, true lioness's, so when the time is right, I want y'all all to manage your own cubs, or new recruits once we get the resources and funds to back such an endeavor." Khan announced while standing at the head of the table and looking each girl in their eyes.

"I'm at the point where I would honestly take a bullet for anyone of you...Y'all are my family and y'all all I got. Just know as long as y'all do right, I'mma do better." A few of the girls started to tear up as Khan walked to the side of the table with all the girls following suit and met for a group hug as everyone in the restaurant looked at Khan and his huddled group of girls like they were insane.

Early the next morning, Khadeja laid in the bed wide awake as the other girls slept soundly. Once she heard the front door slam, Khadeja sat up in the bed and peeped out the window to observe Olivia's miniature body, jumping in the backseat of her cab as she headed to work.

Khadeja slowly eased herself from the bed to avoid waking the other girls, then hopped in the shower to freshen up for her morning routine with Khan. Fifteen minutes later, Khadeja stepped out of the shower smelling like Dove body wash as she wrapped her damp body in a large towel. Her pussy started to become moist from all the lustful thoughts she conjured while walking to Khan's bedroom. Khadeja's smile quickly evaporated when the door knob remained stiff as she tried to turn it to open.

"Why is the damn door locked?" thought Khadeja as she tapped lightly on the door and whispered...

"Khan it's me, the doors locked" she heard footsteps approaching and moments later the door cracked open.

Khadeja was speechless as she was met by a pair of perfectly arched eye brows, a set of high cheek bones, and a wicked smile that made up Rain's flawless face.

"Whad up Dee?" asked a grinning Rain while wearing a police uniform top and a pair of blue thongs to match.

Khadeja couldn't see into the bedroom because of Rain's frame blocking her view. Khadeja tried to remain cool as she spoke.

"I just wanted to let Khan know that I was going to get a head start on networking this morning." Rain smiled at Khadeja's pitiful excuse to save face and decided to call her on her bullshit.

"You had to shower and come see him in a towel in order to tell him that?" questioned Rain with a raised eyebrow. Before Khadeja could respond, she heard another feminine voice call for Rain from inside Khan's bedroom.

"Officer Rain, the suspect is resisting, I need back up!" yelled Heidi, as Rain purposely opened the door a little wider to find Heidi also wearing a police uniform, while riding piggy back on Khan.

Khadeja could tell Khan was high out of his mind as he pranced around the room ass naked with eyes as red as a fire truck. Khadeja prayed that Rain and Heidi wouldn't get Khan hooked on any hardcore drugs that they played with because Khadeja knew this could be certain doom for her new family.

"Well as you can see we're a little busy right now but I'm sure you can handle everything until we're finish, matter fact, I am positive you can…you're his number one right?" before Khadeja could react to Rains spiteful comment she was introduced to the loud slam of the bedroom door.

"That fucking dope head bitch" fumed Khadeja as she stormed off feeling defeated.

"Man y'all two bitches ain't no joke" Khan confessed while breathing hard from the Molly induced threesome.

The girls introduced Khan to a drug called Molly which Khan was a bit skeptical about at first, but when Rain explained that Molly was nothing more than a party drug used to heighten sexual experience, Khan thought to himself…*"One line couldn't hurt"* Khan took the small straw and snorted a thin line of powdered Molly off of his Ninja Turtles 2 DVD case as Heidi and Rain followed suit. One line turned into several more with a few xannies, five blunts and a couple shots of Twenty Grand. Needless to say, Khan was on cloud 9 as Rain and Heidi fucked Khan into submission.

"Okay….Okay…I tap!!!" yelled Khan as Rain sucked on Khan's testicles like an algae eater while Heidi viciously slurped on Khan's extremely sensitive semi hard cock, which only seconds ago just fired off his eighth nut.

"My dick can't take no more, chill!" Khan cried as Rain and Heidi ignored his pleas and continued their synchronized assault.

"Ahh!! I'm good forreal!" Khan yelled as Rain and Heidi had Khan's arms cuffed behind his back and took full advantage of him. Rain finally took Khan's balls from her mouth and asked Heidi…

"Should we let him go?" Heidi stopped slurpin' on Khan's defenseless dick and looked into Khan's pleading eyes.

"I guess…you lucky Rain's so nice because I wasn't gonna stop until you nutted ten times, but if you can't hang then oh well" smiled Heidi but not before sucking on Khan's dick several more times than kissing the tip.

"Had to make sure I got every drop" laughed Heidi as she removed the key from her bra and unlocked an exhausted Khan from his sexual torture.

"Thank you Lawd! Damn I dunno if I can do this every morning." Khan finally laughed while standing up to stretch his cramped legs.

"It's our job to give our daddy total satisfaction and we aim to please." said Rain as she and Heidi stood up from the sex drenched mattress.

"I'm not gonna lie, that role play shit with them costumes was next level….y'all definitely got a talent." Khan admitted as Heidi put on her state trooper style Aviators, then grabbed Khan's dick and gave it one last kiss as the two vixens sashayed to the bathroom to shower, leaving Khan worn out and ready for a nap.

A few days later Khadeja and the rest of the girls gathered in the living room for a house meeting by Khan's request. Khadeja was still feeling a bit salty about Rain taking her morning slot with Khan but chose to keep her thoughts to herself. Khan still managed to find time to break Khadeja off some dick, but it was at random times and different locations. She appreciated the little attention she received but missed the intimacy of cuddling with Khan that their morning rendezvous provided.

"A'ight Pride listen up!" announced Khan while standing in the center of the living room alongside several recently ordered boxes from Amazon.

"We about to step it up a notch….ya girl Rain has hipped me to a different area of the business which caters to fetishes. It's called Cos-Play. It's like role playing, but with costumes and you gotta really be on your actress shit heavy. Make these tricks believe that you are whoever they request." Khan spoke while opening one of the boxes and removing some of the costumes.

"I spared no expense because I have faith that y'all will make a killing from this." Khan smiled as he held one of the costumes up for all to see.

"Now we got ya basic shit like school girl uniforms, we got cheerleader, dirty cop…" Khan winked at Rain.

"And of course some freaky shit like chains and whips for our S&M tricks, but I also got some of my favorite characters that I know will be a big hit with the tricks." Khan opened another box and held several outfits high for display.

"We got Princess Leia, Princess Jasmine, Princess Toad stool, and any princess you can think off, we got Batwoman, Catwoman, Black Widow, I got a costume of one of them African bitches from the Black Panther movie, and my favorite" Khan dug further into the box until he found what he was searching for…

"Which one of you bitches wanna be Harley Quinn?" Khan smiled as he held the black and red lady joker outfit high in the air.

Khan threw the costume on a large pile of multiple disguises and proceeded to search through the inventory.

"Now y'all can't tell me that Nina don't look like a low budget Gal Gadot, so if I gave her this Wonder Woman joint, she would have them comic book tricks paying top dollar." said Khan as Nina laughed out loud at Khan's ambitious statement.

"Long story short….I like when y'all think outside the box because there are a lot of apple head bitches running around selling ass for next to nothing, so in order for us to compete and still maintain maximum profit, we gotta be a step ahead of 'em. So, Khadeja I'mma need you to start networking our new cos-play fetish to go along with our standard promotions. Also, Valita I'mma add you to the networking team to assist Khadeja with my predicted rise in clientele. And last but not least, y'all know I let Slick talk me into battling that nigga ELLL'z tonight so I'mma need y'all to be stupid sexy for this event. It's gonna be at a strip club and even though were gonna be in a club surrounded by naked bitches, I still want all eye's on y'all. Pride dismissed."

Chapter Thirty
WHIP IT LIKE A SLAVE MASTER

"In da kitchen and I'm whippin' like a slave master.../ I'mma whip it, I'mma whip it like a slave master/ Like a slave master (Yup!) like a slave master/ In da kitchen and I'm whippin' like a slave master/

K-Willz spit into the mic as Cannon sat behind the mixing board of K-Willz trap house, studio located in Latrobe Projects.

"You fucking with that hook blood?" asked K-Willz while removing his head phones and sparking a Newport.

"Yea shit cool bossman" replied Cannon while using his Fruity Loops software to put the finishing touches on K-Willz's vocals.

K-Willz walked around the small apartment carefully observing his workers cook crack, and bottle capsules of Heroin. K-Willz felt as if God was on his side, as he again survived another shooting. Neither K-Willz nor any of his crew members were hit from the wild inaccurate shots of the Empire's gunmen. K-Willz decided to get back to the money instead of going into an all-out war with The

Empire. The city was hot and the judges were handing life sentences to young men of color like it was the new trend. K-Willz would get revenge once they city died down, and K-Willz had a long list of people on his shit list….including the nigga that put hands on him during his dispute with Khadeja.

"Hey K-Willz, ain't this the nigga that played captain Save-a-Hoe with ya girl" said one of K-Willz's low ranking flunkies as he passed K-Willz his cell phone which displayed Khan's battle with Crazy Cracker on YouTube.

"Lemme see" said K-Willz while snatching the young kid's phone.

"Hell yeah that's that nigga, damn everybody wanna be a rapper." Laughed K-Willz while listening to Khan's bars.

"Yo jive nice forreal" said the young flunky which caused K-Willz to ice grill him.

"That nigga ain't shit…Khadeja always dick ridding on these wannabe rappers" said K- Willz as he noticed Khadeja standing in Khan's corner for support.

K-Willz jealously was evident as he tried to brainstorm a plan to get his bitch back. K- Willz was still feeling Khadeja, but being a man in his position halted him from showing such emotions. K-Willz had only met Khan twice and already considered him public enemy number one. K-Willz thought the simplest of solutions would be to just erase him from this planet, but figured Khadeja would only detest him even more. So K-Willz thought of another idea to show Khadeja that he was the better man for her.

"Yo scratch that shit Cannon, I am about to put out a diss record." shouted K-Willz.

Cannon gave K-Willz a raised eyebrow as Brent walked out the bathroom and into K-Willz's studio.

"What I miss?" asked Brent while scanning the room of puzzled faces.

"You ain't miss shit bruh, you right on time" said K-Willz with closed eyes.

"On time for what?"

"The return of K-Willz!"

Chapter Thirty-One
EVICTION NOTICE

Khan made his battle with Elll'z seem like child's play and he and his Pride became a highly discussed topic on social media. Khan's girls did as they were told as they commanded the attention of everyone in the strip club including some of the strippers. During the showcase, Khadeja noticed Khan eyeing a very attractive white stripper throughout the night. Khadeja was obsessed with being Khan's favorite girl so she convinced the beautiful young stripper to join The Pride, surprisingly with very little persuasion. When the stripper informed Khadeja that she actually lived with the owner of the club and he basically made her suck and fuck all day for next to nothing. Khadeja couldn't help but smile knowing Khan would be so proud of her as she introduced the Katy Perry look-a-like to Khan.

"Hey Khan, I noticed you watching this girl all night so I figured why not bring her in the family…Khan

I want you to meet."

"Kitty" said Khan while smiling at the sexy white girl Khan saw a while back when he first visited The Oasis during his time on work release.

"Oh...you already know her?" questioned Khadeja.

"Nah, I saw her perform a long time ago but I couldn't come correct 'cause I was busted and disgusted." everyone laughed as Kitty extended her hand to Khan. Khan took her hand and gave it a gentle kiss.

"Money don't mean shit to me Khan, you could've spoke to me, I appreciate loyalty over riches" replied Kitty as Khan nodded in agreement while taking in her runway body.

"Well welcome to the family Miss Kitty cat. I can't wait to get a chance to know you a little better."

Khan worked the stage while the girls worked the tricks. Khadeja also got into the action as she defended her self-appointed title as Queen of the jungle. Khadeja and Khan represented The Pride every time they stepped on stage. The girl's became a hot commodity as their loud cheers and scantily clad attire made them a must see at every event. Khan made sure that Khadeja's bars hit just as hard as his, and this common interest brought Khan and Khadeja even closer than before which allowed Khadeja to get her morning slot back from Rain's freaky ass. Khadeja knew she had to step her game up so she made a habit of bringing Kitty with her to insure Khan had no regrets of choosing her for his morning wake up.

Olivia couldn't go a day without seeing a pair of dirty thongs in the bathroom, or countless used tampons in the toilet. Peace and quiet was as rare as a Big Foot sighting, causing Olivia to work as many extra shifts as possible to avoid being in the chaotic chambers she called home. The only reason Olivia tolerated living in a brothel was because Khan piped her down something serious every night, but lately Khan started being stingy with the dick. Olivia knew that Khan was fucking the other girls in the house because on several occasions she found condom wrappers in her bedroom. Olivia never confronted Khan for fear that he would leave her as she rationed to herself…

"At least he's using protection that means he cares about my health." Olivia forced a smile on her face as she unlocked her front door and prepared to try and relax from a long day of work.

Once Olivia entered her home she was met by a Kitty and Sabrina tag team, on a pale elderly white man stretched out on the sofa bed. The old man smiled when Olivia intruded on his paid session and responded.

"Hey, the more the merrier" Olivia shook her head in disgust as she stomped upstairs to her bedroom.

This was not the first time Olivia stumbled in on the girls turning a trick, but this was the first time the girls paid her no mind and continued like this was their house and they shouldn't even attempt to disguise the offensive acts. Olivia was furious as she walked into her bedroom without knocking to find Suga and Rain giving Khan a full body massage.

"Khan we have to talk" said Olivia as she mean mugged the other two girls until they silently walked out the bedroom.

Khan prepared for the worst as he reached in his basketball shorts and pulled out a cigarette.

"Please don't light that right now, you know I hate the smell." said Olivia while taking a seat on the bed next to Khan.

"Come on mama, it's just a-" Olivia cut him off with a pointed index finger.

"Ands that's what I wanna talk about, it's always just something. I'm not stupid Khan, I know the only people these girls give massages to is you, they hoes Khan, and at first I forced myself to live with that but these bitches don't even respect me no more, shit you don't even respect me. You and I had an unspoken agreement, where I put up with your shit in exchange for my daily dose of dick, but now when I touch you it's obvious your too tired from fucking all these other bitches to handle your business with me. My pussy should be priority. I know you ain't my husband but I thought I was something special to you. And I've put up with a lot from all the dirty laundry to these nasty condoms and tampons to dealing with strangers in my house on a constant basis, but what happened today was the final straw." Olivia fumed.

"What happened?" asked Khan while rubbing her hand before she pulled it away and yelled.

"One of their old ass tricks tried to get me to join in on their threesome!" Khan, suppressed a laugh and tried to take Olivia in his arms.

"I'm sorry mama, and I can see that your very upset and I will tell the girls to get their acts together." Olivia allowed Khan to hold her, then her body suddenly tensed back up and she exploded.

"NO Khan, I need them bitches gone...tonight! You can stay but they gotta go." Olivia cried.

"Mama them girls is my lively hood, you know if they go then I gotta leave with them" said Khan while praying Olivia would reconsider.

Olivia thought long and hard as she slowly spoke her next words.

"Then it is what is Khan, you know my number if you wanna come back" Olivia stood up.

"I'm about to shower and relax, I want these bitches gone Khan" Olivia spoke while leaving the bedroom.

Khan pulled out his phone and found a listing of affordable hotels that were hooker friendly.

"Wow, there's an app for everything" Khan smiled as he called the hotel and booked two adjoining bedrooms with two queen size beds in each room.

"House meeting!" yelled Khan as he stuck his head in the girl's bedroom and headed downstairs to the living room. When the girls arrived Khan got straight to the point.

"Long story short, Olivia wants us out, so pack y'all shit and be ready to leave within the next hour."

Nina was the most upset because losing the house was her biggest fear. Nina was truly alone and couldn't imagine being in the cold streets again.

"Where will we go?" Do you have a plan? I don't vant to be in the streets again" cried Nina as Khan placed a hand on her shoulder.

"I got this mama, this might actually be a blessing in disguise" said Khan to Nina wiping her eyes and ran upstairs to pack.

There was a cloud of uncertainty in the air as the girls all assumed this may be the end of The Pride.

Chapter Thirty-Two
WHEN LIFE GIVES YOU LEMONS

The Pride rode in silence as everyone seemed to be lost in their own thoughts. Khan did his best to keep the girls spirits high by offering them a few words of encouragement, but some of Khan's traits, like the ability to detect bullshit, had rubbed off on the girls. Khan found a hotel which fit his needs perfectly called The American Best Hotel. The hotel offered large rooms at a cheap price and from what Khan read in the reviews, the staff minded their own business. When The Pride pulled up to the lobby entrance of the hotel, the girls jumped out of the truck with their bags and waited for Khan in the lobby as he parked. The second Khan walked into the lobby of the hotel, he knew this was the place to be. For as far as the eyes could see, there were hookers everywhere. Black, White, Spanish and even a few midgets. Judging by their demeanor, Khan had a hunch about these girls and sent Khadeja fishing to find out if he was correct.

Khadeja walked over to a small crowd of girls waiting in line for the vending machine. She made small talk with a few of the girls, smiled and promptly returned to Khan with news that confirmed Khan's suspicions, that the vast majority of these girls were indeed

"Rogue Hoe's".

Rogue Hoes were working girls that walked these dangerous streets without the protection of a pimp. They usually ran with other Rogue Hoes to give them some type of security. The rest of the working girls at the hotel had either a husband or boyfriend. These guys weren't pimps, they were just broke addicts that took advantage of the love their women had for them, and convinced their spouse to trade their bodies to satisfy their own addictions.

Khan licked his chops while surveying what man would consider a pimps paradise. The large lobby had a small waiting area with two sofas that occupied the space. Towards the rear of the lobby were several vending machines which sold everything from sodas, chips to candy and a machine that carried small microwavable sandwiches.

Khan waited for Suga to return from the clerk's desk and took a seat on one of the black sofas. Nina and Sabrina scurried off to the lobby bathroom as Khadeja took a seat on Khan's lap.

"Whatcha thinking" asked Khadeja as she watched Khan's face scrunch with contemplation.

"I think coming here might be the best decision we've made in a long time."

"Yea, why so?" replied Khadeja while searching Khan's eyes.

"You don't see what I see.." asked Khan while pointing in all directions.

"A bunch of dirty bitches in a dirty hotel?"

"No mama, a bunch of answers to our problems. These girls are easy pickings. We could double, no triple our numbers and be on the road to riches in no time"

Khadeja listened as Suga returned with two sets of key cards.

"We in room 810 and 812" announced Suga as she scooped up her bags and handed the keys to Khan.

"I'll explain it once we get in the room" said Khan as The Pride headed to the eighth floor.

"Okay ladies here's the game plan" Khan started as soon as he walked into the hotel bedroom.

"The time to expand is now. There are countless cubs running around this jungle waiting for a strong lioness to give them some guidance. The only job y'all have today is to recruit at least one cub a piece. If you all get at least one girl we will double our numbers, which will double our profits. I was already prepared for a dilemma like this to unfold, so when tragedy strikes, you turn it into a triumph. I wasn't bullshitin' y'all when I said that I have contingencies in play which I have to go check on in a few minutes. While I'm gone, I want y'all to make recruiting your main priority. Just trust ya man and for those who doubt will be surprised and to those who already had faith in me will continue to be a step ahead of the game." Khan's speech motivated the girls to add to the family and consider this nothing more than a minor setback as they each prepared to make Khan proud by recruiting as many girls as they could.

Khan waved to his Pride as he messaged someone on his phone and exited the bedroom, leaving his Pride to handle business.

Michael Pinero or better known as Mikey P was a slumlord that specialized in renting housing properties to criminals and people without proof of income. His motto was "If you can pay the rent, you can live there" no questions asked. Mikey P was also a huge fan of Slick-Talk. Mikey P had been a fan for years and attended numerous events but with the emergence of Gangas Khan, Mikey P's love for battle rap had reached an all-time high. Mikey P was one of Gangas Khan's biggest fans, he even quoted his lyrics to friends and other people that didn't watch Battle rap. Mikey P followed Gangas Khan on all the social media platforms that Valita suggested khan create to develop a fan base, and when Mikey P saw a post from Gangas Khan inquiring about a house for rent, Mikey P jumped on the chance to aide his idol. Khan put the truck in park and stepped out into the darkness of the Hamilton community.

"This look like a pretty good neighborhood" said Khan as he texted Mikey P to let him know he had arrived at the address on Hamilton ave.

"Doors open" responded Mikey P as Khan jogged to the door and entered the large empty house.

If you believed in love at first sight, then judging by Khan's facial expression of the spacious living room alone, told the story of a happy man.

"Wow this place is huge.." said Khan as a stocky white man with a goatee approached him with a half hand shake hug.

"Wait until you see the rest of the place, and it's a pleasure to meet you Mr. Gangas Khan" Khan smiled as his developing celebrity status gave him a high stronger than any drug.

"Back atchu pimp, now let's check out this house"

"Right this way Gangas."

Khan felt bitter sweet about giving Mikey P first month's rent and an additional month's rent for a security deposit, because on one hand, the house was everything Khan imagined with its five bedrooms, two and a half bathrooms, large basement and back yard, but after ordering every item he needed to furnish the massive estate, Khan was broke. This was the biggest investment Khan had ever made. It didn't help that Khan and the girls also picked up some new drug habits thanks to Rain, so that left Khan in a position where he needed these girls to produce.

Khan had faith in his girls and decided to look at this in a positive light as he stepped from the elevator and slid his key card in the door slot to his hotel room. When Khan walked into the room he thought he found the holy Mecca of streetwalkers.

"Wow, I see y'all trying to make me the next Dolemite" laughed Khan as he stood in amazement from the sight of almost thirty women lined up in the hotel room seeking his approval.

"Did we do good daddy?" asked Rain while lighting a freshly rolled blunt and placing it in Khan's speechless mouth.

"Huh….yea…hell yea, fuck yea, how many girls is this" asked Khan while starting to do a head count before Khadeja stepped up and interjected.

"Twenty-seven girls Daddy, and we already started working" said Khadeja as she passed Khan a nice size stack of assorted bills.

Khan's best attribute was his ability to think on the fly, and his thoughts were now running rampant with ways to maximize this opportunity.

"This is wonderful, it really is but there's no way in hell all of you girls are going to eat if you all working the same location. If I combine the girls already on my team that's thirty five women."

"So whats da game plan" Khaedja interrupted.

"First off, don't interrupt me" said Khan while feeling himself as Khadeja nodded and remained quiet.

"Secondly, I may need some more muscle because I plan on spreading y'all out all over the city and the county, and there's no way I can protect all of you at one time. So let me make a few phone calls real quick and we about to get this money forreal!"

Khan made the phone calls necessary to obtain the man power and vehicles required for the next phase of his operation. He reached out to Yella, Swine, and his other brother Scrap, and his cousin D.J.

Khan exchanged info with D.J. at G.P.'s funeral. Before Khan's incarceration, He and D.J. were as thick as thieves. Khan received money orders from D.J. whenever he had the funds and Khan knew that he could trust D.J. Khan had meant to catch back up with D.J. a lot sooner but being homeless has this way of making matters such as rekindling long lost friendships, seem not as important at the time. Yella took Swine and D.J. to the same Rent-a-Car spot that he took Khan to grab a couple SUV's to haul their selected convoy.

Khan split the girls up into five teams, and made Khadeja, Nina, Suga, Rain and Sabrina the team leaders of each respected platoon. Each team was also assigned a male chaperone, which Khan referred to as "A.P.'s" or assistant pimps. Since Khan trusted Khadeja the most, he paired her with Swine because he knew that Swine was the weakest when it came to being around women and keeping his dick in his pants. Khan needed no distractions, because distractions meant mistakes. Khadeja obviously wanted to pair with Khan, but understood Khan's logic. Khan paired Suga with Yella, Nina with Scrap, Sabrina with D.J. and he took Rain which needless to say, felt like a kick in the lady nuts to Khadeja. Khan spread the team out across the town to ensure that any nigga looking to spend money on pussy, would be contributing to Khan and his Pride.

"A'ight lets get this show on the road because I have a special surprise for my girls in the morning."

"What is it daddy?" screamed an excited Rain while rubbing on Khan's arm.

"You'll see soon, now Yella you got Owings Mills, Swine you working out Towson, D.J. you set up shop Downtown, Scrap I'mma send you out Catonsville and I'mma go back out Route 40. We gotta be on our P's and Q's and watch out for them hyenas"

"Hyenas?" questioned Swine.

"The police my nigga, now pay attention" Khan continued.

"I will text y'all the address'es of the hotels I selected for y'all. Please be careful and take care of my women, no fooling around either. I'm not paying you niggas $1500 a day for nothing. Again, stay safe and I love you all."

Khan, along with the other men went to their vehicles and drove to their destinations to set up shop. Khan chose not to operate from The American Best Hotel because once he brought his main girls into their new home, he wanted the cubs to have a place to rest their heads without fear of a possible stalker trick bothering them. Khan saw a bright future ahead of him as he checked into his suite and thought about all the crazy shit he, Rain, and Heidi were about to get into as he popped a Molly and chased it with his favorite Cognac, Twenty Grand.

China, a young half black and Asian girl that Khan nicknamed the moment he saw her in the group of cubs that the girls recruited, walked over to Khan and gave him a seductive look with her exotic slanted eyes and asked...

"Can we take a dip in the Jacuzzi before we start working daddy?"

The thought of China's lean tight body and plump ass cheek's shedding her skin tight jeans caused Khan to stiffen as he looked around the room at Rain, Heidi, and the other four equally attractive young women and said...

"Last one in is a rotten egg!"

Chapter Thirty-Three
TIME TO PLANT THE SEED

The rise in prostitution continued to climb as the department received more and more complaints from local businesses of young women soliciting their customers. Detective Clark recently gave the "go-ahead" for a city wide sweep of hookers, pimps and tricks. The sweep proved unsuccessful as for every suspect they arrested, ten more popped up on the scene. The city was out of control and Detective Clark felt it was time to resort back to the teachings of his mentors' in order to put a stop to the chaotic trend. Clark opened a file on his office desk top which contained an archive of sex workers.

"Who can I get to help bring these low life pimps down?" mused Detective Clark while searching for the most inconspicuous parolee to act as an informant.

Detective Clark's plan was to find a sex worker that received parole or probation, monitor them closely until they inevitably slipped back into a life of prostitution, then personally detain them and threaten them with a harsh prison sentence unless they help to bring down whatever Pimp or Madame ran the organization.

"Oh she looks like a winner. Mallory O'Rilley has been arrested over ten times for prostitution and soliciting. It says she's on parole and faces four years if she convicted of any new charge" Detective Clark smiled like the cat that ate the canary as he continued to inspect her base file and start his due diligence of his potential secret weapon.

K-Willz sat in his apartment which was in the same housing project of his trap house, debating on the right time to release his diss track on Khan. The jealousy and hatred K-Willz had for Khan ate at him like a tapeworm.

"Now niggas saying he the best rapper in the city…Fuck outta here, that nigga ain't shit!" spat K-Willz as Brent nodded in agreement while counting a large stack of money he received from one of the workers.

"When you droppin' that diss track yo?" asked Brent while recounting the cash.

"I'mma do it this weekend, matter fact I'mma have a gansta party for it too!" K-Willz spoke while lighting a blunt of Sour Diesel.

"A gansta party huh…sounds good, we should get some freaks

too" replied Brent.

"Yea I know some bitches from Murphy Homes"

"Nah not them bucket head bitches, let's get some professional entertainment. Like some bitches that will actually put on a show." suggested Brent.

"Where you wanna get them from?"

"Where else…Backpage!"

Chapter Thirty-Four
FAMILY OVER EVERYTHING

"Oh my God, this house is da shit!" yelled Khadeja as she led Khan and the lionesses through the front door of their new home.

"Daddy this is really nice" added Suga while gliding her hand along the soft material of the huge tan suede sectional sofa.

All of the furniture Khan ordered arrived on time to furnish the home before the girls moved in. Khan didn't want to bring his girls into an empty home like he did before. He purchased numerous items to fill the house, but left the painting and décor of the house up to the girls so they would feel a sense of ownership for their new home.

"I got T.V's for each room, silverware and pots and shit for the kitchen, and when it warms up outside we can get a pool for the backyard, but wait until y'all see the upstairs" said Khan as he gave the girls a tour of the first floor.

They left the living room and walked into the dining room

which had a long red wood table that sat ten people. The kitchen had an island in the center with all the up-to-date appliances in a stainless steel theme. The girls opened the backdoor and fell in love with the large backyard, which had an unattached BBQ grill sitting on the patio.

"I can't wait to have a cookout" said Kitty while smiling.

"Me too now lets head upstairs" Khan spoke while leading the way.

When the girls reached the top floor they had no idea which room they wanted to see first.

"Follow me…there are five bedrooms up here, now at first I was going to split y'all up into different rooms but then I said fuck that. There will be no more separation between The Pride. The girls followed Khan as he stopped at the first room and walked inside.

"This is a room I converted into a walk in closet, I ordered all of y'all some new clothes to start up ya wardrobe. I converted another bedroom like this also, four of y'all will share each closet. The room next door is the other walk-in closet, now this room here…" Khan pointed as the girl's noticed countless dumbbells and several pieces of workout equipment scattered amongst the padded floor, along with four treadmills and four stationary bikes.

"This is our personal gym. We gotta keep that ass tight"

everyone laughed excited for what was behind door number 4.

"Now this room is probably gonna be y'all favorite room, this is what I call The Powder Room!" said Khan as the girls observed a room which resembled a make-up prep area behind the scenes at a Victoria Secret show.

The walls were lined with full length mirrors and eight individual make-up tables with vanity mirrors. Hair straighteners and other beauty supplies littered the tables still in there packaging. The girls all had a new found respect for Khan as they all hopped around like crack head rabbits.

"Off to the last room" said Khan as the girls chased behind him in complete bliss.

"Gone are the days of who gets to sleep with daddy, now we all sleep together." said Khan as he led the girls into the master bedroom and proudly presented the girls to his Family Bed.

Khan found the Family Bed on a polygamist website which catered to families of multiple partners. It was twenty five feet wide and could sleep up to ten people comfortably.

There were a variety of unopened boxes containing a television, an alarm clock, and picture frames for The Pride to have a real feel of family displayed on the walls. The spacious bedroom also had three long dressers and two tall dressers. Khan honestly had no idea how to arrange the furniture and decided to leave that up to the girls as well. The master bedroom's best attraction was the attached full bathroom, which Khan had already stocked full of wash cloths, towels, and plenty of hygiene products. The other two bathrooms were addressed the same.

"Oh I almost forgot, there's one more thing I want to show y'all" yelled Khan as he ran through the hallway and down the stairs.

"Wait up!" yelled Nina as she was the fastest of the girls chasing him.

Khan ran down two flights of steps into the lowest level of the house, his basement. When the girls finally arrived, they were slightly winded as Khan laughed before speaking.

"Damn, I'm glad I put a gym in here, y'all young asses should be ashamed of yourselves.

Anyway this is my man cave. The first part here is my game room" Khan had ordered a pool table and three televisions were mounted on the walls.

The center television had a black leather gamer chair in front of it with an XBOX controller resting in the center of the chair, suggesting how Khan spent some of his time at the house before the arrival of the girls. There was a small mini-bar that sat in the corner alongside an empty fish tank.

The girls followed Khan into the next room of the basement which was Khan's studio. He had top notch equipment still boxed up and packaged. Khan bought a dual monitor Alienware desktop, a new interface, headphones, soundboard, and a mixing board. Khan liked the way Yella's Sony microphone sound and purchased one of his own, but unlike the software Yella used, Protools; Khan went with Mixcraft instead. Khan didn't have enough money to buy everything he wanted so he went with the essentials.

"This is my man cave…no girls allowed" laughed Khan.

"Nah but seriously, I hope y'all enjoy the house, we are a family and I understand that y'all have been in and out of houses and shelters, and cars for a long time. Well all that shit is over. We about to run this fucking city. We some bosses now and if anyone tells you different, spit in they face then bring 'em to me."

"Whats in that room back there?" questioned Valita while pointing at the closed door in the rear of Khan's studio.

"Oh that's the laundry room, and speaking of laundry room, the way that you trifling bitches treated Olivia's house will not be how you conduct shit in here. If you bitches don't clean up I will kick you outta the big house and make you live in the hotel with the cubs." Khan laughed as he started removing his studio equipment from the boxes.

"Nah but forreal, I'mma make a schedule of who's gonna clean what and whateva area I give you will be your job to keep that part of the house clean. Now there's only eight girls in here as of now which means there is room for one more girl, if any of you see something in one of the cubs. Don't trip about that right now though, go upstairs and check out some of the clothes I bought y'all and get acclimated with your new home while I set up the Khan cave.

"I'm itchin', I'm itchin', I'm itchin' for that paper/ I'm itchin', I'm itchin', I'm itchin' for that paper/ I'm ridin' round da city and I got my calculator/ I'mma mother fuckin' monsta when it come to getting' paper/"

Future's voice vibrated the truck as Khan and his self-appointed team of Rain, Heidi and the five cubs cruised the highway en route to their Route 40 location. Khan's cubs consisted of China, the first cub that caught Khan's attention, a thick Spanish girl that closely resembled Ashley Graham which Khan named Suitcase because of the large duffle bag sized purse that she toted with her everywhere she went. An African girl from Kenya that Khan called Amber Rose due to her short cut hairstyle, she was tall with small breast a pretty face, and a nice round behind. There was Mute, a quiet gothic looking girl that did a lot of freaky fetishes. She was a very petite girl with an array of tattoo's and piercings that covered her pale white skin, and last was a girl that intrigued Khan the most, she was in her mid-twenties and her red hair and freckles gave away her Irish roots, she reminded Khan of the actress, Julia Roberts in the movie Pretty Woman. She had a swagger to her that oozed sex appeal. She was very obedient and never asked Khan for anything. She managed her money well, unlike the other cubs that quickly gave their daily earnings directly to the dopeman. She could always sense when Khan was horny and attended to his needs without Khan having to ask. She wasn't scared of threesomes or putting on a show with another girl for Khan and she actually low key commanded more of the leadership role which was intended to be Rain's job. She had a mystery about her which lured Khan in, but Khan wanted to learn more about the 5'6 bombshell with thick thighs, nice round ass, and tit's, just big enough for a mouth full. She also had the prettiest feet Khan had ever saw. The young woman's long red hair blew wildly in the wind as she sat in the back seat of the truck making eye contact with Khan through the rearview mirror. When Khan noticed her watching him he gave her a wink and the lovely "Reds" reciprocated by blowing him a kiss.

"Reds I ain't goin' lie, I'm loving how you been getting all these clients for everybody.

You keep it up and you might graduate from cub to lioness a lot sooner than you think."

"And what kinda prize do I get when that happens?" asked Reds while puffing on a cigarette.

"All my lioness's live with daddy in the big house"

"Well I guess I can't wait to get my paws then" said Red's while Rain sat shotgun, silently cursing Reds out in her mind.

The Paw's Red's referred to, were used to signify cub from lioness. Khan took all of his lionesses out to a tattoo shop and each girl got a small lion paw on their right ass cheek. Once you received this stamp, you are now official. Khan got the paw stamped on his neck along with a few other lion paraphernalia tat's on random parts of his body.

"I wanna be a lioness too!" shouted Suitcase from a row of seats in front of Red's.

"Just keep doing what your doing and you'll get there, oh and just to let you know, once you become a lioness, you gotta get rid of that big ass bag." laughed Khan while keeping his eyes on the road.

"Well count me out, this bag is literally my life." retorted Suitcase.

Khan hated when people used the word literally wrong, it was always a pet peeve of his. Khan shook his head as the team arrived at the motel and gave Rain the "Okay" to start networking clients. Khan was the last one to exit the truck as he reached in his pants pocket to retrieve the key card for his suite. The girls rushed in the room racing for the bathroom to freshen up for their dates. Khan took a seat at the small desk located by the television to finish his half eaten Chipotle burrito. Having the munchies made eating the burrito a short lived moment as Khan took off his shoes and laid back on the king size bed. Khan had prepaid for his suite a month in advance, he also had a smaller room next door that he used for a work station for the girls. Khan watched a little Sports Center, then randomly switched through the channels until his burrito decided to fight back.

"Damn...I gotta shit" yelled Khan as he jogged to the bathroom and shoved Heidi and Mute out of the way.

He flopped down on the toilet seat and prepared for the fireworks.

"I guess it was a false alarm" said Khan as he heard the voice of an angel coming from the shower.

"Da fuck?" Khan whispered as the elegant voice recited a beautiful rendition of Tory Lanez's "Say it".

"China, is that you in the shower?"

"Umm yea...is my date here already?" asked China while sticking her head from behind the shower curtain.

"No, I'm more interested in that voice, where did that come from?"

"Oh I just like singing in the shower, it helps me relieve stress."

"Look, I just got my own studio set up in the Big House and I wanna see what I can do with your voice."

"You know I ain't got my Paw's yet, them girls ain't gonna let me in there." said China while rinsing the shampoo from her hair.

Khan was really feeling China, he liked the way she innocently sucked his dick like she didn't know what she was doing, and Khan also had a connection with her that he couldn't describe. Now learning about her musical gifts made Khan's next decision that much easier.

"You moving in the Big House tonight.. I can't let you waste that talent because ..oh" Khan words were cut off by the return of his burrito making its exit as Khan held on tight and braced for dear life.

"China your dates here!" announced Rain as she rushed into the suite.

Rain was on her shit today as she booked clients nonstop for her team. She was hell bent on proving to Khan that she was the head bitch in charge and she refused to be out done, especially by a cub named Reds.

"Coming!" yelled China while putting the finishing touches to her make-up then winking at Khan as she sashayed out the door to service her John. Khan watched the exotic young girl's ass jiggle all the way out the room as he thought to himself.

"Damn, I should keep that bitch to myself, I can't keep letting every Tom, Dick and Harry run up in that fine ass bitch." Rain peeked the exchange between China and Khan as she shook her head in disgust then followed China out the door to await the arrival of other clients.

Khan laid stretched out on the king size bed watching an old episode of The Boondocks as the other girls sat scattered around the room negotiating prices with potential Johns through their text messages. As usual, Reds was the first girl to make her quota, and with Rain posted outside to keep watch over the cubs and the oncoming tricks. Reds took this as another opportunity to get closer to Khan. Reds slowly eased in the bed next to Khan as Khan released his loud goofy laugh to the racially insulting antics of Uncle Ruckus. Khan paid her no mind as he continued to watch his cartoon until she started tugging on his zipper.

"Aww shit now" smiled Khan as he already knew what time it

was.

"Do you mind....zaddy" Reds sang real slow and seductive.

"I would never deny my bitch a meal" Khan replied as he allowed Reds to remove his dick and swallow it whole in front of everyone.

None of the other girls gave them a second glance as they were used to Khan's raunchy exhibitions. Reds sucked on Khan like she had a point to prove and Khan was loving every minute of it. Reds could feel Khan's balls getting tight as she prepared to swallow every drop but suddenly Rain barged in the room with a panicked expression on her face.

"Khan, come quick!" shouted Rain while standing in the door way.

"I'm fixin' to come right now!" yelled Khan through closed eye lids as Reds continued to suck the skin off his dick.

"I'm serious Khan, one of them johns is acting up, he got China helmed up, she needs your help"

Suddenly Khan's dick got soft and he jumped from the bed almost knocking Reds to the floor in the process. After hearing that China was in danger, Khan's entire mood went from joyful to murderous. Khan grabbed his pistol from the nightstand and followed Rain out the door. Rain wanted to put hands on Reds for fucking with her man but knew there were more important tasks to attend to, so she would address it later.

"You got the key card?"

"Yea but I came and got you as soon as I heard her screaming for help" said a worried Rain.

"A'ight watch the parking lot for hyenas, I got this mama" said Khan as he briskly walked to the room which they serviced their clients.

Khan put his ear to the door and heard muffled screams and hollers. He slid the keycard in the slot and quickly turned the doorknob as his heart beat hard for fear of not knowing what he would walk into. The first thing Khan saw once he entered the motel room was a large, muscular, butt- naked man choking the life out of a defenseless China. China's face was starting to turn pale as she could no longer muster the strength to call for help.

"Whoa my nigga, drop the girl!" yelled Khan as he slowly approached the crazed John.

"Nigga, who da fuck is you suppose to be? Her Daddy?" asked the John while applying more pressure to China's tiny throat.

"Yes that's exactly who I am now drop my bitch before shit get crazy." said Khan while standing a few feet away from the muscle bond maniac.

"Mind ya business nigga, that bitch got blood on my dick, now she talkin' bout she ain't giving me my money back, I gotta teach this hoe a lesson!" the John threatened with rage in his eyes.

"A'ight yo, this is my business, and I can clearly see that you one of them hard headed niggas so I'mma have to talk to you in another language" said Khan as he pulled out his .44.

Upon seeing the large hand gun, the John quickly dropped China as she struggled to regain her breath. She slowly stood to her feet and walked over the Khan.

"Put ya clothes on and tell the girls to close up shop, and head to the truck" China simply nodded then shot the John a menacing glare before exiting the room.

"So you like hitting on bitches huh?" asked Khan as he secured the door.

"Nah bruh it ain't even like that, she lied about being on her period and got blood on my shit." pleaded the trick.

"You know what's worst then hitting bitches…." Khan paused as the now helpless John remained silent.

"Hitting one of my bitches" Khan answered his own question as he walked towards the naked man.

"That's my babygirl...that's my princess, and you would've killed my bitch if I wouldn't have run up in here." the trick continued to remain silent.

"So since you think my bitch life ain't worth shit, I'mma show you what happens when you fuck with one of mine." the naked John saw the look in Khan's eyes and knew it was do or die at the moment, so in a desperate attempt to save his life, he charged at Khan with everything he had.

Minutes later Khan finally emerged from the motel room as he jogged towards the clerk's office.

"Hey Abdul, As Salamu Walaakum"

"Waalakum Salam Khan, how can I help you brother?" replied the clerk while sensing something was wrong.

"How much for the security tapes?" questioned a bug-eyed Khan.

"What brother?" stumbled Abdul in his middle eastern accent.

"The tapes Ack...how much?" Khan repeated.

Abdul finally noticed the large blood stain on Khan's shirt and quickly put two and two together.

"Which room do we need to clean Khan" said Abdul.

"212, I need them tapes doe"

"No worries, give me a second" Abdul went to the back of the small shack and returned moments later with the video footage.

"Here, you have done too much for me to charge you. I will take care of everything."

"Thanks Abdul, can you rip that log-in page out also?"

"Already on it" said Abdul as he handed Khan the crumbled log-in sheet with Rains name and ID information.

"Peace bruh" said Khan as he walked out of the shack and jumped into the truck with his girls already waiting for him.

No one said a word as Reds passed Khan a blunt and the Pride drove away to a new motel to set up shop like it was just business as usual.

Chapter Thirty-Five
CAPTAIN SAVE -A- HOE

Khadeja was grateful for the weekends. Khan always gave his girls off on Saturdays and Sundays. Khan enjoyed doing family activities with his lionesses and the girls looked forward to them as well. Sabrina managed to book a few cubs a party for tonight which made Khan feel good that his girls still wanted to put money in his pockets even on their days off. D.J. was scheduled to drop the four cubs off at a party in East Baltimore, and Khan would pick them up. Khan decided to pick the girls up because he only allowed his lioness's to touch his money. Not even his brothers or cousin had that honor, and since no lionesses were attending the party, Khan volunteered his services, to insure no one played with his money. Today was movie night and it was Khan's turn to select the movie.

"What we watching Khan?" asked Khadeja.

"An oldie but goodie….Jungle Fever" smiled Khan while all the other girls had a puzzled look on their faces.

"Whats Jungle Fever?" asked Rain.

"Really?" I forgot ain't none of you bitches a day over twenty-one, y'all make a nigga feel old" laughed Khan while taking a seat in-between Nina and Kitty on the long sectional living room sofa.

"This is some of Wesley Snipes best work, if it wasn't for this movie then most of you mixed bitches wouldn't be here, so all bi-racial girls like Khadeja, Rain and Valita…where's Valita?" said Khan while looking around the living room.

"I think she's still upstairs" replied Suga as Khan paused the DVD then went to check on Valita. Khan found Valita sitting in the powder room staring very intensely at an image on her phone. Khan crept up on her and managed to sneak a peek at the images of younger kids which closely resembled Valita.

"They ya siblings?" asked Khan while startling Valita as she quickly locked her phone and stood up from the chair.

"Yea, it's my little sister's birthday today, I was just checking out some pictures she posted on Instagram of her party." replied Valita with teary eyes.

Khan could tell she was troubled and missed her family, in fact the only reason Khan bought this house, was to give the girls without family, a loving household. If Khan knew that Valita had a family that would accept her, he would've never allowed Valita to travel with them.

"I can tell you miss them a lot" said Khan while wiping a

string of hair from Valita's sad face.

"Yea but my folks won't let Khadeja come back so I'mma rock with her."

"Listen, Khadeja is my family too, she's also grown, and if you have an actual family that loves you and wants you then let me take you to them."

"But what about Khadeja" said Valita as a tear rolled down her face? Khan wiped the tear from her cheek and looked her in the eyes.

"Khadeja will be fine, I might be a street nigga but I'm also a gentleman and I'm a man of my word. I promise I will protect her."

"Okay, let me tell her what's up and-" Khan interrupted her.

"Just pack ya stuff, let me take you home and I'll explain it to her later."

Valita did as Khan said then snuck out the back door and waited at the gas station for Khan. Khan made up an excuse to the girls about having to meet a guy, then met up with Valita and reunited her with her younger siblings. Khan knew this was the right thing to do and felt good on the inside, as he headed to the American Best Hotel to pick up the newest members of the Big House.

"Khan where is Valita? I been calling her like crazy and she's not answering." Khadeja frantically said as Khan walked back into the house.

"Listen, she was homesick so I told her to go home, I didn't know she had an actual home, this life ain't for her, but check this out ladies at first when we had enough bed space for one extra lioness, I made the decision to bring someone, but with the early departure of Valita, that leaves room for two. So without further delay, please welcome China and Reds."

The two women walked into the Big House with smiles on their faces as the girls had mixed emotions about the new lioness's sudden arrival. Khadeja was visibly upset as she didn't even bother to acknowledge the girls and stomped upstairs. Nina, the most obedient of the women, made the girls feel welcomed by helping with their bags and escorting them to one of the walk-in closets. China was ecstatic to live in such a large house as her smile couldn't be contained, while Reds on the other hand had more of a cooler approach about her new scenery. Once the girls were settled in, Khan ordered pizza and the crew continued to watch the movie without the presence of Khadeja.

"How could she just leave me like this?" thought Khadeja while sitting in the exercise room, which was the least frequented room of the house, and Khadeja found solace in its vacancy. Khadeja cried until her phone vibrated alerting her to a new text message from Valita.

"Hey girl, I'm sorry for leaving but I miss my cousins and sister. I wouldn't trip if you did the same, cheer up because Khan is a good man and he told me I can visit whenever I want. I promise I will never miss a battle so keep on kicking ass" Khadeja smiled as she replied with a heart emoji and went downstairs to join her family for movie night.

A little after two in the morning, Khan patiently waited on the Madison St. entrance of Latrobe Projects for his cubs while smoking a Newport 100. Junkies wandered the streets like zombies in search of a come up for their next fix. As Khan watched a Baltimore City patrol officer doze off in his vehicle, a junkie tapped Khan's window, which was halfway rolled down while he smoked his cigarette.

"You got some change black man?" said the ashy skeleton as he fixed a pair of yellow eyes on Khan's cigarette.

"Nah bruh..." replied Khan while growing impatient

"How about a fug?"

"Nah bruh, this is my last one" lied Khan.

"Well can I get a hit from that one" begged the junkie.

"No nigga damn!" said Khan as he rolled his tinted window back up in frustration.

"Where is these damn bitches!" yelled Khan as he pulled out his phone to text the cubs again.

Moments later, Khan saw all four of his cubs walking towards him with a large man in red draped over two of them. The two girls attempted to remove the tricks large arm from their shoulders but he seemed to be using them for balance as the man took slow drunken steps toward the truck. The other two girls quickly jumped to avoid upsetting Khan any further. The girls managed to break free of the drunken tricks grip as they feared Khan would have an attitude, they piled in the back of the truck with a thousand apologizes.

Once the man was close enough to the truck, Khan's entire mood changed as he witnessed a drunk, unsuspecting K-Willz standing inches away from him. Khan's face was hidden behind the darkness of limo tint, as he reached for his .44 magnum. K-Willz was all alone and this would've been the perfect opportunity to get rid of him, but Khan remembered the patrol car sitting a few yards away from his truck. K-Willz continued to tap on the truck to get one of the girls to spend the night with him. All of a sudden the driver side window started to roll down as K- Willz thought this was his lucky day, until he was face to face with a snarling Khan which made K-Willz sober up instantly.

K-Willz left his strap in the house and felt helpless as he watched Khan reach for something on his lap. Khan lifted his arm and pointed an index finger and thumb as if were a gun and fired an imaginary bullet in K-Willz direction.

"Next time nigga" said Khan as he drove off.

K-Willz shook off the shock and extended his arms wide as Khan heard him yelling…

"This is my city bitch…my city ….you'll see!"

After dropping the girls off at the hotel Khan re-counted his money, then jumped back on the highway.

"I'm ready take my blackass to bed" said Khan as he received a text from Khadeja telling him to turn on 92.3 radio station ASAP.

"Let me find out shawty done sent me a shout out on the radio, nigga can't leave for two minutes without these bitches missing me" said Khan while turning on the radio.

"Yo this ya boy, Squirrel Wide and 92Q got something fresh out da frying pan for y'all. We told y'all a few minutes ago that there was a war on these streets and my man K-Willz ain't taking no prisoners. Turn ya volume up for the exclusive new diss track by K-Willz called "Captain Save-a-Hoe"

"Pussy nigga tryin' save-a-hoe/ Blood gang what I'm bangin' hoe/ He talk big but he be bluffin' doe/ I put a bill on ya head like Buffalo/ Da glock hold 15 like Teebow/ you know my team foul, that's why we shootin' all dem freethrows/ Fuck a nigga name Khan and I hope you get da message/ Riding round town fucking wit my sloppy seconds/ If da nigga so hot why he ain't sign no deal/ Fuck how ya feel, I'm just keepin' it real/ We can keep this shit on wax, or we can fight in the field/ And you'll get clip after clip like a highlight reel/ Hey Yo Khan if you really da hottest nigga out why don't you step to a real nigga, you keep battling them bum ass nobodies...whats up nigga, lets put some real bread up! Nigga you can bet ya bitch"

"Y'all heard it live on 92Q, The People's Station"

Khan shook his head in disbelief as his cell phone went off

repeatedly from the hundreds of Facebook notifications from his fan page. It was almost 3am and it seemed as if the entire city was wide awake commenting about the diss track. Even Slick was up going back and forth with Khan's fans on his timeline. Khan decided not to respond and drove back home in silence as K- Willz plan to shake the city up, seemed to be working.

Chapter Thirty-Six
SUNDAY FUNDAY

The upper middle class neighborhood of Hamilton consisted of mostly retired elderly white folks and a few boujee black residents. Winter was knocking on the door as the birds, bees, and other variants of life, scrambled to soak up the remaining warmth of the autumn weather. A rogue ray of sunshine pierced through a small crack of the venetian blinds and found refuge on Khan's face. Khan's eyes slowly opened and his visibility came into focus, as memories of last night's social media drama with K-Willz caused him to frown. Khan became irritated with the numerous posts and comments on Facebook, and decided to turn his phone off for a while. Khan wanted to start this beautiful day off the right way by not involving himself in any stressful situations. Khan glanced to his right and smiled as Khadeja drooled slightly while snuggling under Khan's armpit. Next to Khadija, laid Nina, China, and Kitty. On Khan's left side, Rain had her arms wrapped around his waist as Heidi, Sabrina, Suga and Reds made up the left side of the bed. Khan gently unclasped Rain's arms from around his waist and slithered out of the large bed. China was the only girl to awaken from Khan's evasive moments.

"Hey daddy, good morning" China sat up in a green negligee.

"Hey mama, good morning to you as well" responded Khan while opening a small wooden box on his nightstand.

"Watch doing?"

"About to get blazed and have some family fun" smiled Khan while dumping a small packet of Molly on the surface of the nightstand.

"Oh Yea" smiled China while walking towards Khan.

"Yup, here gut this Dutch for me and roll me a blunt" Khan tossed China the Kush and started doing push-ups.

"Fuck are you doing?" questioned China while breaking up the large sticky clumps of weed.

"Getting ready….I told you we 'bout to have some fun, as soon as this Molly shit hit, I'mma go Hulk on you bitches" Khan spoke while continuing to do push-ups. Khan saw Sabrina stretching then release a loud yawn.

"That's right, getcha big ass up…matter fact all of you hoes get up! I had a rough night so I need a good morning!" yelled Khan as each girl started to stir from their slumber.

"What's going on?" asked a barely conscious Kitty.

"It's Daddy-Time, y'all got five minutes to go brush your teeth and I want all of y'all ass naked front and center.

Once the girls handled their morning hygiene, Khan turned the bedroom into a sweat lodge as he and girls had a small Kush Cypher before the festivities began.

"Alright the Molly has hit me" yelled Khan as he pulled of his polo briefs and laid back on the bed.

"We 'bout to have a Ten-some" laughed Khan as Reds wasted no time inserting Khan into her mouth.

"I want everybody involved on this one, I need y'all to pretend we under water and my dick spits oxygen" Nina observed Khan smiling a little too hard from Red's oral skills as she casually jerked the exposed area of Khan's dick for a few strokes, then his dick made a loud "pop" sound as Nina pulled it from Reds mouth and placed it in her own. Red's smiled at Nina's sly trick, as Red's was not to be outdone. Red's grabbed the back of Nina's ponytail and repeated forced her head further down on Khan's dick. Surprisingly the myth of Nina's un-gaggable throat proved true as she swallowed inch after inch without resistance. Suga decided to get in the action by sliding underneath Khan's testicles and gliding her tongue along his sensitive scrotum which tightened to her touch.

"Sabrina, bring that big ass over here" called Khan as he noticed Sabrina starting to finger herself on the far side of the bed. Sabrina crawled towards Khan and awaited further instruction.

"Put that ass on my face…this Molly got a nigga hungry" smiled Khan as Sabrina proceeded to lift her enormous ass and slowly lower it on Khan's eager tongue.

Khan spread Sabrina's large, plump red buttocks wide as his tongue darted in and out of her pink canal. Sabrina's moans caused every girl in the bedroom to become jealous because Khan rarely used his mouth for anything other than smoking and talking shit. Khan wasn't fond of kissing either, but this new Molly Khan started using had Khan all over his women. Sabrina exploded all over Khan's face as Khadeja, Kitty and China changed shifts with Nina, Red's and Suga.

The trio turned his dick into an all you can eat buffet. The Molly allowed Khan to suppress his threatening orgasm, while he observed Heidi and Rain putting on a two girl show of their own. Heidi had Rain flat on her stomach as she turned the crack of Rains ass into a Lunchable. Khadeja slurped on Khan's dick until she felt it start to pulsate, in which Khadeja positioned her lips to only cover the tip of his dick as she took her hand and glided China's head to the base. China ran her tongue up and down Khan's length at a rapid pace while kitty lightly grinded her teeth into Khan's balls. The sensation drove Khan crazy as he allowed the first of many orgasm's to burst in Khadeja's warm mouth. The Molly kept Khan's rod at full attention as he positioned himself behind Heidi and started working her with slow long thrust. Heidi took the dick like a pro as she continued to eat Rain's ass. Rain was so caught up in the moment, she never realized that Heidi's tongue was replaced by the tip of Khan's dick until he rammed his tool into Rains jiggly ass. Rain squealed like a piglet as Khan punished her brown eye Betty. Reds slid under Rain and nibbled on her clit which made Khan's backdoor intrusion much more pleasurable.

Khan busted another load and made Nina clean his dick off with her mouth. Reds passed Khan another blunt which rejuvenated his stamina instantly. Khan looked like an animal in heat as he scanned the sea of women in search of his next meal.

"Hey Sabrina, bend that ass over" said Khan while inserting his rock hard dick in Sabrina's wet pussy.

"Damn this shit feel good" yelled Khan while gripping Sabrina's waist and slamming into her wetness as her ass jiggled out of control. Khan eventually laid on his back as each girl took turns riding him until everyone reached their climax. After a short nap Khan was ready for round two as he playfully chased the girls around the bedroom screaming.

"Bring that ass here girl!"

Khan showered then got dressed after another short nap. He brushed his freshly cut Caesar while staring at his reflection in the mirror.

"Damn ya mama did a good job" smiled Khan but the very mention of his mother, made Khan a little home sick.

"I'mma go check up on her and kids today" said Khan while snapping on his G-Shock watch.

Khan glanced at his large portrait of Bea Gaddy, he kept hung by the closet. "Good ole Bea" Bea Gaddy was a selfless and caring community activist. She was basically the black Mother Teresa. She fed countless families out of her own pockets and raised money to fund the homeless. Khan reflected back on the days where he and his family stood in line and the late Bea Gaddy blessed them with a hot meal.

"Never forget your roots" mused Khan as he smiled knowing that he had a little over one hundred thousand in his stash. Khan's stash did increase however, so did his bills and expenses. Khan paid Mikey P a little under three grand a month for rent and few extra

dollars to put the deed in a fake name. He struck a deal with the manager at the American Best Hotel to rent out the entire 8th floor to house his cubs for a mere ten bands a month.

Khan paid for all the vehicles from the rent-a-car shop, and he also gave Khadeja's cousin Yemi a nice monthly salary to boost clothes for him and all of his girls. These expenses added up to an extravagant amount, but the price Khan paid for drugs easily tripled that amount.

"I gotta make some changes" said Khan while stealing one last glance at his reflection before leaving his house.

Khan drenched himself in Axe body spray before exiting his truck.

"Can't be smelling like ganja around my mama and nem's" laughed Khan as Khan Jr. spotted his dad entering the yard and drove his bike at top speed to greet his father.

"Daddy!" yelled Khan Jr while racing towards Khan.

"Hey boy, come here" Khan replied while snatching him off his bike and twirling him in the air.

"I miss you Dad"

"I miss you too" Khan said while feeling like an asshole for allowing drugs and hookers to occupy all of his attention.

"Where's grandma and your sister?"

"Everybody is in the house, come on..."

Khan walked into the living room and saw little Khonnie watching SpongeBob on the television. Khan had to walk in front of the T.V. to get Khonnie to notice he was present.

"Daddy!" screamed Khonnie once she realized the large figure that eclipse her view of the television was her father.

"Come here babydoll" said Khan while scooping her tiny body into his arms.

Khonnie planted a huge kiss on her father's right cheek as he playfully scrunched up his face and pretended to wipe off her kiss.

"Why y'all making all that damn noise in my house" screamed Renee while walking into the living room.

"Hey Ma"

"Baby! Hey, I been trying to call you all weekend, what's wrong with ya phone?" asked Renee while giving Khan a hug.

"I been going through some things mama, I cut my phone off for a minute to get my mind right" said Khan as he followed Renee into the kitchen.

"Well I have two things to tell you" said Renee with a look of concern.

"Damn what's up mama?"

"Well my cancer has returned so you gotta get ya shit together. I may not be able to take care of these kids forever. So, we gotta make something happen."

"Well I've been making some moves lately, but damn I thought they got rid of all of ya cancer." Khan spoke while staring at the floor.

"Well its back, no need to trip about it, I'mma just keep fighting until either I win or the cancer wins but what kinda moves you been making?" asked a skeptical Renee.

"Some good moves that will put me on my feet"

"Well it might have been those "Good Moves" that brings me to the next thing I have to tell you…" said Renee as she now stared off away from Khan.

"Whats up" Khan said noticing his mother's change in demeanor. "The police came around looking for you…"

"Damn, for what?" asked Khan while feeling paranoid instantly.

"They wasn't regular cops, they worked for the Department of Corrections, they didn't say why, they just said they wanted you to contact your P.O. ASAP"

"They probably just wanna know where I live now since I moved outta G.P. house." said Khan while feeling a bit more relaxed.

"Didn't you tell your P.O. that you moved?"

"Well….." said Khan while showcasing a smile of guilt.

"Please don't tell me you stopped meeting with your P.O." said an angry Renee.

"I figured if they needed me they would call"

"Khan, you know these people don't play, I need you to stop fucking up because one day you won't have me as your safety net." cautioned Renee while checking on her Pot Roast in the oven.

"Ma, I got this, I will call them in the morning after I drop the kids off at school."

"Oh ok, it must be freezing in hell right now, I get Sunday dinner with my son and he's taking the kids to school….I get to sleep in tomorrow….Yes!!" Renee joked while Khan helped her out in the kitchen.

The two finished cooking and set the table where Khan enjoyed a lovely family home cooked meal and promised to return in the morning.

The next morning, Khan pulled up in a parking spot directly across the street from his mothers' house. Completely oblivious to the all-black Impala that camped outside her home, he proceeded to walk into her yard with several bags of IHOP take out. Khan wanted to surprise his mom with her favorite breakfast meal, then he planned on taking her to her favorite casino in Ann Arundel County. As Khan finally reached the front porch, he heard the gate door behind him fly open as he was quickly surrounded by three D.O.C task force officers.

"Khanstantine Larson, your parole has been revoked."

"For what!" screamed Khan while horse kicking the screen door to alert his mother of his presence?

"Everything will be explained once we get downtown" replied a tall muscular black officer with a box-shaped fade.

"Baby, whats going on?" yelled Renee as the three officers approached Khan.

"They say my parole got revoked…here take my truck keys, I'mma have someone come get it later" said Khan while tossing Renee the keys then surrendering to the officers to avoid making a scene in front of his nosey neighbors.

"I will phone ahead, call me when you get downtown Khan" Renee cried as she tightened up her house gown.

"Will do mama, I brought y'all some pancakes and shit…kiss the kids for me when they wake up"

Khan was shoved in the back of the Impala as one of the officers sat in the back with Khan. Khan was denied his request to smoke a cigarette as the foursome rode in silence. Khan had no idea how the parole board would react to his negligence as he mentally kicked himself for fucking up…yet again.

Chapter Thirty- Seven
THERES A GHOST IN THE BASEMENT

Khan's arrest left the city in shambles. Thousands of "Free Khan" posts littered the newsfeeds of multiple social media platforms. Khan was "The People's Champ" and his absence generated a dismal cloud high above the city's skies, not to mention with the sudden mysterious disappearance of Crazy Cracker, left a void that K-Willz intended to fill. K-Willz jumped on this opportunity by releasing track after track of surprisingly, quality music. Even Slick had to admit that K-Willz stepped his bars up, so much so that Slick considered making K-Willz his main event. Crazy Cracker was set to battle Maniac da Bullet but now with Crazy Cracker not being in attendance, it was K-Willz turn to tangle with the Maniac.

"About fucking time these streets recognize a G" boasted K-Willz while reading all of the love he now received from social media.

"Yea they definitely feeling you now" Brent admitted while scrolling down Facebook on his phone, then picking up a PlayStation controller.

"We on now, and Slick got me the headliner at the next event so I'm about to show out!" K-Willz spoke while grabbing his jacket and keys to his old school, bright red Stingray.

"Where the fuck you going, you know I got some dummies coming through in a little bit" smiled Brent while playing NBA 2K on their trap house television.

"Oh yea?" asked K-Willz while stopping in his tracks.

"Yea that little thick chocolate bitch that be with LaShaye"

"Damn, you talking 'bout Vanessa thickass….damn, just tell shawty I'mma be back later, I gotta go see a nigga about some new…ah beats for my new song" lied K-Willz.

"Oh okay, well handle that because I dunno what's got into you lately but all of ya new songs been straight fire"

"Fuck you talking about….all my shit been fire!" fumed K-Willz.

"If you say so…but these last new joints been next level my nigga" said Brent while concentrating on his virtual free throw shot.

"Whateva nigga…I'm out"

K-Willz hated driving, he'd rather have a gun in each hand instead of a steering wheel whenever he stepped outdoors, but he didn't want Brent to know of his destination for fear of his disapproval. K-Willz slightly out ranked Brent, but he allowed his input nevertheless. Whenever Brent disagreed with one of K-Willz gorilla tactics, he usually nagged and complained until K-Willz eventually gave in. K-Willz was now at a point of no return and couldn't afford to be blocked by Brent if he was to reach super stardom.

K-Willz circled the block twice before parking on the empty streets of Chapel and North ave. Chapel Street was a ghost town, the majority of the houses were boarded up and dilapidated, with very little pedestrian traffic. K-Willz stepped out of his car and looked in all directions before moving briskly towards a large red brick row home with a heavy iron gate security screen door. K-Willz once again checked his surroundings before quickly inserting a key into the screen door and repeating the same process with the wooden oak door.

K-Willz walked into the strong stench of crack smoke and urine. K-Willz heard the static heavy sounds of The Isey Brothers through an old clock radio with blown out speakers as he walked further into the living room to greet the occupants of the decayed dwelling.

"Hey, young Blood" greeted Doc, an O.G. of the Blood gang that allowed addiction to ruin his promising life as a top ranking member in his set.

"What's good O.G." replied K-Willz while stepping over several 40oz bottles of Old English to give the former shell of a man, a quick fist bump.

"I see Ray, done found him a good vein huh?" laughed K-Willz as Ray, the other O.G. which had a similar story to Doc's was leaning over on a milk crate with a long line of drool running down his chin.

"Yea that raw you blessed us with really hit da spot" smiled Doc while firing up another crack rock.

"Say no more, now is that situation down stairs still cool?"

"You paying us too much to fuck that money up young blood, don't worry, we might not look it, but me and Ray still sharp as porcupine pussy" Doc smiled with brown teeth as he meant every word.

K-Willz didn't actually pay them money, he gave them an endless supply of drugs to babysit his insurance policy to take over the Baltimore hip-hip scene.

"Good shit, I'm 'bout to go check on that." said K-Willz while briefly taking in the sights of the trash filled living room.

Two milk crates and an out of commission floor model T.V. which the alarm clock radio sat up on, made up all the décor, as the blanket covered windows acted as a barrier for the sunlight and nosey spectators.

"Cool, let me hold something before you leave nephew" K-Willz shook his head then threw the O.G. a small baggie of Crack Rocks before carefully watching each step and making his way towards the chained basement doors.

After unlocking and removing the heavy chains, the smell of urine increased causing K- Willz to almost vomit while reaching the bottom of the basement. Bound to a wooden chair with thick cattle ropes and a dirty sock shoved in his mouth, was Crazy Cracker. Crazy Cracker was drenched in his own urine and the smell of feces radiated through his soiled garments as his muffled screams increased at the sight of K-Willz.

"Sup playboy" taunted K-Willz as he pulled the funky sock from in-between Crazy Cracker's dry lips.

"Yo you gotta let me go bruh….you doing too much over some rap beef" pleaded Crazy Cracker.

"I told you the deal buddy, since you were the reason for my fall in this rap shit, you will be the reason I rise"

"These people can't be that stupid, they gotta know somebodies ghost writing all ya new songs, because no offense but our styles are like night and day"

"What do you mean?" questioned K-Willz with a serious look.

"Like my bars are fire and your shit is trash" laughed Crazy Cracker.

"I think it's cute that you can still have a sense of humor considering you might die down this bitch" said K-Willz as Crazy Cracker's laughter quickly subsided.

"I just wanna go home bruh…I heard about what you did to my man Jiffy, that's why I fell back from the bullshit" Crazy Cracker explained with tears in his eyes.

"Just continue to write my shit for a while and I'll think about letting you go….and to show my appreciation for the other songs you wrote, I'mma get you some fresh clothes and have my two O.G.'s come down here and give you a sponge bath" K-Willz laughed as he went back upstairs to give his next orders to the O.G.'s as he could feel the shift in star power tilt his way.

Chapter Thirty-Eight
NEVER JUDGE A BOOK BY ITS COVER

"Wow I can't believe I'm locked up with The Gangas Khan!" said Khan's overly excited cell buddy.

"Man chill with that, I ain't no better than the next man" said Khan in a modest response.

"My whole hood fuck witchu Khan, I been rocking with you since you used to the battles at the high school."

"Damn, that was like ten years ago" smiled Khan while looking out the large window of the cell.

Khan was being held at the Department of Corrections Diagnostics intake building, which overlooked the heart of East Baltimore. Khan watched the junkies bop up and down Eager Street while his celly "Lil Bob" continued to fan boy over his lyrical resume.

"And I don't care what nobody says about that battle with Crazy Cracker, you won that shit." Khan took a seat on the toilet to get his thoughts together and lil Bob noticed Khan's contemplation.

"What's up Khan?" lil Bob inquired.

"Shit bruh" said Khan in an attempt to deflect questioning.

"Come on man, it's me...lil Beez-ob" lil Bob was a young brown skinned kid with a short stocky build.

He had a very youthful, jovial demeanor and was always on joke time. He was a very humble young man that got along with everyone, but would sometimes do a little too much to fit in with the "In Crowd".

"Alright man, lets just say that I'm worried if I don't get outta here soon, everything that I've fought so hard to get, will be gone in a blink of an eye."

"You mean ya rap career?" asked a very concerned lil Bob.

"No, not that, I'm talking about ... fuck I almost forgot about that battle!" cursed Khan.

"Who you battling?"

"Slick set me up with Jupiter"

"Jupiter from the Wildin-Out show?" yelled lil Bob.

"Yea his fat ass, but that battle is in two weeks, how long does it normally take to see the parole board?"

"Like three weeks to a month, their so backed up right now that there's really no telling." lil Bob responded honestly.

"Well there goes that once in a life time opportunity." said Khan while standing up to look out the narrow window of his cell door.

The day room was empty as the lone officer sat behind a small desk in the corner reading a magazine.

"What time do we rec?"

"Like right after dinner, so like six-ish" Khan was stuck in processing all day and didn't make it to a cell until after the afternoon shift change which left him no time to use the phone.

"How's the speed on this tier?"

"It's pretty laid back, every now and then them blood niggas be acting up but as long as you stay out the way or in my case, ain't got nothing for them to take, they'll leave you alone" lil Bob didn't have much and didn't have to front like most cats in the city.

"Where you from lil Bob"

"Turner station, born and raised" smiled lil Bob as Khan was starting to take a liking to him.

"My peoples not too far from there, look I'm in a position where money ain't really one of my issues right now. So if you need something, I gotchu" Khan thought about giving the young kid a job but his playful personality led Khan to believe he might be too soft to handle the life.

"You holding up okay?" questioned Khadeja in a sad tone.

"Yea everything is cool, it's the waiting game that's killing me"

"I'mma come see you in the morning, do you need any money on your books?"

"Nah mama, I had a little cash on me when they brought me in, I was gonna take mama to the casino"

"Well is there anything I can do for you?"

"Not right now, I will let you know what I need you to do when I see you tomorrow."

"Okay daddy…I miss you"

"We all miss you!" Khan heard Nina's Russian voice yell in

the background as he smiled.

"Nina misses you too" said Khadeja as she walked away from the nosey girls.

"Tell her I miss her, tell all my babies I love 'em"

"You don't miss me... you miss this mouth" said Khadeja in a seductive manner.

"You better believe it...play with that thang for me real quick" said Khan while placing the phone closer to hear her pussy as her fingers made soft squishy sounds.

Khan felt himself getting caught up in the moment until two inmates walked up on him.

"Daddy you like that?" asked an oblivious Khadeja.

"Hold up mama..." said Khan while turning towards the two intrusive inmates.

"Y'all got next" said Khan thinking that they wanted the phone.

"We want now!" spoke the taller of the two guys.

"Mama I'mma call you back" said Khan while hanging up the phone, sensing something dangerous was about to unfold.

The man that spoke was a tall, basketball player type with long dreads, and the other guy was a little shorter than Khan but was grossly overweight with a short fade.

"What's da issue fellas?" said Khan while standing up to be in a better position if something were to pop off.

Khan noticed the C.O. was in someone's cell doing a shakedown so it was obvious that these guys coordinated this with the officer's rounds.

"K-Willz says hello" said the tall dude with dreads as Khan saw the fat guy pull out a shank.

Fat boy charged Khan as Khan side-stepped and tagged his right side with a quick jab to the eye. The fat nigga stumbled a little as the other guy grabbed Khan from behind putting him in a choke hold as fatboy prepared to plunge the jagged shank in Khan again, lil Bob appeared out of nowhere and caught fatboy with a broom stick upside the head. The fat man fell to the ground on impact and lil Bob quickly retrieved the skank and started stomping fat boy viciously. Khan threw his head back hard and connected with the dread heads nose causing him to loosen up on his grip on Khan's neck, which Khan quickly recovered and started throwing a fury of haymakers until he placed the perfect blow to dread heads chin. Khan watched the man fall and joined lil Bob in the stomping session until someone yelled out "Wop Woop" signaling the C.O. was finishing up with his search.

Khan and lil Bob walked away from the two badly beaten inmates and blended in with the rest of the prison population. Once the C.O. noticed the two bodies on the ground, he called the code on his walkie-talkie and a group of C.O.'s or The Goon Squad rushed to the scene with large cans of mace ready to fire at will. Everyone on the unit was locked down for the next two days since no one wanted to confess or identify the other parties responsible for the gruesome scene. Khan was feeling blessed that he got away scott free and had a new found respect for the man that he once thought of as too soft.

"Yo, I just wan-" lil Bob interrupted Khan.

"No need, you my celly, don't trip" smiled lil Bob

"I'mma give you my info before I leave here, because there's a shortage of real niggas out there."

Khan sat at the small confines of the picnic style table used for visitors. There was a C.O. on both ends of the table as they crammed inmates tightly together to visit with their loved ones. Khadeja, Rain, Nina, and Suga walked into the visiting room looking like steak to an Ethiopian. Khan smiled as some of the other inmates struggled to keep their eyes off his women while in the company of their own girlfriends and wives. Khan gave each girl a long hug and cuffed a little ass in the process before sitting down. Khan made small talk with the other girls before it was time to end the quick visit.

Khadeja instructed Khan to give her and the other girls a nice kiss before they leave. Khan gave her a puzzled look then reluctantly complied. Khan embraced Khadeja and gently pecked her lips, as Khan was pulling his face away she grabbed his head and forced her tongue down his throat.

Khan almost protested until he felt a small balloon floating in her mouth which he sucked out then swallowed. The entire visiting room watched as Khan gave four women long passionate kisses. When Khan said his final good-byes, the C.O. watching from the far end of the visiting room gave Khan a thumbs up as Khan left smiling thinking about his lionesses and the high he was about to experience.

Chapter Thirty- Nine
LADY PIMP

"K-Willz! K-Willz! K-Willz!" chanted the crowd as Slick raised K-Willz's arm in victory.

K-Willz took a moment to bask in the ambience of his new found fame. He already possessed the gangster image which was a prerequisite to gain respect from the streets, but with the addition of his new ghost writer, made him a force to be reckon with.

"You got that one, but please believe we gonna have a rematch" yelled Maniac da Bullet as he walked away from the stage, visibly upset about his loss at the hands of K-Willz.

"Step ya bars up nigga!" K-Willz shouted back while popping bottles on stage with his set and a few groupies.

"So when I walk the girls back to the truck, this nigga Khan bitch ass was behind the window." laughed K-Willz.

"Yea, he was working for me, I asked him to pick them bitches up for me but I ain't know y'all niggas was beefin'" lied D.J.

"Well don't worry about all that, just keep bringing these bad ass bitches to party with a nigga." said K-Willz as he and D.J. started doing business together, shortly after meeting when Khan instructed D.J. to drop the cubs off at the party.

"I got bitches galore…whenever y'all need some hoes, I'm ya man." smiled D.J. as he stood in K-Willz trap house displaying two more cubs that decided to jump ship when Khan got arrested. D.J. was a tall skinny man with long cornrows and a thin mustache. D.J. used to be Khan's right hand, but when Khan started making money, he felt Khan was spoon feeding him and he should've been making the same kind of money as Khan. D.J. started sweet talking the cubs whenever Khan wasn't around, and now with Khan in jail, D.J. could make his move.

"You got my number dug, just hit me up whenever y'all trying to party" said D.J. as he gave K-Willz and his men some dap then headed out the door.

"Fuck do this bitch want?" spat D.J. as he hit the ignore button on Khadeja.

Khadeja made several attempts to get in contact with D.J. after hearing rumors of his betrayal. D.J. didn't feel the need to explain himself to a girl barely old enough to buy alcohol.

"Fuck her, fuck Khan, fuck all them niggas" thought D.J. while making his way back to the American Best Hotel.

Maria aka Suitcase took on the role as D.J's bottom bitch. She knew that she would never make it past cub status because Khan's head was stuck too far up Khadeja's "Phoney Ass". Maria was a county girl hailing from the Towson area. Unlike the other girls, Maria came from a wealthy family. Her parents never gave her much attention because of their careers thus allowing Maria to venture towards the wrong crowd. Maria started experimenting with drugs and developed a shameful reputation which caused Maria's parents to sever all ties with their only daughter. She soon found herself in the streets doing whatever it took to survive. Maria left behind everything in her life accept for the huge Fendi bag her grandmother bought her before she passed away.

"Wanda you should stop fucking with Khan and come join our

team" proposed Suitcase while watching Wanda apply her make-up.

"Khan ain't got no life sentence, he's locked up for a violation, the nigga will probably be home sometime this week" replied Wanda while getting ready for some clients Khadeja booked for her.

"How can a man that's slinging his dick everywhere, make you hoes stay so loyal?" questioned Suitcase with a look of disgust.

"Believe it or not some of us hoes have the common sense to see past go, that nigga D.J. ain't have shit until Khan put him on his feet. Now that nigga wanna do some snake shit while Khan's locked up….man! That nigga D.J. is a…-" Wanda's words trailed off once she noticed D.J. standing by the door of her hotel bedroom.

"I'mma what? Bitch!" questioned D.J. as he slowly walked towards Wanda.

She remained speechless as D.J. backed her into a corner.

"Go-head bitch…I'mma what?" D.J. eyes turned into narrow slits as he quickly brought his huge hand across Wanda's chocolate face.

"Ouch.." screamed Wanda as she slid to the floor holding her burning face.

"That's the problem with you bitches, y'all don't respect real niggas....I told Khan we should be on some gorilla shit but he too fucking soft. I'm taking over this spot now, so if you wanna keep living here you working for me."

"I don't want no problems D.J." whispered Wanda.

"Then learn some act-right" spat D.J. as he turned to leave the room with Suitcase on his heels.

As Khadeja stepped off the elevator, D.J., Suitcase and several other cubs brushed by Khadeja and entered the elevator.

"D.J.!" screamed Khadeja as D.J. simply smiled at her and waited for the elevator doors to shut.

"D.J. we need to talk!" yelled Khadeja as the doors finally closed leaving Khadeja irritated and a bit vexed.

Khadeja could hear the distant sound of crying coming from the cracked door of Wanda's room as she went to investigate.

"Wanda." said Khadeja as she entered the room slowly.

"Huh" responded a disoriented Wanda while staring in the bathroom mirror.

"It's me mama, are you okay?"

"I'm cool Dee, I just gotta re-touch my make-up and I'm all yours" spoke Wanda while forcing a fake smile.

"Did D.J. do this?" said Khadeja while closely examining the bruise on Wanda's pretty face.

"It's nothing…let's just get this money and keep it moving. Tim and Kim, remember?" laughed Wanda.

"Look I'm about to take you outta here, actually I'mma round up all the cubs that ain't flipped on Khan and bring y'all back to the Big House.

"Did Khan say we could go?" asked Wanda through large watery eyes.

"He left me in charge, and I'm sure if he knew that his family and business was at stake, he would do the same."

"Alright, what do you need me to do?" asked an eager Wanda as the news of leaving the cheap hotel brought tears of joy to her face.

"Just start knocking on doors and tell whatever cubs we got left that it's time to roll!"

Khadeja and the nine faithful cubs, loaded up three taxi cabs with their belongings and high tailed it to the Big House. The lioness's were a bit displeased at Khadeja's decision to bring this many girls to their home, but once Khadeja explained the news of D.J.'s deceit, the lioness's came to an understanding and helped clear out some of the closet space in their converted walk-in's to give their new guest a place to sleep. Khadeja called a house meeting once everyone was settled in to explain her plan to keep everything intact while Khan was away.

"As of right now we're a few cards short of a deck, Kitty left us and went back to that strip club and countless cubs showed they true colors. But Fuck 'em. Ain't no more cubs, all y'all is lioness's now, y'all stood strong when the other weak bitches left us on our own, but I like it this way….this the time when the real bitches stand up and keep this Pride alive."

The very next day Khadeja was on her shit. During a morning jail call, she convinced Khan to tell his mom, to give her the keys to his truck, where Khadeja crammed all seventeen girls into the navigator then drove to two of the most profitable locations in the area.

Khadeja had sixteen girls at her command. She split them into two groups of eight and appointed Nina and Reds as the team captains. She considered making Rain a team captain but Rain's addiction increased dramatically in Khan's absence, and Khadeja wasn't in a position to take anymore loses. Khadeja put Nina's team in Owings Mills and took Red's and her crew to Route 40.

Red's turned out to be more than just a kiss-ass to Khan, she was also a great leader that made sure the money was always correct, and had no problems getting her own hands dirty. Her team of Rain, Heidi, China, Wanda and three other cubs nearly doubled what Nina's team made. Nina's team consisted of Sabrina, Suga, Mute, Amber Rose, and three loyal cubs that were fairly new to the game. Khadeja opted not to bother with any of Khan's A.P.'s for protection. She figured if she only booked the girls two tricks at a time, that the combined efforts of eight girls should be more than enough to handle any man.

Khadeja re-located Nina's team to the Catonsville area and they immediately caught back up to Reds team. It was Khadeja's ability to remain cool and calm like Khan taught her, that allowed her to be successful as Khan projected. The expenses that occurred during their temporary pause in action took a big hit on Khan's stash, but slowly and surely, Khadeja managed to climb back out of the hole and bring his total back to its original amount. A few days later she was able to add an additional ten thousand as she smiled while thumbing through a large stack of bills before placing it in the safe. Khadeja then slammed the door shut and flipped the portrait of Bea Gaddy back in its original spot to conceal the safe. As Khadeja turned around to walk out the bedroom, she was startled by a red eyed Rain, who was busy tearing up the bedroom in search of something.

"Oh hey Rain" Khadeja nervously greeted.

"Hey Dee, can't talk, lost my damn syringe" Rain replied without looking at Khadeja.

"Maybe she didn't see the safe, that bitch do stay high 24/7" thought Khadeja while studying Rains movements for any signs of deception.

"When did you come in the room, you scared the shit outta me" said Khadeja while trying to pry a little bit further.

"What? Girl I just walked in like a second ago, look either shut up or help me look for my works" yelled Rain while getting on her hands and knees to search under the bed.

"I'mma check downstairs" replied Khadeja as an excuse to get away from helping Rain.

Khadeja felt satisfied that Rain was still clueless about the safe as she walked in the basement to fool around with Khan's studio equipment.

"Alright China, once we get this Mixcraft shit figured out, we 'bout to make a banger"

"I'm with that" said a smiling China as Nina suddenly appeared out of nowhere.

"Damn, Nina you lite on ya feet" said China while grabbing a spring water out of Khan's mini fridge.

"My bad, you girls make music?" asked Nina

"Yea, if we can figure this shit out" said Khadeja while looking at Khan's equipment like it was from another planet.

"I know how to use" announced Nina as she powered on Khan's interface, then pointed at the microphone.

"China, give me mic check" ordered Nina.

"Testing, testing, Mic check 1, 2" said a nervous China while hearing herself for the first time in headphones.

"We are good to go" smiled Nina.

"Lets look on YouTube for a dope ass beat to use" suggested Khadeja.

"YouTube? Don't disrespect my daddy like that, we are artist no? We make beat not copy" said Nina while sitting down in front of Khan's Casio Keyboard.

"Nina you know how to play that?" asked China.

Nina didn't respond, she simply allowed her fingers to answer as she shocked the girls by playing a more up-tempo version of Beethoven's Moonlight Sonata.

"Where did you learn how to do that?" asked Khadeja.

"I was classically trained in my country" smiled Nina.

"Okay Nina lets create our own beat and China you need to come up with a hook and I will rap a mean ass verse." said Khadeja with sparkles in her eyes.

"Okay!" said both girls as everyone got to work.

"We gonna make daddy proud, let's get this money on the streets and with these beats" said Khadeja as Nina came up with a beautiful melody to kick start their song.

Chapter Forty
FAMILY MATTERS

"*give it away, give it away, give it away now/ give it away, give it away, give it away now/ give it away, give it away, give it away now/ I'm commissary rich, I ain't eatin' trays now/*

Khan did his remix of the Red Hot Chilli Peppers song as lil Bob freestyled a verse.

"*We don't eat them state trays, no no not da Don/ We eatin' like da Mob, thanks to my nigga Khan/ Aye yo its little Bob, Khan gotcha boy a job/ And if its rappin' or its mackin', I'mma get it done/ A nigga ain't got time for these fake friends/ Khan known me three weeks and 'bout to break ends/ I got his back on da streets and in da state pen/ Ya girl want me break bread but I break wind/*

Khan laughed so loud at lil Bob's last bar that his voice echoed out the cell and into the dayroom as the two cell buddies ate big bowls of "Hook up" and got higher than a Mariah Carey falsetto.

"Damn let's chill out before these niggas start tripping about us making too much noise at two in da morning" said Khan while rolling one last blunt of Kush wrapped in paper towel and toilet paper wrapper.

"But I ain't know you could flow like that bruh, I know I got a place for you on the team"

"That's whats up big dug, just don't forget me when you get out tomorrow." Khan was granted time served and issued a warning for failure to meet with his parole officer, due to lack of staff his paperwork needed for release wouldn't be completed until the morning.

Khan wasn't upset because from what he heard, Khadeja had everything under control, plus he had more than enough drugs to get him through the night.

Khan stepped out on Greenmount, wearing a set of D.O.C. blues as he scanned the block for his Navigator. Khan instructed Khadeja to be on the strip no later than four p.m. The time was now 4:45 p.m. and Khadeja nor his truck were nowhere in sight.

"Come on man, I'm not trying to be stuck out this bitch" mused Khan as a money green hellcat with tinted windows pulled up front on him.

"A nigga can't catch a break" thought Khan as he prepared for

the worst.

"Da fuck?" mouthed Khan as the window rolled down, revealing a smiling Khadeja with her hair straightened and a pair of Ray-Bans adding to her sexy swag.

"You like?" said Khadeja while stepping out of the sports car and jumping in Khan's arms.

"I love it, who let you borrow this…and where's my truck?" Khadeja silenced Khan with a kiss which Khan surprisingly didn't protest to, as the two engaged in a passionate lip lock while cars blew their horns at the blockage of traffic.

"Get in, it's yours….and the trucks at the big house" said Khadeja while walking around to the passenger side and sliding in the heated leather seat.

Khan shook his head in disbelief as this young girl not only managed to resurrect his business, but bought Khan his first car in the process.

"You really bought me a car yo?"

"No we bought you a car" Khadeja corrected while checking

on the girls to make sure all was well.

"What? I mean how?" Khan asked still stuck on stupid.

"Straight cash homie, that's how. Yemi put me on with a guy that runs a police auction, and let's just say….it was a steal" smiled Khadeja after looking up from her phone.

"This is my fucking dream car….thank you so much" replied Khan as he realized Khadeja was a lot more than his bottom bitch.

"It's the least we can do…the cars basically brand-new, aside from a few bullet holes in the backseat" Khadeja laughed while rolling Khan a blunt.

"So has D.J. been giving you any problems?"

"Well there's the usual mean mug, if we run into each other at the same hotel but besides that, I think he knows what bitch to play with" Khadeja replied while texting on her phone.

"Fuck you texting?" asked a nosey Khan.

"Boy watch the road, I'm still running the show until you take off them dirty ass jail clothes"

"Shaking my got-damn head" said Khan as he fought the temptation to test the hellcat's powerful engine and maintain the speed limit of 35 mph on the crowded stop and go traffic of Monument Street.

"Welcome home daddy!" yelled The Pride as Khan walked into the Big House. Each girl was dressed in matching cheerleader uniforms as they took formation and did a small routine of kicks, splits and twerking.

Khan was ecstatic as he broadcasted a huge Kool-aide smile while watching some new and old faces work together for the sake of his pleasure.

"Bravo!" yelled Khan as every girl rushed to Khan with hugs and kisses on the cheek.

"Once you get out them clothes and get showered up, the real party can begin" said Reds as she escorted Khan to the bathroom.

Khan went through a weeks worth of Molly in a few hours, as he required extra stamina to make-up for a month without sex. Khan fucked and sucked seventeen different girls until his body cramped up and shut down. Khan was snoring up a storm as the xannies he took finally kicked in. Khan dreamt he was on the couch with Beavis and Butthead as they watched and gave honest reviews to his music video.

Khan smiled as the two iconic musical critics said…

"I need your music in my ears like I need boobs in my hands. Khan was about to go on a crazy adventure with his newest animated fans until Khan was jolted from his sleep with a hard smack of a blunt object.

"What the fuck?" said Khan as his vision took a second to adjust to several figures in his bedroom with ski masks and pistols.

"You know what is nigga" shouted the tallest of the crew, he had a very thin frame and Khan could tell he disguised his voice an octave lower as he spoke.

Khan looked around the bedroom and noticed that every girl was face first on the ground except for Rain and Reds.

"I'mma ask you one time, what is the combo to the safe?" asked the ring leader while snatching down Bea Gaddy's portrait.

"Look don't hurt nobody, ain't nothing but chump change in there….not worth no gun play" Khan spoke while stalling for a way out of this mayhem.

"You got one more time to say something outcha mouth that ain't the combination and I'mma start puttin' holes in you and these dirty ass bitches."

"A'ight man….damn…its-" Khadeja shouted from the floor.

"No Khan, we work too hard for that"

"Shut up bitch!" shouted one of the other masked men in a slight feminine voice, then gave Khadeja a swift kick to the midsection.

"Khadeja!" shouted Khan while instinctively rushing to her aide then was struck again by the butt of a pistol.

Khan laid on the floor next to Khadeja with the top of his head split open and bleeding profusely as he finally gave the masked intruders the combo.

"Its 10-25-96" said Khan while holding his leaking head.

"It's open" said the small masked man that kicked Khadeja.

"A'ight bag that shit up and let's roll!" said the tall ring leader, as the smaller masked man loaded the money into a large designer bag.

Khan's eyes thought they were playing were tricks on him as he noticed the bag.

"Hold up now, I know that big ass bag from anywhere....Suitcase!"

Suitcase pulled of the mask along with the other ex-cubs that held pistols pointed towards Khan and his Pride.

"So I'm guessing the head honcho must be my own blood huh" Khan, shook his head in disgust as D.J. revealed himself last.

"Bitch hurry up with that safe because we gotta smoke this whole room, nigga done seen my face." shouted D.J. while pulling back the hammer and aiming at Khan.

"I hope Khan's ass ain't still sleep, that little thirty seconds of dick he gave me ain't gone cut it" laughed Reds after returning from the corner store to restock on blunts and cigarettes for the house.

As Reds neared the Big House she noticed D.J.'s rental truck parked across the street.

"Why is he here?" questioned Red's as she also noticed Rain sitting in the passenger seat blowing smoke rings out the window.

"And why is Rain in his truck?" Reds sensed there was something strange going on, and decided to enter the Big house from the rear.

Once inside, she could make out D.J.'s voice yelling at someone, which she assumed to be Khan. The girls no longer used the protection of men, so Khadeja provided them with something much more practical...she issued every girl a small can of mace, a switch blade and a mini .22. Reds crept upstairs and slowly towards the master bedroom where she could see the top of D.J.'s head shouting commands at Khan.

Red's inched closer as she used the other bedrooms for cover if detected. Once she was in a comfortable distance, she extended her arms with gun in hand slowly pulled the trigger with her eyes closed.

Pow

A bullet just grazed the top of D.J.'s cornrows as he and the other ex-cubs returned fire in the direction of the unknown gunman. Red's kept her body well hidden behind the door way as she fired off several more shots and yelled....

"This is the police....come out with your hands high"

When D.J. heard the announcement of the police he made a mad dash for the window but not before grabbing Suitcase's bag of stolen cash. Once Red's stop firing, the other ex-cubs followed D.J. out the second story window. D.J. ran to his car as the other girls slowly limped after him because of injury to their ankles from the fall. If D.J. didn't think the girls would identify him to the police, he would've never waited for the girls as Rain watched the scene with a horrific look on her face. Most of the neighbors required the help of hearing aids and had no idea why several people jumped out a window and were jogging to a truck across the street.

"Those niggers are something else" commented Henry, a 75 year old veteran whose day consisted of sitting on his porch and drinking Natural Lite.

"Everybody cool?" said Reds as she ran to the window to confirm D.J. and his band of bitches were gone.

"Yea thanks mama" said Khan while still holding his head.

"We gotta getchu to the hospital Khan" said Khadeja as she ran to her man.

"I'm good, it's just a little cut, I'mma get Heidi to stitch it up for me" some of the girls either forgot or were unaware of Heidi's former medical training.

"Yea I can do that" assured Heidi while examining the damage on Khan's head.

"Damn, I can't believe Rain set us up" shouted Khadeja.

"I can't believe my cousin, oh wait this is Baltimore" laughed Khan as the girls tended to Khan's injury.

Chapter Forty-One
TIME TO WAKE UP

Nearly a little over a week passed since the incident with D.J. and the almost fatal robbery. The once joyful atmosphere of the Big House was now a place of panic and gloom as Khan shut down all operations in an attempt to protect everyone from further danger of retaliation. Khan became extremely addicted to Xanax and other pain pills as he placed himself on an extended bedrest. Lost in a coma of prescription narcotics, Khan would sometimes drift back into consciousness only to implement new house rules. Khan's paranoia and halt of funds caused several girls to leave his once promising organization to try their hands elsewhere, but when Khan proposed that the women should all get "regular jobs" and put this dangerous life behind them, it made the entire house question their loyalty to their once great Pride leader.

"Does ya head still hurt baby?" cooed Reds as she gently caressed Khan's bandages.

Reds made it her business to show Khan her worth by never leaving his side as she nursed him back to good health. Reds knew that Khan was fine and if he wanted to lay in bed all day with her, then she welcomed the attention.

"Yea....I think I need another xanny" cried Khan while cuddling with Reds.

Even Khadeja got tired of Khan's crying and complaining as she allowed Reds to hog her man without protest.

"Where's Wanda, she was suppose to make me some of her special tea." asked Khan while straining to open his eyes.

"Khan that was three days ago, she gone"

"What, damn well tell Mute to make it"

"She gone too" replied Reds.

"Damn, I can't take a day off without bitches jumping ship" Khan shook his head.

"Well it's been over a week Khan, them girls gotta eat, and a lot of them have habits also"

"Who else left?" Khan said while shrugging off her comment.

"As soon as you started talking that "regular job" shit, even Sabrina broke her neck running outta here"

"Not my big baby" Khan said in a sad tone.

"The only girls here are Nina, Dee, China, Suga and me" said

Reds while kissing the top of Khan's head.

"What happened to Heidi?"

"She left late last night, she developed a habit like Rains and that little bit of drugs that Khadeja rationed to her weren't enough"

"Geez, well at least I still got you" said Khan while rubbing Reds ass.

"Can I ask you something?" asked Reds while shifting her long red hair to the other side of her freckled face.

"Yea, whats up mama?"

"Let's run away" said Reds with a serious expression.

"Say what now?" Khan thought he heard her wrong.

"Let's just pick up whateva you got that's valuable, get a couple of fake ID's and bounce"

"You forreal?"

"Yes baby, unlike the rest of these bitches, I managed to save up a nice little nest egg, and I'm ready to move on with my life. I want you to come with me"

Khan took a second as her words danced around his mind. Yes she was everything that Khan ever wanted in a woman, she was smart, sexy, body on point, pretty feet, and not afraid to bust that tooly, but could Khan really just leave everything and everyone behind to venture in the depths of the unknown....

"Mama as good as that invitation sounds, I'mma need to sleep on that" replied Khan while running his fingers in her hair.

"Sleep on it? Khan you've been in bed for over a week baby, just don't take too long because one day I may not be here to take care of you."

Reds stood up and walked towards the bathroom.

"Come on Daddy, time to get up and wash ya ass, you smell like yesterday."

Feeling rejuvenated by Reds sponge bath, Khan decided that today was the day to leave the confines of his bullet ridden bedroom. Khan walked by the exercise room and observed Nina and Suga in the midst of a yoga routine. The girls shot Khan a surprised look as Khan reciprocated with a smile, then made his way downstairs. Khan finally, located Khadeja and China in his basement studio experimenting with the audio software as he crept up on them.

"Whatcha'll doing down here?" shouted Khan.

"Damn nigga you scared the shit outta me!" yelled Khadeja.

"I see you finally woke up" said China while standing behind Khan's Sony microphone.

"Yea, Reds put me on point with all the girls dropping from the family."

"Speaking of Reds. I'm surprised she let you go out of her sights" said Khadeja while rolling her eyes.

"She stepped up to the plate when I was in a funk, so don't come at her like that" Khan retorted.

"And I didn't? I saved this family and put my own life on the line in the process" yelled Khadeja while getting in Khan's face.

"I know mama, I just-"

"You just what? You keep putting all these other bitches over me, do you even know how much money was in that safe?" Khadeja spoke as her nostrils flared.

"How much?" asked Khan reluctantly.

"Almost a quarter million" replied Khadeja.

"Damn" said China while removing the headphones.

"Yup, I found a way to cut out all of those ridiculous expenses like the crazy salary you paid you're A.P's, the entire rental of the 8th floor for the cubs hotel, the truck payments for your A.P's, and I started rationing the drugs for our girls with habits. I was about to make you a fuckin' millionaire but you in my face defending another bitch" Khadeja looked at Khan in an attempt to search his soul for the man she fell in love with as she breathed heavily waiting for his response.

"You right....I'm sorry, sometimes when life hits me hard I just freak out and move without thinking things through. You mean so much to me and I apologize for trying to hide in the pills. I just hate being broke and powerless."

"Khan you don't have to just pimp. Your the most requested rapper in the streets. Go get you money baby." smiled Khadeja as she pulled out her phone and dialed a few digits.

"Who are you calling?"

"Shh, I'm still in charge nigga....hello hey schedule Khan for that battle, of course I have his consent. I'm his manager." Khan had a perplexed look on his face as he waited for Khadeja to end her call.

"Two weeks, alright set it up!" said Khadeja as she sat her phone on the desk of the mixing board then smiled at Khan.

"Okay what just happened?" questioned Khan.

"Well Khan baby, we are damn near broke and with only five

girls, there's no way we could live the lifestyle we were accustomed to. So it's time for the male lion to do some hunting. I told Slick to set up the battle of the century…Gangas Khan vs K-Willz"

"Are you serious…that nigga ain't on my level" spat Khan as he quickly dismissed the notion.

"Khan it ain't about skills, it's about Bills! We don't have enough money to pay rent, for food, for drugs, all the things we need to survive." Khadeja explained.

"But K-Willz though?"

"You been outta the loop for a while but K-Willz has been killing shit lately, he's won every battle since you've been gone, even his music is the most requested on the air…he's got the juice….there's something different about his bars. He's like a different rapper now."

"Okay, well if all that is true then how much is he talking?"

"Twenty-five bands to the winner"

"Oh he's a dead man!"

Chapter Forty-Two
LITTLE CHILD, RUNNING WILD

Valita hated what she had become, as Heidi helped her locate a vein on her bruised forearm. The syringe found its mark as Valita slowly injected the heroin into her blood stream. After a few seconds of a burning twinge, her eyes eventually rolled back in ecstasy as Heidi quickly removed the needle to start the process of her own high.

Valita missed her family dearly, but she also missed the euphoric feeling of the drugs introduced to her by Rain and Heidi. Valita stayed home for only one night before the monkey started to call. Several weeks on the run, she had graduated from the occasional sniff to full blown syringes. Valita was ashamed of her lifestyle and never informed Khadeja of her poor decisions. Heidi did her best to hang in there with Khan, but couldn't function under the small rations of dope that Khadeja provided. Heidi loved Khan and didn't want to abandon him during his time of need, but similar to Valita's dilemma, once the monkey whispers your name, there's no escaping the call.

Heidi ran into Valita on Route 40, Valita was so excited to find Heidi as the life of solitude was starting to wear on Valita.

"It's like a ghost town out here" said Heidi as Valita's high faded off.

"Yea, the fucking police been snatching up all of the pimps and working girls. That's why I stay on the move" Valita stated while lighting her crack pipe.

"Oh well more money for us" smiled Heidi as the two girls waited for a trick in their cheap motel room at the El Rich.

Knock Knock

Sounded the door as Heidi's face lit up with the thoughts of more drug money.

"I got it" said Heidi as she opened the door and let in the short white man with the military style buzz cut, enter the room.

"So what can we do for you?" asked Valita as she attempted to grab the man's crotch.

The man walked away from Valita before she could clutch his penis and asked a stupid question.

"So y'all will have sex with me for two hundred dollars?"

"Um yea…that's what we already discussed" yelled Valita.

"What about your friend?" asked the stand-offish trick.

"Duh...what do you think I'm here for, now can we get this show on the road. I got shit to do" spat Heidi while getting on her knees in front of the jittery jawn only to be deflected again.

"Whatever you have to do will have to wait" laughed the trick while revealing a shiny gold badge.

"Oh shit" screamed Valita as several uniformed officers barged in the room and cuffed the young women.

Officer McFarley escorted the girls to his car as Detective Clark watched the entire arrest unfold.

"Y'all can't do me like this...I'm not one of these regular bitches, I'm one of Khan's! I'm part of the Pride! Lemme go!" screamed a stoned Valita as Detective Clark took note of every comment she made.

D.J. laid on his back as Rain and Suitcase made a full course meal out of his dick and balls, while enjoying the comforts of the luxury suite at the Marriot Hotel. When Rain contacted D.J. about a lick that could have him set for a long time, D.J. wasted no time going after Khan once he was released from jail. D.J. was skeptical about dealing with Rain at first, but when she constantly kept complaining about Khan's relationship with Khadeja, it was apparent that Rains jealousy could be used in D.J.'s favor. Rain told D.J. about robbing them right away, to give them more time to stack money before they made a move. Rain even informed D.J. where the girls hid their guns Khadeja issued them, which also sold for a pretty penny on the black market.

D.J. felt no remorse for robbing and harming the only person in his life that actually broke bread with him because he felt he was entitled to the same life as Khan.

"You wanna go to that battle?" asked Rain in between slurps.

"Hell yeah, we can rob whoever wins" the girls laughed as D.J. was as serious as heart attack.

K-Willz sat in the privacy of his home studying the lyrics Crazy Cracker created for his big showdown against Khan.

"Whad up Slick-Talk nation, this ya boy Slick and I'm coming to you live from the always lit, Latrobe Projects with the great K-Willz. K-Willz we are days away from the highly anticipated battle between you and the peoples champ, Gangas Khan." said Slick while K- Willz stepped in front of the camera.

"Yo he ain't no peoples champ, the people don't even know this nigga. I'm the nigga in these streets. I'm the peoples champ. Khan couldn't even beat Crazy Cracker bum ass, but when I jump back on the scene to finish my battle with that white boy, he all of a sudden get ghost. So I'm willing to bet Khan scared ass do the same thing." K-Willz had the entire projects behind him trying to steal some camera time as D.J. and a few ex-cubs stood in the background looking like royalty.

"I see you got damn near the whole city out here to support you, no doubt this will be the battle of battles. I got people coming from all over to attend this event."

"And they will get their money's worth as long as Khan shows up." interrupted K-Willz while blowing weed smoke into the camera.

"Well y'all heard it, this will be three rounds for a cash prize unheard of on Slick-Talk, we talking a pot worth twenty five thousand dollars! I hope to see all of you there at the next Slick-Talk!"

"Damn this shit is fire" said K-Willz while smiling at the impressive content before his eyes.

What amazed K-Willz the most was the fact that Crazy

Cracker was able to compose bars of this magnitude while being starved to death, tied up in a basement.

Beep, Beep

K-Willz cell phone alerted him to an incoming text message from O.G. Doc. "Fuck these niggas want now?" grumbled K-Willz while reading the text.

"More dope! I just gave these niggas four grams. I'm not giving these niggas shit else, I got what I want from that cracker. That bitch can starve for all I care" shouted K-Willz while ignoring Doc's request and tossing his phone on the floor.

"I got bars for this nigga Khan, but a man in my position can't afford to take chances. I think I might need a little insurance also." K-Willz schemed while thinking of a plan B just in case his bars weren't enough.

K-Willz thought long and hard before it finally hit him.

"I got it….gorilla tactics!"

Chapter Forty-Three
THE FINAL SHOWDOWN

Reds lightly kissed Khan on the lips before quietly tip-toeing out of the bedroom. Before exiting the room completely, she paused and took one final look at Khan as he snored as loud as a grizzly bear. A smile formed on her face as she briefly reminisced about all the good times she shared with Khan. Reds didn't want to leave, but she was haunted by many demons from her past which she knew would inevitably come crashing down on Khan and the rest of the Pride. It hurt her soul to leave a man that she loved so much, but in her heart she knew the shit was about to hit the fan.

"I'mma miss you Daddy" whispered Reds while leaving her emotions behind and walking out of Khan's life forever.

Moments later, Khan sensed something was wrong as he briskly awakened from his sleep. He surveyed the bedroom and did a head count of all his bitches.

"Khadeja…China….Reds…where's Reds?" said Khan as he jumped out of the bed.

He noticed Reds dresser drawer was opened and emptied out as he ran towards the window just in time to see Reds loading her book bag into the backseat of an old station wagon. Khan quickly flung open the window.

"Red's, what da fuck yo?" Khan shouted, not caring that it was 3:00am and his neighbors were sleeping.

"Where are you going mama?" questioned Khan with a look of confusion.

Reds loaded her bag in the back seat then closed the door. Before opening the front passenger side door, she turned around and locked eyes with Khan.

"I'm sorry Khan!" Reds yelled with misty eyes.

"You sorry, come on mama, don't do me like this" pleaded Khan.

"Look, for what it's worth, I really do love you. But shits about to get real and …..and…just tell the girls I'm sorry. Y'all were the only true family I ever had but…I'm sorry…I love you Khan!" Reds had tears dripping down her face as she blew Khan a kiss then jumped inside of the station wagon.

Khan attempted to question her for further explanation but the screeching tires left Khan talking to himself. Khadeja watched as Khan walked back to bed with a stoic expression on his face. All of the other girls were wide awake along with the rest of the neighborhood as Khan sparked an old half blunt, then silently laid in bed and stared at the ceiling. By now all of the girls knew when Khan had "that look", it was best not to disturb him. Everyone laid in silence in an attempt to get some last minute sleep because they were only hours away from one of the biggest showdowns of their lives.

Power Plant live was one of the largest venues in Baltimore. Located in the downtown region of the city. Its platform showcased some of the biggest artist's in the world. The large outdoor pavilion rested upon a huge stage which night clubs and numerous bars surrounded. A small army of security guards manned the long gates of the fenced-in venue as thousands of spectators and patrons of the many hangouts and eateries, roamed the festive grounds.

Khan and his Pride sat behind the tinted windows of the Hellcat while partaking in their usual pregame smoke session in the parking lot. As Khadeja passed the blunt to the girls in the back seat, she looked over at Khan and saw the same blank expression from earlier. Everyone was well aware that Khan was still in a somber mood, and Khadeja had reached her boiling point.

"Khan" yelled Khadeja from the passenger seat.

"Sup" Khan replied nonchalantly without looking at her.

"Look at me nigga!" Khadeja commanded as this finally caught Khan's attention, along with everyone else's in the car.

"Do you realize what's going on right now? Do you know where we are? We parked outside the biggest venue in the city and there are thousands of people from all over the country here to see your black-ass, and your mourning ova a bitch that left ya dumbass while you was sleeping." Khadeja was hot.

"She was good peoples" Khan responded while accepting the blunt from China then stared straight ahead.

"Of course you think she good peoples, she kept ya pockets full and ya nuts empty. You keep letting these bitches get in the way of your priorities."

"And what are my priorities?" asked Khan while facing Khadeja.

"Me nigga!" screamed Khadeja while balling her fist in frustration.

"You…."

"Yes me, me, China, Nina and Suga. The bitches that's been loyal since day one, the girls that put up with all of ya shit and never complained."

"You complain everyday" said Khan with a grin.

"Only when you keep letting these dirty ass white bitches get in ya head, no offense Nina."

"None taken!" yelled Nina in her Russian accent from the back seat.

"Mama, believe it or not, I get emotionally attached to all of you. I don't really have a lot of people in my corner. My family deals with me from time to time but I really can't trust nobody at all. I consider y'all my real family, so I'm sorry if I get a little sad when one of y'all leave me cause y'all all I got."

"Daddy...I was always taught, if they ain't there, they don't care. We gotcha back and I ain't going nowhere

Daddy" said Suga while rubbing Khan's shoulders.

"Thank you baby doll" said Khan while smiling at Suga's reflection through the rearview mirror.

"Me neither!" yelled Nina.

"I'm witchu for life" China assured.

"I appreciate that" Khan said while directing his attention towards Khadeja.

"What?" said Khadeja while giving Khan a puzzled look?

"Oh yea?" questioned Khan with a smirk.

"Fine, you know I'm not going nowhere either...I don't have to say it, its implied." smiled Khadeja.

"I love you. I love you all...now let's go get this money"

After a few more blunts, the Pride's spirits all seemed to be lifted as the team made their way through the parking lot into the entrance of Power Plant Live. Khan and his entourage of bad bitches looked like movie stars as they arrived on the scene. The girls wore matching all black Donna Karen pants suits with a set of bright pink Jimmy

Choo open toe pumps while Khan sported a black Armani blazer and black Armani slacks. He took slow confident steps in his Stacey Adams shoes as everyone in the Pride rocked their signature dark Ray-Ban shades.

"Why you got us all wearing suits and shit?" questioned Khadeja.

"Because baby...we here to handle business" smiled Khan as he took in the scenery.

"Damn this is a lot of people" said Khan as he and the Pride made their way through the herd of viewers and spectators.

"Slick brought the whole city out for this one" yelled Khadeja over the music as she noticed most of Baltimore's elite mingling with fans and admirers.

Celebrities, athletes, artists and other famous fans of Battle rap, paid their respects at the star studded event, as Khan stood in disbelief.

"Yo there go Freeway!" Khan shouted, completely star struck by the famous Philly rapper.

"That is him…Hey Freeway, over here!" screamed Nina as Khan tried to calm her down.

"Chill Russia, we can't be dick riding on these niggas, we gotta pretend like we used to this shit" said Khan while pulling on Nina's arm.

Nina nodded like she understood, but when Khan released her arm she went bat shit crazy again.

"Fuck that, Freeway!" Nina yelled until Freeway and his entourage heard the young Russian and started walking towards Khan and the Pride.

Khan felt embarrassed as Nina made his team look like a

bunch of groupies, but to his surprise, Freeway approached Khan and extended his hand.

"Khan, whats good ack?" said Freeway with a huge smile.

"Assalamu Salam, I'mma big fan"

"You a fan of mine?" asked Khan as he was stunned by Freeways confession.

"No doubt, you out here killing it right now and I can't wait to see what you do to that nigga K-Willz."

"Wow...I'm speechless"

"That's a first!" spat Nina as Khan looked at her and smiled.

"I appreciate the love Free" Khan dapped up Freeway then navigated through the sea of people in search of Slick.

"So you really think you can beat that nigga Khan?" questioned Brent while K-Willz and his team sat in the V.I.P. section popping bottles and talking shit.

"Do I think? Nigga I know" laughed K-Willz as he casually dismissed two Asian girls after a quick lap dance.

"Hows that?" replied Brent while pouring himself a glass of Remy.

"Well two reasons, for one my bars are the shit, and two, I'm going to make him an offer he can't refuse" Brent shook his head anticipating that his partner was up to his old tricks again, as K-Willz smiled and shot Brent a wink.

"Hey excuse me can I get a picture witchu real quick?" asked the young light skinned man in glasses.

"Yea no problem Pimp" replied Khan as he posed for yet another series of flash photography.

"Hey Deja-vu, can I get a couple flicks witchu too!"

"Sure" smiled Khadeja as she and Khan welcomed the new found fame.

"Thank y'all so much, I'm about to fuck Instagram up with these" smiled the fan as he skipped away.

Khan had no idea his popularity had reached such heights. He was so focused on the streets that it never dawned on him that he could become a millionaire without the risk of a hefty prison sentence.

Khan enjoyed the look on his girl's faces as they were treated like celebrities. Even the girls that didn't rap were asked to take pictures by fans of not just Khan and Khadeja, but fans of the Pride and what it stood for. Khan's bladder felt as if it were getting ready to explode from the excitement so he excused himself in search of the restroom.

"Hey I gotta drain the main vein, don't go nowhere I will be right back"

"Okay" said Khadeja while twerking on camera for another fan's Instagram.

Khan finally located a restroom that didn't have a long line to wait in. He darted in the empty stall and took one of the longest pisses of his life.

"All praises due!" said Khan as he exited the stall from relieving himself.

As Khan started washing his hands, he heard the restroom door open and suddenly over twenty niggas in red surrounded him.

"Khan we gotta stop meeting like this" said K-Willz as he stepped into Khan's space.

"Ain't that the truth" replied a nervous Khan.

"Look man, I ain't on no shit right now, I'm here because I

wanna make you an offer" K- Willz said with a wide grin.

"An offer?" questioned Khan while scanning every face around him.

"Yup, a very simple one. Eventually I'mma get tired of all this cat and mouse shit. So one of us is gonna have to go."

"So what is you sayin' dug?" asked Khan now becoming aggravated.

"What I'm saying is nigga, if we beefin', you gonna die… flatout!"

"Ain't nobody scared to die nigga!" Khan retorted with his fist balled.

"I figured that much, but you would be crushed if I went after them little smuts you be with, mainly Khadeja." Khan took a step closer to K-Willz after mentioning her name.

"Chill, there's a way out" said K-Willz.

"You threaten my family, then talk about a way out, nigga fuck outta my face" Khan raged.

"Do as I say and won't no harm come to them bitches, and you know I got the man power to hunt y'all down where ever y'all go"

"And what is it that you want" said Khan while trying to calm down.

"Lose, I want you to throw the battle."

"What nigga? I need this, I need the money and opportunity"

"Well whats more important? Fame and Fortune, or ya lil bitches"

Khan was fucked up mentally and had no idea how to respond. His one shot at giving him and his girls a life they never imagined was about to be over before it even started. He also knew that K-Willz and his crew would end up smoking them before he had the chance to get back to his car. K-Willz had too many soldiers for Khan to go all Rambo on, so he swallowed his pride and put their safety first.

"Yo you a foul nigga, but if you promise to leave my folks alone, I will throw the battle" said Khan while staring at the bathroom floor.

"I knew you would see it my way, and if ya pockets hurting that bad, I could always use a nigga to wash my car" K-Willz laughed as he and his crew exited the rest room leaving Khan feeling completely helpless.

"Move nigga" said Khadeja as she pushed pass one of K-Willz's goons and entered the restroom along with the rest of The Pride on her heels.

"Khan is everything okay?" asked Khadeja while observing the distress on Khan's face.

"Oh yea, we good" lied Khan while attempting to change his expression.

"What was all that about?" asked China

"Oh nothing, he just wanted to make some side bets before the battle" the lied flowed with ease but Khadeja knew something was up.

"I call bullshit, but as long as your safe, let's just get back outside. It's almost showtime" said Khadeja.

"A'ight lemme get myself together and I'll be out in a sec"

The girls reluctantly did as they were told as Khan stared in the mirror contemplating his next move.

"Damn, all I wanna do is smile and a nigga won't even let me have that. Fuck it doe, it is what it is" said Khan while splashing water on his face then joining his girls outside the restroom.

"Remember this battle is three rounds for two minutes a piece. If any M.C. chokes, it's an automatic loss of round. This battle is for twenty-five thousand dollars! And Khan since you're the challenger, you go first."

After Slick made his final announcements he backed away to give Khan, center stage. Khan had a million thoughts running through his mind. To say he was nervous was a complete understatement. This was the largest crowd Khan had ever witnessed, but the lights were so bright that he couldn't see their faces, only their silhouettes. Khan's game plan was to simply choke, or intentionally freeze up twice, to give K-Willz the automatic win.

"Hey yo...." Said Khan as he got his thoughts together while staring at a smirking K-Willz.

K-Willz stood about eight feet away from Khan on the crowded stage. Countless goons stood behind K-Willz as he taunted Khan with a condescending smile. Khan was backed by his Pride as he prepared to give the most shameful performance of his life.

"I say...Recognize my greatness, y'all in da presence of a real nigga/ With a criminal record so fucked up, I couldn't get a job as a drug dealer/ Catch me in purple city, with two birds in purple minks/ In da booth I'm black Panther, cuz I get my power off herbs and purple drink/ Ya bars, put niggas to sleep....ain't no need for da Xanax/ 'cause pussies like you I keep bloody, ain't no need for da tampex/"

Khan went lite with his first set of bars, but the audience was still loving his material as K-Willz started to get agitated.

"*Damn, I guess it's time to fumble*" thought Khan as he continued to rock the stage.

"*But forreal my nigga, you ain't fucking with me/ Because I got.....*"

Khan stumbled.

"*I say because I got a....*"

Again he stumbled.

"Come on Khan" yelled Khadeja.

"*Because I got....*"

Khan really sold the intentional choke as the crowd echoed gasps of shock.

"Fuck!" yelled Khan as Slick approached him holding his hand out signaling him to stop.

"Well y'all know the rules, if you choke it's over, and I must say I would've never saw that coming. Okay K-Willz, if you finish ya round, you up one nothing." said Slick as he returned to the background.

K-Willz couldn't believe that Khan actually choked on

purpose.

"Kill dat nigga K-Willz" yelled one of his goons as K-Willz smiled then walked up on Khan.

"If niggas wanna bet something, then I'm walkin' out with two checks/ My connect love me cause my order fill up like two jets/ Stepping to me is a death sentence, like you claiming two sects/ 'Cause I ain't no referee, but I will put you outta da game with two techs/ We on two different levels, you don't belong on this stage/ I got shooters that'll get Khan-aird like Nicholas Cage/ This ain't no battle nigga, this is a slaughter house/ And when I'm done with you, its big dick in ya daughter mouth/ Come on down Latrobe, I'mma show you what I'm all about/ I'm calling you out, but don't come unless you bringing a live medic/ Because ya sweet ass will get mo' shots than a diabetic/ It's Willz nigga!"

K-Willz winked at Khan as the crowd chanted his name after that stellar performance. Khan felt like shit as he prepared himself to take another dive.

"Khan are you okay?" asked Khadeja while noticing the lack of confidence in Khan.

"Yea, I'm straight…I dunno what came over me. It won't happen again" assured Khan.

"It better not because K-Willz is in rare form. Another round like that and this shit won't make it to round three" cautioned Khadeja.

"I got this….okay!" said Khan in frustration.

"Alright" said Khadeja with her hands in the air, as she retreated to the background with the rest of the girls.

"What's wrong with Khan?" asked Suga.

"I dunno but somethings up, those weren't even the bars he was suppose to rap in the first round. It's like he's changing up his shit" said a confused Khadeja.

"It looked like he choked on purpose" said China.

"What! Fuck no, Khan know we need that money" Khadeja defended.

"Well let's hope not" replied China.

"I can't believe I have to do this shit again" thought Khan as he heard faint chants of encouragement. Khan faked a smile and waved to the audience before getting the "Okay" from Slick to start the next round.

"Yo!" Khan swallowed a large lump in his throat then wiped his sweaty forehead with the back of his hand.

"When my Pimp hand itchin', I need to slap these hoes/

Armani suits got me feeling like a black Gwedo/ I keep that metal on my mind like I'm Magneto/ And ya bitch get wild when I record her, I call her Nat-Geo/

Khan sat the stage on fire as he gave his fans bar after bar but Khadeja could see Khan's demeanor change midway through the round as Khan clenched his teeth while he prepared to deliver the blow that would end his career. K-Willz smiled in anticipation because he also noticed the change of Khan's facial expression.

"*Hurry up nigga so I can win this shit*" K-Willz thought to himself as he impatiently awaited his inevitable victory.

"*I gotchu in my cross-hairs, and I can't wait to pull it/ So when I get....*"

Khan stuttered.

"*So when I get the..../*

He stuttered again as Khadeja lost her shit.

"Say the fucking bar Khan!" screamed Khadeja.

"See what I'm saying" said China while rolling her eyes.

Khan made one last attempt at spitting the bar before dropping his head in defeat and walking back towards his corner of the stage.

"Wow" was all that Slick could muster as he simply shook his head in disappointment then pointed towards K-Willz to finish Khan off.

"I love it when a plans comes together" said K-Willz to Brent as K-Willz immediately went off on a lyrical frenzy making this battle seem as if this was a one sided fight.

As Khan stood in silence, he felt Khadeja burning a hole in the side of his face but he was too ashamed to look at her.

"So you just gonna go out like a bitch huh?" said an irate Khadeja.

"Shit happens" said Khan while wishing this humiliating moment would be over and done with.

"I'm not stupid, we all knew you threw this shit on purpose, but what we don't know is why? Why Khan?" questioned Khadeja with wide eyes that projected anger with a mix of sadness.

"You don't know what your talking about" said Khan in a dismissive tone while pinching the bridge of his nose in frustration.

China watched as Khan and Khadeja went back and forth while she and the other girls stood in silence. China couldn't imagine going back to a life of street walking after all the publicity she received from fans of the Pride. She wanted something better, something meaningful. She too wanted to shine like the star she was born to be, but in order to make that happen, she needed Khan to pave the way.

"Hey Suga....I'm about to try something, just follow my lead" said China as her brain suddenly went for the Hail Mary play.

"Little nigga just sit back, dontchu flinch, move or blink/ Or I ain't taking nothing but head shots....like that bitch pussy stank/"

Spat K-Willz as he now had the entire world in the palm of his hand.

As K-Willz started to give Khan the punchline to finally put him out of his misery, he noticed one of Khan's girls staring at him very seductively.

"She must be ready to jump ship with a real nigga" thought K-Willz as he prepared to deliver the set up to his finishing haymaker. China stared at K-Willz intently with a solid piercing glare. China's half Asian mother passed down a set of eyes that were so breath taking, it made it hard for any man to resist. China was easily one of Khan's most attractive girls, with her exotic look, she slightly resembled Zoey from the TV show Black-ish. Once China realized she had K-Willz's attention, she turned it up a notch by caressing her breast through the thin material of the designer blazer.

"Da fuck is she doing?" thought K-Willz as it seemed as if he was the only person to notice the sexual charades going on behind

Khan's back. She slipped her hand down south and dipped a finger into her honey pot. Completely in a trance, China had K-Willz right where she wanted him as she took her hand from her pants and inserted her wet finger into the awaiting mouth of Suga. Suga slowly sucked on China's finger as K-Willz watched in amazement. The two women fondled each other as Suga licked every trace of China's juices off her finger. K-Willz was so caught up in the moment, he never noticed Slick approach him until Slick placed a hand on his shoulder which brought him back from La-La Land.

"K-Willz? You good bruh?" questioned Slick while standing face to face with a confused K-Willz.

"Huh, yea….I'm ready to rap now" said K-Willz completely lost in the sauce.

"Nigga you was rapping then you stopped which means you choked so we going into the third round."

"What!" screamed K-Willz now fully aware of what happened.

"Well, if you would have finished your round, you would've won and the third round wouldn't be necessary, but it's the first person to win two rounds, so you gotta win the third round to win it all, but if Khan wins the third y'all going into overtime" explained Slick to K- Willz and the audience.

"Them bitches pulled a fast on me" grumbled K-Willz as he

mean mugged a smiling China, then went back to his corner of the stage.

"That was smart thinking" said Suga as she and China gave each other high fives.

Khan couldn't believe that K-Willz choked. He was livid that he had to go through this disgraceful act again as China approached him.

"I pegged you for a lot of things, but never a liar or quitter. Whatever's got you tripping, you need to fix it. I don't wanna walk the streets no more. I got with you because you promised me change, and right now you have the opportunity to make that happen. When all them people was taking my pictures, I felt like I was special."

"You are special princess" assured Khan.

"Not if you lose, if you lose I ain't shit, we ain't shit but hoes and a has been rapper." Khan felt a tear slowly escape his closed eyes as he took a deep breath.

"Listen girls, K-Willz said if I don't take a dive, he's going to come for y'all. And I'd rather lose this battle than my family." Khan confessed as all the girls gathered around a misty eyed Khan.

"Is you forreal!" shouted Khadeja.

"We are all big girls who can handle ourselves."

"She's right, fuck that bitch" co-signed Nina.

"I can't risk it" said Khan while rubbing his 5 o'clock shadow.

"Khan we risk our lives every day, this is nothing new, but I will say this. If you intentionally lose this round, you will lose me in the process" countered China.

"That goes for all of us" announced Suga.

"So y'all just want me to go out there and say, fuck it" asked Khan.

"Our motto is Fuck It!" yelled Nina as everyone laughed.

"Okay, I'm sorry girls. It's time to get back to business."

As Khan returned to the center of the stage, K-Willz could sense the change in Khan's aura.

"Last round nigga, then you can get da fuck out my city." said K-Willz in a low tone.

"Actually theres been a change in plans" smiled Khan.

"What! Nigga don't play with me, because you already know the outcome if you try any funny business" threatened K-Willz.

"I'mma get this money, then I'mma handle you" Khan

retorted.

"Say no more" uttered K-Willz as Slick announced the start of the third round.

"Boo!" chanted the crowd as Khan took center stage.

Khan was determined to win back his fan base, even if it cost him his life. Khan allowed his arms to hang loose as he shook out the jitters then morphed back into someone the world hadn't seen in a long time….Gangas Khan.

"Yo, when you threaten my Pride, you betta off committing suicide/ Because if that four-four don't end ya, it'll leave you breathing through a tube like ya scuba dive/ Nigga I'm do or die, with no regrets or remorse/ I got a shotty they call home wrecker, cuz it'll get ya head and body divorced/ Big pimpin's back my nigga, but I don't do the Gators/ Black, White, Yellow, I got bitches in all different flavors/ So why stress ova a hoe, nigga I get handed groupies/ I got a bitch that'll suck my dick for as long as the Titanic movie/ I got a mean red bone and the streets say she a fan favorite/ I even got a bitch from the Middle East getting that sand paper/ How you been breaking law for so long and ain't neva been knocked, who does that?/ Word on the street is, you been snitchin' since a baby, you little rugrat/ I see that look up in ya eyes, like you really 'bout to go berserk/ Cuz my bars so heavy, I need a spotter just to kick a verse/ Hey, Khadeja, you my baby…that's one honorable bitch/ And if you

harm a hair on her head, I'll have you floating in a bag like a carnival fish/ I don't need niggas to put in work for me, I like to do it all on my own. So when that street sweeper hit ya whip, ya window shield will ressemble a clumsy bitch I-Phone/

"Ya Bitch!" screamed Khan as K-Willz stood infuriated by the reaction Khan received from the roaring crowd.

"That's the Khan I came to see!" shouted someone from the audience as Khan stood stoned faced while awaiting for K-Willz to rap. K-Willz stared at Khan with pure hatred in his eyes but Khan seemed unaffected by his silent threat.

"Let's go Willz" shouted Slick as the crowd started to quiet down so they could hear K- Willz's response.

"Damn" said K-Willz to himself as he shook his head in frustration.

The audience, along with K-Willz's goons and the celebrity guest judges on stage, all anxiously pondered his rebuttal as K-Willz took his time walking towards Khan. Not only did K-Willz not have a third round, he damn sure didn't have an over-time round to go with Khan. He was so confident that his plan would work, the thought of the battle making it past the second round never crossed his mind. K-Willz decided to go for his usual plan B, which was cause a scene so no one would be crowned the winner, similar to how he handled the Crazy Cracker battle. While walking towards Khan, K-Willz noticed an empty beer bottle resting on top of a stage speaker. Freeway, one of the guest judges on stage, peeked the whole scene and grabbed the bottle before K-Willz had the chance.

"Not tonight bull" said Freeway as he passed the bottle to one of his humongous body guards.

"Man fuck y'all!" shouted K-Willz as he stomped off stage with his confused group of flunkies following his lead.

"Hey Khan! Kiss them bitches goodbye!" threatened K-Willz as he made his way through the crowd.

Khan smiled as he allowed the cheers from the audience to distract him from the potential consequences of his actions. Slick walked towards center stage with a manila envelope in his hands and addressed the audience.

"Ladies and Gentleman, the winner by submission and new Slick-Talk champion of the world…Gangas Khan!"

The noise from the venue could be heard from miles away as Slick presented Khan with the prize money and gave him dap. Freeway gave Khan a nod while, him and his bodyguards made their way off stage, leaving Khan and his Pride to have their moment in the spot light.

"My nigga!" yelled Khadeja as the other girls surrounded

Khan with huge smiles.

"Thank you Khan" said China then hugged Khan tightly.

"No, thank you, I couldn't have done it without you" Khan replied.

"Daddy we da shit!" sang Suga as she wrapped her arms around Khan's waist.

"I knew you wouldn't let us down!" yelled Nina as she grabbed Khan's face and planted a huge sloppy wet kiss on Khan's lips.

"Ahh you dirty bitch!" yelled Khan as he chased Nina around the stage.

Chapter Forty-Four
DOUBLE ENTENDRE

Once Khan secured the bag, he and the Pride immediately shook ass to the parking lot while ignoring countless people attempting to flag him down and get his attention.

"Come on y'all, let's hurry up before-" Khan's words trailed off once he spotted K-Willz and his group of gang bangers surrounding his car. Khan instinctively reached to his waist but remembered he had to leave his piece in the car due to heavy security at the gate.

"Damn" cursed Khan as he paused, then huddled up with the girls.

"Look, shit might get a lil nasty, so if y'all wanna try and make a run for it, I'll stall these niggas" said Khan with concern.

"Khan, just because we got pussies don't mean we bitches!" spat Khadeja while preparing to go out swinging with her man.

"Respect" said Khan as the team broke their huddle and proceeded to slowly walk towards a smiling K-Willz and his team of fuck boys.

The Pride approached K-Willz and stood about ten feet away before K-Willz finally spoke.

"I'mma make this quick, which one of these bitches you want to die first?" asked K- Willz while playing "eeny, meeny, miny, moe" with his pistol pointing towards the girls.

"Which bitch do I want to die first huh?"

"How about you?" Khan smirked.

"Bars!" laughed Khadeja as the other girls released a slight chuckle.

"So you still on joke time!" raved K-Willz while walking up to Khan, inches from his face.

"Put the gun down and let's see what's up" challenged Khan.

"Here we go with this shit again" replied K-Willz, clearly avoiding the confrontation of The Fist-ta Cuffs.

"Nah nigga we putting an end to this shit right now" said K-Willz as he pointed his gun at Khan's forehead.

Khan was about to take his chances and charge K-

Willz until someone called Khan's name which caused everyone to look in the direction of the voice.

"Khan!" he yelled again.

Once the figure emerged from the distant visibility, with the help of the parking lot street lamps, Khan could now make out the identity of the welcomed intruder.

"Lil Bob!" shouted Khan as he smiled at the sight of his old cell buddy.

"What da fucks going on out here?"

"You good Khan?" asked lil Bob.

"Mind ya business bruh" shouted K-Willz while focusing his attention back to Khan.

"Oh you got lil Bob fucked up! That's my brova, so that's definitely my business nigga!" retorted lil Bob as he brandished a handgun of his own.

"Nigga please" smirked K-Willz as a few of his goons drew their weapons on lil Bob.

"You gonna need more than that for us, stupid nigga" said K-Willz.

"Aye whad' up Joe!" said another voice from behind lil Bob.

"I know that ain't my nigga Kyree" said Khan as he noticed

several more people approaching the scene.

"Yurrrp!" shouted Swine as he, Yella and Scrap all joined the gathering.

Khan smiled even harder once he saw his father Khalil slowly strutting towards the parking lot with a massive .44 Bulldog.

"Y'all nigga's is still out manned and out gunned" yelled K-Willz while still acting cocky because of his advantage.

"I guess you can't rap or count nigga" bellowed Big Mammoth as he, 9 Milly, Big Pam and a small army of their Empire niggas appeared out of nowhere.

"Oh, it's a party now" laughed Khan as K-Willz was now out numbered. His eyes grew wide with fear as he started to back pedal towards his vehicle.

"Where you going bruh? I thought we had some business to handle?" teased Khan as K- Willz almost tripped over his goons trying to jump back in his truck.

Swine started to blast at K-Willz before Khan stopped him.

"Chill man, it's too much attention out here right now. I'mma handle him on my own" said Khan while scanning all of the faces that showed up to support him.

"Damn, where all y'all niggas come from?"

"We was at the show, nigga's kept calling ya name but once you got the money, yo ass was gone" laughed lil Bob.

"Yea Joe, me and Big Mam got out the same time, ya name was all they was talking about back in da joint" said Kyree as he gave Khan dap.

"Yella, Swine, Pops" Khan greeted.

"You know shawty had the baby, I honestly ain't think she was gonna let me out tonight" laughed Yella as he gave Khan a hug.

"Big Mam, I didn't think you cared" said Khan while giving his former opponent a half hug.

"Well as the saying goes, the enemy of my enemy is my friend."

"Whats that…art of war?" asked Khan.

"Art of War, Bruce Lee, Dr. Phil hell, I dunno" laughed Big Mammoth as members of the Empire showed Khan love.

"You did ya thing on stage son"

"Thank you Pops, I'm glad you got to see me"

"I wouldn't miss it for the world, now I think you should get them pretty girls and that money back home safe."

"Absolutely…. Give me about an hour y'all and let's turn up at the Marriott for the after party!" said Khan as he and his Pride went home to stash his winnings.

"Every day I'm with my team" everyone sang along to the "Creek Boyz" new hit single as Khan pulled up on his street. Khan parked in the front of his home and stuffed the manila envelope of cash in his blazer pocket.

"Y'all hold tight, I'mma stash this cash then we headed straight to the telly" said Khan as he stepped out of the Hell Cat.

"I'm coming in too, I gotta pee" said Suga as she also emerged from the car.

The second Khan closed his car door, he heard the all too familiar sound of a gun click behind his head.

"Just gimme da bread and don't do nothing stupid" demanded D.J. as he held the pistol to Khan's dome.

"Yo, if I get more gun pointed at me.." said Khan.

"Then what nigga!" shouted D.J. as he threatened to pull the trigger at any given moment.

"Here yo" said Khan as he reluctantly gave D.J. the envelope.

"Thank you, but you still got to go fam" said D.J. but right before he pulled the trigger, Suga jumped in-between Khan and the gun.

BOOM

Khan was surprised he was still alive, as he patted his body for proof. Suddenly all the girls from the car started screaming as Khan turned around to see Suga laid out on the ground with a bullet hole in her chest.

"Damn, No. No.No. Suga!" yelled Khan as his eyes turned red with rage.

Khan gave no fucks that D.J. still held him at gun point, Khan was out for blood. Before Khan could make a move, he was interrupted by a group of gang members that he had been trying to avoid all of his life.

"Freeze! Baltimore City Police!"

Instantly the entire block was covered with unmarked cars and patrol officers.

"Drop the gun! And get on the ground!"

D.J. complied because he knew they wouldn't hesitate to blow his head off. Khadeja cried silently as they hauled D.J. and her future husband to the precinct for fear that she would never have the life she imagined.

"You recognize this girl?" asked detective Clark while holding up a picture of Valita.

"Nope" lied Khan as he sat handcuffed to a chair in the interrogation room.

"Are you sure because she sure knows a lot about you."

"A lot of bitches know about me, maybe even yours" Khan smiled.

"Funny, but we'll see how much your smiling when the state gives you a life sentence for trafficking a minor." Clark returned the smile.

"That bitch said she was nineteen" Khan said to himself while still trying to remain cool.

"You are here because I have a reason to believe that you're the head of a very large human trafficking operation."

"And why would you believe such a thing?" Khan replied

slightly appalled.

"Larson, don't get cute with me, we've been on you since day one, you were sleeping with the enemy" said Clark while flipping through a file.

"*An informant!*" thought Khan while trying to catch a glimpse of the names on the file. It seemed as if the detective read his mind as he purposely exposed the document with the informant's government name to Khan.

"Mallory….O'Rilley.. That's some type of Irish last name or something, but I don't know no damn red-head Irish people-" It finally hit Khan.

"Reds! That fucking bitch, that's what she meant by, shits about to get real" Khan surmised while becoming visibly angry.

"I'm guessing you figured it out, we were at your house before you arrived, the only reason we didn't intervene sooner was because we were hoping that other guy would shoot you and save us some paperwork. But when he shot and killed the female instead, we had to take action."

"She really dead?" Khan asked still in disbelief that Suga was gone.

"Yup, that bitch is dead as a door knob. No more cock

swallowing for her" laughed Clark as Khan, fought hard to keep his composure.

"Our informant apparently had a sweet spot for you, she asked if we could wait until after your little hip-hop thingy before we detained you."

"Where's my money?" asked Khan.

"What money? I know you not talking about the twenty-five thousand we recovered for the botched robbery. As far as I'm concerned, that's hoe-money, and it will be held for evidence." Clark smiled even harder.

"Fuck! I need my lawyer!" yelled Khan as he was brought to a large bullpen which a dozen or so inmates occupied.

As Khan waited in line for the phone, he thought his eyes were playing tricks on him.

"I know that ain't D.J. on the phone" said Khan as he slowly rooted the other inmates, he placed his index finger to his lips to indicate for them to be quiet as he approached D.J. from behind.

D.J. was so caught up in his phone call that he never saw it coming. Once in range, Khan swiftly stiff armed D.J.'s head into the hard concrete wall and D.J.'s body dropped to the ground immediately. Khan relentlessly stomped on D.J's head, sending blood, saliva and teeth scattering throughout the bullpen until a team of officers rushed in and dragged a maniacal, laughing Khan to an isolated cell. The medical team had yet to arrive as D.J. laid sprawled out on the floor, motionless in a pile of his own blood as several inmates tried to avoid getting their sneakers dirty by stepping over the body in order to use the telephone.

"Where da fuck Brent at with my food?" whined K-Willz as he impatiently paced back and forth through his living room.

K-Willz felt too embarrassed to hang out with the rest of his team, so he decided to chill at his apartment with Brent and call a few strippers over later on, in the evening.

"How long does it take to grab a chicken box from across the street?" K-Willz was about to call Brent until he heard a knock on the door.

"Finally" spat K-Willz as he walked towards the door and observed Brent's face through the bubbled lens of the peephole. The moment K-Willz opened the door he was met by a cluster of buck shots to his knees causing him to stumble backwards and fall on his butt.

BOOM

Sound the Mossberg Pump as Crazy Cracker entered the living room, carrying Brent's severed head in his other hand.

"What! I thought…" stuttered K-Willz while scooting backwards away from the madman. Crazy Cracker had a deranged look on his face as he watched K-Willz face the Grim Reaper like a pitiful bitch.

"Why did you kill Brent?" K-Willz managed to say.

"Because he has no loyalty. A few days ago, I guess he followed you to that piss hole you had me tied up in. He felt sorry and released me. He told those crackheads you had babysitting me to keep quiet in exchange for a couple bucks. He asked me to skip town so you wouldn't find out about his treachery. I lied of course and stalked him until I found out where you lived, and once I finally caught you without all your goons, I had to take advantage of the opportunity. Brent wasn't loyal, so his life has no meaning. Now it's time for the real show to begin." Crazy Cracker extended the shotgun inches from K-Willz's face as he slightly caressed hair trigger of the pistol grip.

"I'm sorry man, look! I got money" pleaded K-Willz.

"Money, I need much more than that" replied Crazy Cracker.

"What do you want? I'll do anything" K-Willz was going for broke, he knew his life was over.

"Anything huh?" said Crazy Cracker while toying with his

prey.

"Yes man, anything" cried K-Willz as blood poured from his leg like red kool-aide.

"Okay, open your mouth" instructed Crazy Cracker.

"What?" questioned K-Willz.

"Open ya mouth, nice and wide."

"Come on man" pleaded K-Willz.

"Open ya mouth now!" screamed Crazy Cracker as K-Willz closed his eyes and braced for one of the most emasculating moments in his life.

"I'mma just put the tip in" smiled Crazy Cracker as he gently placed the tip of the shotgun in K-Willz's mouth.

"Put some more in ya mouth, I know you can swallow more than that" coached Crazy Cracker as K-Willz relaxed his throat to allow more of the gun to enter his mouth.

"That's a good girl, now suck this shit" screamed Crazy Cracker.

K-Willz started bobbing on the barrel of the gun as Crazy Cracker eased his hands in his pants and fondled his growing erection.

"Yea just like that bitch! Faster!" K-Willz picked up the pace as Crazy Cracker felt himself about to bust a nut.

"Keep going! Faster!" K-Willz eyes started to tear up as Crazy Cracker shoved more of the barrel down his throat while simultaneously jerking his stiff dick at a frantic pace.

"Keep going! Keep going! Look at me bitch while you suck it!" K-Willz complied as he finally noticed Crazy Cracker masternbating to his tourment.

"Almost! Almost! Alm-"

BOOM

The shotgun along with Crazy Cracker exploded sending fragments of K-Willz skull flying across the living room.

"Wheeww.." said Crazy Cracker as he took a seat on K-Willz's plush sofa and threw his feet on his coffee table while pulling out a Newport 100.

"I hope that was as good for you as it was for me" smiled Crazy Cracker as he blew smoke rings in the air and flipped on the television.

Three Weeks Later

Khadeja and the remaining members of the Pride cruised 695 on their way to Essex to meet Olivia. Olivia sent Khadeja a text message, saying that she had some mail from Khan. Khadeja almost broke her neck grabbing her girls and the car keys to the Hell Cat then flying towards the highway.

"Why wouldn't he just mail it to our house?" questioned Khadeja to no one in particular as she pulled up infront of the first home she ever shared with Khan.

"Hey O" said Khadeja as she gave, the still somewhat bitter, Olivia a hug then proceeded into the dining room along with the other girls.

"Hey girls, the letters on the kitchen table, I dunno why Khan mailed it here but you know him, theres always a reason" informed Olivia.

Khadeja quickly opened the envelope and read the short one page letter aloud.

Dee,

It's Crunch Time!! So you're the Captain now! This is just some food for thought because it's definitely the Most Important Meal of the day.

Love

-Daddy

"What?" said a completely confused China as many of the other girls shared the same thoughts.

"I guess Khan's done finally went crazy from all those years in prison" said Olivia while walking into the living room to pet her cat.

"No, not Khan, he's trying to tell me something" pondered Khadeja as she re-read the letter to herself.

"He said that your in charge, what hidden message do you get from that?" asked China while pulling out the Newport from her bra.

"I think Khadeja is right… it's like when Khan raps, his bars have like double meaning" said Nina in broken English.

"Exactly" said Khadeja while pacing through the dining room.

"Okay, its crunch time, I'm the captain now, and the most important meal of the day are all capitalized, and I believe he mailed the letter here because there's something he wants me to get in this house" said Khadeja while everyone but Nina thought she was going crazy.

"Well they say breakfast is the most important meal of the day, right?" asked Khadeja.

"Yea I've heard that before" replied China.

"So let's check the kitchen, does Khan have any special breakfast meals, or request when you cook for him?" asked Khadeja.

"Not really, he just makes me buy that nasty ass turkey bacon" Olivia replied.

Khadeja started rummaging through the cabinets until she stopped in her tracks.

"Who's cereal is this, Olivia?"

"Oh, I almost forgot about that, Khan told me to never touch his Captain Crunch. I dunno why, when I first met him I told him, I hate that stuff"

"Crunch time, I'm the Captain now, most important meal of the day!" said Khadeja as the other girls were now interested in her theory.

Khadeja removed the large box of cereal and noticed it was a bit too heavy to contain just cereal. Khadeja dumped the contents of the box on the dining room table as stacks of bundled up one hundred dollar bills littered the surface of the table.

"Look at all that money" said a shocked Nina as all the girls stood in awe.

"I fucking knew it" said Khadeja as she noticed another note along with a composition note book, buried in the pile of money.

"This must be like a hunnid grand right here" said Khadeja while unfolding the letter as the other girls gathered around.

Dee,

I guess that head of yours can do more than suck dick (lol) I'm kidding mama. It seems your not the only one that can keep secrets. I been stashing a few dollars here and there just incase something bad happened, and if your reading this letter, then indeed something bad happened. There's a little over a quarter million here so please use it wisely. I want a better life for you and my Pride. Give Olivia a few bucks so she can open a hair salon. Don't get lazy, continue to pursue your rap career and help the other girls find their calling. Throw some money on my books and handle any legal fees for me. You got the juice now mama and I'm sorry if I couldn't be the man that you wanted me to be. Learn from my mistakes. Let my mama know I left a little something for her and the kids buried in the backyard. Tell them I love them. Tell the girls I love them. I love you more than you know mama. Also I'm leaving you something worth more than any amount of money, my rhyme book. There are enough punchlines, and creative word play to destroy any M.C. on the face of the earth. You gave my pathetic life meaning, so I shall love you well beyond the grave, and always remember with great bars, come great responsibility.

-Daddy

Khadeja wiped the tears from her face as she and the other girls took a moment in silence to reminisce about the man that each woman in that room fell in love with. Khadeja decided that she should try and build a stronger bond with Olivia out of respect for Khan.

"Hey O, we're about to grab some lunch, you wanna come?"

"Umm….sure, let me feed my cat first and I'll be ready to go"

Khadeja and the girls left Olivia's home moments later. Their first stop would be to go home and put the money away then they planned on grabbing a bite to eat before giving Khan's lawyer a phone call.

Khadeja pulled out of the parking spot, she never noticed the old blue Honda Civic trailing her every move. Fresh out of the hospital, and still recovering from a punctured intestine, Tammy sat behind the wheel, gripping a P89 Ruger, she stole from a "regular" john that picked her up from the hospital. Murder was on her mind as she watched Khadeja and her girls cheerfully sing along to the bass blaring music of the car speakers.

"I got a trick for this bitch" spat Tammy as she waited for the perfect opportunity to extract her revenge.

The End

King 44 is a very talented artist, producer and business savvy entrepreneur from the eastside of Baltimore. Bred from a lineage of ruthless cut-throat hustlers, this self-proclaimed genius now sets his sights on one thing, and one thing only… The World.

On Gawd, this man could literally take ya girl from the confines of a prison cell but luckily for you he's focused on becoming the hottest new author to hit the urban literature scene.

Bars4$ale

We are a team of highly skilled, creative, and witty wordsmiths determined to surpass our goal of customer satisfaction. We will strive for nothing less than perfection and since we're already locked up, we literally have nothing else better to do…

We offer a variety of services such as…

Verses   Battle Rap Bars   Poetry

Jingles   Public Speeches   Monologs

Comedy Skits   Love Letters   Hooks / Chorus

Never panic over penmanship! It's Bars4$ale, don't fight it. Let us write it! Hit us up at DaleeSpitz@gmx.com

You think your pen game is like that? Well contact us and join the team.

Email: DaleeSpitz@gmx.com

IG: DaleeSpitz   Facebook: DaleeSpitz

YouTube: King FourFour …. King 44 vs…

DaleeSpitz

P.O.Box 53

Highspire Pa, 17034

As a token of our appreciation scan the QR code to listen to the bonus soundtrack

1. Dolla at a Time – King 44 (Prison Call)
2. On the Way – Chris Swagg ft Blok1k
3. Modesty – King 44 ft Meeka Monae
4. Running – Cap Yuf ft Master
5. Boulevard – Stew Black
6. Who can I Run to – King 44
7. Remember – Mog Quan (Prod. KGB)
8. Ak12 – Keilago
9. Power – Altuki Samurai ft A Boogie wit da Hoodie
10. My Barz – King 44 ft Big Sin
11. Recognize – Dessi V
12. Letter to Raheem – Glory
13. Good Samaritan – King 44 ft Kevin Warner, Will K
14. Real Women – P Child ft Coldhard of Crucial Conflict
15. Big Mabu – Baltimore Madman
16. Heart and Soul – King 44 ft Tragik
17. Extreme Measures – King 44 ft Lor Ki, Tragik, Dessi V
18. HaveU – Reginald Loud
19. Don't Waste my Time – King 44 (Prison Call)

Made in United States
Troutdale, OR
08/20/2024